About the Author

Marguerite Kaye writes hot historical romances from
her home in cold and usually rainy Scotland. Featuring
Regency Rakes, Highlanders and Sheikhs, she has
published over fifty books and novellas. When she's
not writing she enjoys walking, cycling (but only on
the level), gardening (but only what she can eat) and
cooking. She also likes to knit and occasionally drink
martinis (though not at the same time). Find out more
on her website: www.margueritekaye.com

Regency Scandals

Regency Scandal:

Passion in Spades

MARGUERITE KAYE

MILLS & BOON

First Published in Great Britain 2021
by Mills & Boon, an imprint of HarperCollins*Publishers* Ltd,
1 London Bridge Street, London, SE1 9GF

www.harpercollins.co.uk

HarperCollins*Publishers*
1st Floor, Watermarque Building,
Ringsend Road, Dublin 4, Ireland

REGENCY SCANDAL: PASSION IN SPADES © 2021
Harlequin Books S.A.

His Rags-to-Riches Contessa © 2018 Marguerite Kaye
From Courtesan to Convenient Wife © 2018 Marguerite Kaye

ISBN: 978-0-263-29969-4

MIX
Paper from
responsible sources
FSC™ C007454

Printed and bound in Spain
by CPI, Barcelona

HIS RAGS-TO-RICHES
CONTESSA

For Wendy Loveridge, for being such a loyal and
supportive reader, a wise and wonderful woman,
and a wise and wonderful friend.

Prologue

London—Autumn 1818

The woman The Procurer had come in search of had
once been a regular street performer in the piazza at
Covent Garden. The Procurer had seen her in action
several times, and had been impressed by her skills
and ability to work the crowd, particularly admirable
in one so young. Becky Wickes's looks, no less than
her sleight-of-hand tricks, had always drawn a large
audience, for she was dramatically beautiful, with
huge violet eyes, sharp cheekbones, a sensual mouth
and a lush figure. When she passed the hat round
she garnered a healthy collection of coins, though
about a year ago, by The Procurer's reckoning, she
had abruptly disappeared from her usual pitch. It was
clear now, from the very public scandal in which she
was embroiled, and which the gutter press had naturally made the most of, what she had been doing in
the interim.

The Procurer entered the infamous rookery of St
Giles in the wake of her guide, a local urchin, son of

one of her less salubrious contacts. Her target had not been at all easy to trace, but then people who so desperately needed to disappear rarely were. With very good reason in this case. Members of the royal family, even minor ones, had a long and powerful reach. It had been a very grave mistake on Miss Wickes's part to be caught in the act of fleecing one such.

The Procurer sidestepped the foul sewer which ran down the middle of the narrow alleyway, executing another sidestep in order to avoid landing on the rotting carcase of a small mammal she did not care to identify. A gaggle of rough-looking men were drinking from pewter tankards outside one of the rookery's many gin shops. She could feel their sharp, curious glances stabbing like knives in her back. Her black cloak was plain enough, but the quality of the wool would be sufficient to make her stand out. As would her looks. The Procurer was indifferent to her singular beauty, but she was not fool enough to deny its existence.

As her child guide led her ever deeper into the rookery, the alleyway narrowed. Hatches from the cellars had been flung open to allow the fetid air to escape the subterranean living areas. Even one woman rescued from this ocean of misery and deprivation was a victory, however small. As her guide pointed to the open door of a dark and gloomy close, The Procurer resisted the impulse to scatter her purse of loose change at the feet of the raggle-taggle band of followers her progress had attracted. When she was done here, and returned to safer streets, there would be ample time for dispensing such alms. To do so now might jeopardise not only her mission but her personal safety.

'Stay here and do not move,' she told the boy firmly. 'You remember what you are to do if I do not return within the hour?'

Waiting only on his nod of affirmation, she ascended the worn steps to the third-floor landing, rapping sharply on the first door to the right. There was no answer. Accustomed to encountering both suspicion and fear during this critical first meeting, The Procurer knocked again, listening intently. Yes, there was someone on the other side of the door, she could not so much hear as sense the tension emanating from them. 'Miss Wickes,' she said quietly, her tone conciliatory, 'I come alone, and as a friend.'

After a brief pause, the door opened a fraction. The woman who peered at her in the dim light bore little resemblance to the one The Procurer recalled from Covent Garden. Her formerly glossy mane of black hair was dull, piled in a tangled knot of curls on top of her head. Her violet eyes were darkly shadowed, the slant of her cheekbones so pronounced she looked almost gaunt. 'What do you want? Who are you?' Her panic was evident from the way her eyes darted over The Procurer's shoulder.

'I merely wish to speak to you, Miss Wickes.' The Procurer stuck her foot against the jamb just in time to prevent the door being slammed in her face. 'You need not be alarmed. I am not here to have you clapped in irons, but to put a proposition to you.' Taking the woman completely by surprise, she pushed her way in. 'Now, do you have the makings of a cup of tea? I would very much appreciate one.'

A startled peal of laughter greeted this remark. 'Would you indeed?' Hands on hips, Becky Wickes surveyed The Procurer through narrowed eyes. 'What in the devil's name is a woman like you doing in a place like this? Who are you?'

'They call me The Procurer. Perhaps you have heard of me?'

Becky felt her jaw drop. 'All of London has heard tell of you.' She studied the intruder in her expensive wool cloak more carefully. 'You aren't how I pictured you. I thought you'd be much older. I certainly didn't think you'd be a beauty.'

'Then both our expectations have been confounded, Miss Wickes. Despite your own very striking beauty, you bear little resemblance to the woman I used to admire, performing in the Covent Garden piazza.'

'That's because I ain't working the piazza no more,' Becky said, deliberately lapsing into the harsh accent of her cockney roots. 'What I'm wondering,' she continued in her more cultured voice, 'is what *my* appearance has to do with your appearance here?'

The Procurer, however, did not seem inclined to explain herself. Instead she nodded approvingly. 'I knew, from watching you perform, that you were an accomplished actress. It is reassuring to know that you have also an excellent ear.'

'You saw me on the stage? I've not trod the boards for nearly five years.'

'I was referring to your performances in Covent Garden piazza. I confess, your strong local accent was something which did concern me. I am vastly relieved to discover it is not a problem.'

'That is indeed a relief,' Becky responded in a

mocking and flawless imitation of The Procurer's own accent with its faint Scottish lilt.

'I do not intend any slight or offence,' The Procurer said. 'Firstly, for reasons which will become clear, it is important that your voice does not betray your humble origins. And secondly, I am relieved because your facility with language indicates that you will find a foreign tongue as easy to master as the accent of those who call themselves our betters here in London.'

Becky snorted. 'Judging from your own accent, madam, I'd say that you are in the other camp.'

'I would have thought that you would know better than to judge by appearances, Miss Wickes, for they can be very deceptive. The performer I observed executing those sleight-of-hand tricks was a very confident, almost arrogant individual. Very different from the female standing before me now. Your alter ego had a certain air about her, one may say.'

'One might.' Becky eyed her astonishing visitor with respect. Any doubts she'd had about the woman's claim to be the mysterious Procurer vanished. 'Most people only see what you want them to see.'

'That is my experience, certainly.'

'So there's another woman behind The Procurer, then? I wonder...'

'I suggest most strongly that you dampen your curiosity.' The frigid tone made Becky take an instinctive step back. 'The first of my terms,' The Procurer continued, 'is that you will neither speculate nor enquire about me. And before you answer, let me assure you, Miss Wickes, that I will know if you do.'

Formidable, that was what the woman was. Well, so too was Becky, but she also knew there was a time for facing up to people, and a time for backing down. If she wanted to hear what The Procurer had to offer, then she'd better comply with The Procurer's terms. 'Fine,' she said, throwing her hands in the air. 'No questions. You have my word. And it can be relied on, I promise.'

She was rewarded with an approving smile. 'I believe you. Now, to business. *Do* you have tea?'

'I do, though I reckon you'll think I'm serving you dishwater. If you will sit down I'll see to it.'

The Procurer took a seat at the table, pinching off her gloves and unfastening her cloak, making no effort to disguise her surveillance of Becky's spartan room. That clear, frankly intimidating gaze took in every detail: the rickety bed with its cast-iron headboard and thin cover wedged into the corner; the tin kettle on the hearth and the battered teapot beside it; the mismatched china cups and saucers which Becky set out on the scarred table with the wobbly leg. 'I had heard that until your major faux pas you were rather successful in your... Let's call them endeavours,' she said, as Becky sat down opposite her, 'but I see none of the trappings of that success here.'

'Major faux pas!' Becky repeated scornfully. 'That's one way of putting it, and a lot more generous than some.'

'I've seen the reports in the press. Written with a view to selling copy rather than telling the truth, of course. I prefer to rely on my own sources, Miss Wickes, and I believe I know enough of your circumstances to think that you have been, if you will forgive the pun, dealt a very poor hand.'

'But one I dealt myself,' Becky said bitterly.

'Really?' The Procurer raised one perfectly arched brow. 'I was informed that the plan was hatched by a certain Jack Fisher.'

Becky gave a scornful snort of laughter. 'Your sources, as you call them, are impressively well informed. It was his idea all right.' Her face fell, and her mouth thinned. 'But it was my decision to go along with it, all the same. Even though I knew—but there, it's done now, and at least I've had my eyes opened where Jack Fisher is concerned. I should never have trusted him.'

'Console yourself with the fact that it is a mistake countless women have made with other such charmers.'

Was that the voice of experience she was hearing? Becky opened her mouth to ask, remembering her promise not to do so just in time. 'Well, *I* won't be making that mistake again,' she said instead. 'Once bitten twice shy, as they say.'

'I prefer my own mantra. Onwards and upwards.' The Procurer took a dainty sip of her tea, her face registering mild distaste.

'I did warn you,' Becky said, surprised to discover that she could be embarrassed over a stupid thing like tea. 'Dishwater, like I said, not whatever exotic blend you're used to.'

She expected a polite denial. She was surprised when The Procurer smiled ruefully. 'My apologies. I am fortunate enough to have a friend in the tea trade who indulges my passion for the beverage.' She set the cup to one side. 'Tell me, have you always resided here in St Giles?'

Becky shrugged. 'Here and hereabouts. It's the safest

place to be, for those of us born and raised here, and the most dangerous for unwelcome visitors who were not. How did you find me? Was it Jack who tipped you off?'

'I have not had the misfortune to meet your paramour. In fact I'm reliably informed that he is en route to the New World.'

'I would rather you'd been reliably informed that he was on his way to the underworld,' Becky said sharply. Flushing, she covered her mouth. 'I don't really mean that.' The Procurer raised an enquiring brow. 'Don't get me wrong, he's a lying, cheating—' She broke off, digging her nails into her hands. 'I wish I'd never set eyes on him. I fell hook, line and sinker for his handsome face and his charming ways and his lies. He played me like a fish, and I was gullible enough to believe every sweet nothing he whispered in my ear.'

Becky forced herself to unfurl her fingers, acutely aware of the cool gaze of the woman sitting opposite her. 'I've learnt my lesson,' she said with a grim little smile. 'From now on, whatever happens in the future, it'll be down to me and me alone.'

She'd meant to sound confident. Defiant. But something in her voice or her expression betrayed her thoughts. The Procurer reached across the table, briefly touching her fingers with her own. 'It can be done, Becky. A fresh start. A new you.'

'You sound so certain. How can you be so sure?'

'Trust me, I speak from experience.' The hand was withdrawn. The Procurer was all business again. 'You can escape from here. The proposition I have for you will reward you sufficiently to set you up for life, whatever life you choose to lead, without having to rely on any man. Are you interested?'

'What do you think?'

The Procurer eyed her coolly. 'I think, Miss Wickes, that despite acting foolishly, you are very far from being a fool. A woman from your disadvantaged background, who has survived by her wits rather than succumbing to the many lucrative offers a beauty such as yourself must have been presented with is very much to be admired. I think that you deserve a second chance and I am in a position to offer you just that. As it so happens I am looking for someone with your unique combination of talents.'

A second chance! For two weeks Becky had been in hiding from the authorities, constantly dreading a knock on the door, left to take her chances by the man she had naively trusted, quite literally, with her life as it turned out. Hope flickered inside her. Becky tried to ignore it. 'I want no part of it, if it means using my skills at the gaming tables to line someone else's pockets.'

'Isn't that precisely what you did for Jack Fisher?'

'It is, though I never knew it. Until I met Jack, my only aim was to keep belly from backbone. It was his idea, to move from the piazza to the tables. It took him a year to persuade me, and I only ever did it because I believed the pack of lies he spun.'

'Had you been less principled, Miss Wickes, with a talent such as yours, you would not be living in a place like this. Pray accept my compliments, and my assurances that the assignment I have in mind for you does not require you to use your most considerable skills to enrich my client in any monetary sense.'

'Thank you. I appreciate that. I'd like to know what it is your client does require of me.'

'Some ground rules first, Miss Wickes. I must have your solemn promise that you will never disclose the details to anyone.'

'That I can easily promise. I told you, I've learnt my lesson. Trust no one. Rely on no one except myself.'

'A commendable maxim. You should also know that you have no obligation to disclose any details of your life or your history to my client unless you choose to do so.'

Becky's eyebrows shot up. 'He doesn't know who I am?'

'I have a reputation for making the impossible possible. My clients come to me with complex and unusual problems requiring unique solutions. Solutions they cannot, by implication, come up with themselves. He need know nothing more than you choose to tell him.'

Becky frowned. 'So he doesn't even know you're talking to me?'

'Nor will he, unless you accept the contract offered. The reward for which, as I mentioned, is considerable.'

She quoted a sum so large Becky thought she must have misheard, but when she asked to repeat it, the number was the same. Becky whistled under her breath. 'That's enough to set me up for life, and then some. I'd never have to work again.'

'A life-changing amount.'

'A life-saving amount! Enough to get me far from here before they find me and make an example of me by stretching my neck.' Becky finished her cold tea and fixed The Procurer with a defiant stare. 'Robbery and fraud, they'd hang me for, you know, and they'd have every right. I cheated. It doesn't matter that he could well afford to lose, I still cheated.'

'You did not act alone. Your partner in crime…'

'Is halfway across the Atlantic by now with his pockets full of gold,' Becky said impatiently. 'What a fool I was.'

'Love can make a fool of the best of women, sadly.'

'Love! It doesn't just make a fool of us, it makes us blithering idiots. I thought the earth, moon and stars revolved around Jack Fisher. All I ever wanted was to make him happy. Was that love? I was certainly in thrall to him.' To Becky's shame, tears smarted in her eyes. She brushed them away angrily. She'd cried enough tears to mend the most broken of hearts. 'Never again. I've learnt my lesson the hard way. As you have, I reckon,' she added pointedly.

For the first time, The Procurer failed to meet Becky's eyes. 'To continue with my rules of engagement,' she said brusquely, 'if you accept this assignment, my client will require your unswerving loyalty. He will also require you to complete the terms of your contract to the letter. The terms, as I mentioned, are generous. I should caution you, however, that you will be paid only upon successful completion of your assignment. Half measures will not be rewarded. If you leave before the task is completed, you will return to England without any remuneration.'

'Return to England?' Her anger and embarrassment forgotten, Becky leaned forward eagerly in her seat. 'Where am I to go? Is your client a foreigner? Is that why you mentioned my—what did you call it?—ear for language? I can't imagine—'

'No, I don't expect you can,' The Procurer interrupted, laughing softly. 'Let me enlighten you.'

Chapter One

Venice, Kingdom of Lombardy–Venetia—
November 1818

Drizzly rain was softly falling as Becky embarked on the final stage of her long journey from London, which consisted of the short sea crossing from the nearby mainland port of Mestre to the island of Venice itself. The black gondola which she had boarded with some trepidation a few hours ago made her think of a funeral barge, or some sort of huge menacing aquatic creature with a vicious golden beak. The crossing was choppy, and the *felze*, the poky little cabin which straddled the central seats, afforded her no view of her destination. Clutching gratefully at the gondolier's hand as she climbed the narrow flight of slippery stairs on the jetty, she felt completely disoriented.

The first thing she noticed was that the rain had stopped. The sky had turned from leaden grey to an eerie brackish pink, tinged with pewter. The waters of what she assumed must be the Grand Canal were no longer churning but calm, glinting green and brown and grey, echoing but not mirroring the sky. The air felt heavy, making everything sound muted and muffled. She felt as if she were in a shadowland, as if the gondola had transported her to some mystical place.

Casting around her, Becky began to distinguish the buildings which slowly emerged from the mist, as if voile curtains were being pulled back from a stage set. Somehow she hadn't imagined that the houses would look as if they were actually floating on the water. Their reflections shimmered, creating a replica underwater ghost city. There were palaces as far as the eye could see, jostling for position on the Grand Canal, encrusted with intricately worked stonework as fine as lace, adorned with columns, a veritable menagerie of stone creatures prowling and crouching, standing sentinel on the flat rooftops.

She shivered, entranced, overawed and struck by an acute attack of nerves. She had been travelling for weeks. The journey had been meticulously arranged, leaving her little to do but hand over her travelling papers to be validated, keep an eye on her luggage and get herself from carriage to boat to carriage to boat, the world changing so quickly and dramatically before her eyes that she could only marvel at the different vistas, listen to the changing notes and tones of the languages, all the while trying to appear the world-weary traveller lest anyone mistake her for a flat and try to rob her of her meagre funds.

But now she was in Venice, her final destination, about to meet the man on whom her carefree future depended. Conte Luca del Pietro lived right here, in the Palazzo Pietro, on whose steps she was now, presumably, standing. By the looks of it, it was one of the grandest palaces of all those which lined the Grand Canal. Craning her neck, Becky counted three storeys, which seemed to consist almost entirely of tall glass double doors, separated by columns. A balcony ran the length of the first floor. Lions stood guard all along the parapet of the roof. There was a coat of arms on a shield right above the huge arched double doors, which were being thrown open by two servants in green and gold livery. A third, imperious member of the household, clearly a butler or major-domo, made his stately way to her side. '*Signorina?* If you please, come this way.'

Stomach clenched with nerves, knees like jelly, Becky followed in his wake as the servant led her into the Palazzo Pietro, where she was relieved of her travelling cloak, hat and gloves. The hallway was patterned in a complicated mosaic of black and white tiles. The walls were hung with tapestries. The ceiling, soaring high above her, was elaborately corniced. There was a chandelier so enormous she couldn't imagine how it could be secured so as not to crash to the ground. She barely had time to register anything else as she was swept up a staircase with an intricately carved balustrade, three short flights set at right angles to each other, before they reached the first floor. The middle one of five sets of double doors was flung open.

'Signorina Wickes, Conte del Pietro,' the servant announced, nudging her forward.

The doors were closed behind her. The room in which she stood was staggering. The ceiling was painted with a host of angels and cherubs, peeping from behind fluffy white clouds, gambolling naked in the celestial blue sky, and haughtily strumming on harps and lyres. Another breathtakingly beautiful chandelier glittered and sparkled, reflecting the light which streamed in through the windows on to the highly polished floor. Shelves of decorative china and plates lined the walls. There were clusters of chaises longues, sofas and chairs, scatterings of tables bearing busts, ormolu clocks and garnitures. Outside, the canal had changed colour again, now buttery yellow and seaweed green.

Dazzled, Becky did not notice the man at first. He must have been sitting in one of the chairs facing out of the window. But as he got to his feet and began to make his way towards her, she forgot all about the opulence of her surroundings.

'Luca del Pietro,' he said, making a slight bow. 'I am delighted to make your acquaintance, Miss Wickes.'

Becky dropped into a curtsy, her knees all but giving way. Rising awkwardly, she followed him, taking the seat he indicated by the window, aware that she was staring, but unable to drag her eyes away from the man who was throwing himself carelessly into the chair opposite, one long boot-clad leg crossed over the other. A count, The Procurer had informed her, the product of an Italian father and English mother. Becky had imagined—blooming heck, it didn't matter what she had imagined, this man couldn't be more different.

His hair was raven black, silky soft and too long for current fashion, reaching the collar of his shirt. His brows were thick, fiercely arched, his eyes a warm chocolate brown. A strong nose, sharp cheekbones, a decided chin. A small, meticulously trimmed goatee beard of the style favoured by Walter Raleigh, appropriately enough, for this man looked more like a pirate than a count. Dangerous—yes, very. And wild—that too. Then he smiled at her, and Becky's stomach flipped. Dear heavens, but that smile would melt ice.

'I must tell you, Miss Wickes, that your appearance is not at all what I expected.'

He spoke English with a trace of an Italian accent. His lips were pale pink against the clean, precise line of his beard, sensual, almost feminine. Not that there was anything at all feminine about the Count. Quite the contrary. There was a litheness, a suppleness in the sleek lines of the body lounging with catlike languor in the chair that made her think of him pacing the decks of a ship with the same feline grace. Becky, who had been certain that experience had numbed her to all male charms, was alarmed to discover that she was wrong.

'Conte del Pietro,' she said, relieved to hear that her voice sounded surprisingly calm, 'how do you do?'

She was rewarded with another of those smiles. 'I do very well now that you are here, Miss Wickes. Will you take some refreshment? We have a great deal to discuss. Though perhaps you are tired from the journey. Would you like to see your room first?'

Becky shook her head decisively. She had regained her composure—or near enough so that this stranger wouldn't notice, she hoped. First impressions were more important than anything. This was no time for first-night nerves. The stage was set. Now she had to deliver the required performance. She smiled politely. 'I'm not one bit tired, thank you very much.

What I am is extremely curious to know exactly what it is you require of me. So if you don't mind, let's get down to business.'

Luca couldn't help it, he laughed. Despite all the tales he'd heard of the woman who called herself The Procurer, despite the personal recommendation he'd managed to extract from a very senior member of the British government, and despite the enormous advance he'd already paid, part of him had doubted that the woman would deliver anyone suitable, let alone this extraordinary female sitting opposite him. *To business*, Miss Wickes insisted, but Luca was in no mood to proceed just yet. 'I know from the time I've spent in England,' he said, getting to his feet to pull the bell rope at the mantelpiece, 'that you like to take tea before you do anything. Tell me, how was your journey?'

'Gruelling,' she replied in a tone that made it clear she was in no mood for small talk. 'But I'm here now, so if you don't mind...'

'All in good time,' Luca said as his major-domo arrived with the tea. He could sense her impatience watching the tea service being laid out with the slow, deliberate care with which Brunetti executed every action. When finally the doors closed behind the servant again, he was pretty sure he heard Miss Wickes exhale with relief. 'Would you like to pour?' he asked her, sitting back down.

To her credit, she did not demur. To her credit also, she did not falter in the ritual, spooning the tea from the lacquered caddy, pouring the boiling water into the silver pot, the milk into the china cups with the steadiest of hands. Evidence of her skills with the cards, or a genteel upbringing? Luca wondered. Her accent was not the cut-glass, clipped tone of the English aristocracy which he found so grating, but nor did it have the burr of a peasant woman—which was hardly surprising, and a great relief. Venice was no place for a rustic of any nation. 'You are from London?' he hazarded, since he knew that was where her journey had commenced.

Miss Wickes paused in the act of raising her teacup to consider this. 'Yes.'

'You have lived there always?'

'Yes.' Miss Wickes set down her cup. A lustrous jet-black curl fell forward over her forehead. She brushed it impatiently away, before treating him to a prim smile. 'Something I intend to remedy, with your assistance.'

Luca returned the smile. 'I was under the impression that I was paying *you* to assist *me*.'

She chuckled. Their gazes snagged, and Luca could have sworn there was a mutual spark of attraction. Then she dropped her eyes, breaking the connection, and he wondered if he'd imagined it on her part simply because he felt it. Her beauty was almost theatrical in its nature, the contrast of those big eyes in that small face, the black-as-night hair and her pale northern European skin, the sharp cheekbones, the full mouth. There was a sensuality in the way she moved that seemed cultivated and yet guileless. She looked down her small nose in such a haughty manner it made him want to rattle that air of confidence. Yet now he came to look at her again, her hands clasped so tightly together, her shoulders so straight, he had the distinct impression that she was barely holding herself together.

And little wonder! She had scant idea why she was here or what was required of her. What was he thinking, allowing himself to become so distracted when he had been impatiently counting the days and hours waiting for this very moment to arrive? Luca set his empty cup and saucer down on the table. 'To business, Miss Wickes. Or may I call you Rebecca?'

'I much prefer Becky.'

Most decidedly she was nervous and trying desperately not to show it. 'Becky.' He smiled reassuringly. 'It suits you. And you must call me Luca.'

'Luca. Does that mean *lucky*?'

'Actually it means *light*, but I hope that you will bring me luck, Miss Becky Wickes.'

For some reason, his words made her glower. 'Before you say any more, I should tell you what I've already made very clear to The Procurer. I won't play cards, straight or crooked, just to win you a fortune.'

'Did not The Procurer make it very clear that wasn't at all what I required?' Luca asked, taken aback by her vehemence. 'Do I look like a man of meagre means?'

She flinched, for his tone made it clear enough that he'd found her implication offensive, but she did not back down. 'You look like a man of very substantial means,' she said, gazing around the room, 'but I'll play no part in making you even richer.'

'I don't want you to make me rich, Becky. I want you to make another man destitute.'

Some might say it was the same thing. Not this surprising woman. She uncrossed her arms, frowning, leaning forward in her chair, ignoring the glossy curl that fell over her forehead. 'Why on earth would you want to do that?'

'Oh, I have every reason,' Luca said, the familiar wave of anger making his mouth curl into a sneer. 'He killed my father.'

Becky's mouth fell open. She must have misheard him. Or his otherwise excellent English had deserted him. Though the way he had snarled the words made her wonder if he had known exactly what he had said. 'Killed? You don't really mean killed?'

'I mean exactly that. My father was murdered. I intend to make the man responsible pay.'

Becky stared, quite staggered. 'But if it was murder, then surely the law...'

'It is not possible. As far as the law is concerned, no crime has been committed. I cannot rely on the law to deliver justice for my father, I must provide that myself. With your assistance.'

'Bloody hell,' Becky muttered softly under her breath, as much at the transformation in her host as his words. There was a cold fury in his eyes, a bleak set to his mouth. 'When you say justice...'

'I do not mean an eye for an eye,' he replied with a smile that made her shiver. 'This is not a personal vendetta. It is a question of honour, to put right the wrongs inflicted, not only on my father, but on our most beloved city. Also to avenge a betrayal of the very worst kind, for the man who had my father killed was his best friend.'

Becky stared at the man opposite, utterly dumbfounded. Vengeance. Honour. Righting wrongs. 'The Procurer didn't tell me any of this—did she know?'

'*Si*. It is part of her—her terms,' Luca replied. 'What is required and why. She promises complete discretion. I am relieved to discover that she is a woman of her word.'

His Italian accent had become more pronounced. He was upset. His father had been murdered, for heaven's sake, of course he was upset! 'I'm very sorry, perhaps I'm being slow, but I'm afraid I'm none the wiser.'

Across from her, Luca let out a heavy sigh, making an obvious effort to relax. 'It is I who should apologise. It is such a very painful subject, I did not anticipate finding myself so—so affected, talking about it.'

'Would you like another cup of tea?' Becky said, completely at a loss as to how to respond.

Luca gave a snort of laughter. 'Tea. You English think it is the cure for everything. Do not be offended. I am not laughing at you, but you will admit, it is funny.'

'I suppose it is,' Becky said, simply relieved to have lightened the tension in him. 'You don't mind if I have a second cup?'

'Please.'

She could feel his eyes on her as she took her time pouring, adding milk, wondering what the devil she was to make of what he'd told her. She took a sip, and he smiled at her again, a warm smile that made her wonder if she'd imagined that formidable stranger.

'I have been so anxiously waiting your arrival,' he said, 'so eager to execute my plan, that I forget you know nothing at all. Naturally, you want to ask questions.'

'But I've no right to ask them,' Becky said, re-membering this belatedly. 'You don't need to explain yourself, only tell me what it is you require me to do. I'm remembering, don't worry, that the fee you'll pay guarantees my unswerving loyalty.'

Luca got to his feet, leaning his forehead on the glass of one of the tall windows, staring out at the canal. After a few moments' contemplation, he turned back to face her. 'This is probably going to sound foolish, but I'd much prefer that you helped me because you wanted to, than because you were obliged to.'

'But I am obliged to, if I'm to earn my fee.'

He held out his hand, inviting her to join him at the window. Outside, it was growing dark, the light a strange, iridescent silver, so that she couldn't tell what was water and what was sky. 'My plan requires you to play cards against this man for very high stakes. He is a powerful and influential figure in Venice. He has also demonstrated that he is prepared to be ruthless. It is not without risk. Did The Procurer explain this to you?'

'She told me if I didn't like the set-up I could return to England, no questions asked. I won't be caught, if that's what you're concerned about,' Becky said, dismayed to discover that she didn't feel anywhere near as confident as she sounded. If Jack hadn't given the game away, she wouldn't have been discovered, but it seemed none the less that he'd stolen a bit of her confidence as well as her heart.

'You'll be in disguise, of course,' Luca said. 'It is Carnevale.'

'Carnevale?'

'Carnival. You haven't heard of it? It is the only time of the year in Venice when gambling is permitted—or at least, when a blind eye is turned. You'll be wearing a mask and a costume, like everyone else. You will be Regina di Denari, The Queen of Coins, named after one of our Venetian card suits. I thought it was most appropriate, though if you have another suggestion?'

'Regina di Denari...' she repeated, savouring the sound of it in Italian. 'I think it's perfect. So that's the part I'm to play?'

'One of them.'

'One of them!'

He laughed softly. 'It is a very large fee you are to earn, after all.'

'Not large enough, I'm beginning to think,' Becky retorted. 'How many other roles are there?'

'Only one, but it will be quite a contrast to the Queen of Coins.'

'How much of a contrast?'

'As day is to night. Like Venice herself, you will have two faces to show to the world. You will be two very different women. Do you think you can manage that?'

'Of course I can.' She wished he wouldn't smile at her like that. She wished that his smile didn't make her insides churn up. She wished that the view from the window wasn't so strange and beautiful. She couldn't quite believe that she was here, that *here* was even real.

'I can't quite believe you're here,' Luca said, as if he'd read her thoughts. '*Are* you real, Becky Wickes?'

'As real as you are. And I admit, I'm not at all certain that you are. Maybe this is a dream and I've conjured you up.'

'I'm the one who has been dreaming, dreaming of vengeance. Now that you are here, I can finally act.'

'It's me who has to act,' Becky said, attempting to

bring the conversation back to business, trying to ignore the effect the closeness of Luca's body was having on hers. 'You still haven't told me what my other role is.'

'You will play my painfully shy and gauche English cousin.' He reached out to brush her hair back from her forehead. He barely grazed her skin but she shivered, though his fingers weren't in the least bit cold. 'You are just arrived in Venice,' Luca continued. 'Here to acquire a sprinkling of our city's sophistication, and to provide my mother with some company from her homeland—my mother is English, you know.'

'It's one of the few things I do know.' Becky's head was whirling. 'You want me to play a lady?'

'A young, beautiful lady, who looks out at the world through those big violet eyes with such charming innocence, who understands none of the intrigue going on around her. Venice is a city full of spies, secret societies, informers. Your arrival will have already been noted, so I must plausibly explain your presence, Cousin Rebecca.'

Was he aware that his hand was still resting on her shoulder? Their toes were almost touching. She could see the bluish hint of growth on his cheeks where he had shaved close to his narrow beard. Was this some sort of audition for the part she was to play? But which part? 'In England, if I really were your cousin, you would keep your distance. Are things so very different here?' Their gazes were locked. This was the oddest conversation she'd ever had. Saying one thing. Thinking something else. At least she was, and she was fairly certain he was too. 'The way you're looking at me, it's not at all cousinly, you know.'

He flinched, immediately stepping back. '*Mi scusi.* You must not think I assume because I pay for you to come here that you must…'

'I don't.' It hadn't even occurred to her, though perhaps it should have? But even though she'd only just met him, Becky didn't think that Luca del Pietro was the type of man to take advantage. Not that she'd any intention of allowing him to.

Her head really was whirling. She needed time to think, to try to make sense of all that Luca had told her, and to work out what the many gaps were in his story. She needed time to adjust to her surroundings. She was in a foreign country in a floating palace, for heaven's sake, with a count who wanted to avenge himself on the man who had killed his father. 'This whole situation is very strange,' Becky said.

'Of course it is, and I have not made a very good job of explaining it. I suspect you would benefit from a rest. I will have you shown to your room.'

'Thank you.'

'It will be just the two of us dining tonight. My mother…' Luca hesitated. 'I thought it prudent for her to be otherwise engaged. I was not sure, you see, until I met you…'

'Whether I would pass muster,' Becky said. 'Does this mean that I have?'

'You have, and with flying colours, I am delighted to say, because I don't know what I'd have done if you had not. I think that we will work very well together. And before you say it, I know that I have not explained what it is I want you to do or even why, not properly, but I will. Tomorrow, I promise. You will stay, won't you? You will help me?'

He wasn't pleading, exactly, but he wasn't at all sure of her answer. He wanted her, Becky Wickes, to help him, the Conte del Pietro. More than that. He needed her. It made her feel good. 'Of course I will,' Becky said. 'I've come all this way, haven't I? You think I'd turn my back on the small fortune you're going to pay me?'

'The money means a great deal to you? No, don't answer that, it's a stupid question. You would not be here otherwise, would you?'

'That sort of money, to a woman like me, it's life-changing,' Becky said, using The Procurer's words.

'I have never met a woman like you, but I'm very glad you are here. I think we are going to make an alliance most *formidabile.*'

He lifted her hand to his lips. Still holding her gaze, he pressed a kiss to the back of her hand. The rough brush of his beard, the softness of his lips, was like everything else since she'd arrived, an odd, exciting contrast. Her insides were churning, but Becky managed a cool smile. 'If you'll excuse me,' she said. 'I don't want to be late for dinner, especially since I'm meeting my cousin for the first time.'

Chapter Two

A maid showed Becky to her bedchamber on the next floor of the *palazzo*. As the double doors were flung open, she was about to say that there must have been some mistake, before remembering just in time that she was supposed to be Luca's well-born cousin. She supposed the servants had been informed of this, and wondered what on earth they'd make of the shabby wardrobe of clothes she'd brought with her. Lucky for her that she spoke no Italian. It was best not to know.

'*Signorina?*'

She followed the maid into the room, abandoning any pretence of being at home amid such grandeur as she gazed around her, almost dancing with delight. The vast bedchamber was painted turquoise blue, the same colour seemingly everywhere, making her feel as if she was underwater. Pale blue silk rugs. Blue hangings at the huge windows. They were drawn shut, but Becky guessed they must look out on to the canal. The view would be spectacular in the morning. For now, the room was lit by another of those massive glittering chandeliers. The bed was a four-poster, and bigger than the room in the rookeries she called home. It was so high, so thick with blankets and luxurious quilts, that she reckoned she'd need a step to climb into it. The bed hangings matched the curtains. She couldn't resist smoothing her hand over them. Damask, embroidered with silk. Would there be silk sheets? She was willing to wager that there would be. Never mind playing Luca's cousin, this room was worthy of a princess.

What wasn't blue was gold— no, gilt, that was the word. Little chairs that looked too dainty to be sat upon. A marble-topped washstand. And a mirror. Catching sight of her reflection brought Becky crashing back to earth. She'd bought her dress in a London street market, second-hand but barely worn, using a chunk of the sum The Procurer had given her to cover her expenses. She'd thought it a good buy, but now even the chambermaid looked better dressed. What must Luca have thought? And what on earth did Luca expect her to change into for dinner, which now she thought about it, was bound to be an ordeal. The opportunities to embarrass herself when it came to etiquette were endless. She owned one evening gown, but it had been bought with the gaming hells of St James's in mind. Her card sharp's costume, revealing far more than it concealed, was designed to divert players' attention from her hands. It was totally inappropriate for dinner with Luca. His demure, innocent English cousin would not own, far less wear, such a provocative garment. Thank the stars she hadn't packed it.

There was a copper bath placed in front of a roaring fire. The maid was erecting screens around it, laying out towels to warm. Becky hadn't expected to be living in the lap of luxury like this. Mind you, it was a double-edged sword, for even as she was relishing her surroundings, she was on tenterhooks, terrified she'd make some terrible gaffe that would give her away. If only she could dismiss the maid, she could explore properly, throw herself down on to that huge bed and see if it was as soft as it looked, take off her boots and her stockings and curl her toes into the rugs. There would be time enough, she supposed, when everyone was in bed. Her stay here was going to be short-lived, so she should make the most of it while she could. Though she was definitely not about to permit the woman to undress her. Let her think it was an English peculiarity. She was more than capable of undoing her own stays and garters.

'*No, grazie,*' she said, shaking her head decidedly, slipping behind the screens. Now she could enjoy some privacy, and she wouldn't have to watch the maid's face as she surveyed Becky's meagre wardrobe, searching in vain for evening wear. Quickly ridding herself of her travelling clothes, she sank into the steaming water with a contented sigh. Were these rose petals? And on the little table, beside another jug of hot water, perfumed soap and some sort of oil.

She closed her eyes, allowing the heat to relax her tense limbs and soothe her jangling nerves. She tried to imagine herself playing the lady, all simpering blushes and saucer-eyed wonder. It would be much more of a challenge than the other part she was to play. The Queen of Coins. '*Regina di Denari,*' she mouthed silently. It sounded much better in Italian. Imperious. Seductive. Like this city. And like Luca, a handsome devil, with a smile that ought to be outlawed.

It wasn't like her to be having such thoughts. Perhaps she had become infected by Venice's mystique, the magic in the misty air. She had never been free with her favours—quite the contrary—until Jack came along and stole her heart. It made her cringe now, remembering the way her heart fluttered when he smiled at her, the way she'd gaze at him all starry-eyed, only happy when he was happy, miserable when he was not. She'd loved him, there was no denying it. Their kisses had been lovers' kisses— or so she'd thought. At any rate, they were the only kisses she had shared in all of her twenty-two years, and the only ones she'd been interested in, until now. Luca's kisses, she was willing to bet, would be very different.

Becky's eyes opened with a snap. She was *not* interested in kissing Luca. She was going to stop wallowing in this bath, indulging in idle speculation and slowly turning into a prune. Panicking that she would be late for dinner, she sat up, sending water splashing on to the surrounding mats, and picked up the soap.

'Signorina Wickes, Conte del Pietro.'

Luca, who had been carefully twisting the cork to open a bottle of Prosecco, turned as the library doors closed on the servant.

'Must they announce me every time?' Becky asked, hovering in the doorway.

'I'm afraid formality is the order of the day in palace life. Though I must admit that every time they call me Conte del Pietro, I look over my shoulder expecting to see my father. Are you coming in, or do you plan to have your dinner delivered to you in the doorway?'

'It's just that you're all dressed up and I'm not.'

Becky held out the skirts of her gown. 'I don't have any evening clothes. Sorry.'

She was smiling and glowering at the same time. Embarrassed. Luca cursed his own stupidity for having donned the knee breeches and coat that was the custom for dinner at the *palazzo*. 'It is I who should apologise. This,' he said, indicating his apparel, 'is what my father would have considered appropriate, and my mother still does. Neither are here, for very different reasons. Please, come in. To me you look perfectly lovely.'

'It's the servants' opinions I'm more concerned about,' Becky muttered. 'I didn't know I'd be living in a palace.'

'Venice is a city of many palaces.' Which was true, but hardly the point, Becky was clearly thinking, though she refrained from saying so. As the cork popped from the bottle with a sigh, Luca set it down, torn. The Procurer's terms forbade him from asking any questions. Cursing her strict rules of engagement, he poured two crystal flutes of the cold sparkling wine and held one out to Becky. 'Prosecco,' he said. 'Our Italian version of champagne. Personally, I consider it to be superior. *Salute*,' he added, clinking glasses. 'Here is to your arrival in Venice.'

'*Salute*,' Becky repeated in a perfect imitation of his Venetian accent, taking a cautious sip, screwing up her face in surprise as the bubbles burst on her tongue.

'You've never tasted champagne, I take it?' Luca asked.

'No.' She took another sip. 'But I like this. Have you told the servants that I am your cousin?'

'Yes, of course.'

'What were you going to tell them if you'd decided I wouldn't suit?'

Luca grimaced. 'I have no idea, I preferred not to consider such an outcome. A sudden family illness back in England forcing you to return, I suppose. But you do suit, so fortunately I don't have to tell them anything.'

'Except maybe explain why the cousin of one of the richest families in Venice has the wardrobe of one of the poorest families in England.'

She tilted her chin at him, there was a flash of defiance in her eyes, yet he was certain now that she was embarrassed. 'I'm sorry,' Luca said. 'I simply didn't think. It is easily remedied. *Mia madre*, my mother, she will arrange it.' He shook his head as Becky made to protest. 'We will say that your luggage was lost in transit, or that your parents wished you to be attired on the Continent, since it is well known,' he added with a sly smile, 'that the English know nothing of couture.'

'Yes, but, Luca, I don't have any money.'

'Luckily, I have an surfeit of it. Think of the outfits as your stage costumes. Therefore the expense is my responsibility.'

'Yes, that makes sense,' Becky said, looking extremely relieved. 'Though I don't imagine your mother will be very pleased to hear— Luca, does she *know* why I'm here?'

'*Si.*'

'And what does she think of your plan to avenge your father's—my goodness, her husband's death?'

'She understands that it is a matter of honour, why it is so important to me to see some sort of justice served. It is the least I can do for him.'

All of which was true. It should have been sufficient, but Becky was not fooled. 'You mean she understands but doesn't necessarily agree?'

Shrewd, that was the English word to describe Becky Wickes. Or one of them. An admirable quality in a card sharp, but they weren't playing cards, and Luca was not accustomed to having his motives questioned. In fact he wasn't accustomed to being questioned about anything. 'My mother's opinion should not concern you, since she is not the one paying your fee.' He regretted it immediately, as Becky's expression stiffened.

'I'm sorry. I didn't mean...'

'No, you were right to remind me that it's none of my business.'

She took her time finishing her Prosecco and setting the glass back down on the silver tray before making for one of the bookcases, running her finger over Italian titles which she couldn't possibly understand. Irked by his own arrogance, Luca poured them both another glass of Prosecco and joined her. 'I'm afraid I don't react particularly well to being questioned,' he said. 'But I am capable of admitting to being wrong.'

She took the glass he offered her, touching it to his before taking a sip. 'Not that it happens often, I imagine.'

He laughed reluctantly. 'More often than I'd like. I have always been—headstrong? I think that is the word. Acting before thinking, you know?'

'Not a wise move in my game.'

What was her game, precisely? Where had she come from? What had she left behind? He longed to ask. He hadn't thought that the terms of their contract would be so constraining. He hadn't expected to be so curious. But perhaps if he was a little more honest with her, she would come to trust him. 'My mother does not approve of my plans,' Luca said, 'you were right about that. My father's death was such a terrible shock, she wants to draw a line under the whole ghastly business.'

'When did it happen?'

'In April this year. I was in Scotland, and did not make it back to Venice in time for the funeral.'

'I'm so sorry.'

'Grazie.'

'Was there an enquiry? If he had been murdered, there must have been—I don't know how the law works here. Do you have the equivalent of Bow Street Runners?'

'There was no enquiry, my father's death was deemed to be a tragic accident.' Luca drained his glass, glancing at the clock which was chiming the hour, and on cue Brunetti appeared to announce that dinner was served.

'We can discuss it in the morning, every detail, I promise you,' he said, offering Becky his arm, 'and then I'll introduce you to my mother. She should be home by midday. For tonight, let's take the opportunity to get to know each other a little better.'

The major-domo led them in a stately procession to the room next door. The dining room was another huge chamber, grand to the point of being overwhelming, with a woodland scene painted on the ceiling. Becky made out strange beasts which were half-man and half-wolf or goat, with naked torsos, horned heads, leering down at her, drinking from flagons of wine or playing the pipes. It was enough to put anyone off their dinner, so she decided not to look again.

The table looked as if it could accommodate at least thirty diners. Two places were set at the far end of the polished expanse of mahogany. Torn between awe and amusement, Becky knew enough to allow Luca to help her into her seat, but one look at the array of silverware and glasses in front of her wiped the smile from her face. She watched with growing dismay as Luca sipped and swirled the wine presented to him before his nod of approval prompted the major-domo to fill her glass. Two servants arrived, carrying a silver platter between them. She presumed the major-domo was reciting the contents of the platter. Completely intimidated, Becky simply stared, first at the platter, where she recognised not a single dish, then at the major-domo and then finally at Luca.

Whatever it was he'd noted in her expression, he rapped out a command to the servants. The platter was placed on the table. The major-domo and his consorts trod haughtily out, and Becky heaved a huge sigh of relief. 'What did you tell them?'

'That my English cousin is quite ignorant of our splendid Venetian cuisine, and so I would take it upon myself to make a selection for you. Thus educating your vastly inferior English palate.'

'Thank you.' She was blushing, she could feel the heat spreading up her throat to her cheeks, but there was no point in pretending, it was far too important that she learn while she could. 'You'll need to educate my poor English manners as well as my palate I'm afraid,' Becky said, keeping her eyes on the delicate porcelain plate in front of her. 'I not only have no idea what's on that platter, but I couldn't hazard a guess at what implement I'm supposed to use to eat it.'

'It is the same for all the English who visit Italy you know,' Luca said, getting to his feet. 'Our food, it confuses them. It will be my pleasure to introduce you to it.'

He was being kind, Becky knew that, but she was grateful for it all the same, and extremely grateful that he'd dismissed all the witnesses to her ignorance. As he presented the platter to her, she managed a smile. 'It does look lovely.'

'But of course. The first step to enjoying food is to find it pleasing to the eye. Now, these are *carciofe alla romana*, which is to say braised artichokes prepared in the Roman style—because, just between us, though Venetian cooking is obviously far superior to anything served in England, in Italy, I regret to say that we Venetians are considered to be culinary peasants.' He set a strange off-white chunk of something that looked nothing like the big blowsy green artichokes they sold at the Covent Garden fruit market on her plate.

'Grazie,' Becky said dubiously.

'Now, these are *ambretti all'olio e limone*, which is simply prawns and lemon. Would you like some?'

'They smell delicious. Yes, please.'

'Ostriche alla tarantina.'

'Oysters. I recognise these, though I've never had them hot like this.'

'You'll like them. This is octopus. Try it. And these are *biancheti*.'

'Whitebait,' Becky exclaimed triumphantly after a brief study of the little fish. 'I'll have some of those too, please, unless— Am I supposed to try only one dish?'

'No. This is *antipasti*, the whole point is to sample a little of everything.' Luca sat back down, filling his own plate. 'Use your fingers, then rinse them when you're done. That's what the bowl at the side of your plate is for, see, with the slice of lemon floating in it.'

'Well, I'm glad you told me that or I might have drunk it, thinking it lemon soup!'

'You mustn't worry, Becky. People will expect you to be confused by our customs here. They're very different.'

'Were you the same, when you first went to England? When was that?' She rolled her eyes. 'Sorry, I forgot. No questions.'

'I'm willing to waive that rule if you are.'

Becky examined the chunk of octopus on her plate, then popped it into her mouth. She'd expected it to be chewy, fishy, but it was neither, melting on her tongue, tasting of wine and lemon and parsley. Luca was waiting on an answer, but he could wait. She took a sip of wine. Also delicious. It wasn't that she was ashamed of her humble background, but it was like night and day to all this. Would Luca think less of her for it? In one way it didn't matter, since he'd already committed to her staying.

She picked up an oyster shell, tipping the contents into her mouth, giving a little sigh of pleasure as this too melted on her tongue, soft and sweet, nothing like the briny ones served from barrels back home. Yes, of course it mattered. They were going to be spending a lot of time together. She had warmed to Luca immediately and she wanted him to like her in return. She certainly didn't want him looking down his aristocratic nose at her, but if she didn't reveal a little of her humble origins, he wouldn't know just how much help she was going to need to learn how to be convincing in her role as his cousin. If she had to learn, and make any number of mistakes in the process, she'd rather it was from him, in front of him, and not in public. *And* there was the fact that she wanted to know more about him too.

'Go on, then,' Becky said, 'let's agree to forget the rule for now. But you first. What took you to England?'

'The Royal Navy,' he said promptly. 'When I was twelve, my father sent me as an ensign. When I resigned my commission four years ago, I was a captain.'

'I knew it!' Becky exclaimed. 'When I first set eyes on you, I thought you looked liked a pirate.'

'I think the Admiralty might have something to say about that description,' he answered, grinning, 'though there were times when it was accurate enough.'

Becky pushed her empty plate to one side. 'Have you been all over the world? I can picture you, leaping from deck to deck, cutlass in hand, confiscating chests of gold from the Spanish.'

'You forgot to mention the parrot on my shoulder. And my peg leg.'

'And the lovely wench, swooning in your arms because you rescued her from a rival pirate, who we know must be the evil one, because he's wearing an eyepatch.'

Luca threw back his head and laughed. 'You've watched too many plays.'

'Not watched, but acted in them,' Becky admitted,

smiling at the surprise registered on his face. 'And not any of the kind of roles you're imagining either.'

'What do you think I'm imagining?'

'Breeches roles. Not that I wasn't asked, and not that I bother about showing off my ankles or playing the man, but...' Becky's smile faded. 'It's the assumption associated with those particular roles that I resented. I haven't been on the stage for— Oh, five years now. Since I was seventeen,' she added, 'in case you're curious and too polite to ask my age.'

'It's not the thing in England,' Luca agreed, 'to discuss age or money. But you'll find attitudes differ here in Venice.'

Brunetti, the major-domo, entered the dining room at this point, followed by his minions bearing more dishes, and Luca busied himself with serving her the next course. Risotto, he called it, rice with wild mushrooms, to be eaten with a spoon. It was creamy but not sweet, and though it looked like a pudding it tasted nothing like.

'I think you might be right about Italian cooking, compared to English,' Becky said. 'Not that I'm exactly qualified to compare, mind you. I've never had a dinner like this. All this food just for two people, it seems an awful lot. We didn't even finish the— What did you call it?'

'Antipasti. It will doubtless be finished in the kitchen. Palace staff eat better than most. What kind of food do you like to eat, Becky?'

'Whatever I can lay my hands on, usually. Beggars can't be choosers.' She spoke flippantly. What she'd meant was, *I don't want to talk about it*. Then she remembered that she'd agreed to talk, and that Luca had talked, and it was her turn. 'I don't have a kitchen, never mind a cook. I eat from pie shops. Whatever's cheap at the market at the end of the day, bread—ordinary food, you know?'

He didn't, she could see from his face. 'But you seem... Not comfortable, but you don't seem to be *uncomfortable* with all this,' Luca said, waving his hand at the room, frowning.

'Well, that's a relief to know. The only time I've ever sat at a table anything like this was on the stage, where the food was made from plaster and cardboard. I'm a good actress. Luckily for me, The Procurer spotted that.'

'She saw you onstage?'

Becky shook her head. 'I told you, I've not been on the stage for five years, and The Procurer is...' She bit her tongue, mortified. 'Now, that is one subject I'm not at liberty to discuss.'

'Then tell me instead, what you meant when you said that you resented the connotations of— What did you call them, breeches roles?'

'That's when a girl plays a boy on the stage.' Becky studied him over her wine glass. 'You know perfectly well what I meant. That a girl who flaunts her legs on the stage is reckoned to be willing to open them offstage,' she said bluntly. 'It's what draws most denizens of the pit, with good reason in many cases. But I wanted none of it, and it was easier to remove myself from harm's way than to keep fending them off.'

'Surely whoever was in charge—the theatre manager?—would have protected you.'

Becky laughed harshly. 'Then he would have needed to protect me from himself. He was the worst of the lot. A perk of the job is how he viewed it,' she said sardonically. 'Play nice, you get the best parts. Refuse to let him paw you with his grubby little hands, the work dries up. I decided to take the decision out of his hands by quitting. There are many actresses who are happy to exploit their good looks to their advantage, and good luck to them, but I, for one, refused to. They are the ones being exploited, in my view.'

She was surprised to see that Luca seemed genuinely shocked. 'Which makes you rather remarkable, I think,' he said. 'Was there no one else to look out for you?'

'I was seventeen, hardly a child. You grow up quickly, in that game. If you mean my parents, I never knew my father. As for my mother, she was an actress herself. She lived long enough to put me on the stage alongside her. I was six, maybe seven when she died.' Becky finished her risotto and drained her wine glass, and decided to put an end to this conversation too. She wasn't used to talking about herself. 'I never went to school, but I didn't need to, not with the stage to educate me. Reading. Writing. Manners. Plays of all sorts, from bawdy nonsense to Shakespeare, who can be quite bawdy himself. Anyway, that's quite enough about me for now. I'm much more interested in hearing about you and your life on the ocean wave.'

To her relief, Luca obliged. He was a natural storyteller, transporting her from the dreary dockyards of Plymouth and the grey seas of England, to the azure blue of the Mediterranean, the sultry sun of Egypt, the mayhem of Lisbon and the vast expanse of the New World. There were naval battles, but he glossed over those in a way that she could see disguised pain, suffering, the darker side of human nature. And though he made little of his own role in war at sea, it was clear enough it had been a significant one, that he was not one of those officers who hid behind his men.

'And then, when Napoleon was defeated at Waterloo, it was obvious that there would be no more wars, and therefore no need for a vast naval fleet. The prospect of sitting behind a desk in the Admiralty filled me with dread,' Luca said, 'and so I resigned my commission. Yes,' he added over his shoulder to his major-domo, who had appeared once more, 'we're quite finished.'

Becky looked down at her empty plate. There were fish bones. She hardly recalled being served any fish. Her wine glass was half-full of red, not white. How long had Luca been talking, answering her eager questions? But she wasn't nearly satisfied. 'Why the navy though? And why the English navy?'

'British. Because Venice no longer possesses one. Because I would never countenance serving our usurpers any more than my father would have, whether French or Austrian. Because my mother's family have a proud seafaring tradition. Admirals, and pirates too,' Luca said with a wicked smile.

Shaking her head at the offer of coffee, Becky sat back in her seat with a contented sigh. She'd eaten so much she was sleepy. 'What have you been doing for the last years, then?'

'Learning how to build ships, not sail them,' Luca retorted. 'I spent some time in Glasgow. The Scots are even better ship makers than we Venetians used to be, though it pains me to say it. My father, to my surprise, heartily endorsed my desire to become a shipwright.'

'But why? Noble families like yours don't tend to dirty their hands by becoming involved in trade.'

'We are Venetians,' Luca said. 'We invented trade.'

Becky bit back a smile. He puffed up with pride whenever he mentioned his beloved Venice. 'I'm surprised you ever left the city if you love it so much.'

'We once had a great navy. Our merchant ships travelled the world. But all that was lost as other seafaring nations supplanted us. Venice's reputation these days is based on its notoriety for vice and excess, a city devoted to pleasure. Always, when people talk of her, it is Carnival and nothing else. It is because I am determined to contribute somehow to making this city great again that I left her.'

'But how? Aren't you— Don't the Austrians rule here?'

His mouth tightened. 'For now. Building new ships to re-establish trading routes. That is my dream. Though for the moment, I keep it to myself.' Luca put a finger to his mouth, making a show of peering over his shoulder. 'There is one thing you must never forget about Venice,' he said in a stage whisper. 'There are spies everywhere.'

'I hope you don't ever plan to tread the boards. You're a terrible actor.'

But Luca's expression became serious. 'I mean it. Within these walls it is safe to speak your mind, but in public you must keep your counsel. Intrigue is a way of life and Venice can be a dangerous city for the unwary.'

'How can somewhere so beautiful be so menacing?'

'Because Venice is a city of contrasts. Light and shadow. Beauty and decay. Stone and water.'

'You make it sound fascinating. I look forward to exploring it.'

'It will be my pleasure to be your guide.'

He smiled at her, and she forgot what she was about to say. Sightseeing, she reminded herself, that was what they were talking about, but her eyes were locked on his, and all she could do was stare, mesmerised. She wondered what it would feel like to be kissed by him, and he must have read her thoughts, because there was a gleam in his eyes that made her think he wanted to kiss her too.

The table was in the way, but she was on her feet now, and so was he. He had closed the gap between them. She was lifting her face to his. And then he muttered something, shook his head, stepped back, and at the same time she regained her senses and moved away.

'In the morning, after breakfast,' Luca said, his voice gruff, 'we will draw up a plan of action.'

'In the morning,' Becky repeated, trying to regulate her breathing, 'I will assume the role of your demure cousin Rebecca.'

He looked as relieved as she felt. She wondered if he was thinking the same as her, that it was for the best, since cousins couldn't kiss.

'But in the meantime, you must be tired,' he said.

'Yes,' she agreed gratefully. 'Very tired. I will bid you goodnight.'

He took her hand, bowing over it with a mocking little smile, pressing the lightest of kisses to her fingertips. '*Buona notte*, Becky.'

'Goodnight?' A slight nod, and she repeated the words, enjoying the soft, sensual sound of them. '*Buona notte*, Luca.'

Chapter Three

Becky woke with a start. Completely disoriented by the comforting, heavy weight of the bedclothes, the softness of the mattress, the serene silence, it took her a moment to realise she wasn't in her cramped garret in the rookeries. The room was cool, but nothing like the bone-chilling cold of a London winter morning. There was an ember still smouldering in the fireplace that would take only a moment to relight. Picking up some kindling from the basket on the hearth, it occurred to her that this would be the maid's task, so she put it back.

A narrow shaft of light slanted through the gap in the curtains, but it was enough to allow her to get to the window from the fireplace without bumping into any of the clutter of chairs and occasional tables that littered the room. Gazing out, the canal was shrouded in a blanket of silvery-grey mist. She caught her breath at the sheer beauty of the scene, leaning over the little Juliet balcony to get a better view of the rows of gondolas bobbing gently on the canal banks, to breathe in the salty air, to drink in the utter stillness of the scene, like a painting or a world where she was the only person alive.

Nothing had prepared her for this. In London, no matter the time of day, there was noise, there were people, there was constant bustle. London was a city painted in shades of grey most of the time, the air tasting of the smoke which formed a grimy hem around the cleanest of petticoats. In London, the sky didn't change colour dramatically like this, clearing and lightening to the palest of blue as the sun rose. The fast-running Thames was a muddy brown colour. Before her eyes, the Grand Canal was becoming bluer and bluer, the sunlight painting bright strips of gold on top of the turquoise. It was magical, there was no other word for it.

She watched, fascinated, as the canal came to life, the first gondolas with a lantern in the prow cutting elegantly through the waters, the oar of the gondoliers barely stirring the surface. Only when a man appeared on a balcony opposite hers and blew an extravagant kiss did she recall that she was wearing a nightgown, that her hair was down, that she was displaying herself on the balcony of the Palazzo Pietro like— Well, not like Luca's demure English relative.

Closing the windows, but leaving the curtains drawn back, Becky retreated back into the warm, luxurious nest of her four-poster bed. She had no idea whether she should ring for the maid. No idea whether breakfast would be brought to her, or whether she should seek it out. Reality, long overdue, came crashing down on her. She truly was in another world, one in which she felt completely and utterly out of her depth. Yet she had to convince everyone, from the army of staff at the *palazzo*, to everyone in 'society', whatever Luca meant by that, that she was Cousin Rebecca, born and bred to all this.

Flopping back on to the pillows, Becky tried to calm the rising tide of panic welling up inside her. She'd been on the stage almost before she could walk, and she was an accomplished actress. Cousin Rebecca was just another role she had to play. She could master it if she worked hard enough. So what, if she was living in a palace and not just acting in front of a painted backdrop, acting was acting, wasn't it? And if she thought about it, which she had better do right now, wasn't confidence the key to her success with her card tricks? People only see what they want to see. She'd said something of the sort to The Procurer, and it was true. There was no reason, none at all, why the servants here would look at her and see a card sharp or even just a common Londoner.

She wasn't common; she was extraordinary. Luca had said so. Of course, she wasn't really, it was just that he'd never met anyone like her. She wasn't extraordinary, she was simply different, beyond his ken, as he was beyond hers. It would certainly explain the most unexpected end to the evening last night. Becky burrowed deeper under the covers, pulling the sheet over her burning face. What on earth had possessed her! Her only consolation was that Luca had seemed to be as shocked as she was by that inexplicable almost kiss. He could easily have taken advantage. She would not have resisted him, she was ashamed to admit. Thank heavens the pair of them had come to their senses in time. It must be that strangeness which drew them, two opposites attracted to each other like magnets. She'd simply have to work harder to resist, because the very last thing she wanted was to get burnt again.

Pushing back the bedcovers, Becky sat up to face the cold light of day. She'd learnt a bitter lesson with Jack. She'd given her soppy heart to Jack. Looking back, she couldn't believe she'd been so gullible. All these years fending for herself, and she'd not once been tempted by any of the offers that came her way—though they'd been of the crude sort, and hardly tempting, she was forced to admit. While Jack—well, Jack was a charmer. He didn't proposition her, he—yes, she could admit it, even if it made her toes curl—he had wooed her. Seduced her with compliments and promises, gradually taking more and more advantage as she fell for his weasel words and his false declarations of love. Only then, when she'd handed him her heart on a plate, did he start to use her for his own ends, so subtly she didn't notice until it was too late. It made her blood boil, thinking of the fiasco at Crockford's that might have resulted in the loss of her liberty, if not her life. There was a moment, when it was all tumbling down like a house of cards, when she'd turned to Jack, pleading with her eyes for him to rescue her. Instead of which, he'd turned his back on her and fled to save his own skin. Only then did she realise that it had all been a tissue of lies. Even now, thinking about it left a bitter taste in her mouth. What an idiot she'd been.

But look where it had brought her. Becky propped herself up on the mountain of pillows. If Jack could see her now! She tried to imagine his expression if he walked into the room to see her lying like a princess in this huge bed, but she couldn't. She didn't actually want to picture Jack here at all. In fact the very notion of him being in her bedchamber, seeing her in her nightgown, made her feel queasy, even though he'd seen her in her nightgown numerous times, and had been in her bed any number of times too. But she didn't want to remember that either. Or his kisses, which she must have enjoyed at the time, though the idea of them now... Becky screwed up her face in distaste.

Luca now, she could happily imagine Luca standing here at the side of her bed, gazing down at her in that smouldering way of his. So very different from Jack in every way, Luca was. Kissing Luca would be like walking one of those tightropes acrobats used in the piazza at Covent Garden. Dangerous and exciting at the same time. Thrilling, that was what Luca's kisses would be, because he really was from a different world. A world of luxury and sinful decadence, like the food she'd eaten, the silk sheets she was lying on, the paintings hanging on the walls and the dreamlike city outside her window. A world to be savoured, relished, as long as she remembered it could never be her world.

Outside in the corridor, she could hear the sound of servants going about their business. It was time for her to concentrate on hers. She had to transform herself into the Queen of Coins. She was to play the demure cousin. She was to make a man a pauper to avenge the death of Luca's father. She didn't know how he died or why, or if it really was murder in the first place. There were a great many questions needing answers before she could fully understand her various roles. If Luca's father had been murdered, Luca was entitled to justice, wasn't he? She'd be doing a good deed by helping him, and in the process helping herself by earning a substantial fee. With renewed determination, Becky slithered down from the bed and began to get dressed before the maid arrived with unwanted offers of help.

After breakfast they had retired to what Luca called the small parlour, and though to Becky it looked like a very large one, it could, she supposed, be described as small compared to the drawing room, measuring only about a quarter of the acreage. The chamber was situated at the back of the *palazzo* with a view out to a smaller, narrower canal. The walls were ruby red, and the ceiling fresco relatively plain, with just a few romping cupids and a smattering of clouds. The fire burning beneath the huge white marble mantelpiece, the well-cushioned sofa and chairs drawn up beside the hearth, the pot of coffee on the little table between the chairs where she and Luca sat facing one another, gave the room an illusion of cosiness—for a palace, that was.

He poured two cups of coffee. It was very strong, black and sugarless, almost chewy compared to the drink she was used to, and Becky wasn't at all sure that she liked it. Luca, on the other hand, clearly relished the stuff, draining his cup in one gulp. 'Carnival begins in earnest soon, and we have a great deal to do in preparation for it. But before we get down to business, I would like to sincerely apologise for my behaviour last night.'

'Oh, please, there is no need...'

'There is every need. I did not even think to ask if you were married, though I assumed you were not, else you would have mentioned it.'

'And quite rightly too!' Becky said indignantly.

'What kind of wife would I be, to have encouraged you to— Not that I did kiss you, but…'

'You did not encourage me,' Luca interrupted, mercifully cutting her short. 'I don't know what possessed me.'

'No more do I,' Becky replied, her cheeks flaming. 'Fortunately we both came to our senses. Despite appearances, I'm not that sort of woman.'

'That much was obvious given what you told me last night. You left what I am sure could have been a very lucrative career on the stage precisely because you are not that sort of woman. I am extremely sorry if I gave you the impression that I am that sort of man however.' Luca pushed his hair back from his brow, looking deeply uncomfortable. 'You would be forgiven for thinking that I am just like all those others, seeking to take advantage of an innocent…'

'But you didn't, did you? Take advantage, I mean? And you could have,' Becky said painfully. 'The truth is, if you'd kissed me I doubt I'd have stopped you. But you didn't. You're not a bit like them. It didn't even occur to me to compare you to the likes of them.'

'Grazie.'

She was touched. He'd clearly been agonising over something that was just as much her fault as his. 'I'm not an innocent, Luca,' Becky said. 'I'm not what you might call a loose woman, far from it, but I'm not a Cousin Rebecca either. I knew what I was doing.'

'That is more than I did.'

She laughed, strangely relieved by this admission. 'Shall we forget it ever happened?'

'Easier said than done.'

'Then why don't we concentrate on the job in hand?'

His expression became immediately serious. 'You are right. I will begin, if I may, with a short history lesson, for our city plays a pivotal role in the story. Venice, you see, was once a great city, one of the world's oldest Republics, and one of the most beautiful. Her treasures were beyond compare.'

He began to pace the room, his hands in the pockets of his breeches, a deep frown drawing his brows together. 'My family have always wielded power here. My father, Conte Guido del Pietro, along with his oldest friend, Don Massimo Sarti, were two of the most respected government officials in 1797 when our city surrendered to Napoleon and the Republic fell. Within a year, Napoleon sold Venice to Austria, but before he left, he ordered the city stripped of every asset. Our treasures, statues, paintings, papers, were torn down, packed away and shipped off to France. It was looting on an unprecedented scale.'

Luca dropped back into his chair, stretching his legs out in front of him. 'But they did not steal everything. My father and Don Sarti acted swiftly to preserve some of our city's heritage. Not the most famous works, that would have drawn unwelcome attention, but some of the oldest, most valuable, most sacred. And papers. The history of our city. All of these, they managed to spirit away before the French even knew they existed, to a hiding place only they knew of. It was a tremendous risk for them to take in order to preserve our city's heritage. In the eyes of our oppressors, their actions would be deemed treasonable, and the penalty for treason is death.'

'In England, the penalty for everything is death,' Becky said, curling her lip. 'Whether you steal a silk handkerchief or plot to kill the King.' Or indeed cheat while unwittingly playing cards with one of the King's relatives.

'My father,' Luca said icily, 'did not commit treason. Quite the reverse. It was a noble act born of patriotism. He preserved what belonged to Venice for Venice.'

Becky was about to point out that, whatever his motives, he had stolen the artefacts, but thought better of it. The man, in his son's eyes at least, was obviously some sort of saint. 'What was he planning on doing with all this treasure,' she asked, 'presuming he didn't plan on keeping it buried for ever?'

'They thought, my father and Don Sarti, that the Republic would be quickly restored, at which point they would return the treasures to the city. Sadly, they were mistaken. France gave Venice to Austria. Austria handed Venice back to France. Now, thanks to Wellington, we have lasting peace in Europe, and it looks like Venice will remain as it is, in the Kingdom of Lombardy–Venetia, part of the Austrian empire once more.

'Bear with me, Becky,' Luca added with a sympathetic smile, 'I can see you are wondering what this has to do with your presence here. All is about to become clear. You see, earlier this year my father came to the conclusion that the political situation was now stable enough to negotiate with the authorities for the restoration of the treasures on a no-questions-asked basis.'

Becky frowned. 'Wouldn't that be risky? Since he

had committed treason, according to the law, I mean. Not that I meant to imply…'

'No, you are right,' Luca agreed. 'It was a risk, but one worth taking, my father believed. For those who rule Venice now, it would be a very popular move, to have a hand in restoring what everyone believed lost. But it had been more than twenty years since the treasure had been hidden. Before he broached the idea with the powers that be, my father visited the hiding place, thinking to make a full inventory, only to find it gone. Stolen by the only other person who knew of its existence,' Luca said grimly. 'Don Sarti, his co-conspirator and best friend!'

'Good heavens! But why? If Don Sarti's motives were as noble as your father's…'

'They were, in the beginning, but it seems Don Sarti is in thrall to something which supersedes all other loyalties. Cards.' Luca dug his hands into the deep pockets of his coat, frowning up at the cupid-strewn ceiling. 'When my father confronted him, he confessed to having sold a few pieces each year to play at the *ridotti*, the private gaming hells which operate only during Carnival, hoping each time to recoup his losses.'

'All gamblers believe their next big win is just a turn of the cards away,' Becky said. 'It is what keeps them coming back to the tables.'

'I don't understand it.' Luca shook his head. 'It is one thing to play with one's own money, but to gamble the heritage of our city—Don Sarti knew he was committing a heinous crime. At first, my father thought that everything was lost, but Don Sarti told him he had only recently sold the bulk of the treasure on the black market with the intention of playing deep at the next Carnival, hoping to win double, treble his total losses. He swore it was his intention to gift his winnings back to the city.'

Luca cursed viciously under his breath. '*Mi scusi*, it is difficult for me to talk about this without becoming enraged. The perfidy of the man! To attempt to *justify* his behaviour, to think that he could atone for the loss of irreplaceable artefacts. My father could not believe he had fallen so low.'

'I think,' Becky said tentatively, 'that he probably believed what he said. I've come across men like Don Sarti. It is a madness that grips them. They will beg, steal or borrow to ensure another turn of the cards, another roll of the dice. As long as they have a stake, they will play.' She had always tried to avoid playing against such pathetic creatures. The memory of her time at the tables in the hells was shameful, tinged as it was with the memory of how she had been persuaded to play there in the first place, but that experience was precisely what Luca was paying for. 'I presume,' she said to him, 'that Don Sarti refused to surrender the money into your father's keeping?'

'You presume correctly. My father informed him in no uncertain terms that he would do everything in his power to stop him, going so far as to say that he would make public the story of what they had done, risking his own freedom and his reputation, if Don Sarti did not hand over his ill-gotten gains. The treasure was gone, but what money was left belonged to Venice. Whether or not he would have carried out his threat I will never know, for Don Sarti decided not to take the risk.'

'That was why he had him killed?' Becky whispered, appalled. 'Oh, Luca, that's dreadful.'

'*Si.*' He was pale, his eyes dark with pain, his hands clenched so tightly into fists that his knuckles were white. 'Fortunately for me, unfortunately for Don Sarti, my father wrote to me in desperation as soon as he returned home from that fateful interview, urging me to return to Venice as soon as possible.'

'So that's how you know!' Becky exclaimed, 'I did wonder…'

'But no. I didn't receive the letter. Instead, as I told you yesterday, the summons which reached me was from my mother, informing me that my father had died. He had been dead almost two months by the time I arrived in Venice, in June. As far as I knew, my father had drowned, slipping on the steps of the *palazzo* in the early hours. He was the worse for wine, so the gondolier claimed, and there was a thick fog when it happened. Though the alarm was raised, help arrived too late to save him. When his body was finally pulled from the canal, he had been dead for some hours.'

'How tragic,' Becky said, aware of the inadequacy of her words.

Luca nodded grimly. 'The summons my father sent finally reached me here in July, having followed in my wake from Venice to London to Plymouth to Glasgow and back. You can imagine how guilty I felt, knowing that I had arrived far too late. He had never asked me for help before, and I had failed him.'

Becky swallowed a lump in her throat. 'But even if you had received the letter telling you of Don Sarti's treachery…'

'Ah, no, that letter contained no details, save to bid my urgent return. My father would not risk his post being intercepted. I was not exaggerating when I said there are spies everywhere. No, there was but one clue in that letter. My father said that he had acquired a new history of the Royal Navy, and looked forward to my thoughts on the volume. It was there, in that book in the library, that he had placed the papers relating the whole sorry affair, exactly as I have told you.'

'What about your mother?'

'She knew nothing, until I showed her the letter. She was almost as shocked as I. My father had been preoccupied in the weeks before he died, a delicate matter of city business, he told her, but nothing more. She didn't even know he had summoned me home.'

Luca wandered over to the window, to gaze out at the narrow canal. Becky joined him. The houses opposite looked almost close enough to touch. 'It's a big leap,' she said, 'from learning that your father's been betrayed by his best friend, to assuming the best friend has had him killed.'

'It was only when I questioned the palace gondoliers and discovered that both of them had been suddenly taken ill that day, forcing my father to use a hired gondola, that I began to question events. I can find no trace of the gondolier described by Brunetti. And then there was the timing. It was, according to my major-domo, almost three in the morning when the gondolier roused the *palazzo* to tell them my father had fallen in, yet my father left the *palazzo* where he had been dining with friends at just after eleven.'

'So you think that the gondolier waited to make certain that he was drowned?'

'I don't think he was one of our Venetian gondoliers at all. They are a tight-knit group of men, Becky. Hard-working and honest. If this man who brought my father back had been one of them, they would have known who he was.'

'You think he was actually an assassin hired by Don Sarti and sent to silence your father?'

'My father had threatened to expose him. Don Sarti would have been desperate to avoid that at all costs. Taking account of all the circumstances, I think it is almost certain, don't you?'

'Yes, I'm afraid I do. Is there no way you can bring him to justice?'

'If by that you mean getting the authorities involved, then no. I have no tangible proof of murder, and the only evidence that the treasure was hidden is my father's letter which, if it was made public, would destroy his reputation. I have no option but to find some other way to hold Don Sarti to account. If my father had been less honourable, if he had not tried to prevent Don Sarti from losing everything they had tried to protect, then he would still be alive today.' Luca took a shuddering breath. 'If I had received that letter in time, perhaps he would be alive still.'

'You can't think that way,' Becky said fervently. 'Even if you had received the letter earlier, you still wouldn't have returned to Venice in time to prevent your father's murder, would you?' Which was no doubt true, but for Luca, she understood, quite irrelevant. He would continue to torture himself with guilt until he had found a way to atone. Finally, she understood his plan. 'You can't bring him back,' she said, 'but you can prevent Don Sarti squandering Venice's money, just as your father wished, is that it? You want me to win it back?'

'Yes.' Luca let out a long, heartfelt sigh. 'That is my plan exactly. I want to reclaim the money for my city, and I want to see Don Sarti destroyed in the process. I want to use his vice against him. We will turn the tables on him, quite literally. We will indulge this passion of his until he has returned everything he took from the city. I have to do this, Becky. *Per amor del cielo*, I have no choice. Until it is done, my life is not my own.'

That too she could see, in the haunted look in his eyes. 'How much do I have to win?' Becky asked, knowing already that she didn't want to hear the answer.

'I don't know for sure, but I can tell you what my father estimated.'

He did, and the sum he named made her blanch. 'It sounds like a king's ransom.'

'A city's ransom. It is a dangerous game we will play. If the stakes are too high for you, you can, as The Procurer said, return to England.'

And face the threat of the gallows? Not likely, Becky thought. 'We have a saying back home, as well to be hung for a sheep as a lamb. One—what do you call it?—*scudo*, or a thousand or a million, I don't suppose it'll make any difference, it's all the same to me. It's not my money I'll be staking, and as for the winnings—what are you planning to do with your winnings, Luca, assuming you're not going to litter the streets of Venice with gold for people to pick up?'

'I hadn't thought that far ahead. Does this mean that I can rely on you?'

She knew she should consider more carefully, but what was the point! Luca desperately needed help for a very good cause. She desperately wanted to earn that fee, her ticket to freedom from a life of trickery, and to dodge the noose. It was risky, extremely risky, but there were always ways of managing risk, always ways of making fortune work in your favour. 'If there's a way to pull it off, I'll find it,' she said, 'but you need to understand one golden rule about gambling. Even when the deck is stacked, there are no guarantees.'

'I think I would trust you less if you tried to pretend otherwise.' He kissed her hand. 'You come to me under tragic circumstances, but you are a beacon of light at the end of a very dark tunnel.' He pressed another kiss to her fingertips before releasing her. 'I don't know about you, but I am in dire need of some refreshment before we continue. My mother will be home soon, and we still have a great deal to discuss.'

Luca's idea of refreshment was more strong black coffee. It arrived so promptly when he rang the bell that Becky thought they must have an endless supply on tap in the kitchen. Just a few sips, and she felt her heart begin to race.

'Would you prefer tea?' he asked, already on to his second cup as she set hers aside.

'No, thank you. This stuff might be mother's milk to you, but if I have any more I'll have palpitations.'

'Mother's milk, that is what they call gin in London, isn't it?'

'You're thinking of mother's ruin. And that's not my cup of tea either. Shall we continue?'

He nodded. 'I have been thinking,' he said, looking

decidedly uncomfortable, 'about your role as Cousin Rebecca. If you are to play it convincingly, it is not only a matter of wearing the right clothes.'

'You mean manners and etiquette? How to behave in polite society. I know I need some help, but I'm a quick learner, I promise.'

'Then you won't be offended if I ask my mother to give you some pointers?'

'I would be delighted,' Becky said, heartily relieved. 'I would have asked you myself, only I didn't want you to think I'm not up to the role. Are you sure she'll be willing to help me?'

'Certainly, because by helping you she'll be helping me.'

'She won't be used to mingling with the likes of me.'

Luca smiled faintly. 'I've never met the likes of you. I find you a very intriguing mixture, Miss Becky Wickes.'

It didn't sound at all like a compliment, so it was silly of her to be blushing like a school chit. 'You make me sound like a cake batter.'

He laughed. 'My mother will like you, I am sure of it.'

Since it wasn't in her interests to contradict him, Becky decided to hold her tongue. 'It's not just a matter of how I behave when I'm Cousin Rebecca though,' she said. 'It's about…'

'The cards,' Luca said, pre-empting her.

'Well, yes.'

'We use different packs here, and we play different games, if that's what you were going to ask.'

'I was.'

'I can teach you. I'm not an expert, I'll have to rely on you to determine how to—to…'

'Cheat. You might as well call a spade a spade, if you'll forgive the terrible pun. That's my particular field of expertise. But there's more to it than that. This Carnival…'

'There is nothing like it. It is exciting, it is dangerous, it is a time of intrigue and of decadence. The whole city takes part. You don't know if you are dancing with a countess or a laundry maid, or even,' Luca said with a wicked smile, 'a man or a woman.'

'No! You're teasing me. You're not telling me you've danced with a man?'

He laughed. 'No, I'm not. But there are some women who dress as men to gain access to the *ridotti*.'

'Those are the private gaming hells where I will play?'

'It's where the Queen of Coins will play.'

'Against Don Sarti?'

The teasing light faded from his eyes. 'Eventually. There's much more to discuss, and details to be ironed out. I have the bones of a plan, but I need you to help me flesh it out.'

''If I'm to put my neck on the line, then I'd rather have a say in how I go about it.'

'When it comes to the cards, I will be yours to command.'

She smiled at that. 'I'm betting that will be a first, Captain del Pietro.'

'I mean it.'

For some reason, this brought a lump to her throat. Until Jack, she'd always worked alone. When Jack came along, she'd let him call the shots, not because she thought he was right, but because he thought it was how things should be. Now here was this blue-blooded pirate with his noble cause telling her that he'd defer to her. *'Grazie,'* Becky said gruffly.

'It is I who should thank you. You don't know how much this means to me.'

'I certainly do now.' She smiled shyly. 'And I want to help, Luca, because I understand, not just because you're paying me, though it would be a lie to say that doesn't matter. The fee I've been promised, it might be a drop in the ocean compared to what you're wanting me to win, but it's...'

'Life-changing. That's what you said.'

'Did I? Well, it is.'

'How will you set about changing your life, Becky?'

'Nothing too dramatic. A roof over my head away from the city. Perhaps in the country. Perhaps abroad. Unlike you, I've not travelled to the four corners of the globe. Until I came here, I'd never been further than Brighton.'

'And did you bathe in the sea?'

Becky laughed. 'I wasn't there on holiday, I was there to work. London empties in the summer—at least it empties of those who can afford to leave. And they expect to be entertained in Brighton, just as in London.'

'Ah, so it was in your acting days, then?'

'No, after that. I was what you'd call a street performer. Card tricks, sleight of hand. It's how I earned my corn, after I left the theatre, as I told you, mostly in Covent Garden, which is where The Procurer saw me perform, but I spent a few summers in Brighton.'

'You are full of surprises.'

'I like to think so.'

'You can have no idea, but you'd fit in perfectly with the Carnival, where what you call street performers roam every street and every square. In St Mark's especially, there are tumblers and rope walkers, puppet shows, fortune tellers and any number of men happy to relieve you of your money with the type of tricks you describe.'

'But no women?'

'I've never seen any.'

'I like to think I could best any man.'

'I've never seen you at work, but I don't think I'd like to bet against you.' Luca frowned. 'But you have played in gaming hells too, you said? The *ridotti* will not be alien to you?'

'I played,' Becky said tersely, 'after I gave up working the piazza about a year ago. I won't be sorry if I never have to enter another one of these places again, after I leave here.'

'They would not have permitted you to play, a woman alone, would they? You would have needed a male companion, an accomplice.'

Becky hesitated. She was extremely reluctant to allow Jack any part of this conversation, but she was even more uncomfortable with Luca imagining her playing the tables aided and abetted by another sharp, just like a common criminal. 'He wasn't an accomplice,' she said belligerently. 'You could call him my paramour.' Which is what the press had labelled Jack, making it sound like *he* was the one in thrall to her. She glowered at Luca. 'Not any longer. I'm quite unattached, and I've no desire to ever be anything else. Is that clear enough for you?'

'I beg your pardon. I did not mean to upset you.'

'You didn't.' Which was patently untrue. She forced a smile. 'I don't like to talk about my life back in England. It's over, that's all you need to know.'

'And you have a new life waiting at the end of Carnevale, yes? Which will be early February this year, for the celebrations must end at the beginning of Lent. What will you do with your fee?'

'I'll buy a little cottage and a comfy chair, and I'll keep my fire burning day and night. Oh, yes, and I'll have a larder full of food.'

'You have modest ambitions.'

'Modest by your standards, not at all by mine. It's more than I've ever had. What will you do, when this is over and you've paid your debt to your father and to Venice?'

'I intend to build ships, as I mentioned,' Luca said.

'What about your responsibilities as Conte del Pietro? Won't you be expected to fill your father's shoes?'

'Probably. There have been overtures, but like you, I have not really considered the practicalities. There, that is another thing we have in common.'

Becky laughed nervously. 'We've almost nothing in common.'

He studied her, a half-smile playing on his lips. 'Are you thinking that is what attracts us? The strangeness?'

'Well, yes,' she said, taken aback. 'I was thinking that.'

'And then there is the fact that you are my avenging angel,' he said. 'I would be bound to be attracted to my salvation.'

'I hadn't thought of that,' Becky said. Her own attempt at a smile died on her lips as her eyes met his, and she could have sworn that the air between them positively crackled. It didn't matter how attracted he was to her or how attracted she was to him, she told herself, she could not possibly be thinking about kissing him.

A soft tap on the door made them both jump guiltily apart just as the servant appeared. 'My mother has returned,' Luca translated. 'She is anxious to meet her niece.'

Chapter Four

'Now, make your curtsy as if I was the Contessa Albrizzi, Rebecca. No, not so deep. That is better. Now, let me see you take a turn around the room.'

Contessa Isabel del Pietro retired to her favourite chair in the drawing room, the one by the tall window looking out on to the Grand Canal also favoured by her son, and Becky obediently began to parade in front of her. It was almost two weeks since she had arrived in Venice, almost two weeks of what she called her Cousin Rebecca lessons, and the Contessa was a hard taskmistress with an eagle eye. Becky had had no idea that putting one foot in front of the other could be so complicated. *Back straight! Chin up! Shoulders back but still relaxed!* There were times when she felt as if she were on a military parade ground, except that she was expected to combine all these things with the ability to glide, which meant walking with slightly bent knees. What was more, even though her head was to be up, her eyes were to be down, and heaven forfend that any bit of her swayed or jiggled or caused her skirts to swish.

Cousin Rebecca was proving the most taxing role she had ever taken on in her life. She'd never had to rehearse so much and so often. She was surprised there wasn't a path worn in the rugs in her bedchamber, from her practising over and over in the small hours of the morning. Walking. Sitting. Curtsying. Holding a glass. Holding a knife. Drinking coffee. Sipping Prosecco. So many things to learn in such a short time. The nights weren't nearly long enough. It was exhausting and tedious, but it was worth it, if she was to avoid giving herself away. Becky ended her perambulation, sinking carefully on to the chair in the prescribed ladylike manner.

The Contessa smiled approvingly. 'Well done, you've come on leaps and bounds.'

'Which is, ironically, one of the things I'm not permitted to do.'

The Contessa laughed. 'You are a much-needed breath of fresh air. Shall I ring for tea?'

'I'll do it.' Becky jumped to her feet to tug the bell. 'How I am progressing? Honestly, if you please.'

'You are doing splendidly. Unless one was searching for evidence to the contrary, no one would take you for anything other than what we claim you to be, my niece.'

'But if one *was* searching for evidence…'

'I meant to reassure you, Rebecca. You are too much of a perfectionist.'

'There's no such thing, not when the stakes are so high.'

A tiny frown marred the smooth perfection of the Contessa's brow. 'I hope my son's desire for justice is not placing you in any real danger.'

Clearly Luca had not confided the detail of his plans to his mother. Becky was torn. She did not want to lie, but the truth was that they were going to be playing a very dangerous game. Or games.

'Forgive me,' the Contessa said, sparing Becky the necessity of prevaricating. 'I should not have asked, for it places you in a very awkward position. I commend your loyalty to my son. I hope he has earned it.'

'Luca is paying me handsomely, Contessa. Money that will transform my life.'

'Money is not everything.'

'I beg your pardon, but it is when you are obliged to count every penny.'

The faintest tinge of colour appeared in the Contessa's sharp cheekbones. 'I did not mean to patronise you. You are so very confident, so assured, so quick to learn and assimilate everything I say, and I have been enjoying our time together so much that I had almost forgotten that you are not my niece.'

The Contessa took the scrap of lace she called a handkerchief from her pocket, and began to fold and refold it on her lap. Confident, she'd said. Assured. Obviously none of Becky's doubts and fears had shown through. Pride mingled with relief, but looking at the Contessa's troubled expression, she felt a twinge of conscience. 'I practise a lot,' she confessed, 'in my room, at night. It doesn't come as naturally to me as you might imagine.'

This admission gained her a faint smile, but the Contessa's frown deepened. 'Did you go hungry, Becky?'

More times than she cared to remember, back in the days when she'd found herself suddenly motherless. But Becky chose to forget those days. 'I've never been a charity case,' she said with justifiable pride. 'I'm twenty-two years old. I've been looking after myself perfectly well for most of my life.'

The Contessa flinched. 'I didn't mean to pry, I was merely interested in learning about your life in London. It is a treat to converse with a fellow Englishwoman. I apologise if my curiosity has caused me to overstep the mark.' She tucked her kerchief back into her pocket. 'Your new wardrobe will be delivered tomorrow. I was thinking that...'

Becky listened with half an ear as the Contessa mused on Cousin Rebecca's various toilettes. She never talked about herself. No one was ever interested in her history or her opinions. She couldn't even recall Jack asking her what she thought or felt about anything. Now here were two people wanting to know all about her, wanting to understand her, when she wasn't sure she understood herself.

Across from her, the Contessa had moved on to the subject of footwear. Becky could not accustom herself to this elegantly beautiful, intelligent woman taking an interest in her. Like her son, she seemed to have the ability to read minds too accurately for Becky's liking. Those eyes, so like Luca's, seemingly sleepy, heavy-lidded, were anything but. There were no airs and graces about the Contessa, but despite that, there was something compelling about her. She was the type of person all eyes followed when she walked into a room, just like Luca.

The major-domo arrived with his cohorts carrying the tea things. 'I'll see to it, Brunetti,' Becky said in her best Cousin Rebecca accent, eager to demonstrate that she'd learnt another lesson to perfection. Brunetti, she knew now, spoke perfect English.

'Is everything to your satisfaction, *signorina*?'

Becky inspected the table. She lifted the lid of the little silver salver to make sure there was enough lemon. Just to annoy Brunetti, she shifted the sugar tongs fractionally to the left. 'Thank you,' she said, bestowing her newly acquired demure smile.

The doors closed, and the Contessa chuckled. 'Very good, Rebecca.'

'Becky, if you please. When we're alone and I'm not in character.' She poured the tea, adding a lemon slice to the Contessa's cup, milk to her own, tinkling the spoon against the china in that irritating manner which was apparently *de rigueur*.

The olive branch was noted. The Contessa smiled. 'Then you must call me Isabel. I was telling you that your clothes are being delivered tomorrow. You must be quite sick of being cooped up here in the *palazzo*, with me drilling you for most of the day in etiquette, then playing cards with Luca all evening.'

'Drilling.' Becky grinned. 'I was just thinking to myself that's exactly what it feels like sometimes, being on an army parade ground when I'm with you.'

'Am I a terrible taskmaster?'

'Yes, but that's exactly what I need. Luca's eager to take Cousin Rebecca out into the world, so I need to be ready.'

Isabel sipped daintily at her tea. 'How are you getting on with my son?'

'He's a demanding taskmaster, just like you,' Becky said warily.

'Though neither of us is as hard on you as you are on yourself.'

'I've no intention of picking up a Venetian deck to play for money until I know I can make the cards do exactly what I want them to. I'm very good, but even I need to practise.'

Isabel set her teacup down with a sigh. 'My apologies. I am interfering, and I promised my son I would not.' To Becky's surprise, she reached over to touch her hand lightly. 'I suspect it's because you've given me a purpose, something to focus on since Guido died.'

'I'm sorry. I sometimes forget that it's not just Luca who lost his father. You lost your husband.'

'I find myself with too much time on my hands, but you must not be thinking that my heart is broken.' Isabel's sardonic smile was very like her son's. 'I was fond enough of Guido, but we were never close and had little in common. Our marriage was arranged. Once I'd given birth to Luca, and the lustiest, healthiest of babies he was too, my husband ceased his visits to my bedchamber. It is the custom here, you see, for the eldest son to inherit everything, the Venetian nobility's way of preserving their vast wealth. If I'd had a second son, he would be expected to remain a single man, and as to daughters— Well, dowries for daughters also dilute a family's wealth.'

'But you're not a Venetian,' Becky exclaimed, aghast, 'and the del Pietro family must be far too wealthy to worry about diluting anything. Did you know this when you married him? Didn't you want more children?'

'I would very much have liked the companionship

of a daughter, though I suppose it is a selfish thing to wish.' Isabel smiled sadly. 'In any event, I was not given the choice. Perhaps if I'd explained my wishes to Guido. But, no, that's preposterous, he would not have listened, and I was much too young to make any demands of my husband. Besides, these Venetian traditions, they are very much entrenched. I was expected to be by his side at all times, apart from in his bed. Would you mind pouring me another cup of tea, please? No, no more lemon. Thank you.'

The polite smile was back, making it clear that the subject was closed. Cousin Rebecca wouldn't dream of doing anything but follow her aunt's lead, but Becky was done with Cousin Rebecca for the moment. 'You must have missed him terribly. Luca, I mean, when he was sent off to England at such a young age.'

'Oh, I would not have dreamed of keeping Luca here in Venice kicking his heels. He was bored rigid by school. He has a very restless nature. He reminds me so much of my own brother. A born sailor, is Mathew, and Luca is too. Though, of course,' Isabel added ruefully, 'Guido always attributed every one of Luca's qualities to his own bloodline. Though he is half-English, as far as Guido was concerned, his son could only ever be wholly Venetian.'

'What does Luca think?'

'Come, Becky, you know the answer to that perfectly well. Luca is a Venetian to his core. Why else would he be so set on this complex plan he is embarking on?'

'Don't you wish for justice? Even if you weren't close, your husband was murdered.'

'And I do most sincerely mourn him, but I fail to

see how humiliating Don Sarti will make me feel any better.'

'It's not about humiliation. Luca wants—' Becky cut herself short. It wasn't her place to argue Luca's case with his mother. 'He feels he has no choice,' she compromised. 'I mean, a letter like the one his father left him, from beyond the grave, it's not exactly something he could ignore.'

'I suppose not. And at least it has brought you into my life. I very much enjoy your company. You will see for yourself when you go out in society, that Venice is not a city which invites intimacy of that kind. Confidences can be sold. Secrets can be betrayed. One must always be on one's guard.'

'Luca's forever telling me that. I thought he was being overcautious.'

'I doubt that is possible. It is a relief to be able to talk frankly as we do. I know you are not truly my niece, but I hope you consider me a friend?'

What Isabel had told her of her life, her marriage, made Becky realise she'd assumed an awful lot and been wrong on every count. That a countess living in a palace could be lonely! That she could have let her husband deprive her of children, pack her only son off to England and then deprive her even of being able to claim any of that son's qualities for her own. It took her breath away. 'You know my stay here is a short one,' Becky said. 'By the time Carnival is over at the latest, I'll be gone.'

'And my son, I hope, will finally be able to stop looking over his shoulder to the past, and look forward to the future. Are you worried that I'll become overfond of you, Becky?'

She was startled into laughter. 'I'm worried that I'll get too fond of you!'

'Then we'd better make the most of each other's company while we can.' Isabel got to her feet, shaking out her skirts. 'To work, Rebecca. Let us take a turn around the room together, as two genteel ladies are wont to do, and talk about fashion.'

Becky had mastered the games of Primero and Ombre easily enough, but Trappola was a harder nut to crack. The name meant to cheat or to deceive, Luca had told her. Trappola was unique to Venice, he claimed, and Becky could understand why. She picked up the special deck of cards reserved for the game. Swords, Cups, Coins and Batons. *Spade*, she said to herself as she dealt them out in their suites. *Coppe. Denari. Bastoni.* Each suite had three face cards: the Knave or Foot Soldier, the Knight or Cavalier, and the King. For this particular game, there was no three, four, five or six. And no Queen. When she played Trappola at Carnevale she would be the only Queen of Coins.

Becky shuffled expertly and began to practise her dealing, setting herself more and more complex hands to achieve: dealing from the bottom; dealing herself two cards; making false cuts. This was the easy part, the foundation of all the tricks she had played in her Covent Garden days, and the secret to her winning streaks in the gaming hells. Working with a different pack made little difference to the techniques required.

Bored, she began to build a house of cards. Luca had been called away during dinner by the arrival of an old acquaintance of his father's, newly returned to Venice after a long absence, and anxious to pay his condolences. Becky had assumed that he would join her in the small drawing room as usual when he was free, but it had been an hour since she and Isabel had risen from the dinner table. She should probably go to bed. Isabel was right—she was exhausted between learning to be Cousin Rebecca and practising to be the Queen of Coins. Becky had also been working relentlessly on each role and on the lingo, acutely aware of the clock inexorably moving towards the time when she must make her debut, the weight of responsibility making it almost impossible to sleep when she could be honing her skills.

It was almost ten o'clock, according to the huge clock which ticked quietly in the far corner of the room. The card house was complete. Becky toppled it and began to build another, adding in a second pack of cards. She really should go to bed. The days were beginning to blur one into the other. Had she and Luca really almost kissed in this very room? Maybe she'd imagined it. Certainly, Luca gave no sign of remembering when they sat here, night after night. He was all business. Cards and vocabulary. Vocabulary and cards. The Procurer had been right in predicting that Becky would find the lingo easy. Italian was a lovely melodic language, though the Venetian accent was much harsher. Like cockney compared to the King's English, she thought when she heard the servants speak it amongst themselves, though she wouldn't dream of saying so to Luca.

Another card house was complete. Becky studied it carefully and began to dismantle it, card by card. It was a child's trick, one of the first she'd learnt, but it still made her smile. A question of balance. And of building it just right, of course. There came a point when this card or maybe the next would prove one card too many. A point just before that when it looked impossible, as if the cards on each layer were floating. And then…

She slid the next card out, knowing what would happen, watching with satisfaction as it collapsed in an orderly fashion.

'*Brava.*'

Becky jumped. Luca was standing in the doorway. 'How long have you been there?'

'Long enough to be fascinated.' He walked towards her, pulling out the chair beside her at the card table. 'I take it that you must construct it in such a way that you know which cards are the supporting ones?'

'Something like that.'

'Who taught you to do it?'

'A magician called The Wonderful Waldo. He was a warm-up act in the early days when I was onstage. He wasn't very good, to be honest, but he taught me the basics of card tricks.'

'I'm sorry that I kept you waiting so long. Don Carcolli wished to reminisce of Venice in the old days before Napoleon, when he and my father and Don Sarti more or less ran the city. I thought I might hear something of interest regarding Don Sarti, but like everyone else, Don Carcolli thinks the man a pillar of society.'

'Doesn't anyone know that he plays deep?'

Luca shrugged. 'If they do, they do not speak of it.' He picked up the cards with little enthusiasm. 'We should practise.'

'Yes, we should. Here, give them to me. I've mixed

two packs up.' Becky reached for the cards. Luca's hand covered hers, and she froze. Lifting her eyes to meet his, she could see that he was thinking along similar lines. Not playing cards, but indulging in illicit kisses.

And then he gave himself an almost imperceptible shake before removing his hand. 'Trappola?'

It was a relief to know that he was as determined as she not to be distracted. Except that now she was. 'Trappola,' Becky muttered, preparing to deal, then immediately changing her mind. 'I hope you won't take offence, but I need to pit myself against a more skilled player. Honestly, Luca, speaking as someone who knows, you'll never make a gambler.'

'Am I really that bad?'

She squirmed. 'It's not that you're so very bad, it's just that I'm…'

'An expert. Which is why you and not I will play Don Sarti,' Luca said with a mocking little bow. 'I hadn't considered the need for you to play for real before Carnevale, but I should have. I will think on it. But in the meantime, since I am not worthy to pit my wits against you, will you demonstrate some of your card tricks? Just for fun, mind you. I want you to fleece Don Sarti, not me!'

'I'm already relieving you of a small fortune for my services,' Becky said, more than happy to indulge in a different sort of distraction. 'You can have this for free. So watch carefully.' She shuffled. 'I always started with the flashy stuff. Producing a card from behind someone's ear, that kind of thing,' she said, doing just that, and bursting into a peal of laughter at Luca's astonished expression. 'The aim is to draw an audience, then you can go through your repertoire. The best tricks are the ones that everyone thinks they can see through. Like this one.'

She spread an array of cards on the table. 'Pick one,' she said. 'Now, look at it, and don't let me see. Now, put it back anywhere in the pack.' She performed a complex shuffle, the cards cascading through the air from one hand to the other. One escaped and fluttered on to the table.

'I thought you said you were an expert,' Luca said.

Becky smiled. 'Turn it over.'

'It's my card! That must just be a coincidence.'

Becky arched her brow, then repeated the trick. And then repeated it again. 'You see, you're sure that all it takes is for you to watch me more and more closely,' she said, 'then you'll catch me out.' She turned over the card he thought he had selected freely once again. 'But you won't. And the crowd never did either. At the end, I would pass round a hat. People threw in a few coins, depending on how much I'd entertained them, and how much they could afford to give.'

'If you'd permitted them to bet against you, you could have made a great deal more money.'

'That wouldn't sit well with me.'

'I know, and I very much admire you for that.' Luca caught her wrist as she made to shuffle again. 'Whatever happens, you cannot go back to that life.'

Completely taken aback, Becky let the cards fall. 'If I fail here, I might have no choice.'

His gaze dropped to her hand, where his fingers circled her wrist. He stared at it for some moments, his heavy lids covering his eyes, allowing her no clue to his thoughts. Then he lifted her hand to his mouth, pressing a kiss to her wrist. 'Then we will simply have to ensure that we do not fail,' he said, smiling. 'Show me another trick. This time I am determined to spot how you do it.'

She was unsettled, though she wasn't sure why. Her time in Venice so far, though brief, had been all-consuming. She'd conveniently forgotten it would come to an end and she'd have to consider her future. But there really was no point in worrying about it just at the moment, when what she should be doing was concentrating on earning the money that would at least offer her choices.

She picked up the cards, slipped back into her Covent Garden role and expertly riffled the deck. 'This time, you pick the card and hold on to it. Look at it, remember what it is, then place it face down on the table.' Shuffling—nice, showy shuffling—was required here, to hold his attention. 'The card you selected is the Ace of Cups.'

'How on earth do you know?'

'Because I have it here,' Becky said triumphantly, turning the top card over to reveal the Ace.

'You can't have because I...'

'You have the Knave of Swords.' The way his face fell as he turned over the card made her burst into a peal of laughter.

'How on earth did you do that?'

'Magic.'

'Show me some more,' he said eagerly.

'This one's called Find the Lady,' she said, beginning to enjoy herself as she set out the cards. 'But since we've no Queen of Hearts we'll use the King of Coins, see here? Ready? Now, what you have to do is...'

* * *

'Tricked again!' Luca threw down the card he'd picked in mock disgust. He grinned, pushing back his hair from his eyes. 'Don't explain how you do it, I prefer to believe it really is magic. I would have liked to see you perform in front of an audience. You have a presence—is that the word?—like the best actresses when they come on to the stage, you know?'

'I do, though I think you're flattering me.'

'Not at all. I mean it.' He studied her as she sorted them into their separate suits and packs with speed and dexterity without seeming to look. She was a different person when she worked her tricks, managing to draw him in, making him feel as if she was wholly absorbed in him, only in him, and at the same time creating a barrier between them, as if she were untouchable. He couldn't explain it, he couldn't have said what it was that changed in her expression or her voice or her manner, only that now, as she set the cards aside, it was gone, and she was Becky again. Or the person he knew as Becky, which was different from the one who played Cousin Rebecca so exhaustively during the day and throughout every meal. Was this the real one? He had no way of knowing.

How hard he had worked to stop himself from imagining showering her with kisses as they sat here night after night playing cards. His desire for justice burned ever more fiercely as Carnevale approached, but his desire for the woman who would help him achieve it kept pace with it. It was because she was so very different from any other woman he had desired. It was because he had ruled her out of bounds that he wanted so desperately to break his own rules. It was because she was his avenging angel. He understood all these things, but they did not make his attraction to her any less real.

Becky closed the lacquered box which held the cards. She met his eyes and read his thoughts instantly. He watched, fascinated, as his desire kindled hers. Her eyes became lambent, and her mouth softened, becoming sensuous. Was he imagining it? No, he was sure he was not, and his resolve crumbled.

He pulled her to her feet, wrapping his arms tightly around her. 'I have tried so hard not to think about this.' If she resisted, he would let her go. Sophistry. He knew she would not resist. Her hair had escaped its daytime pinning, forming a cloud of curls around her face. She had such a delightful curve to her bottom that it was impossible to resist the temptation to flatten his hands over it, relishing the little puff of breath that escaped her mouth as he pulled her closer.

It wasn't a good kiss—it was too awkward. She was too small, and he was too tall. They weren't adjusted. They were far too eager. They had waited too long. He lifted his head, saw his confusion reflected in her eyes, wondering how something that should have been so perfect could be so disappointing. Now was the time to stop, Luca told himself, but she made no move to free herself and he was already beyond logic.

Their lips met again. He kissed her slowly, resisting the urge to devour her, sensing the same urge and the same restraint in her. Already he was on fire with wanting her, already afraid that he would lose control. He ran his fingers through her hair, tugging it free of restraining pins so that it cascaded down her back. The skin at the nape of her neck was hot. She watched him, violet eyes under heavy lids, both imperious and sultry. He kissed her again, and she gave a little moan as his mouth found hers, that both reassured and aroused. This was what fire would taste like, feel like, enveloping them both as their mouths opened to each other, as their tongues touched, danced, teased.

He ran his hand down her spine. A perfect curve. She arched her back, pressing herself urgently against him, and their kisses became wild. Her hands tugged at his coat. He shrugged himself out of it and she ran her fingers down his back, clutching at his buttocks, pulling him tighter against her. He managed to steer them both to a sofa, just enough room for him to lie half on her, half by her side, still kissing. Her gown was too high at the neck, but beneath it her breasts were soft handfuls, her corsets barely in evidence. He teased her nipples, watching with a potent pleasure as she moaned, as they tightened, but it was a double-edged sword, for it only served to rouse him to new heights of yearning.

What the devil was he doing? Appalled at his lack of control, and even more appalled at how easily he could have lost control all together, Luca released her, cursing under his breath. '*Mi scusi.* I did not mean…' He stopped short, unwilling to lie, for he had meant, all of it and more. 'I had no right to take such liberties,' he finished lamely.

Becky pushed herself upright, her colour high, gathering up the hair pins that he had scattered so carelessly. 'You didn't take anything, Luca. If I'd asked, you would have stopped.' She took the pin he had found on the sofa, sticking it carelessly into her hair. 'I don't know why I didn't,' she said, shamefaced. 'You won't believe me now, but I…'

'Am not that sort of woman,' he finished for her wryly. 'But I do know that, and it made no difference, though it should have. You are a respectable woman.'

She laughed drily. 'Hardly. I'm a card sharp.'

'One with principles, who does not take *amore* lightly, I think. While I—I have always taken it very lightly.' Luca shook his head. 'We should not find it so very difficult to restrain ourselves.'

She flinched. 'Well, you did in the end, didn't you? I should thank you.'

'I wish I could say you are welcome. By morning, perhaps I will have persuaded myself it was the right thing to do.'

He was rewarded with a mocking little smile. 'Then there's no point in my bidding you to sleep well?'

'None at all.'

'Try the cards,' Becky said, nodding at the box which sat on the table. 'That will take your mind off anything else.'

'Is that what you'll be doing?'

'Tonight, as I do every night. This one is no different.'

The door closed softly behind her. Luca caught sight of himself in the huge mirror above the mantel and grimaced. His hair was a bird's nest, his cravat a tangled knot and his cheeks flushed. Had a servant walked in on them…

He cursed, pouring himself a small glass of grappa. He took a sip of the potent *digestivo*, closing his eyes as it burned its way down his throat, settling in a warm glow in his belly. What had he been thinking to take such an unnecessary risk when so much was at stake? Another sip, and Luca sank down on to the chair at the card table. He hadn't been thinking; that was the point.

They had not been caught, and he couldn't pretend that he regretted it, though it was true, what he'd said to her. Card sharp or no, Becky was a respectable woman with principles and Luca never dallied with respectable women. He enjoyed women's company. He enjoyed making love, though he had never, contrary to what his friends and fellow officers assumed, been the kind of man who took his pleasures whenever and wherever he could. His Italian blood made him passionate, not indiscriminate.

He finished his grappa. He opened the card box and took out a deck, attempting to shuffle as Becky had, but the cards flew from his hand, scattering on to the floor. She was right—he was no match for her, but how to find someone suitable, without giving their game away? Frowning, Luca retrieved the cards and began to sort them into suits.

Looking back over the nights when they'd sat here playing, he realised that though she talked freely enough of what she called her Covent Garden days, she'd revealed little of her most recent history. He knew that she had plied her trade in gaming hells. He guessed, from the way she talked, that she had loathed it. Why then had she given up street entertainment which, if tonight was anything to judge by, she thoroughly enjoyed? The obvious answer was money, but there was nothing obvious about Becky. She did not play to become rich. So why play the hells at all? Was it the man who had been at her side in those hells? A protector, in more ways than one perhaps, and one she had been happy to leave behind, by the sounds of it.

What had made her take the bold step of coming here to Italy at the behest of The Procurer? Again, money was the obvious answer. Yet her needs were modest. A home, a fire, a full larder were the extent of her ambition. It touched him strangely that she should aim so low, pained him that such an extraordinary woman should dream of such a humble life.

Humble to him, but extraordinary to Becky, Luca reminded himself. Who was he to condemn such a choice, to dare to think it unworthy? She would be offended, and rightly so, if she were privy to his thoughts, but still he couldn't help thinking that she deserved so much more. He had never met a woman like her. Perhaps it wasn't very surprising after all that he found her so fascinating and so irresistible. Even though he knew he was playing with fire.

Luca placed the cards back in the box. Tomorrow night, Becky was to make her debut as Cousin Rebecca. In a few weeks, she'd be making her first appearance as the Queen of Coins. The first steps on the path to seeing justice done for his father, the money returned to Venice, its rightful owner. He poured himself another small measure of grappa and turned his mind to ensuring that happened.

Chapter Five

Becky turned the brass handle on the heavy door at the top of the winding flight of stairs, stepped out on to the roof of the Palazzo Pietro and marvelled at the view laid out before her. Roof after roof of red terracotta tiles topped buildings huddled even more closely together than in the worst of London's rookeries, though they looked decidedly prettier. She made her way to the parapet, leaning over to gaze down at the Grand Canal. From this height, she could make out the twists and turns of the channel as it flowed below bridges before meeting the deep blue waters of the lagoon on which Venice floated. Beyond that, a long strip of land which must be the Lido, and clusters of islands. She'd no idea there were so many.

It was a clear day. The sky was pale blue, for once distinguishable from the turquoise waters below. It was Isabel who'd told her about the rooftop garden, accessed by climbing many staircases, past the servants' quarters to the entrance in the attics. Looking around her, Becky didn't think it much of a garden. There were no plants, no greenery at all, just a couple of benches and a table. A waste, she thought. There were any number of other rooftop gardens visible, real gardens, some with small trees, pots, wooden trellises. It would be lovely up here in the summer.

The view was already lovely. There seemed to be hundreds of churches in the city. The huge one, right on the edge of the lagoon with its vast piazza, she knew was San Marco. It reminded her a little bit of St Paul's, but everywhere she looked she could see others, the bell towers marking their locations. The myriad of canals looked like streets from here, winding through the tightly packed houses, some intersecting, some coming to dead ends, the colours dazzling, changing from shades of blue to green to brown, depending on how narrow they were, how high the buildings lining them and the colour of the painted stone. Becky leaned far over the parapet. She'd never seen buildings painted in such bright colours. Golden yellow. Soft pink. Burnt orange. Sparkling white. Though many, when she peered more closely, seemed to be simply stone, and quite decrepit and crumbling at that. Venice, the city of contrasts, was, when it came to rich and poor, not much different from London. There were so very few open spaces though—no parks, only the piazzas, which she now knew to call *campos*.

She was wearing one of her new gowns. A day dress, Isabel called it. White muslin, printed with broad vertical stripes in shades of buff and blue, the skirt hung straight from the fashionable empire-line bodice. The three-quarter-length sleeves were narrow, fitted tight to her wrists. It looked simple enough, but what a palaver it had been to get into it, with all the buttons and loops and ribbons. A soft breeze ruffled the flimsy fabric, which would have been completely transparent, were it not for the many layers of under-clothes which Becky had donned. Chemises and pet-ticoats and a corset laced so tight she'd protested that she couldn't breathe. It certainly helped make sure she sat up straight. She could now appreciate the need for a lady's maid. You'd have to be an octopus to get yourself dressed without help. Perhaps that explained why young ladies like Cousin Rebecca held on to their innocence for so long, it would be too much effort for any man to get through all those barricades. Perhaps if she had been wearing these clothes last night…

Even though she was completely alone, Becky could feel her cheeks flushing. Just as she'd told Luca she would, she had practised cards into the night, fall-ing into an exhausted sleep which left no room for reflections. Then Cousin Rebecca's wardrobe had ar-rived first thing this morning. There had been an em-barrassing amount of clothes to be unpacked. Far too many for one person's needs, though Isabel had as-sured her otherwise. Day dresses and walking dresses, which seemed completely unnecessary since no one could possibly walk any distance in this city without falling into a canal. There were half dresses and half pelisses and half-boots too, though strangely noth-ing called a whole dress or a quarter-boot. Yards of petticoats. Countless pairs of silk stockings so sheer they could pass through a wedding ring. Nightgowns, dressing gowns, evening gowns. Silk and satin and lace, ribbons and buttons.

'What about this one for your introduction into so-

ciety tonight?' Isabel had asked, holding up a pretty
rose-pink gown. 'Or what about this one? Or this?'

White, lemon, sky blue, mint green, the colours
worn by a young unmarried girl, Becky now knew.
They were all beautiful, but none of them were really
hers. She felt a fraud, looking in the mirror just before
she came up on to the roof. Now she was in costume, a
dress rehearsal for tonight, so to speak, she was overcome with nerves, utterly certain she was going to
falter. Isabel, who already knew her far too well for
comfort, had seen all of this in her face, and sent her
up here to get her equilibrium back, as if she was a set
of scales out of balance when what she was, was a girl
from the rookeries, a fish from a very small pond, suddenly cast into a huge ocean. And she was floundering.

She scanned the view, but not even the beauty of
Venice could distract her. Last night, in the small parlour, for heaven's sake, when any servant could have
walked in on them, she had abandoned herself to passion. She had never before behaved in such a wanton
way, had never before lost all sense of her surroundings, lost all sense of herself, been so consumed with
one and only one desire. She simply couldn't understand it. Luca was nothing to her.

No, that wasn't true. Becky paced to the other side
of the roof, gazing sightlessly down at the network
of narrow canals. Luca was a very attractive man,
there was no doubt about that, and she could happily
admit that his particular combination of good looks
and devil-may-care air appealed to her on a visceral
level. This plan he had concocted, it was bold and it
was risky and it was outrageous, as well as honourable. She might be dreading her debut tonight, but she

was relishing the fact that she was vital to him—or rather to his cause. He made her feel powerful. She enjoyed being his avenging angel. After the disaster at Crockford's and Jack's betrayals, Luca's cause and Luca himself were very welcome balms to her shattered confidence.

So it was hardly surprising he aroused such passion in her, Becky reasoned. Indifference would have been more surprising. She smiled to herself at the very idea. Such a potent combination of extraordinary man and extraordinary circumstances, it was no wonder at all that she had lost control last night. In fact it was a perfectly natural consequence, and nothing at all to be ashamed of. Or worried about either, she decided. It wasn't as if she was in any danger of falling in love with Luca. She'd tried love on for size and it wasn't for her. Besides, there could not be two more different men than Luca and Jack. Becky wrinkled her nose in disgust.

A shout from the window of one of the houses on the far side of the roof attracted her attention. Another shout, and then another, saw her pick her way across the roof in search of the source. There were people hanging out the windows on both sides of the narrow canal beneath, shouting abuse and encouragement at the two groups of men and boys clustered on either side of the bridge. She couldn't make out a word of the Venetian dialect, probably because none of the words were polite enough for Luca to have taught her, but it was obvious enough what was going on. Her own early experience had taught her that the less people owned, the more stoutly they defended their turf.

'Becky, come away from the edge.' Luca grabbed her by the waist, pulling her back. 'If you fell, you would be killed.'

'I won't fall, I've a good head for heights,' she said, determinedly ignoring the little surge of excitement she felt at the sight of him. 'Look down there. It's like the Montagues and the Capulets. I wonder if one of the women screeching like a banshee from the windows is the Juliet they're fighting over.'

The fight had died down, with both sides retreating back across the bridge to their own territory. Catcalls and jeers came from the windows. Then as quickly as it had started, it was over. 'It's lovely up here,' Becky said, allowing Luca to steer her away from the edge. 'It's a shame you don't make more of it. If I had a sanctuary like this, I'd want to be up here all the time.'

Luca scanned the rooftop, a slight frown making a groove between his brows. 'How did you acquire your head for heights? In the theatre perhaps?'

'No, by scrambling about on the roofs of buildings when I was a kid. They were our playground, our secret space.'

'There are any number of parks in London.'

'With an army of park-keepers determined to keep ragamuffins out. I was born into the slums, Luca.'

'The rookeries, yes?' His face wrinkled with distaste. 'I had worked that much out for myself.'

'It wasn't that bad, you know.'

'I think it must have been a great deal worse than you would ever admit. How did someone as extraordinary as you survive such a terrible life? And not only survive but—I don't know how to say it without insulting you—but you are so...'

'Assured is what your mother called me.'

'Did she?' He steered her over to the wooden bench, sitting down beside her. 'You certainly can appear to be most assured. It fooled me for a while. That first day, before I knew better, for example, it would not have occurred to me for one minute that this woman was born and bred in the slums of London.'

'What gave me away?'

He shook his head, smiling thoughtfully. 'You are a very good actress, but I— Ah, I admit, I have been studying you very closely. It is in the eyes, I think. There are times when you make me think of a captain readying a warship for battle. He is focused on giving orders, issuing battle plans, organising flags, cannons, ammunition, thinking only of what is to come, thinking only of victory, and then he sees one of his men offering up a prayer and it is a jolt, like a shot across the bows, a reminder of the reality of war. In that instant, just for an instant, he is afraid.'

She'd dreaded seeing pity in his eyes. What she saw instead was that Luca had bared a little bit of his own soul to show her that he understood. It brought a lump to her throat. She reached for his hand, pressing her lips to his fingertips. 'I've never had to face what you've just described. I could never be so brave.'

'You displayed bravery every day, by resisting the temptation to exploit your card skills.'

'It's not a temptation when you know it would be wrong. I'm not brave, Luca.'

'Remarkable, then, if you prefer. What I'm trying to say is that you could be anything you want, Becky.'

'Thank you,' she said awkwardly, because he looked as if he really meant it, and she didn't know what on earth to make of that. 'What I want right now, is to make a success of my debut as Cousin Rebecca.'

'Are you nervous? You've no need to be. My mother has been singing your praises.'

'She's biased, since I'm the product of all her training.'

'You are the product of all your own hard work. I have no doubt you will make a most demure Cousin Rebecca, and a most intimidating and unbeatable Queen of Coins. From the stage of Drury Lane, through the piazza of Covent Garden, the gaming hells of St James's to the salons of Venice and Carnival, Miss Becky Wickes will be a resounding success in every role she plays.' Luca eyed her quizzically. 'There seems to be no end to the masks you wear. One would think you'd been born a Venetian.'

'Since you compare me to your precious Venice, I suppose I should be honoured.'

'You don't like compliments much, do you?'

'In my experience, people only pay compliments to get on your good side, so you'll do what they want.'

'But you're already doing what I want.'

Becky studied her hands. 'You've no need to pay me compliments, then, have you?'

'I wasn't complimenting you, I was telling you the truth.' Luca shifted on the bench, stretching his legs out in front of him. 'I've never met a woman like you.'

'I've never met a man like you.'

'Different worlds. A unique situation. That is what I told myself last night. That is why I don't recognise my behaviour.'

'That's what I told myself too,' Becky said, surprised into a strange little laugh. 'Perhaps it's the truth.'

'Perhaps it is. I tried to take your advice, but I am afraid that cards could not hold my attention,' Luca said ruefully. 'So I spent much of the night thinking about how to find a way for you to play against an opponent.'

'And were you successful?'

'I'm afraid not. I don't think there is any way it can be done safely. Cards are played outside Carnevale at the Contessa Benzon's *palazzo*, I have heard, but Cousin Rebecca could not possibly play, and we could not invite one of the more experienced players here, for we cannot risk anyone knowing of the connection between Cousin Rebecca and the Queen of Coins.'

Becky pondered this disappointing news. 'Would it be permissible for Cousin Rebecca to watch rather than play?'

'Would that help?' When she nodded, Luca brightened. 'I am sure we can arrange that.'

'Excellent, though first I have to get through tonight.'

'One role at a time. Did I tell you that you are extraordinary, Miss Becky Wickes?'

'So often that I'm beginning to believe you after all.'

'I hope so.' Luca reached across to push her hair back from her brow. 'Because it is the truth.'

His lashes were thick and sooty, far too long for a man. In the sunlight, there were streaks of chestnut brown in his hair. Her stomach was fluttering at his nearness. She couldn't break free of his gaze, the heat flaring in his eyes waking a craving for his mouth on hers. He was so close. She only had to move the tiniest bit towards him and he'd know what she wanted, and he'd kiss her. But it was broad daylight. And she was dressed in Cousin Rebecca's costume. Confused, Becky jumped to her feet. 'You haven't told me what you think of my gown, Cousin Luca.'

She waited, eyes lowered demurely, hands clasped in front of her, praying that he would take his cue. And at last he did, getting to his feet, making a bow. 'It suits you perfectly, Cousin Rebecca.'

For her debut in Venetian society, Cousin Rebecca wore white. A silk underdress, an overdress of sarsenet, white silk stockings and white silk slippers. A white shawl of the softest cashmere was draped around her shoulders. Her long gloves where white kid. Chiara, her maid, had powdered her face and shoulders under Isabel's strict supervision, and fixed her unruly hair back into such a tight chignon, using so many pins that Becky's head ached. A white gardenia was threaded on a ribbon around her neck.

'I look like a ghost,' she told Isabel.

'It is a pity that your eyes are such a striking colour' was all that the Contessa ventured. 'You must make every effort to keep them lowered.'

Her nerves, slowly building since this morning, made her stomach roil. As the hour of her public debut drew near, Becky's confidence began to falter. A terror of spattering food on her gloves prevented her from eating much at dinner, though she supposed that was in keeping for the role she was playing. A girl this pale must surely be starving. She wondered what Brunetti would make of her sudden loss of appetite, or indeed what the rest of the servants hovering about the dining room would make of her sudden loss of conversation.

'My cousin Rebecca is a little nervous,' Luca said as the major-domo removed her untouched melting lemon sorbet, as if he'd read her thoughts. 'She is to attend the salon of Contessa Albrizzi tonight.'

'A most formidable woman,' Brunetti said. 'But I am sure Signorina Wickes will make a favourable impression.'

Signorina Wickes was on the verge of losing her nerve completely as she prepared for the short journey, waiting in the reception area in her all-enveloping evening cloak for the gondola to be readied. The Contessa, in a magnificent black gown of silk and lace, her head covered in a veil, looked both remote and terrifying. Even Luca, in his formal evening dress of black silk breeches and coat, silk stockings and shoes rather than boots, his hair slicked back from his high brow, seemed every inch the Count, and several miles in status above her. The gondola, with a light gleaming on the gold-toothed prow, looked even more like a floating coffin than usual.

Climbing into it with Luca's aid, Becky repressed a shudder. There was room only for the two women in the cabin. Venice in the dark was a different place, all looming, sinister shadows and murky waters. She clutched her hands together and sat tensely, mentally rehearsing her role. The gondola glided silently along, and too soon for Becky's peace of mind, came to dock. She felt quite sick now. She was sure that if she tried to stand, her legs would give way.

'Rebecca, are you ready?' the Contessa asked.

Her cue. She remembered then; she couldn't think why she'd forgotten, that it had always been like this before a performance. Every single time. And she remembered too, that the moment she took the first step into the glare of the lights, her stage fright disappeared, and she lost herself in whatever part it was she had to play.

'I am ready, Aunt Isabel.' She got to her feet, wrapping her cloak around her. 'Thank you, Cousin Luca,' she whispered as he helped her ashore. Lights blazed from the first floor of the *palazzo*. Braziers burned on both sides of the doors, which stood open. Luca offered his arm to his mother, casting Becky a worried glance. She saw it, but did not respond, following demurely in their wake, back straight, shoulders back, head up, eyes down.

Contessa Albrizzi was known as the Madame de Staël of Venice. Having had the presence of mind to have her first, unhappy marriage annulled, thus freeing her to marry into one of the city's oldest and noblest of families, she had established herself as a passionate patron of the arts and of artists. Rather too passionate, some said, but as a widow of six years' standing, she was free to bestow her favours as she saw fit. Rumour had it, Luca's mother had informed him, that the English poet Byron had been a recipient, but he took this information with a pinch of salt. Lord Byron's name had been linked with almost every woman in Venice. It was fortunate the man had seen fit to finally quit the city after a mammoth bout of debauchery, rumour had it, at the last Carnevale.

'Contessa.' Luca bowed low over the extended hand. 'You know my mother, obviously.'

'Isabel. It is good to see you out in company again. We have missed you.'

The two women curtsied, and Luca's mother indicated that Becky come forward. 'May I present my niece, Rebecca Wickes, come to us from England to acquire a little of our Italian gloss.'

Luca watched anxiously as Becky made a deep curtsy. 'Contessa Albrizzi, it is a great honour to be permitted to attend your salon. I have heard that the *conversazione* is the most sophisticated and well informed in Venice.' Cousin Rebecca smiled shyly. 'I am neither witty nor sophisticated, but I hope to acquire a little of both in such illustrious company.'

'No doubt Contessa del Pietro will be introducing you to Venice's other *salonista*, Contessa Benzon. You will find good *conversazione* there too, Signorina Wickes.'

'Indeed, I believe that we do plan to attend one of the Contessa Benzon's salons, but I must confess...' Here, Cousin Rebecca seemed to blush, dropping her gaze to her gloved hands, a little intake of breath giving her the courage to look back up. 'I must confess, Contessa Albrizzi, that it is this salon I have been most eagerly anticipating.'

Contessa Albrizzi preened at the compliment, forcing Luca to bite back a smile. He had heard his mother's acid remarks on the rivalry between the two *salonistas*. He placed a small bet with himself that Cousin Rebecca would pay the same compliment in reverse to Contessa Benzon.

'Well, now,' Contessa Albrizzi said, surveying the room, 'let me see who I can introduce you to, Signorina Wickes, to begin your education in the art of *conversazione*. You should be aware that political discussions of any sort are frowned upon.' Cousin Rebecca was treated to a condescending smile. 'Though I doubt very much that politics would interest a chit like you. Ah! Signor Antonio Canova is with us tonight, one of our greatest living sculptors. I will have him show you the bust of Helen of Troy, which he carved especially for me. Signor Canova, if you please.'

The introduction was made. The sculptor was only too pleased to have the opportunity to describe his work in lavish detail to a beautiful young English-woman, placing Cousin Rebecca's hand on his arm and steering her away. Luca's mother was surrounded by a clutch of women all anxious to discover whether her English niece had arrived in Venice with a fortune. 'If you will excuse me, Contessa Albrizzi,' Luca said, 'I should accompany my cousin for propriety's sake.'

'Nonsense. Signor Canova is passionate about marble, not flesh and blood. Though I must say, Conte del Pietro, that if your cousin stood still long enough, one could easily mistake her for being a statue. So cold, these English. It is the climate, I suppose, there is no heat, either in their sun or their blood, if you know what I mean. While we Venetian women— Ah, you must be very glad to be home, though, of course, we would all wish it had been under happier circumstances. Your dear father is much missed. I know that everyone will agree with me when I say that Conte Guido del Pietro was a pillar of Venetian society.'

'*Grazie*, Contessa Albrizzi, but I believe that honour was shared with Don Massimo Sarti. I had hoped to see him here tonight.'

'His wife has a fever. Nothing to worry about I am sure, but Don Sarti is such an attentive husband— provided it is not Carnevale, of course, but then Carnevale excuses us all from our conjugal duties. And on that subject, Luca— May I call you Luca?' Receiving a nod, Contessa Albrizzi smiled winsomely up at him. 'You are the last of our real Venetian men. A seafarer who has seen the world. A man who has only to walk into a room for all eyes to be upon him. And it is not only your very attractive person, but a certain air you possess. Ah, do not attempt to be modest, I am sure that I am not the first woman to tell you so.'

'You flatter me, Contessa Albrizzi.' Luca cast his eyes anxiously around the salon. There was no sign of Becky, and his mother had her back turned to him. 'I fear you must excuse me...'

'But, no, I have not quite finished with you yet.' The Contessa's grip on his arm was surprisingly strong. 'Now that your dear mother has come out of mourning, she will be turning her thoughts to providing you with a suitable wife. I do hope that milksop niece of hers is not in the running? You need a Venetian woman, with fire in her heart to match your own passions. If I were but five years younger, I would offer for you myself. But alas, a widow such as I, though rich in worldly goods and lineage, will not serve for the grand del Pietro name. We must find you a pretty virgin, and I have one such in mind.'

'You are very kind, Contessa Albrizzi, but I believe the honour of choosing my bride rests with my mother, now that my father is no longer with us.'

'Indeed, indeed,' the Contessa agreed. 'I will discuss the matter with her. It does you great credit, Luca, that you honour the traditions. But you have not answered my question. This cousin of yours, I am right in thinking that she is too close in blood to be deemed a suitable bride? Though if your mother had her mind set upon the match, the blood ties can easily be overlooked by a purse of gold passed in the right direction.'

'My cousin is here for a few weeks only, Contessa Albrizzi, to acquire a little polish, just as my mother informed you. Her marriage prospects are no concern of mine.'

'I am very relieved to hear this. My own protégée— but I will speak to your mother, as you suggested. You are anxious to rejoin your cousin, I can see. I suggest you try the second salon on the right, where my Helen of Troy is situated, but before you go, Luca...' the Contessa fluttered her eyelashes '...a lusty man such as you has appetites which cannot await the marriage bed. I think you will find that a woman such as I, of a certain age and experience, would leave you more than satisfied.'

'Of that I have no doubt, Contessa Albrizzi, but I fear you do me too great an honour. Now I really must go. Cousin Rebecca will be thinking I have abandoned her. *Scusi.*'

Thinking that, on this evidence, the rumours about the Contessa Albrizzi and Lord Byron were probably accurate, Luca was too concerned about Becky to feel anything other than faint astonishment at the brazen offer he had just received. Weaving his way through the crowded salon with scant apologies to those who tried to waylay him, he found her, as the Contessa had predicted, standing beside the bust of Helen of Troy listening to its creator's flamboyant description of the lengths to which he had gone to select the perfect piece of marble. Canova, with his back to the doorway, was speaking in impassioned

Italian far too rapid for Becky's developing grasp of the language. Luca watched with amusement as, despite having little or no idea of what was being said to her, she nodded sagely, murmuring, *'Si, assolutamente...capisco perfettamente,'* in a serious, awed tone. He wanted to applaud her, shout *brava* and have her take a bow. Instead, he assumed his role of concerned escort.

'Signor Canova, I must thank you for taking such excellent care of my cousin.'

'Conte del Pietro.' The sculptor bowed with a flourish. 'I must commend you on your relative,' he said, reverting to English. 'For an Englishwoman, and so young, she shows great understanding of our arts. I hope you intend to show her some of our beautiful city's other treasures?'

'Starting tomorrow, *signor.*'

'I am sure I have already seen one of the most beautiful,' Cousin Rebecca said. 'I am honoured to have heard the history of your Helen of Troy, *signor.* It is something I shall never forget. *Grazie mille.*' She dropped into a low curtsy, flashing the artist a smile which made him blink, frown and peer more closely at her, but Becky's face was once more a mask as bland as Helen of Troy's.

'Cousin,' Luca said, struggling not to laugh at Canova's confusion. 'My mother wishes to introduce you to her friends.'

With a huge inner sigh of relief, Becky tucked her hand into Luca's arm and allowed him to lead Cousin Rebecca from the room. 'Thank you. I am not sure how much longer I could have fooled Signor Canova into thinking I understood more than one word in twenty of what he was saying.'

'It seemed to me that you were Signor Canova's perfect audience, Cousin Rebecca,' Luca replied, his eyes twinkling with merriment. 'Awestruck by his genius, and struck too dumb to interrupt the flow of his self-aggrandisement.' He stopped short of the double doors which led to the main salon. 'Your performance as Cousin Rebecca is extremely impressive. Contessa Albrizzi was so taken in, she worries that my mother intends you for my bride.'

'Your bride!' Becky gave a most unladylike snort of laughter. 'If only she knew.'

'I suppose it was an obvious leap to make.'

'Good heavens, why?'

Luca shrugged. 'While my father was alive, there was no urgent need for me to marry. Now that I am the Conte del Pietro, it is my responsibility to ensure that there is another to follow me. I need a son, therefore I require my mother to find me a wife.'

Becky eyed him in astonishment. 'You don't think you would make a better match if you picked your own wife?'

'It is the way it is done here, for parents to select a suitable bride, particularly for the eldest son. My parents' marriage was one of contentment. I trust my mother to find me a bride who will suit me equally well.'

Isabel had said as much to Becky only yesterday morning, but the very notion of someone as decided as Luca permitting anyone to make such an important decision for him was unbelievable. What was more, it didn't sound as if Isabel's marriage had been particularly contented. She opened her mouth to say as much to Luca, then closed it again. Isabel had confided in her as a friend. Besides, Luca's marriage—Luca's future beyond Carnival—was nothing to do with her. 'We should return to the salon, unless you wish people to speculate further about the possibility of you making a match with your Cousin Rebecca.'

'You're right, that would be one complication too many,' Luca said wryly. 'Once we have brought Don Sarti to justice, then I will turn my mind to marriage, but until then, I cannot afford to be distracted.'

He had no sooner opened the door than Isabel, who was clearly getting anxious, signalled them to join her. 'Aunt,' Cousin Rebecca said contritely, 'I am so very sorry to have deserted you, but Signor Canova was so fascinating I found it difficult to tear myself away.'

'He must have been extremely fascinating,' Isabel replied tartly. 'It is quite twenty minutes since Luca went in search of you.'

'Cousin Rebecca was so enthralled, I could not bring myself to cut short her enjoyment. I do beg your pardon, *signore*,' Luca said, addressing his mother's coterie.

'Ladies,' Isabel said, 'may I present my niece. Rebecca my dear, make your curtsy.' She waited as Becky did so. 'My friends have been accusing me of keeping your existence a secret, Rebecca.'

'Indeed, Signorina Wickes, we were most surprised by your arrival. I am Signora Fabbiano, incidentally.'

Becky dropped another curtsy, murmuring that she was delighted to make her acquaintance.

'Contessa del Pietro has spoken often of her brother's children.'

'No doubt because I wrote to her often of them,' Luca said. 'If I have called anywhere home while serving in the Royal Navy, it has been with my uncle, the Admiral, and his family. Indeed, one of my cousins actually served aboard the same ship as me, as my first officer.'

'This we know,' Signora Fabbiano said. 'But of Signorina Wickes…'

'My sister's daughter,' Isabel said. 'I must say, I find it incredible that I have never mentioned her, but perhaps it is because I so rarely hear from my dear sister, for she lives such a secluded life in the wilds of Wiltshire.'

Which was Becky's cue to chime in. 'Dear Papa is a country vicar, and Mama is very much occupied with assisting him in running the parish. She has little time for anything other than good works.'

'So you are the daughter of a man of the cloth?' Signora Fabbiano looked suitably unimpressed. 'You will excuse my asking, Signorina Wickes, but here in Venice we like to understand such matters, it prevents confusion, you see. Your father, then, he is not a rich man?'

'We are poor as church mice,' Cousin Rebecca replied, with a shy smile. 'Were it not for my Aunt Isabel's overwhelming generosity, I would not even own a gown fit to wear this evening.'

'Poor as church mice,' Signora Fabbiano repeated, shaking her head. 'Poor little Signorina Wickes, you must be finding the luxury of the Palazzo Pietro a real treat.'

'It is beyond anything I could have imagined,' Becky replied truthfully.

'Your aunt was telling us that it is your mother's intention to find you a husband when you return to England?'

If I returned to England, Becky thought, I'd be much more likely to find myself in the arms of the law than a suitor. If only she could tell Signora Fabbiano this interesting fact, there would be no need for the tale she was instead about to spout. Isabel had warned her that she would be subject to this kind of inquisition, but she hadn't really believed her. Now she was extremely grateful for her foresight. 'If I could find a man as wonderful as dear Papa I would be very happy,' Becky said soulfully.

'You aspire no higher than a mere clergyman?'

'It was good enough for Mama,' Cousin Rebecca said, trying not to grit her teeth, for Signora Fabbiano could not keep the disdain from her voice. 'I can think of no better example.'

'You will have no cause to wear such a gown as the Contessa del Pietro has provided you with, in the wilds of... Where did you say it was?'

'Wiltshire, *signora*. Perhaps not,' Cousin Rebecca said, 'but I am sure I can cut it down to make the most beautiful christening robe.' Apparently covered in maidenly confusion at having made so immodest a remark, Cousin Rebecca buried her face in her kerchief. Becky was struggling to stay in character. She had no time for these people, they were everything she was not, but it didn't feel right, deceiving them. They had welcomed her into their company, when, if they knew the truth, they'd cross the road—or the canal— to avoid being contaminated by her.

'Well, Contessa del Pietro, and what do you make

of that? To have brought the chit all this way, to our most sophisticated city. Any spit and polish you apply, which is, I believe, the correct English term, will be quite wasted.'

'Perhaps,' Isabel said smoothly, 'but I will have had the pleasure of my niece's company while she acquires it. Rebecca is the closest thing I have to a daughter of my own,' she added.

The warm smile which accompanied this remark served only to make Becky bury her face further in her kerchief, her embarrassment now quite real. Isabel thought she knew her, but she had no idea she was harbouring a gallows cheat. Of course, it was ludicrous to imagine that Isabel could ever think of her as a daughter, but she did think of her as a friend. Which they couldn't be, Becky should have known that. Their friendship, like Cousin Rebecca, was simply an illusion.

'*Si, si...*' Signora Fabianno was nodding. 'Now I understand. A son, even one so handsome as yours, my dear Isabel, is no substitute for a woman's company. So you make a long visit to the Contessa, Signorina Wickes?'

'Cousin Rebecca is with us only until the end of Carnevale,' Luca intervened, to Becky's relief. 'It will be my pleasure to show her our beautiful city, and to rediscover it for myself, through fresh eyes.'

'Though you will not wish such fresh, innocent eyes, to see too much of Carnevale, Conte del Pietro?'

'Indeed not,' Luca said, seemingly quite affronted.

'And you will not, I hope, devote yourself exclusively to your cousin. Charming as you are I am sure, Signorina Wickes, you will understand that the Conte del Pietro requires more worldly company. And there is plenty to be had of it at Carnevale, is that not so, *signor*?'

'Signora Fabianno! If you please, no more in front of my niece.'

'Your pardon, Isabel. Perhaps your niece would like to meet Aurora? My eldest daughter,' she added, smiling at Luca, 'and I must say, without prejudice, one of the most beautiful of Venice's maidens. I am sure she would be delighted to join you on some of your sightseeing trips. You will find her most agreeable, Conte del Pietro.'

Chapter Six

The next morning, Luca informed Becky that he intended to make good on his promise to take her sightseeing. It was a beautiful winter's day, with a bright sun shining in a cloudless sky. Happy to permit Chiara to select an appropriate outfit, Becky wore a white muslin day gown with long sleeves and a small plain collar. Three layers of petticoats, the maid insisted, would provide the necessary protection against the cold, and Becky knew better than to disagree. The dusky-pink velvet half pelisse had a double row of buttons, a military-style cap, half-boots and gloves to match. With her hair gathered at her nape in a deceptively simple chignon, and a pretty but most impractical reticule that was big enough only to hold her kerchief dangling from her wrist, Becky barely recognised herself.

'The colour suits Signorina Wickes very well,' Chiara said, angling the cap at a jauntier angle. 'You look as if you belong here.'

'*Grazie,*' Becky said, smiling to herself. 'That is a bigger compliment than you realise.'

Luca was waiting for her on the small quay outside the *palazzo*, looking very piratical in a short black cloak, black breeches and highly polished black boots, his hair blowing about his face in the breeze, for he wore no hat. 'Cousin Rebecca,' he said with a formal bow, 'I am delighted that you could join me.'

She was surprised to see that this gondola had no cabin, and was therefore completely open to the elements. Following him on to the bobbing craft, Becky was even more surprised when Luca picked up the long oar and took up position at the stern.

'I told the gondolier that his services were not required. Do not fear,' he said, untying the ropes and beginning to row them out on to the Grand Canal. 'I ended my naval career as the captain of a frigate, but I discovered my love of the sea here in Venice. I have been piloting gondolas since I was a boy.'

'I'm simply glad that I don't have to play Cousin Rebecca, since we are alone.' She had to twist her neck to speak to him, seated as she was at the rear of the gondola, facing in the direction in which Luca was rowing. Clutching the side of the narrow boat, Becky clambered over to the other seat, facing Luca. 'Speaking of being alone, I hope you are not planning to take Signora Fabianno up on her offer to foist her daughter on us, not if she is anything like her mother.'

Luca laughed. 'Were you as shocked as Cousin Rebecca appeared to be, by Signora Fabianno's questions? I warned you that we Venetians do not find the subjects of money or marital prospects vulgar.'

'"I think we made it perfectly clear that Cousin Rebecca is not a contender for the position of Contessa del Pietro at any rate.'

Luca smiled wryly, concentrating on steering their gondola further out into the canal. 'My mother tells me that she has already received any number of social invitations which include you.'

'Do I have to go, Luca? I know it's what we agreed, but last night, it felt wrong deceiving all those people.'

'Wrong? A necessary but harmless deception which cost them nothing.'

She frowned down at her hands, as if they could help her divine how much to say without giving herself away. 'If they knew me, the real me, I mean, they wouldn't allow me to step over their thresholds. I'm not your cousin.'

'But it did not occur to any of them that you are not. You played the part to perfection.'

'People see what they want to see, Luca.'

'Accept the compliment, Becky. I could not have imagined a more accomplished performance.'

'Thank you.'

'Are you really so unhappy playing that part?'

Yes was the straight answer. But she'd accepted The Procurer's offer, she couldn't renege on it now. Besides, it wasn't only a case of her fee. Luca had not mentioned his father's murder since the day after her arrival, when he'd told her the story behind his plan, but the pain must lurk, just beneath the surface, carefully tethered. Did he let it loose when he was alone? Did he cry out as she had done, in the days after she'd discovered Jack's perfidy? She couldn't imagine it, somehow. Recalling her own bitter tears now made her cringe inwardly. Jack had hurt her, but how much deeper was the hurt Luca nursed deep within him?

How little she knew of him despite the many hours they'd spent together.

'Forget I mentioned it,' Becky said. 'What matters is that we've taken the first step. I know how much it means to you.'

His face tightened. *'Grazie,'* he said, and the simple word quashed all her qualms.

He had pushed his cloak back over one shoulder, where it fluttered behind him in the breeze. Balanced on the narrow stern, his booted legs braced, both hands on the oar, using an almost circular motion to propel and steer the craft seemingly effortlessly, she could only imagine the strength of his shoulders and arms, the muscles rippling with the effort. The sunlight flickered over the chestnut highlights in his hair. The air smelt so sweet, the motion of the boat was soothing.

'Who taught you how to— Is it called rowing when there is only the one oar?'

'Si. It was one of my father's gondoliers who taught me when I was perhaps seven or eight. Not in a gondola like this, but in a much smaller one, and not so grand. There is no other way to get around in Venice, so many of the footpaths end in blind alleys, or they are flooded at high tide.'

'What about your father, could he row?'

'Yes, but it was beneath the dignity of the Conte del Pietro to break sweat.'

'You are the Conte del Pietro now.'

Luca grinned. 'Not today. Today, I am simply a Venetian showing his beautiful city to a beautiful lady. And there on the left is one of our most beautiful *palazzos* and one of the oldest. It is known as the Ca' d'Oro.'

'The Golden House?' Becky hazarded, though she could see no trace of gold on the ornate exterior.

Luca nodded. 'Home to the Contorini family until the Republic fell. They were the pre-eminent family in Venice until then. Even more powerful than my own. The doge of Venice was effectively the city's prince. You will see his palace facing out to the Lido, where the Grand Canal enters the lagoon.'

Becky gazed around her in wonder. 'Are all these buildings *palazzos*?'

'Not all of them are so grand inside as out,' Luca replied. 'Many are falling into ruin and some even into the canal. And not all are so comfortable to live in as the Palazzo Pietro either. Many of the most venerable Venetian families have become too poor to maintain them.'

'Though they look so very beautiful from here.'

'But as you very well know, appearances, especially here in Venice, can be deceptive. This is the Ponte de Rialto we are passing under.'

The elaborate, covered stone bridge spanned the canal at a sharp bend, rows of shops lining the arches. They travelled on, following another bend in the canal, and the waters changed from turquoise to sea green as the canal became wider and the breeze stronger. Becky listened as Luca pointed out churches and palaces, but there were so many of them, each more awe-inspiring than the next, that she felt quite dazed. Finally, the gondola came to the end of the Grand Canal and the vista opened to one of islands, the Lido in the distance and the sparkling blue of the lagoon. She shifted to the forward-facing seat at Luca's feet to better drink in the view.

'The Giardini Reali,' Luca said, pointing to the first large green space that she had seen in the city, gondolas vying for berthing spaces on the jetty which faced it. 'Built by Napoleon, to compensate us for all that he looted, perhaps.'

But Becky's gaze had already moved on to the elegant tower of the Campanile San Marco, which she had seen from the rooftop of the Palazzo Pietro, and the spectacle of Venice's most splendid square.

'The *piazzetta*,' Luca told her, holding the gondola steady to allow her a better view. 'The Doge's Palace is there on the other side, and the Piazza San Marco leads off the *piazzetta*, with the church…'

'I can see the domes. My goodness, there are so many people here.'

'Wait until Carnevale. This is nothing. I think our street theatre will put anything you have experienced in London or Brighton to shame. The *volo della colombina*, for example, the flight of the dove, where a man dressed as an angel sails down a rope from the campanile to the palace.'

'I would love to see that.'

'You shall. Though Cousin Rebecca cannot risk her innocence at Carnevale under cover of darkness, it would be cruel to deny her the delights to be offered at San Marco in the daylight. Do you wish me to tie up here so you can have a closer look?'

Becky eyed the crowds with little relish. 'We would most likely encounter acquaintances of yours, wouldn't we?'

'I have been away from Venice for so long I doubt

it, but friends of my parents, almost certainly. Would you prefer to go for a stroll somewhere away from the crowds, with no need to play Cousin Rebecca?'

'I'd love to, though I can't imagine where. I thought London was crowded. I've never seen so many buildings crammed into such a small space. No wonder there are so many gardens on the roofs, there's nowhere else to put them.'

'But we do have a beach,' Luca said, turning the gondola away from the view of San Marco, towards the long narrow spit of land known as the Lido. 'The English poet Lord Byron won a swimming race from the Lido to here, I am told. Not content with winning though, he swam the length of the Grand Canal too.'

'Why on earth would he do such a thing?'

Luca shrugged. 'For certain individuals, being notorious is a vocation.'

The breeze freshened and the gondola bobbed on the waves. By the time Luca helped her ashore, Becky was glad to feel solid ground beneath her feet. Though she could see no sign of a beach, the open space, the trees and the absence of crowded buildings were refreshing.

Luca took her arm, leading her along a narrow path directly to the coast which faced out to the Adriatic Sea, and there was the beach. Becky stopped short on the edge of the long strip of golden sand. There were two horse riders galloping away from them in the distance, a clutch of the distinctively shaped fishing boats bobbing on the horizon, but not another soul around. She lifted her face to the breeze, breathing deep of the stinging briny air, pulling off her hat, relishing the way the wind ruffled her hair, tugged at her skirts, making her realise how very constrained she'd been feeling. 'The sand looks so soft, but I don't want to spoil my boots walking on it. Do you think I would be beyond the pale if I took them off?'

'Why not? Though you will find the sand very cold on your feet,' Luca said as Becky perched on a rock and began to grapple with the buttons of her pink boots.

Her hair was escaping its pins, falling in a tangle of ringlets over her face. Her cheeks were pink, her eyes sparkling with anticipation as she set the boots down, wriggling her stocking-clad toes, her smile mischievous as she met his eyes. 'Turn your back,' she said.

He did, most reluctantly, wondering what on earth she could be doing, rewarded, when she caught his arm, with a glimpse of her naked feet, toes curling into the sand. She had closed her eyes, her face tilted up to the weak sun. When she opened them again, her smile was one of pure delight. 'That feels absolutely wonderful.'

She looked so delectable, so innocently joyful, that his heart lifted at the sight of her. He was not conscious of the burden he had carried with him since reading his father's letter, until it lifted momentarily as he smiled down at her, and the world narrowed, so that all that mattered was this moment, this beach, this woman, and the wide expanse of the Adriatic in front of him. The sea had always drawn him. It drew him now, as he caught Becky's hand in his and began to run with her, headlong along the beach, laughing as they stumbled in the soft sand, laughing at her squeal of surprise as it darkened and firmed towards the water's edge, where he stopped short, but Becky did not, picking up her skirts and jumping over a wavelet into the sea.

She yelped. 'It's freezing.'

'I did warn you.'

Another wave caught the back of her legs, making her stagger forward, lifting her skirts higher. Her legs were very pale and very shapely. Luca eyed them appreciatively. 'Don't go any further out. The sand shelves so steeply...'

But it was too late, Becky had already taken another step, which took the water well above her knees. He sprang forward, grabbing her just before she fell.

'Your boots, they'll be ruined,' she said breathlessly as he pulled her back on to the shore.

'I have other boots, but only one Becky.'

Balancing on his arm, she inspected one of her feet. 'I'm covered in sand.'

'You would have been covered in a great deal more than sand if you had fallen in.'

'My hero.' She clasped her hands dramatically to her breast, her eyes dancing with merriment. 'How can I ever thank you, kind sir?'

For answer, he scooped her up into his arms, holding her high against his chest as she wriggled in mock outrage, then clung to his neck as he began to march back across the sands to the shelter of the small dune where she had left her stockings and boots.

'Put me down, sir, put me down at once,' Becky said, in her best outraged-fair-maiden voice, gasping in surprise when he did, letting her slide down to her feet, unfastening his cloak and wrapping it around her shoulders. 'I don't need…' she protested.

'*I* can't afford for you to catch a chill,' Luca said, pushing her hair back from her face. He smiled down at her, quite beguiled. He knew that her life had been a constant struggle. He knew that she must be old beyond her years in many ways, having lived amid so much poverty and suffering, yet she seemed so carefree, took such innocent delight in a walk on a beach. He couldn't bear the notion of her ever returning to that life, though he knew better than to say so.

'What are you thinking, Luca?'

Her smile was dazzling. He stopped thinking. He pulled her tight up against him. He could have sworn the wind dropped as her eyes met his, and the waves grew silent as she slid her arms around his neck, and then there was a rushing, roaring in his ears as their lips met, and they kissed.

She tasted of salt. He licked into the corner of her mouth, relishing the way it made her shiver against him. He slid his hands down her back, beneath his cloak. Her new clothes came with undergarments that deprived his senses of her soft curves, until his hands came to rest on her bottom and blood rushed to his groin in response and his tongue sought hers. Their mouths fitted perfectly, matching kiss for kiss as they stumbled in the sand and then sank on to it, their mouths still clinging as Becky lay back, his cloak spread out on the sand, and he covered her body with his and she gave a soft sigh, pulling him closer.

He dragged his mouth away for the pleasure of looking at her, eyes dark with the passion he knew was reflected in his own, her lips slightly parted. He ran his hand up her flank, past the dip in her waist, seeking the swell of her breast, but encountered only the buttons of her jacket, and beneath that the boning of her corsets.

His frustration must have shown on his face, for she gave a throaty little chuckle. 'The attire of young ladies,' she said, 'is designed to frustrate all but the most persistent.'

Luca groaned. 'It is certainly designed to frustrate.'

'Both parties.' She pulled his mouth back to hers, kissing him fiercely. He felt himself spinning out of control. Their legs were tangled in her petticoats and the skirts of his coat. He wanted to touch skin and soft flesh, but there seemed to be thick folds of cloth between them. Their mouths clung as he rolled over on to his back, taking Becky with him, and he gave a startled cry as the movement freed her to sit astride him, the aching length of his erection between her legs, though still with far too much material between them. He muttered her name, eyes screwed shut at the pleasure, the astounding pleasure, of just having her there, and then flying open as she leaned forward to kiss him again, and the movement made him throb.

He felt such a gut-wrenching desire to be inside her, it was almost overwhelming. When Becky ended the kiss, sliding on to the sand at his side, he was lost for words, breathing heavily.

Beside him, she too seemed to be struggling for breath and control. 'I think it's safe to say that I now have sand almost everywhere.'

He pushed himself upright, shaking the sand from his hair. 'You are not the only one. On the bright side, at least we need not worry about one of my servants discovering us.'

Becky's smile was perfunctory. She busied herself brushing the sand off her feet, and he made a pretence of looking away as she put her stockings back on. 'Is the danger of discovery part of the thrill, Luca?'

'No!' He whirled back around to face her. 'The thrill, as you call it, is you, and nothing else.' Luca picked up a handful of golden sand, letting the grains trickle through his fingers. 'At the risk of repeating myself, I find you extraordinary. And fascinating. And irresistible.'

'You haven't said that I'm irresistible before.'

'But I've proved it, twice in the space of two days.'

'I'm not a hussy, Luca.'

'*Basta!* You think I don't know that? Why would you say such a thing?'

'People assume that women like me, from my background— They think that we're too poor to afford morals.'

Luca opened his mouth to protest, then closed it again. She held his gaze, such a mixture of defiance and pride in her expression that his heart contracted. 'Unfortunately some are,' he said heavily. 'I cannot claim ignorance of such women. I've seen them gathering on the docks as our ship tied up in ports across the world. They do not seek pleasure, such women, they seek money for food, for clothes, for their children. I have never taken advantage of what they offer, and I did not, for one second, think that you were one such, if that is what you are asking.'

Her lip wobbled. 'It would be a natural assumption to make. Let's face it, if I'd really been Cousin

Rebecca and not Becky Wickes, you wouldn't have kissed my hand, never mind…'

'Wanting to kiss you all over?' Luca shuffled closer, covering her hands with his. 'It has nothing to do with where you come from, and everything to do with who you are, can't you see that? I don't think of you as a hussy or a virgin or anything in between. I think of you only as Becky. Unique. And to me, irresistible.'

Slipping her hand from Luca's, Becky leaned back on her elbows, tilting her face up to the watery sun. 'I've never in my life behaved like this before. You've turned me into a wanton.'

'You have had exactly the same effect on me, you know.'

She stole a shy glance at him. 'In a few weeks I'll be gone and we'll never see each other again, and I expect all this will seem like a dream, won't it? Though actually, it seems like a dream to me most of the time already. And when I go, your life will return to normal. Perhaps you'll marry the fair Aurora.'

Luca shrugged. 'Perhaps.'

She eyed him curiously, unable to believe that he was so indifferent to such a momentous event as he appeared. 'You can't truly believe that a wife chosen in such a manner would make either of you happy.'

'Matrimony here is a matter of convenience,' Luca said impatiently. 'I thought I had explained.'

'You did, but— I don't know, it sounds such a cold, calculated arrangement, and you are neither cold nor calculating.'

'*Grazie.* You know, marriage such as the one which will be arranged for me, it will be much more successful than those which are made for love. We will have much in common, my wife and I. Shared heritage. Shared traditions. Shared society. Once we have a son, we will both be free to take a lover. After duty is done, then there can be passion. And when that passion has burned itself out, then there are other lovers to be had.'

He spoke prosaically. His logic, his tone implied, was impeccable. It most likely was, but Becky was repelled. 'Children aren't a commodity, Luca, and nor should wives be. How can you be so sure that when the woman who has borne you a son decides to warm another man's bed, you won't care?'

'You don't understand.'

'No, I don't.' Becky crossed her arms. 'I don't understand why it is you must take a virgin bride, but the moment she's done her duty by you, the chastity that meant so much is completely irrelevant. What happened to the promise to forsake all others, or don't you make that one in Italy?'

'In my experience,' Luca retorted, 'marriages in England are conducted in exactly the same way. The difference being you don't admit it.'

'That may be the case for those with property and bloodlines to worry about, but for most people, marriage is about love. Having a family, not just a son. Being happy with one person, and not taking a string of lovers.'

'For most people, but not for Becky Wickes?'

'What do you mean?'

'You are very determined that marriage forms no part of your future.'

Taken aback at having the tables turned on her, Becky glowered. 'We were talking about you.'

'And now we are talking about you. Love. Marriage. A family. If that makes for such happiness as you declare, why don't you want it for yourself?'

Becky frowned. Surely that was not what she'd said? She had dreamed of exactly that with Jack, it was the reason she'd gone along with his lies for so long, thinking that it might eventually lead her to a happy ending. Aware of Luca's scrutiny, she sought some flippant riposte, but the words wouldn't come. She'd learnt her lesson, but she wouldn't allow Jack to make a cynic of her. 'I'm happier on my own,' she said gruffly.

'Though it was not always so, no? This man, your paramour...'

'Proved just that,' Becky said hastily. 'That I was better off on my own.' She didn't want to talk to Luca about Jack. She was sick of thinking about Jack, and the very notion of him as the loving husband and father she'd once dreamed he would be was ludicrous. Absolutely ludicrous.

She stared at Luca, a smile beginning to dawn. So many times she'd told herself that she was well rid of him, but until now she hadn't believed it. *'Meno male,'* she said, because it sounded so much better in Italian than English. Goodness, it really was true!

'What is it? What are you thinking?'

Becky shook her head, still smiling, as much at Luca's confusion as her own thoughts. 'We should get going, or we'll be crossing the lagoon in the pitch dark.'

'I have done so many times, I could do it blindfold,'

Luca said, though he followed her lead, getting to his feet, shaking out sand from his coat and cloak again, frowning out over the sea as she set about putting on her boots.

He remained silent, pensive, as they retraced their steps back along the narrow path to the other side of the Lido. The lagoon was a darker blue now, the sun beginning to sink. Luca lit the lamp in the prow of the gondola, but as she made to clamber on board, he caught her arm. 'It is different for me. I am not callous but I have no choice but to marry.'

'I do understand that.' She pressed his hand to her cheek. His skin was warm, hers cold. 'It's funny to think, isn't it, that here you are, one of the richest men in Venice, from one of the noblest families, and you don't have a choice in the matter, while I, who don't even know who my father was, can do as I please.'

This time he made no move to prevent her as she climbed into the gondola, leaping lightly in after her, unfastening the rope from the jetty and fitting the oar into the rowlock. The waters were still, the air at that stage between day and dusk where it seemed to be holding its breath. Becky—in the seat facing towards the city, where the lights were beginning to appear—shivered.

'Take this. I don't need it, the rowing will keep me warm.'

His cloak fluttered on to her knees. After a moment's hesitation, she wrapped herself in it, twisting around in the seat to look up at him. *'Grazie.'*

He shrugged, clearly still brooding on their previous conversation. 'For centuries, the Venetian nobility have been arranging successful marriages in the traditional way. Why should I be an exception?'

Her questions had unsettled him. What right had she to question his life, his future? 'It's none of my business, Luca. My only wish is for you to be happy.'

'Why shouldn't I be?'

Why indeed? And why should she care! But she did. Becky sighed, turning her back on him. 'I fervently hope that you will be, Luca.'

Chapter Seven

For her first visit to the opera, Cousin Rebecca wore a rose-pink satin evening gown with an overdress of white muslin embroidered with leaves and flowers. A chemisette made of the same muslin, worn under the gown's low-cut décolleté, covered every inch of flesh at her bosom and protected her maidenly modesty. Becky's hair was pinned so tightly back that it made her feel as if her forehead was being stretched, but she could not deny that the coiffure, along with the face powder, transformed her. And the resultant headache ensured that she did not forget she was in costume.

La Fenice, as the opera house was known, was a short gondola trip along some of the minor canals, which became crowded as they approached the *campo* which fronted the theatre, obliging their gondolier to jockey for position to gain a berth. Becky's stage career had not included the opera, so this was her first experience and she was looking forward to it, having been assured by Isabel that it was perfectly acceptable for Cousin Rebecca to do so.

'The Venetians' claim that their opera is the best in

the world is, unlike some of their other superlatives, most probably true,' the Contessa said, slanting a teasing glance at her son as she took her seat in their private box.

'That, even the English do not dispute,' Luca said to Becky, who was sitting between them. 'My mother's brother, Admiral Riddell, is a connoisseur of the opera. He has been only once to La Fenice, but he still talks of it.'

'In 1792, the year after your birth, and the opening season of the new theatre,' Isabel said. 'I remember it well, though it must be coming up for thirty years ago now.'

'And you have not seen your brother since?' Becky asked.

'Oh, he has visited on a couple of occasions since, but in the summer, outside the opera season.'

'Haven't you ever returned to England since you married?'

'My uncle invited you to visit him several times, to coincide with my ship being docked in Plymouth,' Luca reminded his mother when she hesitated. 'You were apparently unable to oblige because my father insisted he needed you by his side in Venice.'

'Regretfully, that is true,' Isabel replied.

'Didn't you want to see your son and your family?'

Isabel's clear-eyed gaze faltered under Luca's scrutiny. 'You think your father cared that I missed you? He cared only for his position of influence, his precious reputation, and, of course, above all his devotion to his precious Venice. I was a vital appendage, and so in his eyes I could not be spared.' She drew in a sharp breath, immediately contrite. 'I beg your pardon. I should not have spoken in such blunt terms. I do not know what came over me.'

Stuck between mother and son, Becky hardly dared to breathe. Luca, far from angry, seemed thunderstruck. 'Was my father so devoted to Venice as to be completely selfish and intransigent?'

Isabel shook her head. 'He did not see it that way. If I had made more of a fuss—insisted, perhaps—but I did not. I regret it. Of late, there have been several things I have realised that I regret,' she said with a sad little smile aimed at Becky. 'But what is the point in regrets? They change nothing. The future is what matters. Now that I am no longer tied to your father's side, perhaps I will visit England. But for now,' she continued brightly, 'I think we should tell Rebecca the story of Rossini's *Tancredi*, for she may not be able to follow it when it starts. It was the first opera performed here when the theatre opened, and...'

'Were you unhappy, Mama?'

'Oh, Luca, what kind of question is that to ask me?'

'Perhaps one I should have asked long before now.'

Becky sensed Isabel stiffening. 'I spoke to you in confidence,' the Contessa said to her. 'I thought you understood that.'

'I did. I...'

'You are mistaken if you think I'm asking you because Becky has betrayed a confidence,' Luca interrupted. 'I see now though, why she is so very antagonistic towards our Venetian marital customs.'

'We are embarrassing her,' Isabel said tersely. 'And in danger of spoiling the opera for her too.'

'You are right.' Luca made a visible effort to relax as

the orchestra started to tune up. 'Quickly, then, before the curtain comes up, let me outline the plot of *Tancredi.*'

It was, as ever, a bravura excellent performance, but Luca could not concentrate. Beside him, Becky sat leaning forward, unlike him, completely immersed in the opera. It was a rare chance to study her unobserved. Though garbed as Cousin Rebecca, in her fascination with the stage, she was wholly Becky. Emotions flickered across her face, reflecting the mood of the music. Her wide-eyed gaze missed nothing, neither on the stage nor in the wings, somehow anticipating the changes of scenery before the faint grinding of wheels and pulleys began. Very early on, she noticed that the singers took their cues from the conductor, her ear so acutely attuned that she frowned when the chorus came in a fraction too late, making him smile as she nodded her approval when one of the male leads manoeuvred the diva, in the middle of an aria, out of the way of an oncoming prop.

His mother was staring at the stage, but he could tell from her carefully blank expression that she wasn't watching the opera. She had become very fond of Becky. She had confided in Becky what he hadn't even guessed. Had his mother felt her marriage a prison? Had his father been her jailer? An exaggeration, surely? He'd forgotten how hurt he had been, all those years ago, when she had refused the Admiral's first invitation. The second refusal. Yes, he had minded that less. From the first time he set foot on the deck of a Royal Naval frigate, his heart had been given to that life. Venice, his mother, his father, they would always be there, waiting, while the world was his to explore there and then. Duty and desire were serendipitously one, he'd thought, but had he simply been selfish?

A ripple of applause signalled the end of an aria. The first act was nearing an end. Those standing in the pit began to shuffle restlessly. In the tiers of boxes, thoughts were turning to the interval Prosecco, the turning of opera glasses from the stage to the audience. Luca uncrossed his legs. He knew so little of his parents' lives, and it was almost entirely his own fault. He had never asked, never been curious, as absorbed in his own life as his father had apparently been in his.

Did he intend to fill his father's shoes, Becky had asked him. He remembered giving some vague reply about not having considered it, when the truth was he had no idea what it would entail. He had always been so proud of his father, but for the first time that pride sat ill with him.

The singing was reaching a crescendo. Casting an idle glance around the theatre as the curtain came down, Luca tensed. The box next to theirs, in the same coveted position at the centre of the horseshoe facing the stage, had been empty for the first act. His mother had noticed, but chosen not to comment. He had been both disappointed and relieved. With a sense of dread and cold fury, he watched the servant, standing sentinel by the open door, make way for the owners of the box to enter.

'What is it, Cousin Luca?'

Becky was looking up at him anxiously. His feelings must have been writ large on his face. He unclenched his jaw, forcing a rigid smile as he got to his feet. 'Don Sarti and his family have arrived, Cousin Rebecca. His wife must have recovered from her indisposition. Unfortunately we have not time for formal introductions, but I think we ought to make our bows.'

The morning after the opera, Aunt Isabel was confined to her bed with a headache and Cousin Luca had left the *palazzo* at first light, leaving Becky to take a solitary breakfast—if taking coffee and a buttered roll in the company of Brunetti and two other footmen could be called solitary. She went up to the roof afterwards, the only place in the *palazzo* where she ever felt truly alone. It was another bright, sunny winter's day. Simply breathing in the salty air, looking out at the glinting turquoise of the lagoon and the deeper blue of the Adriatic beyond made Becky feel a little better. She had not slept last night, and for once it was not because she had been rehearsing.

The opera had been magical. It wasn't only the music, it was the combination of singing and acting, the complex interaction between the huge chorus and the principals, the dramatic nature of the story, the way that the music enhanced every emotion. For Becky, opera had always been tainted by the bawdy reputation of opera dancers, the notoriety of the green room and the ogling bucks who frequented it. Seeing it from front of house rather than backstage was a revelation. On one level, she couldn't help but be aware of the moving props, the stage directions, the greasepaint and the gaudy costumes, but on anther level she had given herself up to the illusion, lost herself in the story, stirred to her soul by the music.

And then Don Sarti and his family had arrived, and a very different drama began to unfold. It had not been Luca's first encounter with the Don, but it had been his first since concluding that his father's best friend had ordered his father's murder. What had astounded Becky was that he was so unprepared. She herself had felt quite sick, looking at the man that the Queen of Coins was to destroy, thankful for Cousin Rebecca's face powder, and even more thankful that only a curtsy had been required of her. Isabel had appeared the least affected, Becky had thought at the time. Her headache this morning told a different story. Isabel, she knew, had had several encounters with the Sarti family since her husband's death, enough to deaden the blow but not to blunt the impact.

But Luca! If ever Becky needed proof of how much this plan of his meant to him, last night provided it. Barely contained anger had emanated from him in waves for the remainder of the opera, so palpably that Becky fancied Don Sarti must sense it. He held himself so rigidly, she wondered he did not break a bone or grind a tooth to dust. His eyes burned with a fervour that was frightening. Remembering it made her shiver. This was not a game they were playing. In the day-to-day effort to play Cousin Rebecca, she had not lost sight of the Queen of Coins, but she had relegated her to the supporting cast. Soon, Luca's avenging angel was to take centre stage, and Becky had better make bloody sure she didn't fail.

She'd brought the cards up on to the roof with her. Knowing how fond she was of the space, Luca had equipped it with a table, more comfortable chairs and cushions too. One of the *palazzo*'s army of staff must have brought those in at night, for they were never damp. She dealt herself two hands of Trappola and began to pit her wits against herself, but it was no good. Cousin Rebecca would attend the Contessa Benzon's salon tomorrow, her first opportunity to watch others play. It would reduce the risk when the Queen of Coins made her debut, but not enough for Becky's peace of mind.

She was flicking through her sketches for the Queen of Coins's costume when the door to the roof opened, and Luca appeared. He was dressed in long boots and leather breeches, his black hair a wild tangle from the wind, his cheeks bright. To her relief, he was smiling. To her annoyance, his smile set off that distracting fluttering in her belly. 'You missed breakfast, Cousin Luca,' she said, assuming her demure smile.

'I went riding on the Lido. I keep several horses there. It cleared the cobwebs.' He kicked the door firmly shut and strode towards her, ignoring her Cousin Rebecca smile, swept her into his arms and kissed her.

His lips were warm against hers. She closed her eyes, momentarily giving herself up to the delight of their kisses, before dragging her mouth from his. 'Cousin Luca!' Becky said in mock outrage. 'How dare you!'

He tightened his hold, a teasing smile playing on his lips. 'That,' he said softly, his mouth against her ear, 'was most decidedly not a Cousin Rebecca kiss.'

'That is because Cousin Rebecca does not know how to kiss,' Becky said primly.

He nibbled her earlobe. She bit back a tiny moan. His mouth travelled down her throat, stopping at the ruffled neck of her gown. 'On the other hand, Becky most certainly knows how to kiss. In fact I'd go so far as to say that Becky's kisses are the most delightful kisses I have ever enjoyed.'

Her heart was fluttering wildly. Her pulses were racing. Her hands had found their way around his neck. 'High praise indeed, when you must have enjoyed a great many kisses in your time, Captain del Pietro.'

'Not nearly as many as you imagine. In any case, when I look into those big violet eyes of yours, I forget every one of them, and crave only yours.'

It was no use. It was over a week since they had last kissed at the Lido. Telling herself that she'd never be able to concentrate on anything else until she satisfied her own craving, Becky pulled him towards her and claimed his mouth. Dear heavens, but it was sublime. She could drown in their kisses, lose herself in the heady delight of them, her lips clinging to his, relishing the sweep of his tongue, the whisper of his breath, the taste of him. Relishing the way his hands shaped her body, tugging her tight against him. His hair was like silk. His cheeks were rough with stubble, yet his beard was surprisingly soft. They kissed until they were breathless, and when they dragged their mouths apart they stood, locked in one another's arms, gazing dazed into one another's eyes.

And then the grating sound of the door opening made them spring apart. Luca cursed. 'I ordered tea for you. I forgot.'

Becky hastily turned her back, pretending to admire the view as two footmen began to set out the tea things and the inevitable pot of coffee for Luca. Brunetti had decided not to make the arduous climb, she was relieved to note. The major-domo would not have failed to notice Cousin Rebecca's flushed countenance.

'*Grazie,*' Luca said, as the door closed with a creak.

'How did you know I'd be up here?' Becky asked, sitting down to make the tea.

'You feel at home here,' he said simply, helping himself to coffee.

'You find it strange that I should prefer a rooftop to a palace?' She poured herself a cup of tea, adding milk and three sugar lumps since Isabel wasn't there to disapprove. 'There are times when I can't quite believe that I'm staying in an actual palace. I've been here almost three weeks and I don't think I've been in half of the rooms.'

Luca was already pouring his second coffee. 'Would you like a tour?'

'Only if you are sure we wouldn't get lost.'

He grinned. 'It's an alluring prospect, to lose myself with you in an attic somewhere, or in one of the secret rooms behind the panelling in the library.'

'Are there secret rooms behind the panelling in the library?'

'Two. I have no idea what their original use was, presumably to hide valuables.'

'Talking of which…'

'Ah. That is your let-us-turn-our-minds-to-business voice.'

'We have a great deal of business to discuss, Luca.'

'*Si.* Last night, seeing that man…' His mouth tightened. 'Brazenly sitting there in his opera box, waving to the great and the good of the city, his wife and his daughter by his side. It made me feel sick.'

Don Sarti had looked every bit the contented spouse and father, Becky thought. She had imagined a stage villain. Don Massimo Sarti was in fact a handsome man past his prime, with grizzled grey curls, a broad, intelligent brow, a benevolent smile and a quiet yet definite air of authority. This was the inveterate gambler that the Queen of Coins was to bring to his knees. She found it difficult to believe. 'I'm glad he will be in disguise,' Becky said. 'I presume you know *what* disguise?'

'You must not be taken in by the man's appearance. Never forget that he is a thief and a murderer.'

'And a man who, when he has a hand of cards, is in the grips of a compulsion. I understand that, Luca. I am not getting cold feet, it's simply that seeing him with his family last night made what I have to do suddenly very real.'

'And it brought home to me how determined I am that it will be done.' Luca set his cup down on the tray. 'We cannot fail.'

'No, I've been thinking about that.' Becky took a breath to pluck up her courage, but Luca spoke first.

'So have I. It is not enough that you observe the game being played, you must practise by taking part.'

'Yes. That's exactly what I was thinking. But you said…'

'That there is no play, save of the kind you will see tonight, before Carnevale.'

'And since Cousin Rebecca cannot play in the Contessa Benzon's salon…'

'Nor can the Queen of Coins make an appearance there, amusing as that prospect may be.'

'The Queen of Coins cannot make any appearance until she has a suitable disguise to wear. I have some sketches…'

'In a moment.' Luca turned towards her on the

bench. 'Carnevale peaks in the first six weeks of the new year. That is when we will bring Don Sarti to justice. But before then, in December, Carnevale begins, and sport may be found by those who care to seek it out. I have learnt that some *ridotti* will open their doors discreetly some time in the next week or so. The stakes are modest. Like every aspect of Carnevale, the wildness and debauchery escalates as Lent approaches.'

'And you think that the Queen of Coins will be able to gain entry to these places? Who told you of them?'

'My mother. Last night, after you went to bed.'

Becky clattered her teacup into her saucer. 'Isabel! What does she know of such matters?'

'I admit I was surprised. But as we saw last night at the opera, she is more than capable of surprising me.' Luca smiled crookedly. 'You have been here for less than three weeks, and you know my mother better than I do.'

'No, that's not true.'

But he shook his head. 'Perhaps it is because you are both English that you understand each other. My mother freely admitted to me last night that if she had been Venetian, and therefore willing to abide by our marital conventions, she would have been happier in her marriage. But she was neither. I think it was a mistake for my father to choose an English bride. If my mother had been able to bring herself to take a *cavaliere servante*, an established lover, then perhaps things might have been different. I know you heartily disapprove of the way my marriage will be arranged, but at least my wife will be content in a way that my mother was not.'

'Perhaps you're right,' Becky said, though she remained unconvinced. 'Perhaps I simply don't understand how things are arranged here. It is so alien to me, and still is, by the sounds of it, to your mother in some ways. Do you think she will visit her family in England now, as she suggested she might?'

'I have already encouraged her to do so.'

After Carnevale no doubt, Becky thought. After she had brought the husband and father she had seen at the opera last night to his knees. A notion that was beginning to sit a little uncomfortably with her. 'You haven't told me what Don Sartie's Carnival disguise is,' she reminded him.

'You prefer to think of him in character, yes?' Luca asked, proving once again that he saw a great deal more than she would like. 'Very well, it matters not to me how you view him, as long as you win. He wears what is known as a *bauta* mask. It is most commonly white, but a few are gilded. The *bauta* covers the entire face, with only the wearer's eyes on show. Traditionally, there is no mouth, but the lower part of the mask is pointed out, like this,' Luca said, demonstrating, 'so that the wearer can speak, drink, even eat.'

'It sounds grotesque.'

'It is meant to be. The intention behind many of the masks is to frighten as well as disguise identity. The *bauta* disguises the voice to an extent, as well as the face, because of the shape.'

'Why does Don Sarti wear this particular style?'

Luca laughed sardonically. 'In the days of the Republic, the *bauta* and a certain type of black hat, the *tricorno*, and a red or black cloak were worn by all citizens entitled to vote, in order to keep ballots secret. Don Sarti's Carnevale costume is his little jibe at our oppressors.'

'But if many wear that style, how will we know we have our man?'

'We will have to make sure that the Queen of Coins is an irresistible challenge for him. He likes to play deep. We will have to ensure that the stakes are suitably high.'

'Luca, I've been thinking about that. If what you said about the *ridotti* opening in a week's time is true, then the Queen of Coins, by starting small, can build a significant stake and accumulate some experience at the same time.'

'That is a very good idea.'

'It is.' Becky beamed. 'And it gets better. She'll not only be building her experience, but something even more important. A reputation for being unbeatable.'

Luca clapped his hands together. 'Of course! Don Sarti will be unable to resist such a challenge!'

'And when of the Queen of Coins defeats him, what will keep him coming back for more?'

'His arrogance,' Luca said, whistling. 'And the more he loses, the more recklessly he will gamble. We will uses his weakness to relieve him of the money that rightly belongs to Venice. I think you might be a genius.'

'Let's not get too carried away yet. It's a good plan, but before we can get our fish on the hook, we not only have to establish the Queen of Coins as a player, we have to get Don Sarti interested. Society needs to talk, in Don Sarti's hearing, of the invincible card player, a woman no less, who has never been defeated.'

'My mother could help us with this. Thanks to my father, she is extremely well connected.'

'I think that would be a mistake,' Becky said after a moment's hesitation, for Isabel would indeed be ideally placed to help them. 'You know that she doesn't approve of what you are doing. She'd help you, because you're her son and she'd do anything you asked of her but...'

'You think I would be putting her in an invidious position?'

'I do.'

He considered this, frowning down at his hand, which was drumming a tattoo on his thigh. 'I don't understand her reservations, but I know she has them. It would be unfair of me. You're right.'

'I am?'

'Astonishingly, since it means that I must therefore be wrong.'

Becky chuckled. 'I promise, it will be our secret.'

'Che bella,' Luca muttered. 'Do you have any idea what you do to me when you laugh like that?' He leaned over, brushing her hair away from her cheek. 'But I must remind myself that there are any number of rooftops overlooking this one, and that it is almost December and that cold such as this is not conducive to lovemaking.' He kissed her softly, then he released her with a theatrical sigh. 'Tell me instead your thoughts on your disguise as the Queen of Coins. I think you said you had some preliminary sketches?'

'I did. I do.' Becky floundered about for her sketchbook. It had fallen on to the ground. She bent to retrieve it, taking the opportunity to take a couple of deep, calming breaths. Save that they didn't calm her.

It was as well that Luca had demonstrated restraint, as she wasn't sure how she would have reacted had he not. She was strung tight as a bow as she sat back down, her fingers fumbling with the pages of the little book. 'The Queen of Coins,' she said, forcing herself to focus on the first, tentative drawing, turning the page for Luca to see. 'My starting point was the way she's depicted on the cards, obviously, but then I began to think. What is it that we want people to see, what is it that makes her stand out—because we want her to be distinctive, don't we?'

It was working. As she turned the page to the next sketch, she could see that she'd caught Luca's interest. 'We want her to be everything that Cousin Rebecca isn't. Arrogant. Regal. Seductive. But the one thing she has in common with Cousin Rebecca is that no one dare touch her.' She turned the page to the final sketch, watching with satisfaction as Luca's smile dawned. 'What do you think?'

'I cannot imagine anything more perfect.'

Cousin Rebecca accompanied her aunt to Contessa Benzon's salon the following evening. As they entered the room, which was stifling hot and bustling, Becky was assailed by a wave of boredom. Most of the faces looked familiar, some from Contessa Albrizzi's salon, but most from the many calls Rebecca had paid with her aunt Isabel in the intervening ten days. Calls when she had drunk endless cups of insipid tea, for the Venetians could not understand that the leaves must be given time to infuse. She had smiled endless vapid smiles, listening to endless tedious conversations. She tried, when she returned from these excursions, to recall what had been discussed, but it was all a jumble of who was wearing what and tittle-tattle. None of Isabel's acquaintances seemed to *do* anything, save pay calls and gossip endlessly. This life of leisure and luxury, which would have been beyond her own wildest dreams only a month ago, Becky was finding not only wearisome but inexplicable.

'Don't they mind that they serve no purpose?' she'd asked Isabel earlier, as Chiara pattered to and fro with a selection of gowns for Cousin Rebecca to choose from for the coming evening.

Isabel's brittle laugh made her realise how insulting she had been. 'I didn't mean you,' Becky had added swiftly.

'But you make a valid point, Rebecca. Another thing I shall endeavour to change when you are no longer with me.'

Which had brought a lump to Becky's throat. When she was with the Contessa, she increasingly forgot her own sordid history and felt herself truly to be Isabel's friend. She was deluding herself. Though the regal woman in whose wake she was currently trailing was not her friend Isabel, but Contessa del Pietro. 'Contessa Benzon, it has been too long,' she was saying to the statuesque woman who must be their hostess. 'May I introduce you to my niece from England, Signorina Rebecca Wickes.'

Contessa Maria Querini Benzon had once been a famous beauty renowned for courting scandal. She had, Isabel had informed Becky earlier, danced virtually naked around the Tree of Liberty, wearing only a brief Roman-style tunic during the fall of the Republic. A song inspired by this outrageous act was still a favourite with the gondoliers twenty years later. Her latest scandal had been to marry her lover after thirty years together, but her notoriety had more to do with her passion for food than for her husband. The Contessa, a true Venetian, loved polenta so much that she would not leave her *palazzo* without a slice of it tucked into her bosom. The gondoliers called her The Steaming Lady.

As the introductions were made, it struck Becky yet again what a topsy-turvy tangle were the rules and the morals by which these upper-class Venetians lived. A bride must be a virgin, yet a wife was expected to take a lover. Fidelity, that most fundamental virtue in her eyes, meant nothing here. She, who had been true in every way to the man she'd thought she loved, would be perceived as a fallen women by these people, simply because she'd given herself without a formal blessing. Making Cousin Rebecca's curtsy, Becky felt more than ever that she did not belong here.

'I have heard a great deal about you, Signorina Wickes,' Contessa Benzon said with an engaging and refreshingly genuine smile which made Becky's prepared platitudes die on her lips. 'Isabel's little English niece, who dreams of marrying a man of the church just like her papa, do I have that right?'

'Perfectly,' Cousin Rebecca replied, disappointed to see no giveaway trail of steam rising from her hostess's gown. Was that scepticism in the Contessa's voice, or the more usual scorn?

'I confess, Isabel, I was most surprised to hear this story. A niece of yours to marry a man of the cloth! When one would have thought her a perfect match for your son. Oh, I know you will say that she is too close in blood, but we all know that is a rule which can be waived when it is convenient.'

'Rebecca has very modest ambitions,' Isabel replied. 'I would not dream of trying to redirect them.'

'Wisely said, Isabel, but there is one who I think could do so easily, if he chose? What do you say to that, Conte del Pietro?'

'My cousin's mind is quite made-up on the matter.'

'Such a modest young woman, with such modest ambitions, yet she has a will of iron it seems,' Contessa Benzon mused. 'For I find it very difficult to believe she could be immune to your charms, Conte del Pietro. Perhaps he has not tried hard enough. What do you say, Signorina Wickes?'

Thinking sardonically that Luca had barely had to try at all, Becky was forced to look up. 'I do not aspire to such lofty heights,' she said drily.

'But you would like to, no? Who would not?'

Contessa Benzon fluttered her eyelashes meaningfully at Luca, whose manful struggle to conceal his shock at the very obvious suggestion was too much for Becky. She gave a snort of laughter, and though she quickly turned it into a cough, her hostess was not fooled.

'I advise you to look a little more closely at your cousin, Conte del Pietro,' she said with a gleeful smile. 'Appearances can be most deceptive. But I have detained you enough,' she continued, sparing any of them the need to respond. 'Isabel, I see your coterie have gathered over in the corner, you will wish to join them with your niece. Conte del Pietro, my salon is at your disposal. You will excuse me, I have newly arrived guests to greet.'

* * *

The evening continued as all such evenings did, Luca was discovering, with the conversation largely consisting of veiled hints as to his matrimonial prospects, discreet scrutiny of the chances of him following his father into the heart of the city's administration and subtle probing from some as to his inclinations to attend their various societies and clubs. Politics could not be discussed overtly, that much he understood, for the Austrians had spies everywhere, but he was beginning to find the Venetian habit of making an unnecessary mystery of every subject tedious.

Luca had never been much interested in politics, preferring action to words. It was why the navy had suited him, and why he wanted to build ships. What he would do with his fleet was another matter. He had assumed that he would sail with them, but all of Venice expected Conte del Pietro to remain in the city, not absent himself for months, possibly years at a time. He had always known he belonged to Venice, it was in the del Pietro blood that he serve his city, but until his father's life was taken, the date had always been deferred to some mythical point in the future. That was another crime to add to the list committed by Don Sarti. He had stolen Luca's freedom from him.

The man with whom he had been conversing was looking at him expectantly. Luca couldn't even remember his name, let alone what they'd been talking about. Spotting Becky out of the corner of his eye, seated beside his mother and looking as bored as he felt, he made his bow and an apology. '*Mi scusi, signor*, I think my cousin wishes to speak to me.'

He had to suppress a smile, for Becky almost forgot she was Cousin Rebecca in her hurry to get to her feet when he suggested they get some fresh air. '*Grazie*, Cousin Luca,' she said, 'it is true, I am suffocating. From the heat, that is, of course, not from the company, which is as diverting and delightful as always. *Meno male*,' she added for his ears alone as he led her away. 'I thought you would never come and rescue me. Didn't you promise to find a way to let me watch some card playing?'

'It is taking place in another room. We can use the terrace to observe the game. Try looking a little less happy to escape and a little more as if you are about to faint.'

She responded to her cue immediately, and with no questions. Luca watched, fascinated, as Cousin Rebecca's already pale complexion seemed to go grey. Her lids drooped. Her knees began to give way. 'Cousin Luca,' she whispered in a perfect stage aside, 'I fear I am quite overcome.'

She took a tottering step towards the window and Luca, waving aside an offer to help, put a cousinly arm around her waist. 'Some air, that is all she needs.'

'Oh, yes, thank you, just a little air,' Cousin Rebecca said plaintively. The curtain was obligingly held aside, the tall windows on to the terrace opened. 'I am so embarrassed, please excuse— My cousin will take care of me,' Cousin Rebecca implored, and the concerned guest obligingly retreated.

As soon as the curtains fell back together, Becky straightened up. 'Which way? Oh, Luca, what if the curtains to the room are drawn?'

'They are not. They were, but I remedied that.'

'Excellent. Are you sure we won't be spotted from inside?'

'If anyone looks up, you can faint into my arms.'

'Magari,' Becky said with an impish grin, using one of Chiara's favourite words. 'I wish!'

'Not as much as I do,' Luca muttered under his breath, following in her wake as she crept light-footed along the narrow balcony, past the second set of windows belonging to Contessa Benzon's grand drawing room, to the light streaming from the card room, where she stopped short.

'This is perfect,' she whispered as he stopped beside her. 'Both tables closest to the window are playing Trappola. You don't have to watch. Just keep a lookout for me, and be prepared to catch me if required.'

She turned her attention back to the room, and was immediately rapt with concentration. Two floors below, Luca could hear the rush of the waters of the Grand Canal that told him the tide was on the turn. He would not build his ships at the old docks, he would build a new dockyard, modelled on the one on the River Clyde in Glasgow, where they constricted ocean-going clippers, faster than any other. He would send his fleet across the world to trade in silks and in tea, in spices and tobacco, bringing trade back to his city and much-needed work. In the cool night of the last days of November, Luca leaned on the low edge of the balcony and gazed out to sea, indulging himself in his dreams.

'I hope you employed someone more attentive to act as lookout when you were at sea.' Becky's voice in his ear startled him from his reverie. 'Don't worry,' she said, flashing him a smile, 'no one has come in search of us, but I think we'd better return to the drawing room before they do.'

'Was it helpful, even though they were playing for pleasure, not money?'

'Yes. The two ladies in particular were very skilful players. Do you think you can persuade your mother to leave now? I don't think I can bear...'

'Not yet,' Luca said curtly, ushering her through the still-open window. 'Look over there. Don Sarti has arrived with his family.'

'Luca...'

'I am more prepared this time,' he told her with a grim smile. As he propelled Cousin Rebecca towards the Sarti family, his stomach was clenched in a tight ball, but his fists were determinedly unfurled, even though every instinct urged him to grab the man by the throat and throttle the life out of him.

'Luca.' Don Sarti held out his hand. 'I was saying to my wife, when we saw you at the opera the other night, how good it was to see your mother back in circulation. I believe the credit belongs to this young lady, her niece?'

'Allow me to introduce Signorina Wickes,' Luca said, discovering that he was loathe to do so.

'Signorina Wickes, it is a pleasure. I confess, I was not aware of your existence until you arrived in Venice. May I introduce you to my wife, and to my daughter, Beatrice.'

'I hope your aunt will bring you to tea, Signorina Wickes,' Donna Sarti said, after Becky made her curtsy. 'Beatrice will be happy to have a new acquaintance, won't you, my dear?'

'Indeed, Mama,' her daughter murmured, looking,

to Luca's eye, every bit as demure and colourless as Cousin Rebecca, and on the face of it, a perfect match.

It was not a friendship he wished to encourage, though he could think of no way to curb it without raising suspicion. He would have a word with his mother about it. He couldn't risk Becky being too much in Don Sarti's company. Only then did it occur to him to wonder how much of Donna Sarti's company his mother usually kept. Were the two women friends? He was about to find out.

'Anna. And Beatrice. How lovely to see you.'

He watched his mother greet both Sarti women warmly, and he had his answer. It surprised him, for his mother had not alluded to any such friendship, though it was natural enough, he supposed, for the wives of two old friends to be on good terms.

'Don Sarti, good evening.'

His mother's greeting was significantly cooler, but the Don didn't appear to consider this unusual. 'Contessa.'

Was Sarti looking ill at ease? Was his conscience bothering him in the slightest? Luca couldn't decide.

'I will leave you to catch up with Isabel,' Don Sarti was saying now to his wife. 'I believe there are cards underway in the other salon. No,' he added swiftly, as his wife's face fell. 'Of course, I am not going to play, my dear. What is the fun in playing without a stake to risk?'

As he excused himself, making for the connecting door, Luca saw Donna Sarti's eyes following her husband, her mouth pursed into a tight line.

Chapter Eight

The sky was gunmetal grey and lowering two days later, when Luca took Cousin Rebecca out on the pretext of another sightseeing trip, though the real reason for their expedition was to visit the mask-maker. Once again, they were in the open gondola with Luca taking the oar himself. Becky, swathed in a woollen hooded cloak, sat once again in the seat facing him rather than the direction in which he was rowing. They headed away from the Grand Canal, through a confusing network of tributary canals which gave her a completely different impression of the city. Although some of the buildings were clad in gaily painted stucco, all were decrepit and in varying states of decay.

The buildings towered high over the canals. It seemed to Becky, craning her neck, that the narrower the strip of water that separated them, the taller they were built, as if reaching desperately for the remote sky. The bridges were not ornate but simple low spans, requiring Luca to duck as they passed underneath. Moss grew thick on the steps, a deep, vibrant green, while the canals themselves reflected the colours of the surrounding buildings—muddy brown and dusky pink and milky grey. Where there were walkways they were precarious and narrow, connected by shallow flights of steps. It would be very easy to lose one's footing on the damp cobblestones, even easier for the unwary to slither down those treacherous little steps and plunge headlong into the murky water.

There were few people visible, yet Becky had an acute sensation of being watched, from behind green shutters, from just around the corner of the warren of passageways. Voices echoed, but they seemed to emanate from far away. Cats sat on the top of the steps leading down into the waters, on the window ledges, in the doorways, watching. It was eerie and beautiful, haunting and frightening. 'I wouldn't like to come here on my own at night,' she said to Luca, keeping her voice low, in tune with her mood.

'I would not advise it, especially not on foot,' he replied. 'Even Venetians can get lost and end up walking around in circles. You can be five minutes from your destination, and it can end up taking you an hour or more.'

Becky shivered. 'I feel like there are eyes everywhere. It's like walking through the rookeries at night. You know the place is overrun with people but you can't see them, not unless you know where to look.'

'I don't like to think of you alone in a place like this, day or night.'

'It's safe enough if you are known,' Becky said. 'Most of the time,' she added with a wry smile. 'When you live there, and you don't know any different, it's not so bad. Now— No, I wouldn't go back even if I could.'

'Could?'

'It's just a saying,' she said hurriedly, cursing herself for the stupid mistake. Trust Luca to notice it! 'What I'm saying is, I don't aspire to live in a *palazzo*, but I don't want to live in a slum.' She leaned back, gazing up at the narrow grey sliver of sky. 'I'm beginning to think that I need to broaden my horizons a bit though. I don't just mean travel, which I *have* been thinking about, thanks to you, but... It was something your mother said, about wanting to be useful.'

'Talking of my mother, I've written to my uncle, asking him to arrange safe passage for Mama to England as soon as he can.'

'Luca!' Becky jumped up, causing the gondola to rock wildly before sitting down again immediately. 'Sorry, I forgot we were on a boat! I was going to hug you.'

'Then far be it from me to stop you.'

'It would be most improper of me to do so,' Becky said primly. 'Have you told Isabel that you've written to her brother?'

'No, I want it to be a surprise. I've forgotten why I came to mention it now.'

'I was talking about wanting to be useful. The problem is that I have no idea what I mean by that. Have you thought about what you're going to do with the money we will win back for the city?'

'I have. In fact, we're nearly at our destination. If you don't mind a short detour, I can show you.'

'Please,' she said, intrigued, since they were in one of the dingiest and most run-down districts of Venice she had seen so far.

Making sure that her hood covered most of her

face, Becky clutched Luca's hand gratefully as she stepped on to the slimy cobblestones. She would have missed the narrow passageway had she been alone, would have fallen in the sudden gloom were it not for his support, and was dazzled when they emerged suddenly into a large *campo* with a bustling market. The stalls were covered in garish canvas awnings, the vegetables and fruit, considering the time of year, ripe and brightly coloured, but it was the plentiful mounds of unfamiliar fish which intrigued Becky. 'I don't think I know what half of these are. What is that horrible thing with the gaping mouth full of sharp teeth?'

'*Coda di rospo*, which means tail of the toad. You don't eat the ugly bit,' Luca said. 'These are all various species of octopus, which you've had in antipasti, but not these little ones, which are called *folpeti* in Venetian.'

'And these... Are they snails?' Becky asked, eyeing the writhing mass of shells.

'Sea snails,' Luca answered, laughing at her expression. 'We call them *bovoleti*.'

'They sound much nicer than they look.' They carried on, past stalls selling bread and wine, and many more fish stalls. 'There's no meat for sale,' Becky observed.

'This is one of Venice's poorest quarters. They can't afford meat,' Luca replied. 'Many here have no work. There was once a charitable school and a hospital, but the funding for both dried up. Now these people are struggling to survive.'

It was horribly familiar, yet it seemed so much worse for such poverty to exist in such beautiful surroundings—and there was beauty everywhere, Becky noted, gazing around her. A portico carved with vine leaves, elaborate latticework in an arched window, coloured glass in a fanlight, a wooden balcony tilting precariously. Venice, even in her pockets of decay, was beautiful. Though beauty provided scant solace to an empty belly or a cold hearth, she knew all too well. 'Do you plan to help them?'

'By restoring the schools and the hospitals which have fallen into disuse, for a start.'

'And more appreciated I'm sure than some old paintings hanging in a gallery.'

'My father's motives were noble but you have a point.'

'Perhaps I will follow your example and use my windfall for a good cause. Establish a school? I have no idea what it would cost. Or I could fund a refuge for young girls. You know, a safe house.'

'The kind of sanctuary which wasn't available to you, Becky?'

She coloured. 'Could I afford that, do you think?'

'Easily, but don't spend it all on other people.'

'Are you worried that I'll get a taste for the high life?'

He laughed. 'Your favourite place in my *palazzo* is the rooftop. You already have a taste for the high life.'

'I think of it as my little kingdom.' They had come to the end of the market. On the far side of the *campo*, three children were throwing a stick for a scrawny dog to fetch. It was starting to rain. 'What people want, in my experience, is not charity, Luca. It's the ability to earn a living. You'll do more for these people by building your dockyard and creating jobs than handing out alms.'

'Or building them a fountain?' he asked with a mocking smile. 'It was one of the things I'd thought of. Beautiful and also practical. Clean drinking water is in scarce supply.'

'Who'd have thought that spending money would be such hard work?' Becky said. 'If you're not careful, it will take over your life and your shipbuilding plans will remain a pipe dream.'

'All of it will be a pipe dream if we don't get the Queen of Coins's costume made. The studio is not far from here.'

It was ironic, Luca thought as he guided Becky the short distance to the mask-maker's studio, that while her horizons were rapidly expanding, his were narrowing alarmingly. Would dispensing all this money become a burden? What was the point in worrying about it now? he thought impatiently. After Carnevale was time enough. Though after Carnevale, the time when his life would begin afresh, was beginning to feel like the time when his freedom would be surrendered completely. The point when he would assume the mantle and the responsibilities of being the Conte del Pietro. Justice would have been done—yes, that was still a most uplifting prospect. But Becky, through whom justice would be served, would be gone.

There were weeks and weeks left before then. They had barely begun. 'This is it,' he said, stopping abruptly in front of a shuttered window.

'There's no sign. It doesn't even look like a shop. Are you sure? And are you absolutely certain that this man can be trusted?'

'The mask-maker knows the identity of every Venetian who wears his creations. In his own way, he is even more powerful than my father was. His family have been creating masks for generations, and for generations have kept the owners' identities secret. I would go as far as to say that if there is one man in Venice who can be trusted, it is he.'

Becky still looked dubious, but from the moment she stepped through the door and into the studio she was, as Luca had known she would be, completely enraptured.

Bartolomeo, the only name the mask-maker was ever known by, locked the door behind them, bowing low. 'Conte del Pietro. It is an honour. I don't believe I have created a mask for you before.'

'I require only a *volto*,' Luca said, pointing at an example of the simple white ghost mask. 'It is the *signorina* who has a more specialised request. Show Bartolomeo your design,' he added in English to Becky.

She did so, and as he had expected, the mask-maker eyed the drawing with delight, exclaiming in a stream of excited Italian which Luca translated for her. 'The *colombina*, a classic half mask extended over the forehead, an excellent choice! The *colombina* should be worn only by the most beautiful women, it will suit the *signorina* to perfection, such a mouth as she has, and a very shapely chin. She must decide whether to fix it with laces, which is what I would recommend, though some do prefer the baton.'

'Laces, please tell him,' Becky said. 'I need to have both hands free.'

But Bartolomeo had already moved on to the particulars of the design, poring over the sketch, making several drawings of his own, then, with a brief *'mi scusi'*, tilting Becky's face this way and that, nodding in satisfaction.

'The *signorina*'s eyes,' Luca translated, 'have a sparkling quality. We will highlight this with the application of crystals of blue like this.'

Becky pored over the redrawn design, entranced by the subtle changes which the mask-maker had made. As he began to position crystals in shades of blue over what she could now see was a template, her belly fluttered with excitement. 'It is wonderful,' she said to Bartolomeo in Italian. 'Absolutely superb.'

'No ostentatious feathers for the *signorina*. Her perfect beauty means she has no need of any further adornment. You agree?'

'What did he say?' Becky asked, after Luca had nodded his agreement.

'He said he was ready to begin your first fitting.'

The mask-maker sat Becky down on a stool. Several heavy clay models were placed over her face, until both Bartolomeo and Becky were happy with the fit and level of comfort. She listened, fascinated, as he explained the process which would follow, with Luca translating. 'This will be the mould. He will then make your mask using layers of special paper and a glue which is the most secret of formulas, to make a very light mask, which will be further shaped and trimmed, then decorated to your design. And it will be delivered in…?'

'For you, Conte del Pietro, and for the very beautiful *signorina*, I will work through the night. The mask will be ready in three days. The delivery will be to yourself at the Palazzo Pietro? And you wish a *volto* for yourself? The most popular mask. I have some already prepared in various sizes. Come, let us see what is the best fit.'

It was late afternoon by the time they left Bartolomeo's studio, for the mask-maker was also liaising with the dressmaker who would fashion the Queen of Coins's costume. The market in the *campo* had long ago been packed up and closed for the day. They crossed the now-empty space, littered with detritus, to reach the passageway which would take them back to the gondola, their footsteps echoing, accompanied only by a small tabby cat. Above them, the sky was still pale blue with wispy clouds, but the waters of the canal were darkening to an inky colour.

'There will be a beautiful sunset in a little while,' Luca said, helping Becky back into the gondola. 'I know a place not far from here where we can watch it if you like.'

'Yes, please, I'd like that very much. I don't want to return to the *palazzo* just yet. I'm enjoying being outside in the fresh air.'

Musing that what he enjoyed was the pleasure of her company, regardless of the location, Luca rowed them to a junction where two canals crossed, then tied the gondola up facing west before joining Becky on the bench. 'The sunsets at this time of year are dramatic but are over very quickly,' he said, risking putting an arm around her to pull her closer, her thigh against his, his arm on the curve of her waist, an exquisite torture.

The canal turned darker as the sun sank, the shadows cast by the overlooking buildings disappearing.

Above, the sky became almost colourless, the air around them cooling abruptly so that their breaths began to cloud, and then the show began. A tinge of pale pink low in the sky streaked with white, turned the canal into a mirror of pewter and silver. On the horizon, pink darkened to violet, and the fast-sinking sun streaked orange and vermilion. As the mantle of night fell, making black hulks of the buildings, the remnants of the setting sun produced blindingly vibrant hues. And then it was over, as dramatically as it had begun.

The air hung heavy and silent, expectant, for why else would a sun set so ravishingly if it was not to encourage a kiss? They were not alone, Luca knew that, but it felt as if they were, and that was all that mattered. His heart began to thump as their lips met. If kisses could speak, this one surely spoke of yearning. Of wanting. Of passion too long pent up. There was so much restraint in their kiss, in the clutch of their hands, in the tensing of their muscles, as if every ounce of effort was needed to suppress something wild. Such longing.

Their kiss came to a reluctant end, leaving them facing each other, their expressions cloaked by the gloom, only their quickened breathing and the gentle rocking of the gondola against its mooring to betray them.

Becky had been on tenterhooks for the last four days, waiting anxiously for Luca to decide the time was right for the Queen of Coins to make her debut appearance. Finally, that time had arrived. As the clock struck eleven, she ceased her anxious pacing. She was already wearing undergarments beneath her dressing gown in preparation. She had piled her hair high on her head, allowing it to trail in wild curls down her back and over one eye. Placing her powder and rouge in her pocket, she quit the room.

The corridor was dark, but years spent creeping back to her lodgings from the theatre at night meant Becky could see as well as a cat in the dark. The staff of the Palazzo Pietro went early to bed. There was only one night porter on duty in the reception hall three floors below. Becky glided silently down from the second to the first floor, making for the library.

Luca was waiting, dressed in his customary black, looking decidedly raffish rather than sombre. 'Everything is prepared,' he said, offering her a fortifying glass of wine, which Becky refused.

'I need to keep my wits about me.'

Butterflies began to flutter in her tummy as Luca pulled a book from the lower shelf of one of the bookcases and twisted a lever to open the door of the secret chamber. 'Your boudoir awaits,' he said.

Becky stepped into the square, windowless room, where a lamp was already lit on the table. It was warm from the huge fire which burned in the adjoining library wall. The costume, swathed in muslin, was laid out on a chaise longue. On the table beside the lamp was her mask. A gilded chair beside the table, and a full-length mirror were the room's only other furnishings.

'There's a handle on your side of the door,' Luca said. 'I'll wait in the library.'

He closed the door. Becky carefully removed the muslin from her gown. With only her sketches to work

from and not a single fitting, there was every chance
that it would fail to meet her expectations, or fail to
fit. But the costume revealed made her gasp with delight. It was as if the dressmaker had been able to read
Becky's thoughts. Whoever she was, the woman was
a genius.

She cast off her dressing gown and picked up the
tunic. Made of cobalt-blue silk, it had been inspired
by the costume Becky had once worn to play Queen
Guinevere, with long tight-fitting sleeves, a very low
neckline and a full skirt. Black lacing was sewn into
the waist, like a corset on the outside of the gown. She
pulled it tight, pleased to see that the effect was exactly
as she'd imagined, making her waist look impossibly
small, her cleavage almost too plentiful for the gown,
in comparison. The overdress which would serve as
a coat was made of black silk lined with cobalt blue,
with long pointed sleeves trailing medieval-style almost to the ground. It had a wide hood that would conceal the Queen of Coins's face and protect her from the
elements. A broad band of silver embroidery trimmed
the overdress, and a wide sash of black silk embroidered with silver sat like a girdle on her hips. Black
boots with pointed toes were adorned with crystals
which matched those on her mask.

Becky applied a dusting of powder to her neck,
throat and bosom, and a coating of rouge to her lips,
before she tied her mask in place. Pulling a swathe of
her curls over her shoulder to trail provocatively over
her cleavage, she fixed the hood in place with some
pins, and stepped in front of the mirror.

She barely recognised the creature reflected there.
Her eyes, glittering behind the mask, seemed more

blue than violet, picking up the colour of the gown. The vivid colours—black, blue and silver—were a stark contrast to the pale lustre of her skin, the vermilion slash of her lips. The Queen of Coins was a sensual creature, but she was also intimidating. She was mysterious, regal, remote, yet there was something about the hood and the mask, the shadowed face and the exposed bosom that beckoned, hinting at intimacy. She was a woman of contrasts, like the city she was to conquer. If Becky could have imagined the perfect role for herself, it would be this one. The costume made her feel strong, powerful even. Luca's avenging angel. She smiled at herself, a slow, deliberately provocative smile. She was ready.

As she opened to door back into the library Luca turned quickly, setting the wine glass which had been raised to his lips quickly down. '*Che meraviglia,*' he said with a soft whistle. 'I don't know whether to throw myself at your feet or into your arms.'

Becky couldn't resist giving a little twirl. 'You like?'

'I like very much,' he said. 'And you, I think, much prefer to be the Queen of Coins than Cousin Rebecca?'

'Let's just see if the Queen of Coins is successful first.'

'I do not see how you can fail. No man, seeing you in this most delectable outfit, will be looking at your hands,' Luca said, quite blatantly eyeing Becky's breasts. 'I presume that was a deliberate ploy?'

'To distract my opponents, not my protector,' she said pointedly.

He laughed. '*Mi scusi*, but I am not yet dressed for the role. One moment.' He threw his long black silk cloak over his shoulders, fastening the silver buttons at the neck. The *volto* mask was chalk white and completely plain, covering his entire face apart from his chin. The black tricorn hat placed on top made him unrecognisable and slightly intimidating. 'Now,' Luca said, 'we are ready. Tonight, I very much hope, signals the beginning of the end for Don Sarti.'

They left the *palazzo* through a door at the back of the secret room that opened on to a narrow canal. The air grew noticeably colder as they descended a steep flight of steps. Luca held the lantern high, revealing a gondola tied to a rusty iron ring. 'Who left the boat here?' Becky asked.

'One of the gondoliers. I told him I had a lover's tryst.' Luca was already on board, holding his hand out for Becky. 'He won't say anything, don't worry. I think he was surprised that I hadn't asked for the boat before. This secret entrance has always been used to enter or leave the *palazzo* undetected.'

Becky took her usual seat facing him, accustomed now to the gondola's motion. Luca picked up the oar, set it into its lock, untied the rope and kicked the boat out into the canal. It was a dark night, the thin strip of sky visible too dark with clouds for any stars to shine. If there was a moon, it was in another part of the heavens. Luca was a dark, sinister shape on the stern, his *volto* mask eerily pale under the black shadow of his hat. He could be anyone, a complete stranger, as could she, she supposed, in her Queen of Coins costume, hiding behind her mask. Yet the enveloping night encouraged confidences. 'Have you had many lovers, Luca?' she asked.

'None since my return to Venice. Before then, a few, though not so very many. We went our separate ways when passion died, as it always does.'

'Does it?'

He did not answer until he had steered the gondola under one of the low arched bridges, so low that it forced him to duck his head. 'That has always been my experience.'

Becky tilted her head back to search the sullen sky for pinpoints of light, but found none. She had no previous experience of passion. Her desire for Luca burned so persistently that she found it difficult to believe it would die. But then, there had been a time not so very long ago when she'd thought her love would never die, and a time even closer to hand when she'd thought her heart was broken. She'd been wrong about both. Startled, she tested herself, but though the bitterness of that final betrayal which threatened to put a noose around her neck was still every bit as strong, she felt nothing else save a sense of relief that her eyes had been well and truly opened. What an escape she'd had! Were it not for the fact that she was a wanted criminal...

Her eyes flew open as the gondola bumped against a wooden jetty and Luca jumped out to secure it. As she followed him on to dry land, something brushed past her gown, making her jump. 'Where are we? Where is the *ridotto*? I can't see any lights.'

'It is a short walk from here. Are you happy with the plan?'

She ought to be, it was her plan, and they had discussed it often enough. She opened her mouth to reassure him, only to be assailed by a memory of the last time she had played the tables. She screwed her eyes shut, trying to will it away but it persisted. When she had realised what had happened, there had been a moment of shocked disbelief. All eyes were on her, but time seemed to stand still, and her mind was quite frozen. Jack, she'd thought, where was he? Only the scuffle, the shout, as he fled startled her into action, too terrified that the hands reaching for her would catch her to concern herself with the act of betrayal.

'Becky?'

Her mouth was dry. Her knees were like jelly. Sweat trickled down her back. Under the shadow of her hood, impeded by her mask, she tried to take calming breaths. Tonight she would not fail. Tonight, the Queen of Coins would triumph. She would not let Luca down. She checked the strings on her mask. She placed her hand on Luca's arm. *'Andiamo,'* she said. 'Let's go and win some money.'

Chapter Nine

It was still dark when they left the *ridotto*, though dawn was not far-off. Becky felt as if she was floating, as if she had drunk a magnum of Prosecco. She couldn't stop smiling. She jumped down into the gondola, making it rock wildly. 'We did it.'

Luca was unfastening his mask, casting it with his tricorn hat on to the other bench and running his fingers through his flattened hair. 'You did it.'

'*We* did it.' Becky threw herself on to the bench, making the heavy purse containing her winnings clunk against her thigh. 'You selected the opponents, the Queen of Coins vanquished them one by one.'

Luca cast off and began to turn the gondola. 'Though there were moments when it seemed to me that the Queen of Coins was the one about to lose.'

Becky chuckled. 'Oh, that is all part of the act. You have to give your adversary hope. You have to lead him to believe that he can beat you, else he will not be tempted to play on.' Her face fell. 'That sounds very callous.'

'I think you were fair, in the circumstances. You

did not permit the stakes to go anywhere near as high as some of the more reckless gamblers wished.'

'That is true,' she said, brightening. 'Do you think the Queen of Coins is being talked about already?'

'From the minute she walked into the room she was a sensation, and I believe I played my part in stirring up interest. By the end of the night, I had the pleasure of several of my stories regarding the identity of the mysterious Queen of Coins being quoted back to me along with various other speculations not of my devising. The runaway Bulgarian princess was my personal favourite.'

Becky let out a peal of laughter, which echoed around the narrow canal. 'I know we must repeat our success several times over before Carnival starts properly, but we did make an excellent start, didn't we?'

'A dream start.'

'All of this feels like a dream.' She lay back on the bench, watching starry-eyed as Luca rowed the gondola back to the *palazzo*, the sky lightening just enough for her to see his handsome countenance.

He was smiling as he tied the boat up, carefully securing the oar before helping her out and lighting the lamp. 'Are you tired?'

Becky shook her head. 'I feel like I'll never sleep again, though I will be very relieved to take off this mask.' She followed him back up the steps to the door of the secret room, pulling the pins that secured her hood and untying her mask with a happy sigh as Luca locked the door behind them, placing his hat and mask on to the table. 'A nightcap to celebrate, I think,' he said. 'Wait there.'

Becky pulled the purse containing her winnings

from the secret pocket inside her overdress and put it beside the masks. After the cold outside, the room felt warm. She untied the sash and slipped out of the outer dress of her costume, and then sank on to the chaise longue, wriggling her numb toes inside her boots and loosening the laces at the front of her tunic. All her fears were completely unfounded. Not one of her many opponents had suspected foul play for a moment. True, they had none of them been experts, she was already far more skilled than any of them, but it was reassuring all the same. Much more reassuring than she had realised.

'I thought it was time that you tasted grappa.' Luca, now cloakless and coatless, was carrying two small glasses. 'It is distilled from the skin and the seeds of grapes which are leftover from winemaking. Don't screw up your face. It tastes good, I promise.'

He sat down beside her, handing her one of the little glasses. 'To the Queen of Coins. *Salute.*'

'*Salute.*' Becky took a cautious sip, gasping as the fiery liquid hit the back of her throat. 'That is a great deal stronger than wine.'

'It is not to your taste?'

She took a second cautious sip. This time, now that she was prepared for it, she enjoyed the tingling warmth. 'It is good, though I don't think I'd manage more than one glass, it would go straight to my head, and I'm already a little bit drunk on success.'

'Well-deserved success. All your hours of practice have paid off.'

'This is only the first step, Luca.'

'I know, but it is a truly wonderful feeling to have finally taken it, to be one step closer to my goal.' He threw back the rest of his own grappa, turning towards her as he set the glass down on the floor. 'Thanks to you.'

His leg was brushing against hers. A long strand of silky hair fell over his brow. His smile was warm, his brow for once free of even the faintest trace of a frown. It was as intoxicating as grappa, to bask in her success, the relief of it, the outrageousness of it. And now that it was over, the vicarious thrill of it, made all the more thrilling by knowing she was winning for Luca.

'I couldn't have done it without you,' Becky said, reaching up to brush his hair back from his forehead.

He caught her hand, pressing a kiss to her palm, and the warmth of admiration in his eyes changed to a different sort of heat as their gazes clashed and held and Becky's heart began to race with a very different kind of excitement. His mouth lingered on her palm. He licked his way up her thumb and his lips closed around it. She shivered in sheer delight and everything she had been feeling merged, transforming itself into the burning heat of desire.

Yet she couldn't move. Luca's gaze was scorching, transfixed on hers as he licked the tip of her index finger, drawing it into his mouth. She had only to blink to stop him, to pull her hand free from his, but it didn't even occur to her. She was positively smouldering, every lick, every kiss, the sweet dragging of his mouth on her fingers sending sparks of heat through her veins to concentrate in an aching drag of desire low in her belly.

His breath was shallow, his pupils dilated as his mouth closed on her little finger, and Becky shuddered, released from her trance, falling towards him on the chaise longue. He let out a low groan as their lips met, their tongues met, their bodies met in a tangle of wild kisses and feverish hands. She stopped thinking, surrendering herself to the spinning, urgent need for skin to touch skin, plucking at the buttons of Luca's waistcoat, tugging his shirt free from his pantaloons to run her hands up his back, thrilling at the ripple of his muscles beneath her palms and the shudder of delight which coursed through him at her touch.

When he dragged his mouth from hers, her whimper of protest turned into a sigh of delight as he kissed his way down her throat to lick into the valley between her breasts, tugging at the loose fastenings of her tunic enough to slip it down her shoulders. More kisses, on the exposed flesh of her breasts, her nipples hard and aching inside the constraints of her corsets. He was murmuring in Italian, words she didn't recognise, but which sounded like pleas and promises she longed for him to fulfil.

She stood up to wriggle free of her tunic. Luca cast off his waistcoat and then, at her urging, pulled his shirt over his head. His torso was smooth and tanned, his skin gleaming in the lamplight. Entranced, Becky traced the muscles of his shoulders, down the slight swell of his chest to the dip of his belly, relishing the way her touch made him shiver. She pressed her mouth to his skin, tasting salt and soap and heat. His fingers were running through her hair, spreading it out over her naked shoulders, his hands on her back, then on her arms, then on her breasts, cupping them through her corset, making her cry out with delight, arching against him, her mouth desperately seeking his, and finding it in a deep, urgent kiss.

She could feel the distinctive evidence of his arousal pressing between her thighs through the single petticoat she wore over her pantaloons. Mindless, she clutched at the firm flesh of his buttocks. Staggering backwards, she found herself pressed against the door which connected with the library, and still they kissed feverishly. Luca's hand was under her petticoat now, and instinctively she wrapped her leg around his, yanking the thin cambric higher in the process. He muttered her name, one hand braced against the door behind her, the other between her thighs, finding her flesh between the split in her pantaloons, his fingers sliding into her, forcing her to cling frantically to the last remnants of self-control. She was strung so tightly that it would not take much to set her over. She was torn between wanting to fall headlong into her climax, and to cling on, to enjoy and endure for as long as she could.

But Luca gave her no choice. Kisses, his tongue matching his fingers, stroking, thrusting, making her tighten, surrendering herself to the spiralling, twisting tension inside her, arching against him as it took her, making her cry out, cling to him, pulsing and throbbing in complete abandon.

When it was over, she clung limply to him, drained and sated. Luca was still unmistakably aroused, yet he was gently disentangling himself from her. Confused and fast becoming embarrassed by her state of undress and her wanton abandon, Becky grabbed her dressing gown, belting it tightly around her. 'I think the grappa must have gone to our heads, after all,' she said, because she had to say something.

'If anything went to my head, it was you. Now, please, go to bed before I lose what very little is left of my self-control.'

When Becky awoke it was already light. The curtains in her bedchamber had been drawn to show one of those misty days, where the sky and the canals seemed to merge. Sitting up in bed, she saw that the fire was burning brightly in the grate, and even as she peered over at the clock trying to make out the time, Chiara crept into the room, bearing a huge tray.

'*Buongiorno*, Signorina Wickes. It is not like you to oversleep. I have brought you breakfast.'

'The Contessa! I was to accompany her on her morning calls.'

'Conte del Pietro has accompanied her instead. Do you want breakfast in bed or do you wish to sit by the fire?'

'By the fire, I think,' Becky said, appalled by the idea of getting breadcrumbs between her silk sheets. 'Just set it down, Chiara. There is no need for you to stay, thank you.'

Becky wrapped herself in her dressing gown and sat cosily by the fire. In addition to tea things, the tray contained warm bread rolls wrapped in a cloth, butter, apricot and cherry jam, several mouthwatering sweet pastries and the little biscotti filled with raisins which the Venetians called *zaletti*. Her tummy rumbling as she brewed her tea, Becky broke off a piece of pastry and popped it into her mouth, closing her eyes as it melted in buttery flakes on her tongue. A flurry of rain spattered against the window. She curled up on the chair, tucking her bare toes under a velvet cushion. There was something quite delightfully decadent in being inside in front of a blazing fire with a tray of good things to eat while outside the weather turned nasty. When Carnival was over, when she was rich enough to have her own little cottage somewhere, she could probably sit like this all day every day if she wished, getting fat on sugary treats and...

And what! Wishing her life away? Ignoring the world outside, caring nothing for it, as long as she was warm and well fed? Becky wrapped her hands around her teacup in a way that Isabel would deeply disapprove of, and sighed to herself. Her little pipe dream was just that. She'd be bored rigid within a few days—say a week at most. And as for eating herself fat, something she used to dream of when she went to bed ravenous, while buttering a roll and smearing on a dollop of cherry jam was still novel enough to be a real treat, it was no longer the limit of her ambitions.

Becky topped up her tea from the pot, and topped up the pot from the hot-water kettle. It was Luca's fault. He'd opened her eyes to possibilities she could never have envisaged on her own. A world to explore and people in it she could help. Though she still had no idea how to go about such an undertaking. Or even where. Because she was fooling herself, thinking it could ever be in England.

Setting her cup back on the tray along with her empty plate, Becky padded over to the window. Her breath steamed up the cold glass. The rain had settled in, the heavy sky turning the canal below a dull pewter. It was one thing to escape, but another to admit that she couldn't risk going back. And it was one thing to imagine herself free to travel round the world, but to know that she had no home to return to—not that she ever wanted to return to the home she had left.

Despite the rain, Becky opened the tall windows and stepped on to the narrow balcony. She had never been one to indulge in self-pity, and she wasn't about to do it now, especially when she had less reason than ever to do so. She had no ties back in London. Hers had always been a solitary life and she'd liked it that way. Funny, but even at her most besotted, there had always been a part of her that had resented the changes she'd had to make to accommodate Jack. Funny, now she thought about it, how little changes she'd actually made. The trauma of their parting had obscured the fact that she hadn't really missed him. She'd miss Isabel a great deal more. And Luca…

Oh, Luca. Last night, he had been utterly transformed by their success. Last night, she had seen him carefree, lit up, happy. It was an infectious mix. Very infectious. Wrapping her arms around herself, Becky slipped back inside, sinking back down beside the fireside. Her utter abandonment still astonished her, but she was no longer embarrassed, nor could she bring herself to regret it. This extraordinary situation, this extraordinary man, were an all-too-brief departure from the natural order of things. At the end of Carnival they would part, their respective futures taking them in radically different directions. But that was still weeks away.

Becky closed her eyes, letting herself drift into a delightful dream of last night. Passion was such a very different thing to love. A very much more delightful experience, where instinct ruled, and pleasure was the only thing that mattered. It would pass, Luca had said, and she hoped fervently that he was right, at the same time hoping fervently that it would not fade too quickly. He had opened her eyes to a whole new world of gratification last night, a world she was eager to explore.

She'd never taken a lover before Jack wormed his way into her affections, so there had been no one for her to compare him to. Becky winced. She didn't much like the thought of doing so now. Perhaps it was because she had been so anxious to please, that she hadn't been so very satisfied herself back then. That would certainly be one explanation. Another would be that Jack had been as selfish in her bed as he'd been in every other aspect of her life, interested only in what she could provide him with, and giving back in return the bare minimum he could get away with. Now, that, unfortunately, rang very true.

While Luca— Oh, Luca was a very different matter. The next time—Becky smiled to herself, unfurling her legs from beneath her and stretching her toes to the fire, yielding to the temptation of imagining just exactly how the next time might be.

It was late afternoon by the time Luca and his mother arrived back at the *palazzo* in the pouring rain, leaving little time to change for dinner. He had spent most of the day taking tea and making polite conversation, with frustratingly few opportunities to bolster the legend of the Queen of Coins, his mother's friends being far more interested in stakes of the matrimonial kind. Accepting an *aperitivo* from Brunetti, he took his usual seat by the window in the otherwise empty drawing room.

Brunetti hovered, adjusting cushions, tending to the fire, waiting on the ladies' arrival. Luca stared out at the dark sweep of the Grand Canal. A few sleepless hours of contemplation in the early morning had left him baffled by his behaviour last night. Not what had happened, so much as what had not. Becky was entirely beyond his ken. He had no one to compare her to, nor did he wish to. The situation presented them such limited opportunities to indulge their mutual passion, last night's conflagration was inevitable, he had concluded. What confused him was why he had not taken matters to the ultimate conclusion.

Not because of lack of desire, that much was certain. He had never wanted anyone the way he wanted Becky. And she had wanted him every bit as much, he didn't doubt that either. As a result, they were both behaving out of character. She, who was not in the habit of offering, would have given him all, and he, who was in the habit of taking all had demurred. He was, for the first time in his life, uncertain of his own feelings. He didn't doubt what he wanted, but he wasn't sure it would be a good idea for either of them. Familiarity bred not contempt but indifference, had always been his experience. But the more he knew of Becky, the more he wanted her.

Whether their mutual desire would persist or fade was a moot point, however. At the end of Carnevale Becky would leave Venice, and he would take up the reins of his new life in the city, his duty to his father done, justice served. He would build his ships. He would restore the stolen treasures to Venice in a new form. He would step into his father's shoes. It was all he had dreamed of, all he had wanted, since he'd read his father's letter, yet all he could think of was that Becky would play no part in it.

He would miss her! There, he could admit that much. But it would pass—it would have to. And in the meantime, instead of dwelling over Becky's looming departure, what he ought to do was enjoy the time they did have.

The door opened, Brunetti bustled over to greet his mother and her niece, and Luca got to his feet. Becky was dressed in lemon tonight, one of Cousin Rebecca's simple gowns with a demure neckline, though it seemed to him, as she stepped lightly towards him, that it clung in a very far from demure way to the curves he had explored so delightfully last night.

'Good evening, Cousin Luca.'

Her smile was tentative as she made her curtsy. He couldn't resist taking her hand, pressing it fleetingly, smiling into her eyes in a most uncousinly way. 'Cousin Rebecca,' he said, 'as always, it is a pleasure to see you.'

'Your absence was much commented on today, Rebecca. I was forced to make your excuses at every call we made.'

'I am very sorry.' Becky pushed her untouched wine aside. Isabel, who had been rather silent throughout dinner was, now that the servants had departed, sounding decidedly waspish. 'I will ask Chiara to wake me if it ever happens again.'

'Please do. Now that it is widely accepted that I

have a niece, I would rather she did not garner a reputation for being either sickly or unreliable.'

'Mama, that is most unfair of you,' Luca said mildly. 'You must know perfectly well why Becky was so tired.'

'Presumably she was playing at a *ridotto* in her other guise,' Isabel replied tetchily. 'Though why you should imagine that I know this *perfectly well* when you have been at great pains to keep your plans from me, I do not know.'

'I have kept my plans from you because you expressed a desire not to know,' Luca retorted coldly. 'Despite having read my father's letter, despite his desperate plea for justice, you would rather sweep the entire matter under the carpet.'

'For very good reason.' Isabel picked up her napkin and began to pleat it. 'I apologise for my harsh tone, Rebecca.'

'I shouldn't have overslept.'

'Oh, it's not that.' Isabel threw her napkin down and took a sip of her wine. 'Anna Sarti was at the Fabbiano *palazzo* this afternoon. The poor woman is on tenterhooks knowing the start of Carnevale is fast approaching.'

'She knows, then, that her husband is a reckless gambler?' Becky asked with a sinking feeling in the pit of her stomach, though she had suspected as much from a remark made by the Contessa Albrizzi.

'Of course, she knows and dreads the coming weeks, though there is nothing she can do.'

'For which we should be grateful,' Luca said tersely. 'You know that the money he will stake belongs to Venice, not to Sarti.'

'Of course.' Isabel took another sip of wine. 'I also understand your desire to put right a terrible wrong.' She smiled weakly. 'Unfortunately, it is not only Don Sarti who will pay the price.'

'That is a matter for Don Sarti's conscience, not mine.'

Isabel nodded again. Luca poured himself a cup of coffee. Becky's conscience niggled her. Why did Isabel believe Donna Sarti would also pay, if the Queen of Coins took only what the Don had stolen? The winnings would be put to good use too, she reminded herself. Schools and hospitals for the people, Luca had said. If Anna Sarti knew the truth...

'Rebecca, I see from that fierce frown that I have upset you.' Isabel leaned across the table to press her hand. 'I promised not to interfere. I beg your pardon, Luca, you must do as you see fit to honour your father's memory. And when you have, Rebecca will be free to return to England. We will miss you. Do you have plans?'

'Nothing cast in stone,' Becky said vaguely. 'Though I'm not sure I want to go back to England,' she added, which was at least close to the truth.

'Really? But you must have family there?'

'Unfortunately, I don't. I am quite alone in the world.'

'You poor thing! Even though I have not seen my own family for decades, at least I have the consolation of knowing they are alive and well.'

'I'm well used to being on my own. In fact, I prefer it.'

'But you are still very young, with your life stretching out in front of you. Perhaps you'll marry, have a family of your own. Though I would not recommend a country vicar,' Isabel said. 'That may very well suit my niece, but…'

'That is a very poor attempt at a joke. If I wished to marry—which I do not—no man of the cloth would take me. You have no idea—' Becky broke off, appalled, suddenly on the brink of tears.

Isabel flinched. 'You are right, I do not. It was presumptuous of me to put myself in your shoes.'

'Yes, it was. You no more understand my life than I do yours, nor would ever want to. Your life may well be one of privilege, Isabel, but it's also mapped out in advance for you. I may not have much, but I do have the freedom to choose.'

Becky hadn't felt so completely out of place since the first night she'd arrived. After a day so foolishly anticipating seeing Luca again, all she wanted was to be alone. Without waiting for either mother or son to fill the astonished silence, she pushed back her chair and got to her feet. 'I'm here to carry out a specific task. When it's completed, I'll be gone. It will be as if I was never here in the first place. It cannot be any other way and that is for the best, for all of us. *Buona notte.*'

Chapter Ten

It had been raining overnight. The rooftop terrace was damp underfoot, though the sun was making a determined effort to break through the grey cloud. Becky gazed out morosely over the rooftops towards the Lido, where, Isabel had informed her, Luca had gone riding. Her mood, in contrast to the sparkling blue lagoon, was as grey and gloomy as the leaden sky above her.

She had waved away Isabel's attempt to apologise over breakfast. There was nothing to apologise for, after all. They had not quarrelled. Isabel had simply been curious. Becky preferred to keep her plans to herself. If they had really been friends it would be a different matter, but they were not friends. Last night, what Becky had said was a timely reminder for all of them of the real reason for her presence here. She had shocked them both with her vehemence, but it was for the best. She didn't belong here, nor would she ever.

'And I'd better make bloody sure I remember that from now on,' she muttered to herself. The arrival of a tea tray—courtesy of the Contessa, the servant informed her—made her feel like an ungrateful wretch.

Passing on her thanks, pouring a very welcome cup of piping hot tea and adding three sugars, Becky steeled herself. Isabel, she could keep her distance from. Cousin Rebecca was in awe of her aunt anyway. But Luca was another matter.

She curled her fingers around her cup, sitting back on the bench. Only yesterday morning, lolling about in her bedchamber in the aftermath of their lovemaking the night before, she'd been imagining all sorts of passionate couplings between them, quite forgetting the sole purpose of her being here. Nothing mattered more to Luca than his quest for poetic justice. Becky was his means to achieving it, and anything else she was to him was merely a product of this. When Carnevale was over, Luca would have no further need of her. His suggestion that she gaily set off to travel the world, it occurred to her now, reflected his own passion for travel, not hers. She was even entertaining the notion to please him, giving no thought to the practicalities, or the reality of travelling alone as a single woman. Her inexperience, ignorance of the world beyond London coupled with the sense of isolation she would feel, made it a daunting prospect.

But there was an even more scary thought. By his own admission, Luca indulged in dalliances, whose passion always died sooner or later. There wasn't anything wrong with that. It wasn't that she was in danger of falling in love with him, but that didn't mean she was immune to being hurt. In the cold light of day, her behaviour in the secret room behind the library appalled her. It wasn't what she had done, it was why. Because Luca mattered.

She was not as far gone as to be foolishly thinking

there could be any sort of future together for them, nor even to want it. She hated this world he inhabited, the stifling drawing rooms and the conversations where one thing was said and another meant entirely. Masks were not only worn during Carnival. Beneath that rich, sophisticated veneer of polite society, as far as she could see, there were a lot of unhappy people. She didn't understand the Venetian ways, Luca had said, and she never wanted to. She was glad she'd never be anything other than an impostor here. She liked Luca. She admired him and she found him fiercely attractive, but she didn't like his world and she couldn't believe a man like him could ever be happy in it. Though that was for him to discover, long after she'd left.

In the meantime, he was a distraction she really could not afford. Luca wasn't Jack, but if she wasn't careful, history could repeat itself. If the Queen of Coins failed, not only would Becky fail to earn the fee which would change her life, she could lose her life if she were caught manipulating the cards. She needed to concentrate totally on the task at hand, and so did Luca. She had not come to Venice to find a friend in Isabel or a lover in Luca. She'd come here to fund a new life for herself, and that was the thing she'd lost sight of these last few days. Her hard-won freedom depended on it. She was determined she wasn't going to lose sight of that again.

Becky was leaning out over the parapet when the door to the roof terrace creaked open. Before she turned, she already sensed it was Luca. He was looking particularly windswept, his eyes and cheeks glowing with the exercise and fresh air, his hair tangled, and despite herself, she felt a lurch of excitement at the sight of him. 'I hoped you'd find me here,' she said. 'I want to talk to you.'

He muttered something under his breath, striding across the roof to her, and clasped her hands. 'Please, I know what you're going to say, but I beg you not to do anything rash before you hear me out. Last night at dinner, it was clear that my mother's misguided concerns for Donna Sarti were making you uncomfortable. And then her misguided attempt to speculate about your marital prospects appeared to make things worse. But what wasn't clear to me until later, and it should have been,' he said wretchedly, 'was that I was at the root of your strange mood. I got carried away, Becky, and though you too seemed to be more than willing—I should have known you'd think differently in the morning. Please, tell me you're not thinking of leaving. It won't happen again.'

He had reached exactly the same conclusion as she, though via a very different route. She snatched her hands free. 'I didn't think differently in the morning, Luca. Quite the contrary. Heaven help me, I actually dreamed of more.'

She had the satisfaction of seeing him look astonished. 'So did I,' he said with a crooked smile.

If only he hadn't said that. But it made no difference. 'We can't always have what we want,' Becky said brusquely. 'Especially when it gets in the way of what we really want, and that's what's in danger of happening. You're a distraction I don't need, and frankly, I'm a distraction you can't afford. I'm not leaving. I'm staying, but there's too much at stake to risk letting passion cloud our judgement, Luca. You were the very one who pointed out on the first day we met, that we are playing a dangerous game. If I am caught...'

'You won't be.'

'No, I won't, because I'm going to do everything in my power to make sure I'm not. And so are you. I'm not going to fall into the same trap as last time.'

His eyes narrowed. 'Last time? What do you mean?'

Her stomach roiled, her heart felt as if it was in her mouth, but she met his eyes unflinching. 'That's what I want to talk to you about. Perhaps it would be better if we sat down?'

'I have a feeling this requires fresh tea. I am sure that I will need coffee.'

In something of a daze, Luca went inside to summon a servant. Becky wasn't leaving. Becky was staying. Becky thought he was a distraction. Becky didn't want to make the same mistake as last time, whatever that meant.

She was right, he thought with a sinking feeling. They had become distracted. It was a timely reminder that Becky was not here to play Becky, but the Queen of Coins. And a timely reminder that when she was done with that role, she would leave Venice.

Giving his instructions to the servant, Luca found himself wondering how many more times he'd order a pot of tea for Cousin Rebecca along with his own coffee. It was a sobering thought but, for the moment, quite irrelevant. Becky was waiting for him, and whatever she was about to tell him, she was dreading it. The answer to the question of why she had left England, he guessed. An account of what became of the man she referred to as her paramour, he suspected. The past that Becky had been so reluctant to talk about.

Luca paused on the final step to the terrace. He had no idea what to expect, but whatever she wanted from him, he needed to be able to provide it. He had come too far to give up now.

He opened the door, crossing to the bench, handing Becky the cloak he'd asked the servant to bring. 'I know you say you never feel the cold, but I have a feeling we're going to be here for a while.'

'*Grazie.*'

She wrapped herself in the voluminous garment, sitting on the edge of the bench as if readying herself to fly. Her skin was pale. There were dark circles under her huge violet eyes. The usual strand of glossy black curls had escaped to trail down her cheek. With difficulty, he resisted the familiar impulse to tuck it behind her ear. She looked at the same time both terrified and resolute. He wanted to reassure her, but knew better than to offer empty platitudes, knew that she was in fact quite capable of shocking him. So he kept his counsel until the tea and coffee came, watching the familiar hesitation before she decided to add a third sugar lump, the little smile of satisfaction that always greeted the first sip, the way she held the cup between her hands to warm them. The habit of a woman who had grown up in cold, damp, inadequate accommodation, he finally realised. How little he really knew of her or her life.

Becky took another sip and angled herself towards him, clearly bracing herself. 'My story centres around Jack, though I expect you've guessed that.' She took another sip of tea before setting the cup down with trembling hands. 'My paramour, they called him in the scandal sheets, though I thought of him as my husband. Not that we were really married, but I've never seen the need for a bit of paper to confirm what you already know. Or think you know,' she added with a bitter curl to her lip. 'I was twenty when I met him, and I prided myself on being worldly-wise. It turned out I was wrong.'

The tale she told was sparse on details, for which Luca was grateful. She said enough for him to imagine the charming rogue who had first seduced her, and then used and abused her. He had to work hard not to curl his hands into tight fists as Becky made light of her lover's greed, blaming herself for her own gullibility in not challenging his duplicitous lies as he lured her away from the streets where she had been content to perform her tricks and into the murky gaming hells of St James's.

'He told me that the money was to pay his father's debts,' she said. 'His father was in prison, his mother and brothers left without food, fearing eviction. How could I refuse to help him when I had the ability to do so?'

How indeed, Luca thought, his lip curling. The scurrilous bastard had clearly known Becky well enough to detect the tender heart beneath the gritty veneer. He hated the man for that and was uncomfortably aware that there was also, lurking beneath his contempt, something akin to jealousy.

'I couldn't make enough in the streets for what he claimed he needed,' Becky continued, 'so he taught me how to play the tables—he saw, you see, just how easy it would be to turn my hand, literally—from card tricks to card sharping. But no matter how much I won, it was never enough to satisfy his demands. There was always another debt to be paid, rent, food, clothes to buy and schooling for his brothers and sisters too.'

'It didn't occur to you that he should have taken responsibility for his family rather than you?'

'He was, he said, by allowing me to help them. I know it sounds so pathetic—but I was pathetic. And every time I protested, there was a new tale of woe. You'll think me a fool, but I believed him. I had no reason not to, Luca, and he was very convincing. He could have had a career on the stage.'

He belonged in the gutter, Luca thought with a horrible premonition of what was to come. 'And then, inevitably, one day his greed caused both your downfalls, I take it?'

Becky's cheeks were chalk white. She nodded, swallowing several times before she continued. 'Crockford's,' she said, her voice barely more than a whisper. 'That's where he wanted me to play. Have you heard of it?'

'Yes.' The elite of St James's hells, where there were no limits on the stakes, where men lost and won fortunes on a nightly basis. Men like Don Sarti. The parallels were beginning to make Luca feel sick. 'Go on,' he said.

'I didn't want to. I told him I wouldn't. It was far too dangerous. They have people walking the floors, constantly on the lookout for sharps operating. And the players—they're men with influence and a long reach. I didn't want to risk it.'

'But he told you a tale which melted your heart,'

Luca said viciously. Becky flinched and he cursed his insensitivity. 'Forgive me, but I find the way this man used you difficult to stomach.' Even as he uttered the words, he wondered if he was being a hypocrite.

Becky, however, shrugged. 'I let him use me. It was my own fault. I knew what he wanted me to do was wrong. I knew it was dangerous, but I did it all the same. It took him some doing to persuade me, but I was persuaded. He told me that his father had died in prison, leaving his mother and brothers destitute with no prospect of any income now the family breadwinner was dead. Jack wanted to raise one final significant sum, enough to pay for them to travel to Ireland, where they had relatives, and establish them there. After that he would have discharged his duty and I would no longer have to play the hells, and we could concentrate on building a life together. So...'

Becky's composure snapped. A tear trickled down her cheek, but she brushed it away angrily, shook her head when Luca reached for her hand, though she accepted a fresh cup of tea. 'So we duly visited Crockford's,' she said. 'And I was winning. Jack was with me. As you know, I couldn't have crossed the portal of Crockford's without a male escort. But he was nervous. I was playing for such high stakes and it showed on his face. I was so focused on the cards, I didn't notice, but one of the Crockford's men did, and they watched Jack watching me. Their suspicions were raised. Well, it was only a matter of time before they were on to me.'

Becky drained her tea. She was staring out at the sky, her eyes unfocused, lost in what was, judging by the way she clutched at her empty teacup, a terrifying memory. 'Jack gave the game away but it was me who paid the price. I felt a hand on my shoulder. I looked up, thinking it was Jack, but he was already halfway out the door with my winnings and making a run for it. I shook myself free. Someone shouted, "Stop, thief!" from the other side of the salon—they'd noticed Jack running by then. It was enough of a distraction for me to be able to flee out of a window. It was my only bit of luck, for it faced out on to the back of the building.' Becky's smile was mocking. 'My head for heights came in very handy. I escaped across the rooftops and finally made it home, where I waited, my nerves shredded, for Jack to turn up.'

'A wait that continues to this day, I'll wager. If he is ever foolish enough to break cover, mine will be the last face he sees.'

Becky shivered. 'Then I'm very glad he's not here. Oh, don't get me wrong,' she added hurriedly. 'At the time I would have happily ended his miserable life myself. But coming here in search of a fresh start has made me realise something. It is done, and cannot be undone. It's futile for me to rail against the past or seek revenge. The future is what matters.'

Luca stared at her in amazement. 'The man betrayed you. He lied to you. He deserted you.'

'And he broke my heart too, or I thought he did. It's mended now, thanks to you.' Becky coloured. 'I mean thanks to your faith in me. I haven't told you the worst part yet. I went in search of him. Of course I did. That's when the house of cards came tumbling down, so to speak. The landlord at his lodging house informed me there was no family, never had been. Jack had left for America, leaving nothing behind but an unpaid rent bill. All that money I'd won, he'd been salting away. Right from the moment he set eyes on me at Covent Garden, he'd been planning it, I reckon. Making me fall in love with him, leading me on, before leaving me high and dry and with a price on my head to boot. The man I had been fleecing when I was caught cheating turned out to be a member of the royal family! The full fury of the establishment was turned on me, my name blackened and my crime plastered all over the scandal sheets. The Runners were set on me, and if they'd caught me…'

Luca stared, utterly horrified. 'They would hang you?' he whispered.

'In a heartbeat.'

'That is what you meant when you said you couldn't go back to England, even if you wanted to?'

'When The Procurer found me, I was in fear of my life, Luca. I don't know what I'd have done if she hadn't offered me this opportunity. You saved my skin.'

He poured himself the dregs of the cold coffee, unsurprised to see that his hand was not quite steady. He pictured the guillotine in Piazza San Marco. 'Only to put it in danger again.'

'No,' Becky said firmly. 'That's what I'm determined won't happen. That's why we can't afford to be distracted, not when we're in the *ridotti.*'

The coffee was cold and gritty, but it was sufficient to calm him. 'I would never abandon you to your fate.'

'Of course not!' she exclaimed scornfully. 'You're not Jack, you couldn't be more different. I've known that from the start.'

'*Grazie mille.*'

'I mean it.' Becky smiled painfully. 'I hated working with him, he was always the weak link, but I couldn't play without him. I know I can rely on you. I can trust you, because I understand, I truly do, why it matters so much to you to make amends for what happened to your father. I brought what happened to me on myself—most of it,' Becky said. 'My form of atonement is to move forward, to claim my life back on my own terms. It's—what do you call it?—serendipity that I'll be able to do that by giving you your life back too.'

'You are a very brave woman, Becky Wickes. I know no one like you.'

She blushed, shifting on the bench. 'Well, that's just the problem though, isn't it? I've never met anyone like you, and together we've both allowed that fact to…'

'Get in the way?'

'We can't risk getting any closer. Do you see?' Her cheeks were fiery red, but Becky continued determinedly. 'Passion always fades, you said, but it doesn't feel like it's fading at the moment, and I think it's time we made an effort to put the fire out, rather than to stoke the flames.'

He laughed drily. 'Sometimes you sound as if you are speaking in a play.'

'Sometimes playwrights say it better than I ever could. To put it bluntly, I need to stop thinking about anything other than what you brought me here for.'

Luca sighed heavily. 'You are right,' he admitted most reluctantly. He couldn't argue with her. Her confession had shocked him to the core, but her determination and courage were admirable. 'You have already risked your life once. I have no wish to jeopardise it a second time.'

'But when you wrote to The Procurer, you must have known that whoever she sent you would be risking their life?'

'Not in such stark terms. It is like the difference between drawing up a battle plan and fighting a battle. The danger only strikes home when hostilities commence. I don't know that in all conscience I can make you...'

'I wish you would rid yourself of the notion that you can make me do anything. You didn't make me come here. You didn't make me deceive your mother's friends into thinking I'm your cousin. You didn't make me kiss you. You can't force me to play the Queen of Coins. It's my choice, Luca. And, yes, it's a risk, but it's a manageable risk.'

'Provided we refrain from complicating matters.'

'Now you understand. It's your future at stake here as well as mine. You told me, remember, that you couldn't build your ships until this was done. Think of those ships, Luca.'

She was persuasive. And heaven forgive him, but he wanted her so much. He couldn't bear to be responsible for putting her in danger. Yet if he did not, he would be denying them both their futures—for he knew that she would accept no money from him if they abandoned their plan. His head was spinning. 'I need time to think.'

'A luxury we don't have. We return to the *ridotti* tonight, Luca. We need to agree...'

Looking into her pleading eyes, he felt his heart skip a beat. He could happily forget everything and everyone when he looked into her eyes. And that was when it finally struck home what she had meant about distraction. This wasn't mere passion. Something much more fundamental had developed between them. Something that could easily grow into a heart-breaking problem if they let it. Something that could very easily lead to their downfall in the *ridotti* too.

Luca released her, getting to his feet again. 'Your anonymous playwright is in the right of it,' he said. 'We must snuff out this fire burning between us.'

Chapter Eleven

Carnevale—January 1819

'You remember the secret signal?' Luca asked.

'Yes.' Becky checked the ties which held her mask in place. They were perfectly secure, as they always were. It was a habit, this little ritual she performed as Luca steered their gondola to the jetty. Check the ties. Check her secret pocket. Check the laces on her gown. Unnecessary, since none of them ever needed adjusting, but it had become something of a superstition. As if, somehow, if she forgot to do it, her luck would change. Luck did not enter into it, she reminded herself. She and Luca had proved such a successful duo that all of Venice was talking about the Queen of Coins and her mysterious protector.

'You have the stake?' Luca asked.

'Yes.' He too had a routine, questions in his case, to which the answers were always positive. He always had an escape plan worked out too, meticulously re-evaluated for each of the *ridotti* they visited, the number growing as Carnevale progressed. Becky had lost track of the different locations. Each night he made her recite a different set of precise directions, designed to lead her to a rendezvous spot, where she could safely wait for him to find her in an emergency.

It was reassuring, for it proved he never underestimated the dangers they faced. But every night, just at this moment as they stepped out of the gondola on to a jetty or a walkway, when he could legitimately allow his hand to clasp hers, when she could legitimately allow her fingers to twine with his, there was a frisson. Not of danger, but of awareness, of the passion still smouldering between them, which lurked, barely contained, beneath the surface. And then he let her go, and she gathered the Queen of Coins's skirts up to protect them from the perpetual damp of Venice's watery landscape, and it was over.

'Will Don Sarti be here tonight, do you think?' Becky asked.

'The play is deep here, deeper than any of the salons we have so far visited, so it's highly likely,' Luca replied. '*Bene.* You are ready?'

'Ready.'

It was the final part of their litany. Luca led the way through the gloom, to a double door under a portico far more elegant than any they had visited thus far. As usual, the windows were heavily curtained, the merest flickers of light showing. As was always the case, a burly sentry stood guard, giving them a knowing glance before ushering them in. As she always did, Becky took a moment to accustom herself to the blaze of light, the heat, the air redolent of scent and wine and nervous excitement. And as usual Luca stood at her side, a solid, comforting presence, achingly familiar, agonisingly remote. But as they made their way into the first salon, Becky sensed instantly that this was a *ridotto* in a very different league from all the others.

The room was huge, lit by several glittering chandeliers. A great many of the clientele were women, perhaps as many as half, as far as Becky could see. Many wore a simple *moretta* mask of black velvet covering most of their face, their hair concealed under a flowing veil, but there were several much more elaborate constructions, half- and full-face. Feathers, turbans, silk flowers and spangled scarves were variously utilised to make elaborate coiffures. Though dominos were the most popular garment, some of the female clientele wore gowns so low-cut that they revealed far more than they concealed. Her own costume was positively demure in contrast. The prize in some of these games, she suspected, watching a very dishevelled couple emerging from a door at the rear of the salon, was a currency very different from gold. This was a very decadent Venice on display, a city of excess and vice.

'I should have warned you,' Luca whispered. 'You need not fear that you will be propositioned.'

'I do not,' Becky replied. Few men dared to importune the Queen of Coins, her haughty demeanour being sufficient to warn off all but the most ardent, and when it was not, a few choice words from her protector sufficed. Only once had Luca been forced to manhandle a would-be seducer, and it had been carried out with such astounding efficiency that the man was on the banks of the canal before Becky had even called for help.

'We won't find our prey in this salon,' Luca said. 'Let's try upstairs.'

The chamber on the first floor was a very different place. Dimly lit, chequered with card tables and their players, the atmosphere had the distinctive hush and almost palpable tension that accompanied serious gambling, the acrid tang of fear a top note to the sweeter scent of perfume and powder. Their entrance caused a stir. Though not every occupant of every table looked up, most did. As Luca led their customary progress around the room, dealing with the various discreet overtures from those eager to pit their wits against the Queen of Coins, Becky maintained her aloof bearing, though her heart was pounding. It always did at this point in proceedings, marking her entrance on to the stage, her assessment of her audience, her prelude to the show, but tonight there was a sharper edge to her nerves. Don Sarti was here. She was sure of it.

A table was set out for her. Several fresh decks were placed upon it. A man sat down with a nod and flexed his fingers. The little finger on his left hand was crooked, the nail missing. Becky made a point of remembering such things. If their paths crossed again she would remember his style of play. He was not a poor player, certainly no novice, and was cautious at first, but as he began to lose he became more reckless.

The stakes here started high and the man opposite her wanted to raise them again despite his already heavy losses. Entry to this *ridotto*—which was, like all the other Carnevale *ridotti*, essentially a private gaming hell—was limited by the mysterious hosts to those who could demonstrate the means to play. Becky was

torn, unwilling to take any more gold from her opponent, unable to force him to leave the table until their
agreed number of hands were completed, unable, in
her role as Queen of Coins, to deliberately lose. She
hated this aspect of the game they played. She could
ensure that she did not play this man again, but there
were nights in the *ridotti* when it seemed to her that
Venice was populated entirely by such men, set not
upon winning but playing, their world narrowed to
the turn of a card, the gold they staked of no impor-
tance at all, save only to provide their quota of danger and excitement.

Luca didn't understand. He thought they had a
choice, but the worst of them had no more choice than
an opium addict, inexorably drawn to their preferred
drug. He thought Becky's conscience would be eased,
knowing their losses were added to the coffers to be
returned to Venice. It helped, but only a little.

Her opponent was betting wildly now, his concentration so entirely on his own cards that it would have
been easy to turn the deck in his favour for the last
two hands, reducing the point differential in the final
tally, thereby curtailing his losses somewhat. But there
were too many onlookers for that. When he tried to
insist on playing on, Becky gave the secret signal to
summon Luca. She had no idea how he did it, cloaked
and masked, but the authority which must have made
him a formidable captain in the navy made him a very
formidable protector. With a final mumbling protest,
the man left the table. The used deck was replaced.
Luca discreetly pocketed her winnings and summoned
her next adversary.

She did not need the fleeting touch on her shoulder to warn her. She knew as soon the black-cloaked figure with the white *bauta* mask approached that it was Don Sarti. His walk betrayed his sense of superiority, the arrogant tilt of his head, the length of his stride, the faux-humble way he clasped his hands. She had studied him closely on the few occasions they had met socially, her actor's eye noting what others might have missed. He made only the briefest of bows to the Queen of Coins before taking his seat. She wondered briefly what had betrayed his identity to Luca.

She was glad to have one game against a wild player already under her belt, to have had the opportunity while doing so to observe the room, to have settled her customary stage fright. The endless nights of playing at the other *ridotti*, Luca's endless hours of meticulous preparation, her complete trust in him as her protector, left her free to concentrate on the turn of the cards now. She did not know where he stood now, but she knew wherever it was, he would be on hand if she needed him. He seemed never to watch the play. No chance of her protector being accused of aiding or abetting. Not this time.

Becky deliberately allowed Don Sarti to win the cut for the privilege of dealing the first hand. He was not wearing his heavy gold ring with its flashy diamond, but he couldn't remove the tiny mole on his right knuckle she had noted previously. He dealt the cards for the first hand, and she turned her mind to the game.

'We did it!' Luca exclaimed triumphantly, appearing in the doorway of the secret room behind the library with a tray containing a bottle of grappa and two glasses. His eyes blazed with excitement. 'All our hard work—all your hard work, I should say—has paid off. Tonight, for the first time, Don Sarti crossed swords with the Queen of Coins and lost. I think that deserves a toast.' He poured two glasses of grappa and handed one to Becky, who was seated on the chaise longue, having just removed her mask. 'To the Queen of Coins, Don Sarti's nemesis and my avenging angel. I know we have only taken the first step, but there is no doubt he'll be back, and he'll keep coming back until he has returned all of Venice's money. We have him, Becky. *Salute.*'

'*Salute.*' Becky took a cautious sip, coughing as the fiery liquid burned her throat. 'Assuming it was Don Sarti?' she teased.

Luca laughed. 'I spotted him the moment we walked into the salon. It took all my self-restraint not to approach him before he approached me. I did not have to wait long.' He lifted his glass to Becky and tossed the remainder of the contents back. 'He tried, but he could not contain his own eagerness. Your reputation for invincibility has him in thrall already.'

Becky tipped the remainder of her grappa into her mouth. The tension of the night, the strain of the many games she had played after Don Sarti had departed, began to ease as the *digestivo* hit her stomach. She relaxed back on to the chaise longue. If she needed any reassurance as to how much this meant to Luca, she had it now in the form of his euphoric expression. A glow of satisfaction suffused her, and she smiled at him, quite forgetting that she had resolved not to smile in that particular way at him again.

Ever since her first outing as Queen of Coins and

the aftermath in this very room, Luca had taken to bidding her a curt goodnight, leaving her alone immediately upon their return. Now here he was, smiling back at her, and her heart was racing, and she was thinking about all the things she had been trying so hard not to think about. Becky sat up abruptly. 'It's late,' she said meaningfully.

But Luca for once didn't take his cue. 'What kind of player was he, Becky?'

'He's very good. Possibly the best I've played.'

Luca frowned. 'Yet he loses.'

'Everyone loses if they play often enough. Trappola is not only a game of skill. All card games involve an element of chance.'

Within the confines of the little room, they were as far apart as it was possible to be, but it was still too close. Or not nearly close enough. She mustn't think this way.

'You never lose,' Luca said.

'Because I remove the element of chance. I control the cards. Or, to put it another way, I cheat.' Let him leave now, Becky thought, though she wanted him, she so desperately wanted him to stay. Five weeks since they made their pact not to distract one another, and only that one sign, when their hands touched as he helped her from the gondola, suggested that they had not successfully doused the flames.

'If he is such a good player, why doesn't Sarti quit when he is winning?' Luca asked, still showing no signs of departing.

'He is not content with winning,' Becky replied. The reality of the situation was beginning to dawn on her. *We have him, Becky.* Her excitement began to fade. 'The more he wins, the more he wants to win. Tonight I kept the point difference between our scores low to encourage him to believe he could beat me when we meet again.'

Luca leaned back against the door to the library. It clicked shut, but he didn't seem to notice. 'I still don't understand. As a skilled player, he should win more than he loses when he plays anyone other than you.'

He truly didn't understand, Becky thought, despite her attempts to explain. His poetic justice would destroy the man and possibly also the man's family. And she was aiding and abetting him.

We have him, Becky. Justice required a price be exacted, she knew that, but still, it left a nasty taste in her mouth, that her role should be so ambiguous. 'When he loses,' she said, 'he cannot resist the urge to recoup those losses. When he wins, he foolishly believes he is fated to win more. Don Sarti, like the first man I played tonight, is irrational when in the grip of gambling fever. He must feed his craving. It is why he will come back to the Queen of Coins again and again, as a drunkard will to the bottle.'

'If Sarti lived in London, he'd have been ruined years ago,' Luca said, shaking his head. 'Only Venice's strict rules, which limit gaming to Carnevale, have spared him until now. Yet ironically, it is our city which funds his play. Tonight we made a start on taking back from him everything he has stolen.'

'You mean your father's estimate of what he stole. You can't know the exact figure, Luca. Black-market fences—men who deal in stolen goods—they don't pay the full value, far from it.'

'Sarti is hardly likely to have sold Venice's treasures through a common— Fence, did you call it? Many heads of state throughout Europe are renowned collectors. The Russian emperor, for example, is an avid acquirer of important artefacts.'

Sometimes the gulf in social class between them seemed like a chasm, Becky thought. 'Regardless of who bought them, they will not have paid the full value,' she said patiently.

'What Don Sarti was paid is immaterial. What matters is what my father believed the treasures were worth. And the truth is they were priceless.'

Becky sighed. 'So we must take everything he has. His *palazzo*? His wife's jointure? His daughter's dowry?'

'The crime is Sarti's. If others suffer, then the blame lies squarely with him.'

She could point out that Luca was in the grip of a compulsion of his own, so intent on his thirst for vengeance that he did not care if innocent people were caught in the crossfire. *We could aim lower*, she wanted to say, but what would be the point? He wouldn't listen, any more than the man who had been the Queen of Coins's first victim tonight, and she was too tired to argue. She didn't want to argue at all. Especially not with Luca.

He had taken off his mask and his cloak, loosened the buttons on his coat and waistcoat. His hair, limp from the heat of the salon, flopped over his brow. Their eyes met, and he smiled, and her tummy flipped. She hadn't forgotten that smile, but she'd tried very hard not to think about it.

'You saw the darker side of Carnevale tonight,' he said. 'I am sorry I had to expose you to it.'

'It was all a game to them, in that downstairs salon, wasn't it? I thought the females were doxies, at first, but they weren't.' Becky wrinkled her nose in distaste. 'I thought I'd seen it all, but otherwise respectable women gambling their favours just for the hell of it, hiding what they no doubt call their minor indiscretions behind a mask, that was something new to me. I'm not sure I like this Carnevale very much.'

'That's because you've not seen the lighter side.' Luca sat down on the chaise longue beside her. 'Would you like to?'

'Very much.'

'Would Cousin Rebecca like to see the sights tomorrow?'

'I'm due to visit...'

'I'll clear it with my mother. You've earned a break, Becky, and it would be a pity if your memories of Carnevale were restricted to its scamier side.'

'Thank you. I will look forward to it.'

'We'll be amongst the crowds,' Luca said with a small smile. 'Quite safe from temptation.'

For the second time that night their eyes met and held. For the second time that night, Becky's stomach lurched, and now her pulses began to race, her blood heat. Just one kiss, surely just one kiss would do no harm. She forced herself to remain perfectly still.

'I know how they feel, those men who look at the Queen of Coins,' Luca said. 'Forbidden desire. A seductress who cannot be touched. I know how they feel. I wish I did not want you so much.'

'All passion dies,' Becky said. 'You told me so.'

'I did, and it was the truth until I met you.'

He reached out to push her hair back from her brow.

His fingers trailed down the column of her neck to rest on her bare shoulder. She could tell herself that his hand compelled her to lean towards him, but it would be a lie. 'I'll be gone soon,' Becky said.

'Yes. You will.'

She caressed his cheek with the flat of her hand. It was rough, his beard soft in contrast. Her touch made him exhale sharply, and the warmth of his breath made her lean into him, and their lips met. For an agonising moment, they were quite still, each waiting on the other to break the contact, neither able to move. And then it was too much. She opened her mouth to him, he opened his mouth to her, and they kissed.

It was a searing kiss, dark with desire and over before it had begun. They jumped to their feet. Becky's heart was racing. Luca, hands shaking, poured two more glasses of grappa. 'Another toast,' he said with a mocking smile. 'This time to the beginning of the end.'

It was very cold the next day, the sky leaden, turning the Grand Canal a palette of brown tinged with copper, pink and grey. Though Isabel had appeared content to release Rebecca from her scheduled round of social calls, Becky knew better. The Contessa was going along with her son's plan, but under duress. The lure of spending the day with Luca was a much more attractive proposition than a tedious day spent making calls, however. Becky slipped into her warmest coat of dusky-pink wool. With a dove-grey velvet collar, belt and cuffs, gloves, boots and a charcoal-grey hat, she looked as if she had chosen her outfit to complement the colours of the canal.

Luca was waiting on the jetty, dressed in his customary black, but a long greatcoat with several capes replaced his preferred short cloak. There was no sign of the gondola. 'I thought we'd walk, if you're amenable,' he said.

'Very. It will be a relief to feel the ground beneath my feet for a change.'

He tucked her hand into the crook of his arm and led her away from the Grand Canal, along a footpath which followed one of the narrower bodies of water. 'Though Carnevale is not so celebrated as it was in the last century, it is still a festival of the people, as you will see today. Unlike the *ridotti*, the spectacle at Piazza San Marco is open to everyone, and a good many go in disguise.'

'In masks, you mean? In the daytime?'

'And costumes far more elaborate than any you have seen in the *ridotti*, where they would make some of the nocturnal activities somewhat problematic,' Luca said drily. 'In Piazza San Marco it takes the form of an informal parade. Of course, part of the fun is that no one knows who is parading. It has been known for a high-born *donna* and her maid to wear the same costume on different days. At Carnevale you must be on your guard. You never know who you're talking to.'

'Or liaising with? Are you speaking from experience?'

Luca laughed. 'No. It is true that some people take pleasure in such encounters, and many more visit Venice during Carnevale with such encounters in mind, but I am not and never have been one of them.'

He pulled her away from the edge as a gondola bedecked in garlands swept past, waiting for the wake splashing on to the walkway to die down. 'You take such enormous pride in being a Venetian,' Becky said, 'but there are times when I wonder if you are a Venetian at all.'

She'd meant to tease him, but he took her seriously. 'While I was away, I thought myself Venetian to the core. Now I am not so sure. I think perhaps there is more of my mother's blood in me than I realised.'

'It is your mother's blood that sent you to England and then to sea.'

'I always thought that was my Venetian blood,' Luca said, taking her other arm as they resumed their walk and the pathway tapered, placing her on the inside, away from the canal. 'Because that was what my father always insisted.'

'It seems to me that he made sure your mother had very little influence on you, even as a child.'

'A son is raised by his father,' Luca said, frowning. 'It is the custom here, especially for an eldest son. And you forget I was sent to England with my mother's blessing.'

'It's true. Isabel said that you were so restless no school could contain you.'

He smiled at that. 'And for many years, my mother's family gave me a home, so you see, she has had a great deal of influence on me.'

'Yes.' Becky concentrated on the shallow, moss-covered flight of steps which led first down and then straight up again, before the walkway came to an abrupt halt and they were forced to turn sharply through one of those dark passages populated by feral cats and no doubt a quota of rats. Fortunately, this one was short, emerging in a run-down *campo* with an empty fountain.

A flock of startled pigeons flew up into the air. Luca made for the canal at the other side of the *campo*. 'You do not sound convinced.'

'I suppose it's because I could never be happy with this way of life. I can't see that you could either.'

He stopped at the edge of the canal, where a humpbacked bridge to the other side seemed to be the only route. 'You are referring to my marriage. You know it's not exactly imminent. In fact I've been thinking that it would make sense to concentrate on putting our winnings to good use before considering anything else. A year, perhaps two or three, to accustom myself to the idea.'

'Don't you think it's significant that you feel the need to accustom yourself, Luca?'

He laughed shortly. 'I can trust you always to get straight to the point, Becky.'

'That's because I'm not Venetian.'

'No.' They climbed the steps up to the top of the bridge. There was an odd little stone bench built into the centre of it. Despite the cold, of one accord they sat down. As ever, the green shutters of the overlooking houses seemed to Becky like closed eyes. Beneath them, the canal reflected the crumbling stone, the grey lowering sky. 'You're right,' Luca said. 'I'm not as wholly Venetian as I imagined I was. I don't want a marriage such as my father's, I do not think that my mother is more suited than I to select a wife for me.' He slanted a smile at her. 'You see, Becky, I do listen.'

'What do you want, then?'

He sighed impatiently. 'I will know that nearer the

time, I hope. I must marry to continue the line. My wife must possess suitable lineage. But at this moment—since I have no idea how I, as Conte del Pietro, wish to live my life—I am hardly in a position to say how I expect my wife to live hers.'

'You don't think she'd wish to have a say in it?'

He laughed. 'She will not be Becky, determined to lead her own life on her own terms.' His smile faded abruptly. 'She will be as unlike Becky as it is possible to be.'

Something she'd always known, but for some reason the words were like a punch in the stomach. 'I should think not,' she said with an attempt at a smile. 'A woman who was dragged up rather than raised, who doesn't even know who her father is, who's made a living by cheating gullible men.'

'Don't say that.' Careless of the fact they were in public, Luca grabbed her hands. 'You are the bravest, most honest, most loyal woman I've ever met. With your talent, you could have made a fortune for yourself, whereas the truth is I suspect that there are times when your principles have left you both cold and hungry.'

Lord, she wished he didn't understand her so well. She wouldn't cry. Not here. Not in front of him. 'You make me sound downright noble,' she jested.

'You are.'

'A noble savage, perhaps,' Becky said sardonically.

'I wish you would not demean yourself. You are extraordinary, and I will be forever grateful to have known you.'

A lump formed in her throat. Her heart felt as if it was being squeezed. She had a horrible premonition of what life was going to be like without him. 'Better not to say that, not until the Queen of Coins has finished her task,' Becky said brusquely. 'And better we don't sit here any more, lest people think we're taking advantage of Carnevale, only without our masks.'

She got to her feet and Luca followed suit, but before she continued over the bridge he caught her arm again. 'I meant it, every word,' he said. 'You have to believe me.'

She didn't doubt him, not the way he was looking at her. 'I know you do,' Becky said, blinking away a tear. 'It would be better for both of us if you didn't.'

Piazza San Marco was crowded, the cafés which lined the terraces packed. Becky, clutching Luca's arm, eyed the huge sea of colour and faces in astonishment. 'It's like Covent Garden multiplied a hundred times,' she said. 'No, that's not true. It's like all of the theatres in Covent Garden had spilled all of their actors on to the piazza in their stage costumes. I had no idea it was going to be so spectacular.'

When Luca had likened it to a parade, she hadn't taken him literally, but that was exactly what it was. A couple strolled past, clad in cloaks of scarlet and black silk stripes, beneath which they were dressed like court jesters. Huge feathered hats sat upon their heads. Chalk-white masks covered their faces. They were identical save that one was clearly a man, the other equally clearly a woman. There were a great many hooped gowns in garish colours, blue teamed with gold, cherry with emerald, red with burnt orange. The wearers swayed seductively, their tall powdered wigs adorned with stuffed birds and dried flowers, their masks, the type attached to a baton, painted to match their gowns. Not all of them were female, Becky realised, as one picked up his skirts to show a decidedly masculine pair of legs. He ran at speed towards a petite figure dressed in a vaguely Turkish outfit of scarlet spotted with gold, a gold mask on her face, a gold turban trailing a long red scarf on her head.

As they made their way slowly around the perimeter of the piazza, Becky noticed a good number of people in similar costumes. 'Characters from the *commedia dell'arte*,' Luca explained. 'That is Mattacina, all in white, save for his red shoes. Then over there, you can see Pantalone, the emblem of Venice, in a red waistcoat and black cloak. In fact, you can see several more of them over there,' he added, pointing at a group of men all dressed very similarly. 'The costume preferred by those lacking in imagination, I think.'

Becky laughed. 'What about that one?' she asked, nodding at a man in an outfit patched with red, green and blue triangles which bordered on the obscene, so tightly did his pantaloons and jacket fit.

'Arlecchino,' Luca said. 'You might know him as Harlequin.'

'I doubt *he* shares his costume with anyone else,' Becky said wryly, 'unless he has an identical twin.'

A woman began to sing an aria, her voice amplified by the arcade under which she stood. As they proceeded up towards the imposing arches at the entrance of the basilica, Becky was slightly shocked to see coloured booths set up on the steps of the church. There were turbaned fortune tellers in bright silks with tarot cards and shimmering crystal balls. There was a man with skin like parchment clad in a sorcerer's gown offering horoscope readings. Quacks stood on

wooden boxes, proclaiming their wares, offering elix-
irs and pills which would cure baldness and child-
lessness, which would make an angel of a harridan, a
daredevil of a coward. A tooth puller stood outside his
tent, wielding a terrifying pair of pliers. A slight man
clad only in a pair of white drawers and a turban was
seated on the cobblestones. To Becky's astonishment,
as he began to play a discordant tune upon a pipe, a
snake emerged from the basket in front of him. Poets
declaimed, minstrels sang and played, adding to the
cacophony of sound.

By the campanile, on a high rope strung between
two poles, two men were balanced precariously, juggling wooden clubs. Beneath them, a group of child
acrobats climbed on to each other's shoulders to form
a pyramid, waiting only for a smattering of applause
before they leapt down, tumbling and leapfrogging
each other in a blur of sequins and satin. Then came
the magicians, the illusionists and the conjurors. A
pierrot rolled up the sleeve of his tunic, brandishing
a knife. The crowd gasped as he sliced into the flesh
of his own arm, and blood seemed to gush from the
wound. Cheering and applause followed as he towelled
the arm dry to reveal not a trace of a scar.

Becky, who had seen such tricks before, was more
interested in the next stall. A white *volto* mask and a
plain black domino was the magician's disguise. His
props were as simple. A ball. Three large cups. 'He'll
find someone in the crowd to shout out which one the
ball is under,' Becky whispered to Luca. 'There, see.'

A well-dressed youth stepped cockily forward and
proceeded to wrongly guess the location of the ball
every time the magician moved them around. Becky

whispered the correct location to Luca and the crowd jeered at the victim's every mistake. 'If he's wise,' Becky said, noting that the lad was becoming aggressive, 'he'll allow him one win.' Almost before she had finished her sentence, the magician did exactly that.

Luca chuckled. 'A pacifier before he passes the hat round, I think.'

'Exactly.'

They moved on, past a man juggling knives and a puppet show to another magician with a pack of cards, and Luca stopped. 'He's doing your trick,' he said, 'the one where I had to guess the card. Do you think Cousin Rebecca might take him on?'

She was tempted, remembering how impressed Luca had been that night by her silly card tricks, confident, watching him, that her own skills were superior to the sharp plying his trade. 'No,' she said firmly, turning away. 'This is his pitch, Luca, his livelihood.'

She was rewarded with a warm smile, the slightest pressure on her gloved fingertips. 'I should have known,' he said. 'My most honourable card sharp.'

She couldn't help but laugh at that, trying to ignore the glow inside her, caused not only by his admiration but by his nearness, for the continually jostling crowd had forced them more closely together. At least that was what she told herself.

It was a perfect day out of time. Against the odds, they did not encounter a single acquaintance. As a result, Becky forgot to be Cousin Rebecca and was herself for the duration, embracing the spirit of this bright, alluring side of Carnevale with the same innocent, endearing joyfulness Luca remembered from their trip to the Lido.

It was infectious. He found himself calling out a warning to Pulcinella's wife at the puppet show, surprised to discover that Becky was as familiar with the characters as he was, for it was a popular show in Covent Garden, she told him. They shared a bag of roasted chestnuts, which he had the tortuous pleasure of peeling for her, popping them into her mouth in order, he claimed, to save her from soiling her gloves. They watched a balloon ascend from the centre of the piazza and come perilously close to colliding with the campanile before it disappeared over the rooftops, apparently intending to land on Guidecca, though the stiff breeze seemed intent on taking it directly out to sea.

Florian's was crowded, but for once Luca was happy to be recognised, the Conte del Pietro and his cousin being ushered into the warm interior to a quiet table where Becky marvelled at the gilded ceiling and frescoes he was so familiar with as to fail to notice, leaving him free to marvel at her, her cheeks pink with the cold, her big violet eyes bright with delight as the waiter set a hot chocolate and sugared pastry down in front of her. She ate delicately but with relish. It touched his heart to think that this too was a result of deprivation. He couldn't bear to think of her, a young, vulnerable version of the glowing woman beside him, fending for herself, peering into the steamed-up windows of cafés such as this one.

As the sun sank, the atmosphere in the piazza subtly altered. The necromancers and the quacks packed up. The music became seductive, in tune with the changing mood of the crowd, now seeking entertainment of a very different nature. 'We should go back to the *palazzo*,' Luca said reluctantly. 'My mother will be expecting us for dinner.'

'Our little holiday from reality is over. It's been truly wonderful Luca, a day I'll never forget.'

The way she smiled up at him gave him that odd sensation again, as if his heart was contracting. It was because he'd miss her, he thought. Of course he would. After all they had been through it was natural enough. Something of his thoughts must have shown on his face. Becky looked away, started walking, forcing him to follow, away from the throng, out of the piazza, back in the direction they had come, though she faltered at the first junction, and he took the lead once more.

The air was heavy and still, the sky already darkening to night, the temperature plummeting. They walked on, their steps muffled. He thought it was rain at first, the cold sensation on his cheek, but Becky's surprised exclamation made him stop, look up at the sky.

'It's snowing,' she said, her voice hushed.

She tilted her face up to the sky, closing her eyes as the snow began to fall thick and fast, flakes landing on her cheeks and her lashes. When she opened her eyes again and turned to him, smiling, he caught her in his arms. Time stopped. It truly felt as if time stopped as he held her, as she reached her arms up to twine around his neck, tilting her face to his with an inevitability that could not be resisted.

And then they kissed, cold lips meeting, melding into the sweetest of kisses, warming his blood, stirring him into an aching desire. It was wrong, yet when it was over their lips clung, the tips of their tongues touching. And then came more kisses. Little kisses that shouldn't mean anything, butterfly kisses that were surely harmless, though the way they were pressed together now, her back against the stone wall of a shuttered building, his body covering hers, hers arching against his, though there were layers and layers of clothes between them it felt as if they were stripped bare.

Their kisses deepened, their tongues tangled and he gave himself up to the moment, forgetting everything save for the taste of her, the heat of their kisses, the agonising delight of them, so longed for, so illicitly dreamed of and so much better than any dream. Drugging kisses, impossible to resist, so sinuously, deceptively languorous that he could pretend he wanted nothing more than this, just this, warm lips, tangled tongues, cold snow framing their faces.

But he wanted a great deal more. He was so hard he was throbbing. Dragging his mouth from hers, Luca saw his own desire clearly writ on Becky's face, her big eyes glazed, her cheeks flushed. There was nothing to be done about it, nothing to be said. She slipped her hand on to the crook of his arm, and they continued the short walk back to the *palazzo* through the swirl of the softly falling snow.

Chapter Twelve

'My mother sends her apologies,' Luca informed Becky when she joined him in the drawing room before dinner. 'She has gone to comfort a sick friend and will not return until tomorrow.'

Their escape from reality was not over after all, Becky thought. The Fates were conspiring to test their resolve.

Her evening dress was one she had not worn before, of turquoise silk trimmed with silver ribbon. 'Your gown is the colours of the canal on a winter's morning,' Luca said, handing her a glass of Prosecco.

His hair was still damp from his bath. His cheeks were freshly shaved, his beard neatly trimmed. Their eyes met as their glasses touched in a silent toast, and she knew that he, like she, was thinking of those kisses in the snow, so achingly sweet, a refrain of longing and yearning. A refrain which surely deserved to be sung to the end, just once.

Smiling inwardly at this flight of fancy, attributing it to her new-found passion for the opera, which she had now been to see six times, Becky made for the windows, pulling back one of the heavy curtains which had been drawn against the cold of the winter's night. It was still snowing heavily, huge flakes tumbling like snippets of lace, coating the moored gondolas in a cloak of white, giving an eerie light to the night sky.

'It's so beautiful,' she said, entranced by the view, still caught up in the enchantment of the day, acutely aware of Luca standing just at her shoulder. 'Even more unreal than usual.'

She felt the whisper of his lips on the nape of her neck. She felt the whisper of his breath on her ear. She turned, lifting her hand to caress his cheek, the merest touch causing such an upsurge of longing as to make her catch her breath. 'Luca,' she said, and he reached for her, and then the door opened, and they jumped apart as Brunetti appeared to announce that dinner was served.

But still the heightened mood lingered as they ate, scarcely aware of the servants pouring the wine, bringing the different courses, leaving them, at Luca's behest, to serve themselves. The fates continued to smile, Becky thought to herself, as she sampled some of her favourite dishes, *calamaretti*, the little baby squid fried in batter, the razor clams which the Venetians call *capelonghe* cooked in butter and parsley, the baked fish which they called John Dory at home and which here was known as *sanpiero*, served with a fragrant pesto.

They talked of Carnevale, of the sights they had seen in the Piazza San Marco. A perfectly innocuous conversation to anyone listening, but there was another unspoken conversation continuing between them all the while. It was there in the slanted glances, in the lingering gazes, in the grazing of their fingers as they passed the dishes. The day was far from over.

After dinner, they retired to the small parlour, where the dark red walls, the tightly drawn curtains and the well-stoked fire gave the palatial room an illusion of cosiness. They had sat here many times before, practising cards, but tonight there was no question of cards.

They sat on the sofa facing the fire. Becky knew that nothing had changed, that nothing could alter the ending which loomed, but tonight she didn't care. This was a moment out of time. Tomorrow, they would return to reality, see the dangerous game they played to its conclusion and then she would leave Venice and Luca for ever. Tonight was their only chance. She knew that if she didn't grasp it, she would regret it.

Luca poured them each a cup of coffee, downing his in one gulp as usual. 'I shouldn't stay here like this, alone with you. I can't trust myself to keep our promise if I do.' He shifted on the sofa, his knees brushing hers. 'We agreed,' he said, 'that we must extinguish the attraction between us.'

But the fire was burning in his eyes even as he spoke. His hand was already covering hers, he was already leaning towards her. 'Do you think we've succeeded?' Becky asked.

His laugh was a low growl. 'We've succeeded in making it burn ever brighter.'

She leaned closer, so that they were within kissing distance. 'Do you think if we allowed ourselves this one night, it would douse the flames?'

They both knew her question was sheer sophistry. Luca was more honest than she. 'You know it would not be enough, Becky.'

Her fingers tightened on his. 'But if it is all we can have?'

'Then I would rather have this than nothing.' His free hand touched her cheek, pushing her hair back behind her ear. 'Are you sure?'

Looking into his eyes, she felt such a surge of emotion that it twisted her heart. She knew then, though she refused to acknowledge it, that something profound had just occurred. She reached for him, twining her arm around his neck. 'I'm absolutely certain,' Becky said, and then she kissed him.

He kissed her back fiercely. The restrained yearning from those earlier kisses in the snow was unleashed as their mouths clung, ravaged each other, desperate to sate the hunger which had been far too long suppressed. It was as well that Luca, tearing himself free, retained a modicum of sense. 'The door,' he said, dragging himself away from her to lock it, but when he returned to her, instead of more kisses, he pulled her to her feet. 'We have waited so long,' he said with a smile which made her burn inside. 'We can wait a little longer.'

He kissed her again, but slowly, smoothing his hands over her back, as if to calm her. He shrugged out of his coat and his waistcoat. Turning her around, he kissed the nape of her neck, the pulse at her collarbone, untying the laces of her gown, sliding it down her shoulders, over her hips. She had never been undressed before, not by anyone. She was facing the mirror above the mantel. She could see her reflection,

Luca behind her, his hair dark against her skin, his hands cupping her breasts over her corsets. She shuddered. She arched her bottom against him, feeling the ridge of his arousal, and shuddered again.

He released her only to untie her corsets. When he cupped her breasts again, there was only the thin film of her cambric chemise between them. In the mirror, she could see his thumbs circling her nipples, felt her nipples harden, saw the result in the mirror, felt and saw his sharp intake of breath, and then he turned her around and their mouths met again in a savage kiss.

She tugged his shirt free of his breeches, gazing hungrily as he pulled it over his head, her hands already roaming over the muscle-packed flesh, pressing wild kisses over his chest, relishing the way her touch made him groan. The bow which held her chemise in place was undone, the garment slid down her arms to pool on the floor beside her gown, and for a moment Luca simply gazed at her breasts, and the stark longing in his eyes swept away any embarrassment, and then he pulled her into his arms, naked flesh to naked flesh, and Becky thought she would die with the bliss of it.

They sank to the rug. He eased her on to her back and he kissed her, her mouth, her throat and then her breasts, making her writhe and beg, making her moan and arch under him, his mouth tugging at one nipple, his fingers tugging at the other until she thought she could take no more and told him so. And he laughed, telling her that she could, and kissed her again. The valley between her breasts. Her belly.

They were both breathing heavily now. She could see the beguiling rise and fall of his chest in the firelight. His cheeks were slashed with colour, his eyes dark pinpoints. He sat up to remove his boots and pantaloons. She stared unashamedly, hungrily, at the sleek lines of his body, the muscled buttocks, thighs, and as he turned, the thick curve of his erection. She wanted him so much. She ached for him to enter her, was twisted so tight with desire that she needed him inside her before she unravelled. When he knelt between her legs, covering her body with his, his erection pressing between her legs she moaned, their kiss a deep, passionate prelude of what was to come next.

Save it did not. Luca smiled at her, a wicked smile which made her heart bump, and began to press kisses down the length of her body again, and this time he did not stop at her belly. The strings of her drawers were undone. Her undergarments were tugged down her legs, and Luca's kisses began again. The backs of her knees. The inside of her thigh, and only then did she realise his intention, crying out a startled protest which instantly became a moan of delight as his mouth covered her sex, and he licked into her.

She clutched at his shoulders. She bucked under him. She clenched her teeth in an effort not to fall immediately over the edge, for his tongue worked such delicious, delightful magic, making her feel as if she were being turned inside out, licking and kissing and stroking, making her so tight she could not bear it. She clenched her fists. Tight, tight, tight, so sweetly aching she was inside, and then he sent her over the edge with one last flick of his tongue. Becky spiralled out of control into a climax so intense she was senseless, pulsing, throbbing, tugging mindlessly at him, begging him equally mindlessly, 'Now, now, now.'

'You are sure,' he panted, his voice rough, and she

could only nod, urgent for him to be inside her, needing him to be inside her.

'Sure,' she said.

He kissed her mouth. She could feel him shaking. And then shuddering. Bracing himself. And then shuddering again. And with an agonised groan, he lost control, collapsing on top of her as his climax shook him.

Luca was mortified. Sitting up, he found his handkerchief and mopped up the evidence of his shame, cursing under his breath. 'I am sorry,' he said, forcing himself to meet Becky's eyes. 'That has never happened to me before.'

To his utter astonishment, Becky laughed. 'That is one compliment I'm more than happy for you to pay.' Sitting up, she wrapped her arms around him, nestling her breasts against his back. 'That has never happened to me before,' she whispered, nuzzling his ear. 'What you did to me, I had no idea it could feel like that.'

'So I pleased you?' he asked, already feeling considerably better.

She laughed again, and her breasts shook delightfully. '*Pleased* is not a remotely strong enough word to describe how you made me feel.'

'I am sorry,' he said again. 'Witnessing you achieving satisfaction, well, it was too much for me.'

'Luca, just kissing you was almost too much for me. All this waiting,' she said, nipping his earlobe, 'it was too much for both of us.'

'But I wanted it to be perfect.'

She chuckled. 'It will be. We agreed to one night, not one act.'

And then she kissed his neck, fluttering kisses with her lips and her tongue, tasting the hollow at his shoulders, and Luca felt, to his astonished delight, that it would not be long at all before he was ready to remedy matters. She slid her arms around him, stroking his nipples, tugging at them, mimicking what he had done to her, and his shaft stirred into life. She slid out from under him, laying him on his back and rolled on top of him, her smile playfully wicked, a smile she had never bestowed on him before, and the blood surged to his groin.

Becky's eyes widened. 'An encore, so soon?' Then she kissed him, and Luca forgot all about his untimely release and felt only the most aching of wanting, wanting such as he had never felt before. He was urgent to be inside her, but once again she took her cue from him, slowing their kisses, sliding down his body to kiss his neck and his chest, to kiss his nipples, down his belly, wriggling further down until she was between his legs and her breasts were grazing his skin making him writhe beneath her, and then he felt her hand on his shaft.

She stroked him, watching him, and he groaned. She stroked him again and felt him getting harder in her hand, and so did he. She dropped her gaze from his eyes to his shaft, watching the effects of her touch with a fascination that aroused him even more. And then she dipped her head, and her tongue touched his tip, and Luca cried out. She stopped. Studied his face. A slow smile dawned on hers. She licked him again and then again. Sweet torture. Luca clenched his fists. He curled his toes as she licked again and again, and then she took him into her mouth and he knew it would not be long before she sent him over the edge, and he was determined that that was not going to happen again.

When she released him, he took her by surprise, rolling her on to her back, wrapping his legs around her. His shaft nudged at the heat between her legs. She shuddered. They kissed. He thrust his tongue into her mouth, and he entered her, just enough to make her cry out, to arch her back, and he pushed higher. She was so hot and so wet and so tight, he was almost overwhelmed. He waited, bracing himself on his arms, and they kissed again. Slow kisses, slow thrusts, each one making her tighten around him, making him throb, and then harder thrusts, and she wrapped her legs around him, her heels digging into his buttocks and he could thrust higher, and their kisses became frantic as she opened up to him and tightened around him, until he felt her shudder and heard her cry out, and her climax shook her and he felt his own gathering, tightening, pulling himself free with a cry as it shook him, from the depths of his being, and he held her tightly against him, skin against skin. He had the absurd notion of wanting to climb inside her, felt as if they could never, ever be close enough.

Becky watched the dawn arrive, huddled in her dressing gown. The snow had melted. The Grand Canal was grey, the sky iron, but she was still glowing from their lovemaking. And it had been true lovemaking, on her part at least. She was in love with Luca. She loved him with her heart and her soul. Hugging her precious secret tightly to herself, she couldn't help smiling. She loved him so much, she thought she might burst with it.

Leaning her forehead on the cool glass, she closed her eyes, remembering last night. It was like nothing she had ever experienced before, beyond anything she could have imagined. Such passion. Such intensity. Such complete closeness. There were times when she felt as if they truly were one. No need for words. Only afterwards—lying in his arms, sated—she had struggled not to say those particular words. She loved him so very much.

I have never lost myself so completely before, Luca had said, looking embarrassed, with no idea just how much his words meant to her. He didn't love her, but she was like no other woman, unique to him. It was more than she had allowed herself to wish for. Besides, she would not truly wish for him to love her, for they must part and she couldn't bear to hurt him.

This sobering thought forced her eyes open, sent a chill running down her spine which the draught seeping through the tall windows never did. Shivering, Becky stoked the embers of the fire and curled up on the chair by the hearth, for once heedless of what Chiara would think when she arrived with her morning tea. Luca didn't love her, but after last night, knowing her as he did, there was a danger that he would realise that she had fallen in love with him. He must not know how deep her feelings ran. He would feel sorry for her. He would worry about hurting her. Those were complications they could not afford.

She groaned. Had it been wrong to surrender to her feelings last night? But yesterday had been so perfect and so magical, and it truly had been their one and only chance. She'd been fooling herself for so long that she didn't care for him, telling herself that it couldn't be love because it wasn't what she'd felt for Jack. Though she hadn't known it at the time, she'd been playing a part with Jack, imagining herself in love, acting her heart out in an effort to make reality fit her idea of what love should be, seeing Jack himself through her misty-eyed vision. He'd lied to her, yes, he had, and he'd used her too, but as to breaking her heart—no, she'd done that herself, by trying to mould him into her idea of a perfect man.

While Luca was anything but perfect. There were aspects of Luca's character she didn't agree with— this thirst of his for vengeance, for example, and his misguided belief that doing his duty would make him happy. No, Luca was far from perfect, but she loved him, every bit of him, exactly as he was. How long had she loved him? For ever. At least from the moment she met him, it seemed now. It didn't matter. She loved him, and when he kissed her in the snow yesterday, her heart had, ironically, simply melted along with her resistance. She loved him. She had made love to him.

And now it was over. *Time to stop dreaming*, Becky told herself sternly. In a sense, nothing at all had changed. She loved Luca, but it was a love with no future. There was no need to recite the many facts which made her an impossible bride for him, because even if she truly was his virginal, well-born cousin Rebecca, it would make no difference. This stifling life was not for her.

It was time to face reality. No more distractions. And no more questions either. She might not like his plan, but it was what she'd signed up to see through. Don Sarti's family was, as Luca repeatedly said, his own concern and none of hers. Vengeance in Venice, she thought with a twisted smile. It sounded like a play. If that was all she could do for Luca, then she'd better make sure she did it properly because it was her future she was gambling with too.

It had been a very successful night at the *ridotto*, Luca thought to himself as he rowed the gondola back to the *palazzo*. The second time Don Sarti had sought out the Queen of Coins, the second time she had beaten him. Sarti's losses were bigger tonight, for the stakes Luca had agreed had been higher. So why was he not more elated? His satisfaction was muted, his thoughts far from the card tables of the *ridotto* and centred on Becky.

He had not allowed himself to dwell on the previous night. Not with this night looming. But now it was over, he could hardly believe it had happened. Their lovemaking had been even more passionate than he had imagined. His loss of control was no longer embarrassing but part of what made the entire night unique. It frightened him now, looking at Becky, head back on the seat, clutching her mask, exhausted, the feelings she roused in him. He wanted her even more, his body craved her, but there had been moments, in the aftermath of their lovemaking, when he'd wanted to cradle her close, to keep her safe, to keep her with him and never to let her go. Those moments scared the hell out of him. He had known from the instant he met her that Becky was unique. He had nothing to compare his feelings for her with. But he knew, in his gut, that he had to put a stop to them before they got any stronger. On both their parts. Because he knew, knowing Becky, that she would not have made love to him unless she cared a great deal for him. And if she cared deeply, it would pain her to leave him. He didn't want to hurt her. She was his path to the future but she couldn't be part of it.

He knew this, but it made him sick to his stomach all the same, making him lose his hold on the oar. The gondola bumped against the side of a bridge, startling them both, and Luca caught the oar just before it fell into the canal.

Becky sat up, blinking staring around her. 'I fell asleep.'

Hardly surprising, he thought but did not say, for they had agreed, in the hour before dawn when they finally parted, that they would not mention what had happened. 'We'll be back at the *palazzo* soon.'

Becky nodded.

'You played Don Sarti perfectly tonight,' Luca said.

'Yes.'

'Four more weeks and Carnevale will be over. More than enough time for us to take back what he stole,' Luca said, because he needed to say it aloud.

'I would prefer it if that were sooner rather than later.'

'Are you anxious to be on your way, Becky?' he asked, thinking only that it meant she wanted to leave sooner.

'Oh, Luca.' She shook her head, her mouth trembling. 'You know what I think. I agree Don Sarti must pay, but do we have to bleed him dry?'

'Don Sarti!' he exclaimed, realising that they were at cross purposes, annoyed at himself for his contrariness. It would probably be better for both of them if

Becky left as soon as possible. 'I thought you under-stood why I must aim so high,' he said.

'I do understand.'

They had arrived back at the *palazzo*. He tied up the gondola, but when Becky made no move to get out, he sat down opposite her. 'What is it?'

'You thought I meant that I wanted to leave, didn't you?'

He sighed, smiling ruefully. *Trust Becky to say what anyone else would have left unsaid.* 'Yes. I have waited so long to see justice done for my father, if you had asked me when you first arrived, I would have said the sooner the better. But now—now I will speak the plain truth to you, and prove once again that I am not the true Venetian I thought I was. It is inevitable that you leave, but...'

'We have so little time to accustom ourselves to it,' Becky finished for him, 'that we would feel cheated if we deliberately cut it short.'

'Yes.' He covered her hands. 'Though if you feel differently...'

'No.' Her fingers tightened on his. 'If this is all we can have—and I know it is—then I want it all.'

Which ought to set alarm bells ringing in his head, but which instead made him giddy with some other feeling he did not care to scrutinise. 'When you do leave, what will you do? Clearly you cannot return to England.'

'Oh, maybe some day I will, when the dust has long settled on my indiscretion.' She extricated her fingers from his. 'The truth is, Luca, I'm someone who wants to be settled. It's what most women like me yearn for. To have a roof over my head, to be safe and warm and not hungry. When Mum died, it was the workhouse or the streets. For a while, it was the streets. Eventually I scraped enough from my acting to rent a room in the rookeries but many other less fortunate urchins slept rough under the stars. They deserve better, and now I might be in a position to help.'

'The world you describe, it's beyond my comprehension,' Luca said, both appalled and touched.

'Exactly, while I understand it all too well. Which is why I'm thinking of doing something about it. I don't know what, precisely, but I'd like to give people a place to go when they need a roof over their heads. Do you see?'

Luca was beginning to, and he was beginning to think himself very ignorant. 'I think that you would make a far better fist of spending Venice's money than I ever will.'

'You're doing yourself a disservice. Hospitals, schools, fountains supplying fresh water, the things you're contemplating, they aren't high-minded, Luca. They're very much needed and they'll cost a lot more money than I have. I'm thinking smaller. Refuges, I suppose you could call them. Safe havens where women and children can go without fear they'll be separated, without being judged for not being able to make ends meet. Rooms that are home until they're on their feet again or fit to fend for themselves.'

'Where will you found such places?'

'Oh, I don't know. Wherever I lay my hat, as the saying goes. I don't suppose London is any different from other cities. You could probably do with a few here in Venice.'

'And you, Becky? What will you do once you have established these places?'

'Sit by my fire and eat sweetmeats,' she said flippantly, getting to her feet. 'I won't be doing any of it if I don't earn it.'

She jumped on to the jetty, and he followed her. She made her way swiftly up the stairs to the secret room. He hesitated. He wanted to kiss her. But it would be wrong. Utterly wrong. And Becky—honourable, admirable, fearless Becky—deserved to be treated with the utmost respect.

Bidding her goodnight, knowing he would be unable to sleep, Luca returned briefly to his own bedchamber to change, then quit the *palazzo* once more, this time by the front door, taking the night porter by surprise. He headed along the wide banks of the Grand Canal all the way to the lagoon, past the Doge's Palace and on to the Arsenal, the district known as the machine, once the greatest shipbuilding concern in the world. It had been dubbed the eighth wonder of the world in its heyday, the engine that made Venice a world power. Now, in the grey light of the early winter's morning, it looked exactly what it was: outmoded, run-down, a ghostly reminder of past glory, the few ships still constructed here like dinosaurs of ancient times. The proud *arsenalotti* who built the ships lived in poverty now, in an enclave set apart from the city, struggling to survive without work or any prospect of it.

The ships Luca would build, modelled on the sleek, modern Clyde clippers, would require very different skills. He'd have to remodel the whole dockyard, buy and assemble new, modern equipment. The *arsenalotti* notoriously resisted change. His father had been disparaging of them, urging Luca to import Scottish labour, certain that the Venetians would refuse non-traditional work. What basis had his father had for such sweeping assumptions? Luca had not thought to question him. Wandering morosely around the crumbling extent of the Arsenal, he saw that he'd been more concerned with building his ships than with who would build them. Ships would make Venice great again, his father had said. Luca had sailed in the finest vessels of their day, fought some of the greatest battles. Ships were his life, but oughtn't he be more concerned, as Becky would be, with the power in his gift to grant new life to the people who would build them?

Unaware of the cold and the rain which was starting to drizzle down, he propped himself against one of the docks' defensive towers and gazed out sightlessly to sea. Thoughts of the future, of the daunting task which lay ahead of him, of putting Venice's money to good use, were depressing rather than uplifting. He'd assumed he knew what was best for Venice because that was what he'd been raised to believe. It had been his father's tenet, his raison d'être, working for Venice, thinking only of Venice, risking his life to keep Venice's treasures safe, at the cost of all else. Was it arrogance? Or a compulsion, like Don Sarti's fascination with gambling? The comparison made Luca deeply uncomfortable, but it could not be ignored. His father had wanted to restore a Republic that no longer existed. He'd claimed he was working towards a new future for the city, but it was in reality a shadow of the past. He had spent his life looking backwards. His last act, or at least his last words to his only son, had been an exhortation that he do the same. His father wouldn't approve of Luca's charitable intentions. His father had wanted Venice's treasures restored, her heritage, her history reinstated, regardless of the fact that her people needed food and work and schools and clean water.

Becky saw that clearly enough. How was it that it had taken Luca so long to see with equal clarity? Surely he couldn't question his father's motives, his father's principles, his father's ideals? Guido del Pietro had loved Venice so much that he had put his own life in danger by threatening to expose Don Sarti. And also the life of his wife. And to an extent Luca's life too, for if his father had been tried as a traitor along with Sarti, he would have forfeited everything. Just as Don Sarti was risking forfeiting everything, his wife, his home, his children's future, by gambling.

But, no, the two were not the same. Luca jumped down from the high wall on to the muddy shoreline, where the retreating tide exposed the detritus of Venice's shipbuilding past in the ribs of a rotten galleon. He was not thinking clearly, the result of two nights without sleep. He had been planning Don Sarti's downfall for months. He had to honour his father's wishes before he faced any sort of future. Those were the facts, he reminded himself, picking an ancient rusty nail out of the sand, turning it over and over in his hand. His plans was too far advanced to contemplate rethinking them now.

It was Becky's fault. He cast the nail into the shallows. Becky, who said she understood his desire for justice but whose wrong-minded doubts were encouraging doubts of his own to surface. He had to put a stop to them, else where would he be? Justice would not be served.

And Becky would still be gone.

He didn't want her to go. Luca stumbled, only just preventing himself from falling into the mud. He didn't want her to go, she didn't want to go, yet go she must.

What was it she had said? *If this is all we can have, then I want it all.* He swore viciously. He didn't want to hurt her, but it was already too late, he saw that now. Too late for Becky, because what was that other than a tacit admission of love? And too late for him. Because he loved her with every fibre of his being.

Luca staggered back up the muddy shore, hauling himself on to the sea wall. He loved her. Love was the cause of all the feelings he'd never felt before, for the way his stomach churned and his heart protested at the thought of her leaving. He loved her, and it was utterly impossible for him to love her, because even if he'd been asked to specify the most unsuitable woman in the world for the Conte del Pietro to fall in love with, he doubted he'd have invented one less suitable than Becky Wickes.

Or more perfect. For a few blissful moments, Luca allowed himself to imagine a future with Becky by his side. Becky, the antithesis to all that was Venetian, forthright and outspoken, an old-fashioned woman who believed in love and fidelity and marriage and family, who was, contrarily, a card sharp and, if seen through the eyes of Venetian society, a low-born wanton. And yet he loved her.

There was no question of her becoming his wife.

She was not even suited to become his established lover, for her lowly birth made her utterly ineligible. Besides, the idea was repugnant to Luca now. He understood, finally, Becky's own repugnance at the arranged marriage he must make, the loveless future which lay ahead of him. Whatever happened, he knew that he could no longer go through with that.

Which left him where, precisely? A man with a duty to discharge to his father, justice to dispense, whose life was on hold until he had done both, which he was well on the way to achieving. A man with a vision for the future which would also serve his city and the needs of many of her people. Which was all very well and very noble, but he couldn't be the one person he wanted to be above all else. A man who was proud to call Becky his wife.

Chapter Thirteen

Two weeks later

Becky was alone in the small parlour. Cousin Rebecca was required to pay less and less house calls as Carnival progressed. There were almost no evening parties now—at least none of the respectable kind. All of Venice was immersed in the festivities. The canals resounded day and night with music as revellers called to each other from their garlanded gondolas. There were bull runs in the narrow streets, too terrifying and too cruel to be classed as entertainment, in Becky's view, after she had witnessed the start of one from her rooftop viewpoint. The fireworks, on the other hand, which she also watched from the terrace, she would never tire of. She watched all of it unfold alone.

Luca was distant and morose, in her company only as her protector at the *ridotti*, or as her cousin, in the servants' presence in the *palazzo*. It was how she ought to want it. There was a good chance he had guessed the depth of her feelings for him—if not that she had actually fallen in love with him, at least that she cared far too much. He wanted to spare her any further hurt, she guessed, or perhaps he was simply paving the way for the day when they would never see each other again. She missed him dreadfully. Her heartache was like a nagging toothache, a constant unignorable presence. Luca dominated her thoughts, taking up every free moment, until she wanted to scream or to weep or to seek him out and throw herself into his arms in a desperate search of oblivion.

She did none of these things. Instead, she practised her cards. She tried to plan her unimaginable future. She watched Carnival play out on the streets and canals below her from her rooftop kingdom. She had never felt so alone.

In the last two weeks, the Queen of Coins had played Don Sarti seven times, his losses increasing incrementally with each game, his desperate determination to win increasing at the same rate. She dared not even think about the sum they had amassed, the gold which must by now surely have filled the coffer which Luca kept hidden somewhere in the *palazzo*. He never told her the exact total, only that they had not yet reached his target. She loved him, but this aspect of him, his determination to see his plan through to the last *scudo*, she could no longer sympathise with. Though he insisted it was justice, to Becky it was beginning to seem like a vendetta, an aspect of his Venetian heritage that did him no credit.

She was reminding herself yet again that Luca's motives were of the purest, that the money would be well spent, that Don Sarti's family was Don Sarti's responsibility, when the door to the parlour opened.

'Oh, Rebecca, I didn't realise you were in here.'

Isabel stopped short on the threshold. 'Do not let us disturb you,' she said as Becky got hastily to her feet. 'Come, Anna…'

But Donna Sarti had already entered the room. 'To what do we owe the pleasure of your company?' Becky asked nervously, concerned that Isabel's horrified expression was going to betray her.

Donna Sarti was always pale, but today her complexion had an ashen hue. There were dark circles under her eyes. 'I have come to discuss a matter of some delicacy with your aunt. I would not wish to burden you with the unsavoury details.'

Without another word, Donna Sarti left the room, Isabel in her wake, only to reappear alone half an hour later. 'She is gone,' Isabel said, sinking down on to the sofa in front of the fire. 'Poor woman. She is at her wits' end over her husband's gambling.'

'She would be better served raising the matter with her husband, rather than sharing her concerns with you,' Becky said with a sick feeling in the pit of her stomach. She didn't want to have this conversation with Isabel. It was bad enough that she had it with herself almost every night.

'It would be futile. He won't listen. He believes that the next night he will win, the next night he will make good his losses, the next night will see him triumph. Which he might do, who knows, if the cards were not stacked against him.'

Becky flinched. Isabel's eyes were hard, her mouth set into a tight line. She was very much the aristocratic Contessa, not at all Becky's friend and confidant. 'You know why the cards are stacked,' she said evenly. 'You know too, that this is Luca's doing, not mine.'

'Luca is not the one taking Don Sarti's money from him.'

This was Luca's game. If Becky did not play it, she would be left with nothing except a broken heart. 'Don Sarti took the money from Venice.' It was Luca's argument, not hers, but she had no option save to repeat it.

'Venice!' Isabel jumped to her feet. 'I am sick to death of hearing about Venice. I have sacrificed everything for Venice. Years spent doing my duty at my husband's side, time I could have spent with my son, or my own family. I surrendered the opportunity to have more children for Venice. I listen to Anna Sarti's descriptions of her husband's blind obsession, Rebecca, and do you know what it reminds me of?' She smiled bitterly. 'I can see from your face that you do.'

'Your husband, Isabel, he— I imagine he always did what he thought was for the best. He was not like Don Sarti…'

'Not true.' Isabel sank back on to the sofa, wringing her hands. 'That is not true. Anna's husband will ruin her life and blight their daughter's future with his gambling. In the same way, my husband's obsession with Venice dictated our lives, and by writing that damned letter, threatens to destroy our son.'

'Isabel!'

'No, listen to me, Rebecca.' Isabel clutched at her wrists, her carefully manicured nails digging into the soft flesh of Becky's skin. 'You can stop him. He'll listen to you. You can put an end to this.'

'I've tried, but my words have fallen on deaf ears. He desperately wants to put things right, Isabel. Let's not forget that Don Sarti had your husband killed for the sake of those treasures.'

'If Guido had left well alone, he would still be alive.'

'And Don Sarti would have gambled away Venice's heritage,' Becky said. 'At least, thanks to Luca, the money will benefit the city. Some good will come of it. Do you have any idea what you're asking me to do? If I don't fulfil my part of the bargain, I get nothing.'

'I have funds…'

'I don't want your money. I thought you knew me better than that.' Tears welled in her eyes. Becky brushed them furiously away. 'If you wish to discuss the subject further, I suggest you speak to your son. Now, please, leave me alone.'

She waited, dimly aware of the irony of ordering the Contessa from her own room, but though Isabel got to her feet, she did not leave. When she spoke, her tone was not cold, it was worse. It was full of pity. 'You don't approve of his plan, any more than I do, do you?'

'It doesn't matter what I think. Luca has my loyalty, he knows that.'

'Does he know that he has also captured your heart?'

It was quite beyond Becky to deny it. 'It's true, but it's also irrelevant.'

'You will not believe me, Rebecca,' Isabel said with a twisted smile, 'but I am truly sorry for that. Contrary to your very low opinion of me—one which I fear is at least partly justified—I have a very high opinion of you. If you were truly my niece, I could think of no more suitable wife for my son, and would have made every effort to make the match our society has assumed I'm trying to make from the moment I introduced you. But as you say, unfortunately the circumstances render your feelings irrelevant. I have said more than enough, forgive me.'

The door closed softly behind her. It was so unfair of Isabel to challenge her, even if Isabel did say what she was already thinking. Don Sarti would ruin his family, because she, as the Queen of Coins, would ensure he continued to lose. That Isabel had, at the same time as condemning Becky's actions, demonstrated her true affection made everything much more painful. If only she had been Isabel's niece! Ridiculous, preposterous thing to wish for. Luca would never have cared for such a one as Cousin Rebecca. Not as he cared for Becky. And he did care. She knew he did.

The air in the parlour was suddenly stifling. She felt as if the *palazzo* itself was closing in on her. Becky threw open the door of the parlour and ran full tilt down the stairs, making for the front door. The footman called to her. She had no hat or coat. Standing motionless on the jetty, she hesitated for a moment as the sleet fell, then turned away from the Grand Canal and began to run, with no thought as to where she was going.

She was very quickly lost and disoriented. Narrow pathways came to sudden dead ends, forcing her through dark passageways, down shallow steps, across one bridge, back over another. The momentary relief of a courtyard that seemed familiar turned into panic as the narrow passageway she was sure took her back to the *palazzo* instead took her back to the same dead end she had reached fifteen minutes before. She met not a soul as she ran, though as ever she felt a thousand eyes watching her from behind the shutters of the shadowy buildings looming over her. Her footsteps echoed too loudly, pigeons scattered at her approach. The sound of the canal water lapping at the crumbling brickwork took on an eerie, beckoning quality. As she stood, trying to remember which of the exits from a deserted *campo* she had already taken, the thick silence was pierced by a wail that made her jump. A child, she thought, but it was only one of the feral cats. The sound of footsteps gave her hope, but when she followed them, called out, there was no one there.

Thoroughly frightened, chilled to the bone from the mist which was swirling around her, Becky sat down on the rim of a dried-up fountain. Silent tears streamed down her face. Anxiety gnawed at the pit of her stomach. Isabel's words rang in her ears. Donna Sarti's face swam before her eyes. She had no reason to feel guilty, she told herself. She was not forcing Don Sarti to play. She had justice on her side—or at least Luca's form of justice. This was not her plan. She was merely the executioner.

A sob escaped, quickly stifled, but it echoed around the *campo* all the same. She thought she'd come so far from London, left that poor shattered Becky who had been Jack's puppet far behind her. She'd known instinctively that what Jack wanted her to do was wrong, yet she'd done it, thinking she loved him, thinking that what she was doing was for a good cause. Was it happening all over again?

'No!' Her voice, echoing again, made her jump. Luca's cause was real, it was just, it was no lie. And her love for Luca—that was real too. So very, very real. So why, then, did she have this awful feeling that there was something wrong? She covered her face,

hot, bitter tears seeping through her fingers, and surrendered to despair.

He might have been a ghost, the tall, cloaked figure who appeared at the far entrance to the *campo*, but no ghost walked so purposefully, and no ghost made her heart leap the way it did, and as she threw herself into his arms, no ghost felt so solid and so reassuring. 'I got lost,' Becky mumbled, wriggling closer, as Luca pulled his cloak around her.

'You're safe now,' he said.

There was a crack in his voice that made her look up, and his expression squeezed her heart, for she saw her own feelings reflected there. 'Oh, Luca, I—'

'Don't say it.' His arms tightened around her. 'Please, don't say it.'

Perhaps it was to stop her declaration of love, or to stifle his own. It didn't matter. Their lips met. They kissed and their kiss said more than words ever could.

There was only a week of Carnival left. The Queen of Coins and her protector chose not to take the gondola that night, but walked instead, taking a circuitous route from the back entrance of Palazzo Pietro which led to the side entrance of another *palazzo* only a short distance away, facing the Grand Canal. They were infamous now, ushered past the downstairs salon where the play was neither deep nor serious, up the wide marble staircase to the first floor. The salon they entered must look out on to the canal, but the crimson damask curtains were firmly drawn across all the windows. Their arrival caused a stir as it always did. They stood just inside the doorway as was their custom, allowing them both the opportunity to assess the room in their different ways.

Though Becky had grown accustomed to the opulence of the various Venetian *palazzos*, this room was so sumptuous as to be worthy of one of the former doges. High above her, bordered by a cornice of white and gold more elaborate and deeper than any she had seen, the ceiling was painted with a bloodthirsty hunting scene. On each wall was another such scene, presumably depicting a story from antiquity, the characters probably members of whichever aristocratic family owned the palace. There were six chandeliers, making the room garishly bright, and two fires blazing in the hearths at opposite ends of the salon made it uncomfortably hot, the heat blending the scent of perfume and sweat and red wine, and the peculiar, dusty smell of masks worn too often, into an unpleasant miasma that had a metallic quality.

She knew Don Sarti was already there. The hairs on the back of her neck alerted her to his piercing gaze before he made his way across the salon towards them, the small cluster of other gamblers vying for a game with the Queen of Coins parting to make way for him. There was no pretence now, that she would pit her wits against any other. All of Venice knew that this was a duel. All of Venice watched each fresh game with bated breath.

She sensed the change in Don Sarti immediately as he took his place opposite her at a table in the centre of the room. Luca took up his usual position, close enough to be at hand should he be needed, distant enough to avoid any accusation of collusion. The tension which usually crept up on Don Sarti as he lost was there from the beginning tonight as he cut the cards. She let him win, allowed him to deal the first hand. The sense of anticipation, the confidence with which he began every game between them was also absent. He sat too straight in his chair, his voice was strained, he dealt the cards with a snap.

'We do battle again, Queen of Coins. I hope that tonight the outcome will be very different.'

Beneath his mask, his eyes glittered feverishly. Tonight, he was afraid to lose. Becky suspected he would not be staking Venice's gold but his own. Total ruin was, quite literally, on the cards.

Don Sarti played with a recklessness born from desperation. When it came to Becky's turn to deal, she gave him a hand where Swords was the obvious suit to lead with, for he held the Foot Soldier, a ten and a seven. Yet he instead chose Cups, in which he held only the Ace. By the time all the cards of this hand had been played, she could tell without having to add up the complicated scoring system, that he had already lost deep.

The sixth hand was the last, and Becky was once again the dealer. Their audience was two deep now. Luca had been forced to move away from the door to a further corner of the room in order to maintain his view of the table. When she first played, what seemed like a lifetime ago now, Becky thought as she shuffled the deck, he had been nervous of any witnesses, afraid that her tricks would be detected. But though some clearly suspected her reputation as being unbeatable relied on some trickery and watched her closely, she was too skilled to betray herself, and Luca realised that the audience lent her credibility.

She wanted it over. Having shuffled the cards into the order she required, the Queen of Coins executed another fancy false shuffle and dealt. Four cards to Don Sarti, a mixture of suits, all low save one Cavalier. Four to herself, all Batons. Five more to Don Sarti. Another five to herself, including two Kings and two Foot Soldiers. As she expected, Don Sarti discarded all nine of his cards, drawing the next nine blind from the pack, calculating the odds were good that he would select more of one suit or higher value cards, oblivious that the odds were fixed. His hand was shaking. His fingers left damp traces on the cards. A bead of sweat trickled down from his mask on to his neck. She waited, for he had the right to discard one more time, but he did not.

The game was over very quickly after that. With a sick feeling in the pit of her stomach, Becky totted up the scores, adding in the extra points for three of a kind, for court cards taken, for the tricks won with a deuce, all the extra points she had engineered for herself, which she had ensured Don Sarti could not win. The total brought a gasp from the crowd. Hoarsely, his voice muffled by his mask, Don Sarti demanded the paper from her and began to recount. Unable to reduce the tally, he threw the pencil across the table, pushing back his chair so violently that it toppled over.

'I will give you your winnings before tomorrow night's play.'

At his words, Luca stepped forward. 'You have no right to play if you cannot pay.'

His voice was softly menacing. Don Sarti took an involuntary step back. 'You have my word as a gentleman,' he said and then, taking both Luca and Becky by surprise, made a lunge across the table, leaning so close that the grotesque nose of his mask almost touched Becky's. 'Tomorrow,' he hissed, 'I will return, and vengeance will be mine.'

'Did you hear him?' Luca asked with derision as Becky removed her mask in the secret room hours later. 'Little does he know that the vengeance being administered is mine, not his.'

'The entire salon heard him. Haven't we punished him enough?'

'Not nearly enough.'

'Will it ever be enough, Luca? He's sick. He can't help himself. He'll keep coming back to the Queen of Coins until he has absolutely nothing left.'

'This sickness you claim he suffers from is what compelled him to steal from Venice, to have my father murdered. It is only right and proper that the same sickness brings about his downfall.'

'But it will eventually, regardless of what we do, can't you see that?' Becky exclaimed wretchedly. 'Perhaps not at this Carnival but the next or the one after that, depending how deep his pockets are. He'll engineer his own downfall, he doesn't need you or me to do it for him.'

'I am honour-bound to do see this through to the bitter end,' Luca said. 'It was my father's last wish. I thought you understood that.'

'I understand it's what you believe,' she whispered. 'Hasn't it occurred to you that your father was every bit as reckless as Don Sarti? That he was in the grip of his own compulsion to restore Venice to some mythical vision of the past? And you too. Don't you think that this compulsion to do your father's bidding is misguided?'

Her words, spoken only in desperation, made him flinch. Luca was leaning against the door, his mask dangling by its strings from his hand, his cloak over his arm. 'I am neither blind nor obsessed,' he said.

'No.' Becky swallowed. 'That's not what I'm saying.'

'All I'm doing is seeking to right a wrong.'

'I know.' She couldn't take her eyes from him. She loathed the fact that her words must hurt him. His cause was just, she still believed that, but his method— Oh, why the devil had she started this conversation? 'I'm sorry.'

'What for?'

For no longer being able to be completely on his side. But she couldn't say that. For falling in love with him. But she could never regret that. She shook her head helplessly. Did he love her? A week ago, when he had rescued her, kissing her so desperately at the fountain, the question had crept into her mind, but she had instantly shied away from answering it. Best to leave the impossible unsaid. But he must have read it in her eyes, for his own darkened, he dropped his cloak and mask, moving towards her as if in the grip of an irresistible force.

'The only compulsion I have is for you,' Luca said.

Becky's heart was pounding. She felt both sick and giddy. She loved him so much. This was so wrong, yet it was so right. The only thing she was certain of at this moment was that she loved him and she was incapable of denying it. One more time, she thought desperately, lifting her face to his, just one more time.

There was no finesse to their lovemaking. Their kisses were frenzied, the kisses of two people at the ends of their tethers, made frantic by the knowledge that soon they were to be parted for ever. Passion ripped through them as they tore at each other's clothes, as they ravaged each other with kisses, as they clawed at each other's skin, wanting to mark and to claim, seeking to merge, to lose themselves in each other. Becky kicked her way clear of her costume as Luca pulled his shirt over his head, kicked off his boots.

She scattered wild kisses over his torso, breathing deep of the heat of his skin, her hands restless over his back, his buttocks, the tautening response of his muscles rousing her as much as his mouth on her breasts, licking, then tugging on her nipples, setting up the sweetest, most aching, dragging tension inside her. She flattened her palm over the ridge of his arousal, felt him pulse at her touch through his breeches, and then she could wait no longer, pulling at the buttons, an agony of suspense as he freed himself, the sweet delight of him, silken and hard as she curled her fingers around him, the rasp of his breath, and then the drugging rapture of his kisses as he sank down on to the chair, pulling her on top of him, sliding inside her.

She shuddered. She wrapped her arms around his neck, claiming a deep, thrusting kiss, and then it began, the frenetic ascent to completion. His arms were on her waist, lifting her as she tightly clung then thrust, drawing a feral groan from him, taking him so deeply inside her that she cried out, tightened around him, felt the first prelude to her climax, clung more tightly. Another thrust, and she was already lost, pulsing around him, but as he lifted her, she thrust again, panting, kissing, clutching, saying his name over and over as wave upon wave caught her, and still he thrust until a hoarse cry was ripped from him and the pair of them tumbled to the floor together as his own climax shook him, and still they kissed, clutched, kissed, clung and kissed.

For a few perfect moments they were one. Becky lay on top of Luca, their skin slick with sweat, her face hidden in his hair, thinking of nothing, save how much she loved him. And then she opened her eyes, and saw such devastation in his and she knew it was over. All of it.

'I don't know what I'm going to do without you,' Luca said.

Becky sat up. The room was lit by a single lamp, but it felt like a blinding light. Save that she wasn't blinded. She saw painfully clearly what she must do. 'I'm sorry,' she said, this time utterly sure of what it was she apologised for. 'I'm so sorry, Luca. I love you with all my heart, but I can't be party to this, not any more. The Queen of Coins has played Don Sarti for the last time.'

Chapter Fourteen

'**W**hat do you mean?' Hazy from their lovemaking, Luca watched in a daze as Becky jumped to her feet and began to gather various bits of her costume from the floor, where they had been discarded.

'Exactly what I said.' She turned to him, clutching a handful of silk and ribbons, her hair dishevelled, her eyes blurry with unshed tears. 'I'm not winning another *scudo* from Don Sarti.' She began to fold up the bundle of clothes in an alarmingly final manner, as if she were already consigning the Queen of Coins to the history books.

Luca cast about for his own clothes, hastily pulling on his breeches and shirt while Becky, taking off the tunic of her costume, tied the sash of her dressing gown securely and made to leave the room. He caught her by the wrist. 'You don't mean that. We are so close to achieving our goal…'

'No! Luca, I'm sorry, but I simply can't do it.'

Her reservations had grown steadily, she'd told him so often enough, but he'd always been able to persuade her she was wrong. Or at least to persuade her to continue, which was the same thing. Wasn't it? 'What has made you change your mind?' he asked, trying to ignore the sinking feeling in the pit of his stomach.

'It was obvious tonight that he desperately needed to win, Luca. You must have sensed that.'

'He always needs to win. It's what drives what you call his compulsion.'

'But tonight it mattered in a different way.' She spoke gently, and gently led him over to the chaise longue where she sat down. He didn't like the way she looked at him, as if she pitied him. 'Tonight I'm convinced that Don Sarti was playing with money he didn't have. Not Venice's money, Luca.' Becky held her hand up when he made to speak, shaking her head. 'You have this fixed notion that when we reach a certain sum, you'll no longer feel guilty for not being able to prevent what happened, that it will compensate you for the loss of your father, for the loss of your freedom—because that is part of it too, isn't it? Your father's death has forced you to give up the life you love.'

'It's not about that.' But even as he denied it, Luca knew in his heart she was right.

'This quest of yours has become all-consuming, and I think you resent that more than you're prepared to admit.'

She had no right to question his motives, he thought frantically. He just needed her to do what she had been hired to do. Anger, a blessed relief from doubt, began to take hold. 'You can't leave until you have completed the terms of our contract.'

Becky flinched. She paled. But she did not falter. 'I'm aware that I'll forfeit everything.'

'I didn't mean…' He stopped. What had he meant? Not to send Becky away with nothing. No, no, no, a thousand times no! She could not go back to that life. She could not go back to England, where the shadow of the gallows loomed over her.

Luca jumped to his feet. 'You don't mean this. You're overwrought. I've asked too much of you, pushed you too hard. I see that now. There's still a week of Carnival left. We can leave Don Sarti in suspense tomorrow night, you can take a well-earned break, rest…'

'Luca, you're not going to change my mind.' Becky hadn't moved from the chaise longue. She looked at him, those big violet eyes of hers unwavering, her expression quite tragic, and he knew she meant it. He thought he was going to be sick.

'You don't need to ruin Don Sarti,' she continued, still in that soft, inexorable voice. 'He'll destroy himself, sooner or later.'

'But what about justice?'

'Your quest for justice has turned into a vendetta I want no part of. It's wrong, Luca. It's as simple as that. I feel it here,' Becky said, placing her hand over her heart. 'Once before, I allowed my feelings to override my conscience. I can't do that again.'

'You are comparing me to that lying toad?'

'No! I would never compare you to Jack, never. What I feel for you is utterly different to anything I've felt before, but if I carry on doing what you ask of me, I'll never be able to look myself in the eye again. Can't you see?' Becky got to her feet. 'Please think about what I've said. More than anything, what I want is for you to be happy.'

'Happy?' He stared at her as if she were speaking a foreign language.

'Forget Don Sarti. Build your fountains and your hospitals and your schools in your father's name, and build your ships in your own. Stop allowing your father to dictate your life from beyond the grave, Luca.' Becky took his hand. 'Stop looking over your shoulder. What is done is done. I love you so much. I beg you, find a way to be happy. Trust me, my darling, this is not the way.' She lifted his hand to her mouth and pressed a kiss to his palm. A tear splashed on to his fingers. She let him go. He watched, stunned, frozen to the spot as she left.

He lost all track of time. For moments or minutes or hours, Luca stared in utter disbelief at the closed door of the secret room, telling himself foolishly that as long as he stood still there was a chance Becky would return. The sound of someone moving about in the library gave him a brief, flaring hope, but then he heard the rattle of the brass curtain hooks on the pole, the clatter of a bucket on the grate, and realised that it was one of the chambermaids doing her early-morning chores. Quickly and quietly he finished dressing, now desperate to escape. It was nearly dawn as he untied the gondola, snow falling from the lightening sky. He began to row, making instinctively for the lagoon, the freedom and privacy of the Lido.

A vigorous gallop did not clear the fuzziness in Luca's head. Over and over, as his horse pounded the length of the Lido and back again, all he could think of was that Becky was leaving. Which made him miserable to the core of his being but was hardly helpful. Becky was always going to leave, he'd known that from the start.

Handing his steaming horse back to his groom, Luca made his way disconsolately down to the beach, throwing himself down on a sand dune. A foolish mistake, for the place was redolent with memories of Becky. Becky laughing as she curled her toes into the wet sand. Becky's innocent joy as she tried to hurdle the waves. Her surprise when the force of one of them nearly toppled her over. The way she had wrapped her arms around his neck when he caught her, teasing him. Then kissing him. The wild rush of pleasure as he touched her, lying right here in the sand. How long ago? A decade. A minute.

He dropped his head into his hands, groaning aloud. Why the devil did he have to love her so much? Why the devil did she have to be so stubborn? And so damned sure she was right. Because she wasn't right. Not about any of it. Save that she loved him. His chest tightened. She loved him. So why wouldn't she do what he wanted?

That she had dared to compare him to Jack Fisher! Luca swore viciously, curling his hands deep into the damp sand. But she hadn't, not really, he was forced to acknowledge, recalling her exact words. It wasn't her feelings she was comparing, it was her conscience.

If I carry on doing what you ask of me, I'll never be able to look myself in the eye again. Can't you see?

He did see. He didn't want to, but he did, and he was filled with awe at her bravery. She was willing to sacrifice everything, all her dreams to help others like herself, and, worse, her own security, in order to stand by her principles. He couldn't let her do that. For the first time since their return from last night's *ridotto*, Luca was certain about something. He could not let her do that. No matter what.

But what did that mean? The truth was...

His heart began to race. The truth was, he didn't want her to go anywhere. The truth was, he wanted her to stay with him, by his side, for evermore. For a glorious moment it seemed that the grey snow-laden clouds parted and the sun came out as he imagined that happy fate. He and Becky, together. He and Becky married. He and Becky with a brood of little children cast in their image. He smiled, half mocking himself for this sentimental vision, but at the same time tears stung the backs of his eyes. Becky loved him. Becky wanted to make him happy. And what would make him happy, he saw now, wasn't vengeance or justice or whatever name he wanted to give it. It wasn't even building ships. It was Becky.

He jumped to his feet, running down to the shore, stopping just short of the waves, staring out at the Adriatic, past the white-crested waves, as if there was an answer somewhere on the horizon, if only he looked hard enough. Even if he could reconcile himself to giving up on his plan, to failing to complete the task his father had bequeathed him—yes, she was right about that too—there were so many obstacles keeping them apart. Conte del Pietro could not marry Becky Wickes, a wanted criminal and one born without a father's name to call her own. What was more, Becky Wickes wasn't in the least bit interested in becoming the Contessa del Pietro and living the stifling life of a Venetian society hostess. Luca grinned at the very notion of it. No, Becky would not endure that life any more than he would.

He wasn't his father. He was not going to live in his father's shadow. Becky—forthright, clever Becky, who knew him better than he knew himself—had opened his eyes. It was time for him to stop looking over his shoulder and start looking forward. To claim his life back. He had no idea how. He had no idea what it might mean, but by the stars, he was going to do it. It had been so long since he had faced the challenge of overwhelming odds that he'd forgotten that stirring in his blood, that grit inside him that relished a fight. There must be a way to make it right. There had to be a way, and he had to find it quickly, because he couldn't let her go. He simply couldn't countenance losing her.

It was the early hours of the afternoon before a heavy-eyed Becky finally forced herself to leave the sanctuary of her bedchamber. Outside, snow clouds filled the sky, the Grand Canal below her window as grey as her mood. She had a headache, she'd told Chiara, and wished only to be left alone. But the maid, most likely concerned by Becky's red-rimmed eyes and chalk-white colour, besieged her with tisanes and teas and cold cloths and hot broth and fruit until Becky had no option but to claim she felt much better.

She felt, in fact, utterly devastated, and though her conviction that she was right was unshaken, she couldn't think about the consequences without trembling. She had been in worse straits, she reminded herself, significantly so. In the years immediately after her mother died, for example, when she hadn't even a room of her own, when she'd left the theatre at night with no idea where she was going to sleep. And more recently, hiding out in the rookeries following Jack's betrayal. Yes, she'd been considerably worse off, she told herself stoically. Even if her dreams were well and truly shattered. Even if the vision of a future free from trickery and cold and hunger had taken root. Even if she must leave the man she'd given her heart to, knowing that she could not give him the one thing he thought he craved. And so Becky steeled herself, as she made her way out of her bedchamber and down the stairs, to ask Isabella to help her to leave Venice for a destination unknown, as soon as practicable.

She entered the drawing room to discover the Contessa deep in conversation with a stranger, and would immediately have left with an apology for interrupting, had Isabel not beckoned her over, smiling. 'My dear Rebecca, come and be introduced to my brother, Admiral Riddell. Mathew, this is Rebecca, who is, as you know very well, *not* your long-lost niece.'

Mortified, Becky made a very shaky curtsy, her cheeks flaming with embarrassment, but to her consternation and surprise, Admiral Riddell seemed not to care a jot that she was an impostor. 'My sister has informed me of the reason you are here. I must confess to finding the tale reminiscent of something from a lurid novel. Odd sort of plan that my nephew has concocted, I think he must be turned in the head, to imagine— But there, none of my business.'

The Admiral was a tall thin man who bore a strong resemblance to his sister, though the same features which made Isabel beautiful, made him appear more formidable than handsome, his nose tending to hawkishness and his chin to squareness.

'Please join us, Rebecca. I have ordered tea,' Isabel said. 'Mathew has come all the way to Venice to escort me to England for a visit. Luca wrote to him. I had no idea. It is a lovely surprise. I was just saying to Mathew that his timing could not be better, for he plans to take in the remainder of Carnival, to set sail at Lent, which means we will be back in England for Easter.'

'I see,' Becky said vaguely.

'No, my dear, you don't. It means we will be able to take you with us. You won't have to travel back to England alone. How you made the journey yourself in the first place... But now I don't have to worry about your safety.'

'Oh.' Brother and sister were gazing at Becky expectantly. Becky bit down on the hysterical bubble of laughter which rose as she contemplated informing them that the Royal Navy would be transporting a capital criminal back to face trial. She couldn't possibly go with them. 'Thank you,' she said.

The door to the drawing room opened. Thinking that it would be the tea Isabel had ordered, Becky got to her feet to help with the tray, only to drop back down on to her chair as Luca entered the room. He was soaking wet. He had not shaved. He was still wearing last night's clothes. Where had he been? Her hand lifted, beckoning him. Their gazes locked. He took two steps towards her then stopped, shook his head, little sparkling crystals of snow scattering on to the floor. 'Uncle,' he said, extending his hand, meeting the Admiral in a warm embrace. 'I've just been informed of your arrival. I did not expect you so soon.'

'Isn't it marvellous, Luca, a wonderful surprise,'

Isabel said, beaming. 'And such fortuitous timing, I was just saying to Becky, it means we can take her back to England with us. What do you think of that?'

'Not a lot.'

Becky jumped. Isabel's mouth fell open. The Admiral, however, simply narrowed his eyes. 'I understood from your mother that this odd undertaking of yours would be completed by the end of Carnival.'

'This undertaking, as you call it, has turned out to be a damn sight odder than my mother could possibly imagine,' Luca said with the strangest of smiles. 'And if I have my way, it will be over today.'

'Today!' Isabel clapped her hands together. 'Luca, do not tell me that Rebecca has persuaded you to—' The Contessa broke off, covering her mouth.

'I didn't speak to him on your behalf, Isabel,' Becky said dully, wondering how much worse this conversation could get, 'but on my own. It made no difference.'

'But it did.'

Luca was smiling at her now. There was a light in his eyes that she didn't recognise and didn't dare name. It made her silly heart leap. It made her think that perhaps love did conquer all, just as it did in the theatre. And then she remembered that this wasn't a play, and before she could stop them, tears began to cascade down her cheeks. She covered her face, but not before she saw Isabel's horrified expression, the Admiral's perplexed one. She stumbled to her feet, muttering her excuses, making for the door. A strong arm guided her from the room. She wanted to burrow her head into Luca's shoulder and sob, but what would be the point. She shook herself free.

'I listened, Becky,' he said urgently, holding her

by the wrists. 'I don't know how yet, but I'm going to find a way to resolve this mess. I love you so much.'

She couldn't wish the words unsaid, but she wished he had not uttered them, all the same. 'I know you do, but it doesn't make any difference.'

'It will,' Luca said fiercely. 'I'll ensure it makes a difference. We'll talk later, *cara mia*, and I'll explain, but I have something I must do first.'

She watched him go, fighting the ridiculous thought that she'd never see him again as he hurtled down the stairs, still unshaven, still wearing last night's clothes, throwing open the door before the footman had a chance to reach it and disappearing, hatless, back out into the snow.

Unable to face more of Chiara's ministrations, Becky joined Isabel and her brother for dinner. They were then heading off to La Fenice to see a rare revival of Vivaldi's *Griselda*. Becky excused herself on the grounds of a headache, and Isabel, who had several times during dinner asked her to explain Luca's strange behaviour, questioned her again.

'Let the lass alone,' the Admiral intervened, much to Becky's relief. 'Can't you see she's as much in the dark as you? I dare say I know that son of yours better than you do yourself. His methods are not the most conventional, I'll grant you, but by heaven, Luca gets results, and he's as straight as the day is long. So we'll leave them in peace to sort things out between them while we're at the opera. I can't tell you how much I'm looking forward to it.'

The Admiral steered his sister out of the door. Becky retired to the library, pulling one of the huge leather chairs forward to the fire, curling up there with a book of librettos, which she failed to open. Her mind darted about like a starling trapped in an attic. She struggled to make sense of Luca's remarks, for while her silly heart veered off in the direction of unrealistic hope, her head veered in the opposite direction, telling her there could be none. Luca loved her. In the end, as the clock struck eight, Becky wrapped this knowledge around her like a soft woollen blanket. He loved her. Until he returned, she would allow herself the bliss of pretending that was all that mattered.

She must have dozed off, for she did not hear him entering the library, opening her eyes to find him standing over her, gazing down at her with the most tender of smiles. Still caught up in her dream, Becky scrabbled to her feet, allowed him to wrap his arms around her and to hold her tightly against his chest.

'Becky,' he said as she gently freed herself. 'Becky, I've just confronted Don Sarti.'

She dropped back down into the chair, her legs giving way under her. 'Please tell me you didn't do anything foolish.'

Luca poured himself a glass of grappa, drinking it in one gulp before pouring another and taking the seat beside her. 'I didn't need to. You were right,' he said heavily. 'He needs no one's help to destroy himself.'

'Tell me what happened.'

He did, recounting the full, sorry tale, in stark terms that left her in no doubt that, finally, Luca understood the true nature of Don Sarti's compulsion. 'I thought he'd deny it all,' he said. 'The theft. My father's murder. But he didn't. He cried like a baby when

I told him that the Queen of Coins was my avenging angel…'

'You told him! Why, Luca? That was never part of your plan.'

'No, no, it wasn't, but it should have been.' He set down his glass, a heavy frown marring his brow. 'Having spoken to him, I can see what you have seen all along. He is already a broken man.' He shuddered. 'He was even pathetically grateful that we had saved him from himself, taught him a lesson he would never forget. Not that I believe we have.'

'No. He won't be able to resist returning to the tables,' Becky said sadly.

'No. I pity him, but I pity his family more, for he will take them down with him. I dreamed of serving poetic justice,' Luca said wryly, 'but it was already being served by the culprit himself. I can never forgive Don Sarti for having my father's life snuffed out, but I am done trying to avenge it. My father's legacy will be hospitals and schools and freshwater fountains for the poor of the city, not paintings and artefacts. Venice is nothing without our people. You've made me see that, Becky. I've been trying very hard to avoid thinking about having to step into my father's shoes. I've decided that I'm simply not going to.'

'Luca! I am so happy to hear that.'

'Are you, *cara mia*? I hope that you're going to be a great deal happier when you hear what else I have to say. You said that all you want is my happiness because you love me? I finally saw, this morning, on the beach at the Lido, that the only thing that would make me happy was you. But how to make you happy—that was a very different problem.'

He was clasping both her hands now. The tenderness in his eyes as he looked at her was almost more than she could bear. 'You can't,' Becky said, too upset to prevaricate. 'All I want is you, and it's impossible.'

'That's what I thought.' He released her to get to his feet, leaning his back against the wall beside the mantelpiece. 'I will be a very different Conte del Pietro than my father, but as conte I am required to marry well. I must produce an heir. I must make my life in Venice. You could not be less suitable in the eyes of the world, yet you are the only woman I will have as my wife, Becky.'

'Oh, Luca, that is the most— But it's impossible. I wish you had not...'

He dropped to his knees in front of her. 'For myself, I've come to realise that I don't give a damn for any of these traditions. What matters to me is not my wife's pedigree or her innocence. What matters is that her heart is the truest and the bravest I've ever known, that I will be the last man if not the first for her. That she loves me, not for my name or my money but for myself, just as I am. That she wants what I want, to be always by my side, to make a family with me, not for the sake of the del Pietro name, but for the sake of our love. That's what I want, Becky, and that's why I want you and only you. But the world would not see the things that matter. They would judge you on the things that don't. Which is why, though I am determined to marry Becky Wickes, as far as the world is concerned, I'm going to marry my cousin Rebecca.'

'You don't have a cousin Rebecca.'

'I know that,' Luca said with a mischievous smile, 'but no one else does.'

'Save the most important people, your immediate family.'

'My uncle was very taken with you. He would have no objection.'

'How can you possibly know that?'

'I've been to the theatre to speak to them.'

'And your mother? She's sacrificed her entire life to the Venetian way. What does she think?'

'She does not want my wife to be unhappy as she has been, but more importantly, what she wants is for you to be happy. She's become enormously fond of you, I think you know that.'

'She guessed my feelings for you,' Becky confessed.

'She told me. She was delighted to hear that my feelings for you were exactly the same, though extremely concerned about what society would say, as you can imagine. My proposal for countering the gossip tickled her.' Luca smiled. 'Not only would she much rather have you as her daughter-in-law than her niece, she can now happily claim that she has, as is the convention, chosen a bride for me.'

'But I'm not who people think I am.'

'This is Venice in Carnevale. No one is who you think they are.' Luca took her hands again. 'When Cousin Rebecca arrived in Venice, the world assumed my mother had brought her here to be my bride. The world assumed, despite Cousin Rebecca's pious claims to have no ambitions beyond marrying a rural English clergyman, that my charms would prove to be irresistible.'

'As indeed they have,' Becky said shyly.

'So Rebecca fell secretly in love with her dashing cousin Luca. But it was only as she planned to leave, to journey back to England with her aunt, that Luca realised that she would be taking his heart with her. And so he told her.'

Becky felt giddy. Her heart was fluttering and jumping and racing with joy, and she was trying desperately to rein it in. The grey fog which had enveloped her since the early hours was lifting, replaced with a bright, golden light that seemed to be taking its place. Her heart was bursting with love, and a huge bubble of joy was threatening to burst inside her. 'What did Cousin Luca say to her?'

'He said I love you with all my heart. I cannot let you go. If you will promise to be my wife, I will spend every day of my life trying to make you happy. I will be true to you always and for ever. My darling Rebecca, please say you will marry me.'

'Oh, Luca. Oh, my darling, if only...'

'No, no, those aren't your lines. You must ask me how I can possibly make you happy as Contessa del Pietro, when it would stifle you, to live as my mother does.'

'And what is your answer to that?'

'That you are no more obliged to live in my mother's shadow than I am to live in my father's.' Luca grinned. 'My father, along with Don Sarti, was the most influential man in Venice. I'm his son. If I choose, I can wield just as much influence. Where the del Pietro family lead, society will follow. We will set a trend, my darling, for fidelity and for togetherness in our good works. You understand, in a way that I never could, what it is to suffer, and what is needed to alleviate it.' He laughed, embarrassed. 'That sounds very worthy, very stuffy. I don't mean to imply that we'll be either, but…'

'You want me to help you?' Becky squealed.

'I want you to be at my side, to realise both our dreams, not only mine.' His smile faded. His frown returned. His clasp on her hands tightened. 'Would that make you happy, Becky? Do you think that we could forge a life together here?'

'I can't even begin to imagine how happy I would be to— But, Luca, how are we to be married? Not here, in a church— I don't know what official documents are required, but I doubt I have them.'

'We will be married at sea by my uncle, who, fortunately for us, has the power to do so invested in him as a ship's captain. We will honeymoon in England, and when we return, the story of our shipboard romance will be old news.'

'England! I can't go to England.'

'Becky Wickes most assuredly cannot go, but the Contessa del Pietro can have nothing to fear. I want you to meet my mother's family, Becky. I want you to feel part of my family, before we make a start on establishing our own.'

Heat flamed in her cheeks. 'I can't believe what you're saying.'

'I mean every word,' Luca said fervently. 'I know it must sound as if I've turned everything I believe in on its head, but I feel quite the opposite, as if I'm seeing straight for the first time since I returned to Venice, and it's because of you. This morning—was it really only this morning?—when you said you were leaving, I knew that I couldn't bear to let you go. On the beach later, I still had no idea what I needed to do, only that I must do something. I love you. It changes everything—or at least it means that I'm willing to change almost everything to have you by my side. I love you. The future is ours to shape together. Becky, if you are willing to take the risk.'

'Luca, I've been trying to reconcile myself to a future without you, without the means to put a roof over my head, in a foreign country...'

'Then marry me. At least that way you'll always have a roof over your head.'

'I'd prefer to live *on* the roof here.'

'That can be arranged. Anything you wish, if only...'

'I wish only for you, Luca. And—and not to be the Contessa del Pietro like your mother. I can't quite believe this is happening.'

Luca pulled her to her feet. 'The Procurer has a reputation for making the impossible possible. I remembered that today, and I thought, if she can do it, why, then, can't we? Do you love me, Becky?'

She twined her arms around his neck. 'With all my heart, Luca.'

'Will you marry me, Becky?'

Finally, she allowed her joy to burst through, allowed her love to show in her smile. 'Yes, my darling Luca, I will marry you.'

He pulled her roughly into his arms, holding her so tight she could barely breathe. 'I promise you that you will never, ever regret it,' he said, and then he kissed her. Tenderly at first, almost tentatively his lips touched hers, his hands crept up to cradle her face, but as Becky pressed herself against him, as their tongues touched and their kiss deepened, passion flared.

Enveloped in the sweet delight of a love they had

both come so close to losing, they surrendered to each other on the hearth in the library of the *palazzo*, affirming their love for each other over and over as they kissed, as their limbs tangled, as their bodies merged, climbing together to their climax, clinging together as one, as they would be for the rest of their days.

* * * * *

Historical Note

I've never been to Venice, but thanks to Peter Ackroyd's *Venice: Pure City* and John Julius Norwich's *Paradise of Cities*, I feel as if I have. Any inaccuracies or mistakes about the Venice of Luca and Becky's time are all my own doing.

Norwich mentions Contessa Isabella Teotocchi Albrizzi, and I came across her again in Benita Eisler's epic biography of Byron, *Byron: Child of Passion, Fool of Fame*. Known as the Madame de Staël of Venice, hers was only one of two surviving salons from the heyday of the Republic. The renowned sculptor Antonio Canova was a regular there, and the bust of Helen of Troy, which he is delighted to show to Becky, was a gift from him to his hostess.

The other salon was run by Contessa Maria Querini Benzon. Byron, on his last visit to the Venice Carnival, decided that hers was more interesting than her rival's, perhaps because the Contessa was happy to include his low-born mistress into her drawing room. Contessa Benzon was notorious for having danced in a skimpy tunic around the Tree of Liberty, and she did indeed inspire a ballad, 'La Biondina in Gondoleta', which, according to Norwich, is still sung by today's gondoliers. In Becky and Luca's time she was more fond of food than dancing, particularly polenta, which she carried around with her, stuffed into her ample cleavage in winter—hence the name the gondoliers gave her: El Fumeto, The Steaming Lady.

Gambling was illegal in Venice in 1819, though a blind eye was turned during Carnival, when many of the large *palazzos* opened up private gaming hells called *ridotti*. Both women and men could play, provided they were masked, and the stakes were not always financial but a very different currency indeed.

Much of the Carnival atmosphere, both seamy and fiesta, I've taken directly from Byron's descriptions quoted in Benita Eisler's book.

Byron—obnoxious man, but excellent source—called marriage Venetian-style a social convenience rather than a sacrament. Though he was more than happy to avail himself of the custom for married women to take a lover, he was hypocritically scathing of the practice. By the time in which my book is set Venice was very much in decline, and the rich were forced to be careful with their wealth, thus the custom to try to limit the number of sons who could inherit, and the expectation that only the eldest would marry.

Regular readers of my books will notice that shipbuilding is a recurring feature, and in particular Clyde-built ships. The reasons are simple: my paternal grandfather built ships on the Clyde, my maternal grandfather captained them, and my writing view is of the Clyde estuary. If you'd like to read about an actual Clyde shipbuilding hero, then I can offer a choice of two: Iain Hunter in *Unwed and Unrepentant* and Innes Drummond in *Strangers at the Altar*.

Finally I owe a debt to Jeffrey Steingarten, for his exhaustive index of Italian and Venetian terms for all things from the sea in *The Man Who Ate Everything*. I had enormous fun creating dinner menus—and worked up a huge appetite in the process!

FROM COURTESAN TO CONVENIENT WIFE

For Paris, City of Light, city of romance,
and my favourite city in the world. Je t'adore.

Prologue

London—May 1818

The house that was her destination was located on Upper Wimpole Street, on the very edge of what was considered to be respectable London. The woman known as The Procurer stepped down lightly from her barouche, ordering her coachman to wait until she had successfully secured entry, then to return for her in an hour. An hour, The Procurer knew from experience, was more than sufficient time to conclude her unique business. One way or another.

Number Fourteen was situated at the far end of the terrace. A shallow flight of steps led to the front door, but the entrance to the basement she sought was around the corner, on Devonshire Street. The Procurer descended the steep stairs cautiously. Despite the bright sunshine of the late spring morning, it was cool down here, dank and gloomy. The curtains were pulled tight over the single, dirty window. A fleck of paint fell from the door when she let the rusty knocker fall.

There was no reply. She rapped again, her eyes on the window, and was rewarded with the ripple of a curtain as the person behind it tried to peer out at her unobserved. She stood calmly, allowing herself to be surveyed, sadly accustomed to the reticence of the women she sought out to welcome unsolicited visitors. The reasons were manifold, but fear lay at the root of all of them.

The Procurer offered an escape route from their tribulations to those women whose particular skills or traits suited her current requirements. The exclusive temporary contracts she offered provided those who satisfied her criteria with the funds to make a fresh start, though what form that would take was always entirely up to them. The unique business she had established was very lucrative and satisfying too, on the whole, though there were occasions when The Procurer despaired of the tiny impact her altruism had, when set against the myriad injustices the world perpetrated against women. Today, however, she was in a positive mood. A new client, another extraordinary request to test her reputation for making the impossible possible. She had heard of Lady Sophia Acton's spectacular fall from grace and had wondered, at the time, what had been the cause of it. Now, thanks to her spider's web of contacts, she understood only too well. Her heart was touched—as much as that frozen organ could be, that is.

The Procurer gave a little nod to herself. She could not, she thought wryly, have designed a more appropriate task for the woman if she tried. Who had by now,

she judged, had more than sufficient time to decide that
her visitor was neither her landlady come to evict her,
nor a lady of another sort come to harass her. It was
time for Lady Sophia Acton to come out of hiding and
return to the world. Albeit a very different one from
that which she had previously inhabited.

The Procurer rapped on the door again, and this
time her patience was rewarded, as she had known it
would be. The woman who answered was tall and wil-
lowy, dressed in an outmoded gown of faded worsted
which might originally have been either grey, blue or
brown, and which was far too warm for the season.
Her silver-blonde hair was fixed in a careless knot on
top of her head from which long, wispy tendrils had
escaped, framing her heart-shaped face. The wide-
spaced eyes under her perfectly arched brows were extraordinary: almond-shaped, dark-lashed, the colour of
lapis lazuli. There were dark shadows beneath them,
and her skin had the fragility of one who slept little,
but none the less Lady Sophia Acton was one of the
most beautiful women The Procurer had ever encountered. It was an ethereal beauty, the type which would
bring out the protective nature in some men, though
more often than not, she thought darkly, the fine line
between protection and exploitation would easily be
crossed. Men would assume that Lady Sophia Acton's
fragile appearance equated to a fragile mind. Meeting
the woman's steady gaze, The Procurer thought very
much otherwise.

'Who are you? What do you want?'

The questions were perfunctory, the tone brusque.

Lady Sophia had no time for social niceties, which suited The Procurer very well. She insinuated herself through the narrow opening, closing the door firmly behind her. 'They call me The Procurer,' she said. 'And I want to put a business proposition to you.'

Sophia stared at the intruder in astonishment. *This* elegant, sophisticated woman was the elusive Procurer?

'You are thinking that I look nothing like the creature of your imagination,' her uninvited guest said. 'Or perhaps I flatter myself. Perhaps you have not heard of me?'

'I doubt there is anyone in London who has not heard of you, though how many have had the honour of making your acquaintance is a another matter. Your reputation for clandestine dealings goes before you.'

'More of the great and the good use my services than you might imagine, or they would care to admit. Discretion, however, is what I insist upon above all. Whatever the outcome of our meeting today, Lady Sophia, I must have your promise that you will never talk of it.'

Sophia laughed at this. 'Madam, you must be aware, for since you know my name you must also know of my notoriety, that there is no one who would listen even if I did. Those with a reputation to guard will cross the street to avoid me, while those who wish to further tarnish my reputation have no interest in my opinions on any subject.'

As she spoke, she led her visitor into the single room which had been her home for the last three weeks. The fourth home she had occupied in the months since her return from France, each one smaller, dingier and less genteel than the preceding one. It was only a matter of time before she was expelled from her current abode, for London, despite being a big city was in reality a small place, and London's respectable landladies were even smaller-minded.

'I am afraid that my accommodation does not run to a parlour,' Sophia said, drawing out one of her two wooden chairs. 'A woman in my position, it seems, has no right to comfort.'

'No.' The Procurer took the seat, pulling off her kid gloves and untying the ribbon of her poke bonnet. 'A woman in your position, Lady Sophia, has very few options. I take it, from your humble surroundings, that you have decided against the obvious solution to your penury?'

'You do not mince your words,' Sophia replied, irked to feel her cheeks heating.

'I find that it is better to be blunt, when conducting my business,' The Procurer replied with a slight smile. 'That way there is no room for misconceptions.'

Sophia took her own seat opposite. 'Very well then, I will tell you that your assumption is correct. I have decided—I am determined—not to avail myself of the many lucrative offers I have received since my return to London. I was forced into that particular occupation for one very important reason. That reason...'

Despite herself, her throat constricted. Under the table, she curled her hands into fists. She swallowed hard. 'That reason no longer exists. Therefore I will never—*never*—demean myself in that manner again, no matter how straitened my circumstances. So if you have come here in order to plead some man's cause, then I'm afraid your journey has been a wasted one.'

Tears burned in her eyes, yet Sophia met her visitor's gaze, defying her to offer sympathy. The Procurer merely nodded, looking thoughtful. 'I have come here to plead on behalf of a man, but my proposal is not what you imagine. The services he requires of you are not of that nature. To be clear, you would be required to put on a performance, but quite explicitly not in the bedchamber. The role is a taxing one, but I think you will be perfect for it.'

Sophia laughed bitterly. 'I am certainly adept at acting. The entire duration of my last—engagement—was a performance, nothing more.'

'Something we have in common. I too have earned a living from performing. The Procurer you see before you is a façade, a persona I have been forced to adopt.'

Which remark begged any number of questions. Sophia, however, hesitated. There was empathy in the woman's expression—but also a clear warning that some things were better left unspoken. Locking such things away in the dark recesses of memory, never to be exposed to scrutiny, was the best way to deal with them, as she knew only too well. Sophia uncurled her fists, clasping her hands together on the table. 'I will be honest with you, Madam, and trust that your reputation for discretion is well earned. A woman in my position has, as you have pointed out, very few options, and even fewer resources. I do not know in what capacity I can be of service to you, but if I can do so without compromising what is left of my honour, then I will gladly consider your offer.'

Once again, The Procurer gave a little nod, though whether it was because she was satisfied with Sophia's answer, or because Sophia had answered as she expected, there could be no telling. 'What I can tell you is that the monetary reward for the fulfilment of your contract, should you choose to accept the commission, would be more than sufficient to secure your future, whatever form that might take.'

'Frankly, I have no idea. At present, my only future plans are to survive day to day.' But oh, Sophia thought, how much she would like to be able to discover for herself what the future might hold. Six months ago, bereft and utterly alone, raw with grief, she had been so low that she had no thought at all for the future. But life went on, and as it proceeded and her meagre funds dwindled, Sophia had not been able to look beyond the next month, the next week, the next day. Now, it seemed that a miracle might just be about to happen. The Procurer, that patroness of fallen women, was sitting opposite her and offering her a chance of redemption. 'I have no idea what the future holds,' Sophia repeated, with a slow smile, 'but I do know that I want it, and that whatever it is, I want it to belong to me, and to no one else.'

'Something else we have in common, then, Lady Sophia.' This time The Procurer's smile was warm. She reached over to touch Sophia's hand. 'I am aware of your circumstances, my dear, including the reason you were compelled to act as you did. You do not deserve to have paid such a high price, but sadly that is the way of our world. I cannot change that, but I do believe we can be of mutual benefit to each other. You do understand,' she added, resuming her business-like tone, 'that I am not offering you charity?'

'And I am certain that you understand, for you seem to have investigated my background thoroughly, that I would not accept charity even if it was offered,' Sophia retorted.

'Then indeed, we understand each other very well.'

'Not quite *that* well, Madam. I am as yet completely in the dark regarding this role you think me so perfectly suited for. What is it that you require me to do?'

But The Procurer held up her hand. 'A few non-negotiable ground rules first, Lady Sophia. I will guarantee you complete anonymity. My client has no right to know your personal history other than that which is pertinent to the assignment or which you yourself choose to divulge. In return, you will give him your unswerving loyalty. We will discuss your terms shortly, but you must know that you will be paid only upon successful completion of your assignment. Half-measures will not be rewarded. If you leave before the task is completed, you will return to England without remuneration.'

'Return to England?' Sophia repeated, somewhat dazed. 'You require me to travel abroad?'

'All in good time. I must have your word, Lady Sophia.'

'You have it, Madam, rest assured. Now, will you put me out of my misery and explain what it is that is required of me and who this mysterious client of yours is.'

Chapter One

Paris—ten days later

The carriage which had transported Sophia all the way from Calais drew to a halt in front of a stone portal surmounted by a pediment on which carved lions' heads roared imperiously. The gateway's huge double doors were closed. Was this her final destination? They had passed through one of the entrance gates to the city some time ago, following the course of the bustling River Seine, which allowed her to catch a glimpse of the imposing edifice which she assumed was Notre Dame cathedral. Despite this, Sophia still couldn't quite believe she was actually here, in Paris.

The days since her momentous meeting with The Procurer had passed in a blur of activity as her papers were organised, her travel arrangements confirmed, and her packing completed. Not that she'd had much packing to do. The costumes required for her to carry out her new duties would be provided by the man who presumably awaited her on the other side of those doors. The man to whom she was bound for the duration of the contract. The shudder of revulsion was instinctive and quickly repressed. This contract was a world away from the last, less formal and much more distasteful, one she had reluctantly entered into to, she reminded herself. The Procurer had promised her that her stipulated terms would be honoured. Though she must do his bidding in public, this man had no right to any part of her, mind or body, in private. So it was not the same. This man was not Sir Richard Hopkins. The services he was paying for were radically different in nature. And when it was over, she would be truly free for the first time in her life.

The butterflies which had been slowly building in her stomach from early this morning, when she had quit the last of the posting houses to embark on the final leg of her journey, began to flutter wildly as Sophia saw the huge doors swing inward and one of the grooms opened the carriage door and folded down the steps. Gathering up the folds of her travelling gown she descended, glad of his steadying hand, for her nervous anticipation was palpable.

'*Monsieur* awaits you, *madame*,' the servant informed her.

'*Merci,*' Sophia replied, summoning up what she hoped was an appropriately eager smile, thanking the man in his own language for taking care of her during the journey. The servant bowed. She heard the carriage door slam, the clop of the horses' hooves on the cobblestones as it headed for the stables.

Bracing herself, Sophia prepared to make her entrance. The *hôtel particulier* which she assumed was to be her temporary home was beautiful. Built around the courtyard in which she now stood, there were three wings, each with the steeply pitched roof and tall windows in the French baroque style, the walls softened with a cladding of ivy. The courtyard was laid out with two parterres of box hedging cut into an elaborate swirling design which, seen from above, she suspected, would form some sort of crest. The main entrance to the *hôtel* was on her left-hand side. At the top of a set of shallow steps, the open doorway was guarded by a winged marble statue. And standing beside the statue, a man.

Late afternoon sunlight glinted down, dazzling her eyes. She had the absurd idea that as long as she stood rooted to the spot, time would stand still. Just long enough for her to quell her fears, which were hardly unjustified, given her experience. Men wanted but one thing from her. Despite The Procurer's promises and reassurances, until she could determine for herself that this man was different and posed no threat to her, she would, quite rightly, be on her guard.

Though she must not appear so. Sophia steeled herself. The future, as she had discovered to her cost, did not take care of itself. This was her chance to forge her own. Though she had assumed her new persona in Calais, now she must play it in earnest. She had coped with much worse, performed a far more taxing role. She could do this! Fixing a demure smile on her face for the benefit of anyone watching from the myriad of windows, she made her way across the paved courtyard.

The man she approached was tall, sombrely dressed, the plain clothes drawing attention to an impressive physique. Black hair. Very tanned skin. Younger than she had anticipated for a man so ostentatiously wealthy, no more than thirty-five, perhaps less. As she reached the bottom of the steps, he smiled, and Sophia faltered. He was a veritable Adonis. She felt her skin prickle with heat, an unfamiliar sensation which she attributed to nerves, as he descended to greet her.

Jean-Luc Bauduin, The Procurer's client and the reason she was here, took her hand, making a show of raising it to his lips, though he kissed the air above her fingertips. 'You have arrived at last,' he said in softly accented English. 'You can have no idea how eagerly I have been anticipating your arrival. Welcome to Paris, Madame Bauduin. It is a relief beyond words to finally meet my new wife.'

Jean-Luc led the Englishwoman through the tall doors opening on to the terrace, straight into the privacy of the morning room. 'We may speak freely here,' he informed her. 'Tomorrow, we will play out the charade of formal introductions to the household. For now, I think it would be prudent for us to become a little better acquainted, given that you are supposed to be my beloved wife.' Thinking that it would take a while to accustom himself to this bizarre notion, he motioned for her to take a seat. 'You must be tired after your long journey. Will you take some tea?'

Though he spoke in English, she answered him in perfect French. 'Thank you, it has indeed been a long day, that would be delightful.'

'Your command of our language is an unexpected bonus,' Jean-Luc said, 'but when we are alone, I am happy to converse in yours.'

'You certainly speak it fluently, if I may return the compliment,' she said, removing her bonnet and gloves.

'I am required to visit London frequently on matters of business.'

The service was already set out on the table before her, the silver kettle boiling on the spirit stove. His wife—*mon Dieu*, the woman who was to play his wife!—set about the ritual which the English were so fond of with alacrity, clearly eager to imbibe. In this one assumption, at least, he had been correct.

Jean-Luc took his seat opposite, studying her as she busied herself making tea. Despite the flurry of communications he'd had with The Procurer, there was a part of him that had not believed the woman would be able to deliver someone who perfectly matched his precise requirements, yet here was the living, breathing proof that she had. In fact, in appearance at least, the candidate she had selected had wildly exceeded his expectations. Not that her allure was the salient factor. Finally, after all these weeks of uncertainty and creeping doubt, he could act. Recent events had threatened to turn his world upside down. Now, he could set it to rights again, and the arrival of this woman, his faux wife, was the first significant step in his plan.

Her name was Sophia, one of the few facts The Procurer had shared with him. Of her origins, her life, past or present, he knew nothing. His request had been for a woman whom the society in which he moved would accept as his wife without question, a woman he could credibly have fallen deeply in love with, enough to cast caution to the winds and marry post-haste. His request had been more than satisfied. The woman The Procurer had sent him was the answer to prayers he hadn't even said.

He had assumed she would be an actress, but looking at her he found it difficult to believe, though he could not say why. Her beauty was quite dazzling, but it was fragile, sylph-like, ethereal, with none of the overblown showiness required to tread the boards. She was slim as a wand, and looked as if she could slip through rain, as the saying went. Her hair seemed almost silver in the glare of the sunlight behind her, her skin almost translucent, her lips soft pink. But it was her eyes which drew the attention, an extraordinary shade of blue, like the Mediterranean in the south, though he would not call it turquoise or cornflower or even azure. He had never seen such a colour.

To his embarrassment, Jean-Luc felt the first stirrings of desire. It had not occurred to him that he would find the woman he had come to think of as his shield attractive. Her stipulation that there should be absolutely no physical intimacy between them had surprised him. His expectations of the role his wife would play most certainly did not extend to his bed, but on reflection, he thought it wise of her to clarify a matter which could easily be open to misinterpretation, and had agreed without hesitation. Though he did not doubt his ability to honour his promise, he wished that The Procurer had not sent him a woman who was the perfect embodiment of desire—or of his desires, at any rate. He did not wish to be sidetracked by passion, even if it was destined to remain utterly unrequited. He could only hope that the amount of time they would be forced to spend in one another's company would cure him of such inopportune thoughts. What mattered was not what she was, or what effect she had on him, but what she appeared to be to everyone else.

Accepting the Sèvres cup of tea reluctantly, Jean-Luc's fingers brushed hers. She was icy cold. She had flinched, out there in the courtyard, when he had affected to kiss her hand, though she had tried to conceal it. She was nervous, he expected. Well, so too was he. There was a great deal riding on her arrival.

On her wedding finger, she wore the simple gold band he had asked The Procurer to purchase on his behalf. She sipped her tea delicately. There was a poised refinement in her manner, that made him wonder if her birth was numerous rungs up the pedigree ladder from his own. But why would a gently born and raised female agree to play a French wine merchant's wife? An intriguing question, though one he had no time to pursue. Whatever her origins, what mattered was that she was here, allowing him to establish his own. The Procurer had chosen well, as he would expect, given her reputation and the large fee she had demanded. A fee he'd happily pay twice, thrice over, if this masquerade of theirs proved effective.

Unthinking, Jean-Luc took a sip of the dishwater so beloved of the English, and immediately set the cup down with an exclamation of distaste. 'So, *madame*,' he said, 'to business. Perhaps we could begin with what it is you know of the task which lies ahead of you?'

Sophia set the delicate Sèvres cup down carefully. Despite the tea, her mouth was dry, her heart thudding. To business, he had said, the identical cold phrase that Hopkins had used. But this time she was no ingénue. She cleared her throat. 'Before we start, Monsieur Bauduin...'

'Before we start, *madame*, I think we should agree to address one another less formally. We are, in the eyes of the world at least, married. My name is Jean-Luc. I would ask that you use it.'

'Jean-Luc. Yes, I am aware. And I am Sophia.'

'Of that I am also aware, though I know no more.'

He waited, one brow slightly raised. His eyes were a very dark brown, the lashes long, thick and black. One could not describe a man's eyes as beautiful, and in any case, this man was too—too masculine. His jaw was very square. There was a permanent furrow between his brows. Not an Adonis, she had been mistaken to label him that, and not handsome either, if one took Lord Byron's classic perfection as an example. This man who was to be her husband for the time being was not at all like Byron or Adonis or any other model of perfection, but in another mould altogether. Memorable. A vibrant presence one could not ignore. If one was inclined to find a man attractive, then this was undoubtedly such a man. But she was not so inclined. Nor was she about to satisfy his curiosity about her surname either, especially since he was a regular visitor to London. So she met his gaze blankly and said nothing. She was good at that.

'Simply Sophia it is, then,' he said eventually, with a casual shrug that might have been defeat, or more likely indifference. 'Will you at least deign to tell me, Simply Sophia, what The Procurer told you of this assignment?'

Was he teasing her or mocking her? She couldn't decide, and so decided not to care, which was always the safest thing to do. 'I was told very little,' Sophia replied stiffly. 'Merely that you require me to play the part of your wife, and that I must convince everyone that it has been a love match. The reasons for my presence here, and my duties, she said would be explained by your good self, as would be the terms upon which our contract is to be deemed complete. In short, she was not forthcoming at all, though she assured me that you had disclosed all to her, and that she believed me to be an excellent match for your requirements.'

'Her reputation for discretion appears to be well founded.' Jean-Luc twisted the heavy signet ring he wore on his right hand around his finger. 'It is ironic, that I must explain myself to you, while you are not obliged to tell me anything about yourself. Not even your surname.'

Ironic, and very convenient for her, but, judging by the tension around his mouth, extremely inconvenient for him. Why did a man like this—rich, confident, successful and, yes, Sophia could admit it to herself, extremely attractive—need to *pay* a complete stranger to act as his wife?

He was still eyeing her expectantly, waiting for her to fill the silence with the answer to his implied question. Sophia kept her expression carefully neutral. 'If I am to fulfil my role convincingly, then, painful as it may be to explain yourself to a complete stranger, it seems you must.' And painful as it might be, she must first ensure that her own terms were clearly understood. 'Though before we proceed, I would like to discuss the conditions which I stipulated.'

'I am not sure what there is to discuss,' Jean-Luc answered. 'I accepted them, as you must know, else you would not be here.'

Sophia smiled tightly. 'In principle, yes. But I find it is best to be crystal-clear about the detail.'

His brows shot up. 'You find? You have entered into contracts such as this previously?'

'I have never before entered into an arrangement such as this one,' she said stiffly, which was after all the truth, but he need not know the precise nature of her previous *arrangements*. 'What I meant was, that I find it is—I think it would be best for us both to be absolutely clear, before we start, as to the extent of our—our intimacies.' Sophia squirmed inwardly. She sounded like a prude. 'If I am to play your wife, I presume it is for the benefit of an audience, and that therefore there will be some displays of affection required? I would be obliged if you could explain in plain terms what form you anticipate those taking.'

'I confess, I had not thought so specifically—but you are right, it is best to be clear.' Jean-Luc stared down at his signet ring. 'Very well, in plain terms then, our marriage will be for public consumption only. In private, you have my word of honour that I will make no physical demands upon you of any sort. For the sake of appearances, in public and in front of my servants, our "intimacies", as you refer to them, will be confined to only those acts which can be performed in public with propriety. Do you wish me to be any plainer or is that sufficient?'

'It is more than sufficient.' And an enormous relief. Some of the tension in her shoulders eased. Her instincts told her that she could trust him to keep his word, though her instincts had proven to be fallible in the past. Disastrously so. 'You understand that any breach of these terms would render our contract null and void? Not only would I leave immediately, but you...'

'I would be obliged to recompense you with the full amount. I am aware. I have already given you my word that I will not breach the terms, Sophia, I'm not sure what else I can do to reassure you, save to tell you that my reasons for bringing you here in the first place are, *en effet*, life-changing. This charade of ours must succeed. I have no intentions of doing anything to endanger it. You understand?'

'I do.' A little more of the tension eased. She allowed herself a small smile. 'And I can assure you, *monsieur*—Jean-Luc—that I will also do all I can to ensure that our charade does succeed.'

'*Eh, bien*, then I trust that is an end to the matter?'

'Thank you, yes.'

He returned her smile, but only in a perfunctory way. 'You must understand though, Sophia, that it is vital that we are convincing? I do not expect you to make love to me, but I do expect you to appear as if you wish to, or better still as if you just have.'

'Of course.' She could feel the slashes of colour stain her cheeks. It was mortifying to discover that even after all she had been forced to endure, her sensibilities could still be so obviously inflamed. It would be considerably easier than she had expected to spend time in his company. It might even be—no, it was too much of an exaggeration to say enjoyable, but it would be no hardship. 'Though I'm still not at all clear,' Sophia said, flustered by her thoughts, 'as to why you need a wife? And why must it be a love match?'

'Oh, as to that, it is quite simple. Love,' Jean-Luc said with a wry smile, 'is the only credible explanation for the suddenness of our union, and the suddenness of our union will come as a great surprise to all who know me.' He frowned, choosing his words with care. 'It is not that I am against marriage. It is an institution I have always planned to embrace at some point in the future, but for the time being, it is well known that I am effectively married to my business. Ironically, my passion for my business has largely been responsible for my success, which in turn means that I am rather inconveniently considered a much sought-after marital prize.'

His tone made his thoughts on this state of affairs

clear. 'Yet you have so far evaded capture,' Sophia said. 'I cannot believe that you have employed me in order to ensure that you continue to do so. You do not strike me as a man who could be persuaded to do anything against his will.'

'Not so Simple Sophia after all,' Jean-Luc said, smiling. 'You are quite right. It is precisely because I will not have my hand forced that you are here.'

'Good heavens,' she exclaimed, startled, for she had spoken mostly in jest. 'You can't possibly mean that you are being forced to marry someone against your will?'

His smile became a sneer. 'There is indeed a woman attempting to do exactly that. Whether she is a charlatan or simply deluded I cannot decide, but whichever it is, she is doomed to failure. I intend to prove to her that her various claims are utterly without foundation. Producing you as proof that I am already married is just my first salvo across her bows.'

Sophia was gazing up at him, her extraordinary blue eyes wide with astonishment. 'I don't understand. One cannot be *forced* into marriage, not even when— not ever,' she said, hastily amending whatever it was she had been about to disclose. 'This woman, she can hardly hold a gun to your head and force you to take her hand in marriage.'

'But she does have a gun, and she has been holding it at my head since April.' Jean-Luc laughed grimly. 'It is loaded, she thinks, with a silver bullet which will be the answer to all her problems. You are the armour I need to deflect that bullet'

Sophia shook her head in bewilderment. 'I still don't understand. Why not simply tell her that you won't marry her?'

'Because it is not that simple. I'm sorry, I have been living and breathing this farce for so long, and now you are here, I am so eager to put my plans into action that I forget you know nothing of them.'

She smiled, her first genuine smile, and it quite dazzled him. 'Let me reassure you, I am just as eager as you are to begin. So why don't you tell me more about this woman who wishes to be your wife. Starting with her name, perhaps?'

'Haven't I told you?' Jean-Luc rolled his eyes. 'Juliette de Cressy is her name, and she turned up, quite unannounced on my doorstep six weeks ago. Until that point I had never heard of her.'

Sophia wrinkled her brow. 'But if she was a complete stranger, why did you grant her an audience?'

'One of the many things which makes me ambivalent about Mademoiselle de Cressy is that she appears, on first inspection, to be eminently respectable. She called with a maid in tow. She had a visiting card. I have an enquiring mind and was intrigued enough to hear what she had to say. When I did, my immediate reaction was simply to dismiss her tale out of hand. In a bid to take the wind out of her sails I told her that she was wasting her time, as I was already married.'

'I take it she didn't believe you? Hardly surprising, considering what you have more or less confessed to being known as a dedicated bachelor.'

'Yes, but it was more than disbelief. She was—I

don't know, it is difficult to explain. At first she was quite distraught, but she very quickly recovered. That is when she produced the legal documents—her silver bullet—which she believed would substantiate her claim. And that is when I realised she was not, as I had assumed, simply a brazen and audacious opportunist who would be put off by the threat of an invisible wife. It wasn't only that she didn't believe I was married, you see, it was that she was extremely convincing in the strength of her own case. Of course, the chances were still high that she was an extremely convincing charlatan, but…'

'It occurred to you that she might simply be, as you said, deluded.'

'Yes, that is it. Either way, it was clear that she was not going to go away.'

'And you were faced with the problem of admitting that you had lied when you said you were already married, or coming up with the evidence to back up your fiction.'

'Precisely, though I did not immediately rush to The Procurer for help. My next step was to test her resolve by telling her that I wished my lawyer to examine the papers she had to support her claim. She handed them over willingly, informing me that she had expected no less. It was clear she had faith in their authenticity, and equally clear that it had not occurred to her that I might simply destroy them.'

'Any more than it would have occurred to you, I assume?'

'You assume correctly.'

'That is reassuring,' Sophia said, with an odd little smile. 'So, Mademoiselle de Cressy's seemingly innocent trust in you was, then, another point in her favour?'

'It was.'

'And the documents, whatever they are?'

Jean-Luc rolled his eyes. 'Most likely genuine.'

'So you hired me to prove to Mademoiselle de Cressy that regardless of these documents she has, she is, as we say in England, barking up the wrong tree? You cannot marry her, because you are already married?' Sophia frowned down at her hands. 'You have gone to a great deal of trouble and expense to call this woman's bluff. Couldn't you simply have paid her off?'

'I offered to do just that, to make the problem go away, but she refused. She said she wanted what was rightfully hers, not blood money. As you will have realised by now,' Jean-Luc continued, 'the matter is complicated, and I am aware that you have only just arrived. You have not even seen your room.'

He sat at an angle to her, his long legs tucked under the sofa, which had the effect of stretching his pantaloons tight over his muscled thighs. He might not look like an Adonis, but his build was reminiscent of one. His physical proximity made Sophia uncomfortable. Not unsafe, she was surprised to notice, but—odd. Her pulses were fluttering. It was because he was so close, a warning sign, she supposed, though she felt no inclination to move. 'All in good time. I take it your plan is to introduce me to Mademoiselle de Cressy sooner rather than later?'

'All in good time,' he answered, smiling. 'My plan for what remains of today is to allow you time to rest and recover from your journey. There is a good deal more to this tale, but it can wait.'

Jean-Luc took her hands between his, a light clasp from which she could easily escape, which meant she had no need to. 'I will have them bring you dinner in your room, and water for a hot bath, if you wish?'

Sophia couldn't imagine anything nicer. His thoughtfulness touched her. It had been so long since anyone had thought of her comfort, for in the end even Felicity…

'That would be perfect,' she said, desperately trying not to let fall the tears which suddenly stung her eyes. 'I think I am a little fatigued after all. *Merci*, Jean-Luc.'

'It is my pleasure, Sophia.' He pressed her hands. Then he let her go.

Chapter Two

Jean-Luc was in his working in his office the next morning when his new wife appeared, looking much refreshed.

'May I come in?' Sophia asked. 'The footman told me that you don't like to be disturbed, but I thought…'

He jumped to his feet to pull out a chair for her. 'Remember that you are my wife, as far as the footman and every other servant is concerned. This is your household to command. In any event, you are not disturbing me. I am far too distracted to work, thanks to you. Are you rested?'

'Fully.' She took the seat he indicated, opposite him, but moved it forward, so that she could rest her hands on the desk which separated them. 'Before you relate the rest of your story, I think it only fair that I reassure you, since you were so patient in reassuring me yesterday.'

'Reassure me about what?'

She smiled at him faintly. 'You said that your reasons for bringing me here were life-changing. I should tell you that my reasons for agreeing to come are also life-changing. Coming to Paris, taking on this role, contract, commission, I'm not sure what to call it—this false marriage of ours, if I make a success of it, and I am determined to do just that, the money I will earn will allow me to quite literally change my life.' She bit her lip, considering her words carefully. 'I will be free. Free to make my own way in the world, on my own terms. For the first time in my twenty-six years I will be able to live only to suit myself, to finally discover what it is I like, what I want, what makes me happy. So you see, the stakes are too high for me to fail. You can have no idea how much that means to me. I won't let you down.'

There was a sparkle in her eyes, a tinge of colour that was not embarrassment in her cheeks, giving him a tantalising glimpse of the woman she could be, or would be, if she achieved her goal. He had thought her beautiful before, but seeing her like this, she positively glowed. 'I can see for myself how much it means,' Jean-Luc said, quite beguiled. 'Thank you. May I say that I can think of no one I would rather pretend to be married to than you.'

She laughed. 'We have not even been married two days. I will be more flattered if you still think so in a week's time.'

'Actually, as far as the world is concerned, we have been married since March. But I get ahead of myself. Are you comfortable? Because the tale I'm about to relay is long and convoluted.'

'I don't know what to say,' Sophia said some time later. 'I am utterly confounded. Juliette de Cressy not only claims that you are contracted to marry her, but that you are a duke!'

'Of all the preposterous things this woman alleges, the lunatic notion that I might be the long-lost son of an aristocrat who went to the guillotine—' Jean-Luc broke off, shaking his head. 'Me! It is simply ridiculous.'

'You know, most men would be both delighted and flattered to be informed they were of noble birth.'

'Even if it means disowning the parents who raised them, who loved them and who tried to give them the best life possible in difficult circumstances? No.' His mouth firmed. 'I know who I am. My father—yes there were times when we did not agree, when I thought that he did not care for me, that he—he somehow resented me, but that is normal, for a father and a son, as one grows older, and the other stronger.'

'I can imagine it would have been normal for you. I expect you were very sure of yourself, even as a boy.'

Jean-Luc laughed. 'What was your upbringing like? No, you need not answer,' he added hurriedly, 'I did not mean to pry.'

Sophia hesitated. She was under no obligation to tell him anything, but it seemed wrong to shut him out completely when he had just confided so much to her. 'My relationship with my father was difficult. He wanted a son. As a female, I was of limited use to him.'

'But you knew he cared for you?'

She knew he had not. 'I never doubted he was my father,' Sophia said, unwilling to lie.

'You refer to him in the past tense.'

'He died four years ago. My mother many years

earlier. To return to the matter in hand,' she said hurriedly, 'are you saying that, thanks to Mademoiselle de Cressy, you are doubting your own parentage?'

'*Mon Dieu*, no! The difficulties I spoke of were a long time ago. My father was very proud of my success. He told me not long before he died, ten years ago, just nine months after Maman, that he could not have asked for a better son.' Jean-Luc's hand tightened around the quill he had been fidgeting with. 'For my father, that was quite an admission, believe me.'

'More than I ever got,' Sophia said with feeling. 'My father never missed an opportunity to tell me that he had never wished for a daughter of any sort, never mind...' *Two*. The pain took her by surprise, making her catch her breath. All too aware of Jean-Luc's perceptive gaze on her, she took a firm grip of herself. 'Never mind my father,' she amended lamely. 'We were talking of yours.'

He waited, just long enough to make it clear he knew she was changing the subject, then set down his quill. 'My father, Robert Bauduin, you mean, and not the Duc de Montendre.'

'Indeed. May I ask how you plan to prove your heritage? I'm assuming that you doubt a simple introduction to me will send Mademoiselle de Cressy running for the hills. That you require me to be by your side to maintain the façade, in order to buy yourself the time you need to gather the evidence to quash her claim completely?'

'Ah, you do understand.'

'But of course. If a wife does not understand her

husband, then she is a poor spouse indeed,' Sophia quipped.

Jean-Luc smiled, albeit faintly. 'I must confess, I'm concerned as to how she will react when she does meet you. To date, she has quite simply refused to accept that I have a wife.'

'Then we must hope that she does not try to eliminate me—an outcome not at all unlikely in the context of this tale, which is worthy of Shakespeare himself.'

'Or perhaps more appropriately, Molière,' Jean-Luc said drily, 'for it has all the hallmarks of a farce. It is, to say the least, inconvenient that the agent which Maxime—Maxime Sainte-Juste, my lawyer, that is— sent to Cognac to retrieve documentary evidence of my birth, came back empty-handed.'

Sophia wrinkled her nose. 'You don't find it odd that he couldn't locate the certificate of your baptism?'

Jean-Luc shrugged. 'I was surprised, I had assumed that I was born in Cognac, and my parents had always lived there but they must have moved to that town when I was very young. I was born in 1788. It was a time when there was much unrest in the country, crops failing, the conditions which resulted in the Revolution. There could have been any number of reasons for my parents to have relocated.'

'What about your grandparents then? You must know where they lived.'

'I don't. I never knew them, and have always assumed they died before I was born, or when I was too young to remember them.'

'But there must have been other relatives, surely? Cousins, aunts, uncles?'

'No one.' Jean-Luc twisted his signet ring around his finger, looking deeply uncomfortable. 'When you put it like that, it sounds odd that I never questioned my parents when they were alive, never even noticed my lack of any relatives at all when I was growing up.'

'But why would you? Your parents are your parents, your family is your family.'

'Yes, but most people *have* a family,' he said ruefully. 'It seems I did not, though of course I must have relatives somewhere. Unfortunately, I have no idea where I would even begin to look in order to locate them.'

'What about family friends, then?'

But once more, Jean-Luc shook his head. 'None who knew my parents before I was born. You're thinking that is ridiculous, aren't you? You are thinking, there must be someone!'

'I am thinking that it is extremely awkward for you that there is no one.'

'Extremely awkward, and a little embarrassing, and very frustrating,' he confessed. 'I cannot prove who I am. More to the point,' he added, his expression hardening, 'I cannot prove to Mademoiselle de Cressy who I am, which means that...'

'You must prove that you are not who she says you are, the long-lost son of the fourth Duc de Montendre.'

'*Exactement.*' Jean-Luc grimaced. 'Unfortunately, not as straightforward a task as you might imagine. I have, however, made a start on testing the veracity of Mademoiselle de Cressy's documents. Unlike me, she does have a baptism certificate. Maxime's agent has been despatched to Switzerland to check it against the relevant parish records. If it proves to be legitimate, then his next task will be to attempt to obtain a description of Juliette de Cressy. As the only child of the recently deceased Comte de Cressy, there must be someone in the neighbourhood where she says she lived for all her twenty-two years who can shed some light on her.'

'So she was born after her parents left Paris?'

'If her parents were the Comte and Comtesse de Cressy—who were, incidentally, real people, that too I have established—then she was born six years after they arrived in Switzerland, fleeing Paris in the days when it was still possible to do so, before The Terror.'

'And the marriage contract, it was written when?'

'It is dated 1789, the year of the Revolution, and one year after I was born—not that that has anything to do with it.' With an exclamation of impatience, Jean-Luc got to his feet, prowling restlessly over to the window to perch on the narrow seat in the embrasure, his long legs stretched in front of him. 'The marriage contract appears to be signed by the sixth Comte de Cressy and the fourth Duc de Montendre. It stipulates a match between the Duc de Montendre's eldest son, whose long list of names does not include mine, and any future first-born daughter of the Comte de Cressy.'

'And this fourth Duc de Montendre was killed during the Terror?'

'As was the Duchess, some time in 1794. This much

Maxime has been able to discover, though the circumstances—there are so few records remaining, so much has been destroyed. It may be that the witnesses to the contract also—if they were loyal servants…'

'They too may have gone to the guillotine?'

'Like so many others. The final months of the Terror following the Revolution saw mass slaughter, so many heads lost for no reason. Maxime thinks that trying to prove Mademoiselle de Cressy wrong could turn into a wild goose chase.'

'A whole flock of geese, by the sound of it. It sounds daunting in the extreme.'

Jean-Luc grinned. 'There is no finer lawyer than Maxime, and no better friend, but the reason he is so successful in his chosen profession is because he is a cautious man, and the reason I am so successful in my chosen profession—or one of them—is that I recognise when it is necessary to cast caution to the wind.'

He returned to his seat behind the desk, picking up his quill again. 'Maxime is right, though, it will not be a simple matter to prove I am not this Duke's son. There have been many cases in France over the last few years, of returning *émigrés* or their apparent heirs, claiming long-lost titles and estates. With so many of the nobility and their dependents dead, so many papers lost, estates ransacked, it is very difficult to prove—or to disprove—such claims. And even if they prove to be true, in most cases, the reward is nothing, or less than nothing, you know? What money existed has long gone, along with anything of value which could be sold or stolen. No one really cares, you see, if Monsieur le

Brun turns out to be the Comte de Whatever, if only the name is at stake.'

'So it would be, ironically, easier for you to accept the title than to reject it?'

'Equally ironically, acquiring a title, especially such a prestigious one, would, in the eyes of some, be of value to my business. It would,' Jean-Luc said with a mocking smile, 'be more prestigious to buy wine from the Duc de Montendre that from Monsieur Bauduin.'

'But it is not a mere title which *mademoiselle* would have you claim, but a wife. And another family. Another history.'

'None of which I desire.'

'No, but Mademoiselle de Cressy does. Which begs the question, if she is the real Juliette de Cressy, and the contract is valid, if her father really was the Comte, then why didn't *he* pursue it when he was alive?'

Jean-Luc nodded approvingly. 'A good question, and one which you can be assured I asked her. She told me that her parents vowed never to return to France. For them, the country was tainted for ever by the Revolution, which is perfectly understandable—Paris must for them have been a city redolent with terrible memories. Her betrothal to the son of the Duke who was the Comte's best friend, was a sort of family myth, she said, a story that she was told, and that she believed to be just that—a story. It was only when her father died, and she discovered the marriage contract in his papers, that she realised it was true. His death, she openly admits, left her penniless, for his pension died with him.'

'So she came here, to Paris, to claim her only inheritance, which is you.'

He shook his head. 'According to her family tale, as Mademoiselle de Cressy tells it, the Duke sent his son to Cognac in the very early days of the Revolution, to keep him safe, to be raised in secret by a couple named Bauduin, until such a time as he could safely reclaim him. Only his best friend, the Comte de Cressy, was aware of the ruse, and the Comte and his wife fled France around about the same time as their daughter now claims I was sent to live in Cognac. And so it was to Cognac Mademoiselle de Cressy went first, when her father died. And from there, she claims, traced me to Paris—not a difficult thing to do, since my business originated in that town and the office which I keep there today bears my name. This element of her story is, obviously, the most dubious, and equally obviously, impossible to either prove or disprove.'

Sophia frowned, struggling to assimilate the tangle of implications. 'You think she had the contract and the baptism certificate in her possession, and that she targeted you to play the long-lost heir?'

Jean-Luc spread his hands on the blotter. 'I am one of the wealthiest men in France. My parents are dead. I have no siblings. And she believed me to be single.'

Sophia couldn't help thinking that when Jean-Luc himself was added to the equation, it was not surprising that Mademoiselle de Cressy had elected him. 'Do you think she has taken account of the risk that the real son of the Duc de Montendre might turn up in Paris?'

'It is fifteen years since Napoleon allowed the first of the *émigrés* to return, and almost four since the Restoration. If the fourth Duc and Duchess of Montendre had a son—something which is still not verified—and if he is still alive, I think he would have surfaced before now.'

Sophia shook her head. 'If it is a scheme, it is very ingenious, and Mademoiselle de Cressy must be very bold to attempt to carry it off.'

'Or very greedy.'

'Or very desperate.' As she had been. Desperate almost beyond reason, and utterly heedless of the consequences. Sophia's stomach churned at the memory, that constant feeling of panic as she searched for a solution, any solution to her own dilemma.

'Sophia?' Jean-Luc lifted his hand from hers as soon as she opened her eyes. 'You look as if you are about to faint. Can I get you some water?'

'No.' She clasped her hands tightly together, trying to disguise the deep, calming breaths she was being forced to take. Never again. That was why she was here, wasn't it? Never again. She could not afford to draw parallels between herself and this Juliette de Cressy, must not allow herself to imagine that they had anything in common. More than anything, she must not allow any sympathy for the woman to jeopardise her own future. 'I'm fine,' she said thinly. 'Perfectly fine. So, where do we go from here?'

He looked unconvinced by her smile, but to her relief, he did not question her further. 'Establish you as my wife, first and foremost. Introduce you to Mademoiselle de Cressy, which will be in in the presence of Maxime. Try to verify the existence of the lost heir. Try to verify the marriage contract. I have a very long list of tasks, which I will not bore you with.'

'I won't be bored. I'd like to help.'

He looked startled. 'Your role is to play my wife.'

'Doesn't a wife help her husband? What do you envisage me doing, if not that?'

Jean-Luc shrugged in a peculiarly Gallic manner. 'What does a wife do? I have never been married, perhaps you can tell me.'

Almost, she fell for the trap he had laid, but she caught herself just in time, and smiled blandly. 'Why don't you let me think about that, come up with a plan of my own, which we can discuss.'

He laughed, holding up his hands in surrender. 'Very well. I have made arrangements for you to visit the modiste to select your trousseau tomorrow. There will be time before that for me to introduce you to the household. The day after that, a tour of the *hôtel*. And after that, I am happy to hear your ideas. I do have a very competent housekeeper though, I'm not expecting you to burden yourself with household matters.'

'At the very least she will expect to take her instructions from me.'

'Do you know enough of such things to instruct her?'

'I would not offer if I did not.'

He leaned forward, resting his head on his hand to study her. 'I was expecting The Procurer to send me an actress.'

'I'm sure that there are some actresses capable of managing a household.'

'You are not an actress.'

She rested her chin on her hand, meeting his gaze, reflecting the half-smile that played on his lips. 'A better one than you, Jean-Luc, for your motives are quite transparent.'

'But I'm right, am I not? You are not an actress?'

'I have never been on the stage.'

'No, I thought this morning, when I first caught sight of you, that your beauty was too ethereal for the stage.'

She could feel herself blushing. She ought to change the subject, to break eye contact, but she didn't want to. 'I'm tougher than I look.'

'Of that I have no doubt. To come all the way to France, alone, even with the assurance of The Procurer's contract, demonstrates that you are made of stern stuff. And now you offer to help me with my search for the truth, too.' He reached over to cover her free hand with his. 'Beautiful, strong and brave, and clever too. I am very glad to have you on my side, Sophia.'

For some reason she was finding it difficult to breathe. 'We are both on the same side, Jean-Luc.'

'I like the sound of that. I am not so arrogant as to imagine that I and only I can resolve this mess, Sophia. It's true, I am accustomed to making all my own decisions, but one of the reasons they are sound is that I take account of other opinions. I would very much appreciate your help. Thank you.'

'Thank you.' No man had been interested in her opinions before. No man had been interested in her mind at all. That's why she was feeling this strange way, light-headed, drawn to him, even enjoying the touch of his hand on hers. Until he withdrew it, broke eye contact, and sat up straight.

'We are agreed then. However, before we begin the difficult task of proving that Mademoiselle de Cressy's story is without foundation, there is the small matter of convincing Mademoiselle de Cressy that we are married.'

'Can we do that? We don't have any paperwork. What if she tries to verify our story while you are trying to prove her story wrong?'

'My lawyer has informed her that we were married in England. As to paperwork, it hasn't occurred to her to ask, perhaps because she doesn't believe you exist.'

'So, when do you plan to produce me as evidence?'

'As soon as we can prove to ourselves that we can be convincing.'

Sophia pursed her lips. 'You think we need some sort of dress rehearsal?'

He smiled at that. He really did have a very nice smile. It was easy to return it. 'Tonight,' Jean-Luc replied. 'We will have dinner, just the two of us, with the attendant servants looking on. It will be a gentle introduction.'

'You think so? In my experience, servants are the group most difficult to fool.'

'Then we will know, after tonight, that if we can fool my household we can fool Paris society, and more importantly, Juliette de Cressy, yes?'

'Yes.' Was there a chance that Paris society would

contain any visiting English society likely to recognise her? She could not possibly enquire, for to do so would be to betray herself. But The Procurer would not have sent her here if she had considered it a possibility, would she, for then she would have failed in meeting Jean-Luc's terms, and The Procurer was reputedly infallible. She had to take confidence from that.

'What is worrying you, Sophia?'

She gave herself a little shake. 'Nothing. Save that we must concoct a love story, mustn't we? People will ask how we met, won't they, and how our whirlwind romance developed.'

'Whirlwind romance,' Jean-Luc repeated slowly. 'I am not familiar with that phrase, but it is—yes, I like it. We will come up with a love story tonight worthy of your Lord Byron,' he said, his eyes alight with mischief. 'We dine at seven. I took the liberty of sending your maid out for an evening gown. I had no idea whether you would have anything suitable with you. I hope you don't mind.'

'There was no need. I do possess an evening gown, you know.' Albeit a very shabby and venerable evening gown.

'Don't be offended, Sophia. Think of it as your stage costume,' Jean-Luc said. 'When you put it on, and not your own clothes, then it will help you, will it not, to play your part?'

How on earth had he guessed she had used that trick before? She had left her previous costumes behind in that house in Half Moon Street, but when she'd worn them—yes, it had been easier to pretend. 'Thank you,' Sophia said.

Jean-Luc got to his feet, holding out his hand. She took it. He bowed over it, kissing the air just above her fingertips. '*À bientôt.* I look forward to meeting my wife properly, for the first time.'

Chapter Three

The evening dress that Jean-Luc had thoughtfully provided was deceptively simple in its construction, consisting of a cream-silk underdress, and over it a very fine cream muslin cut in the latest fashion, the waist very high, the sleeves puffed, the skirts fuller than had been worn a few Seasons before. Gold-figured lace in a leafy design formed a panel in the centre of the skirt at the front and the back, with twisted gold and cream lace on the décolleté, and a matching trim on the hem.

'Ça vous plaît, madame?' the dresser asked Sophia, fussing with the bandeau which was tied around her hair.

'C'est parfait,' Sophia replied in her softly modulated French, twisting around in front of the mirror to take in the back view.

It was indeed perfect. The most expensive gown she had ever worn as well as the most chic. Madeleine, the dresser recently employed by Jean-Luc for his new wife, had excellent taste. She would have Madeleine accompany her, Sophia decided, when she visited the mediate tomorrow to select the remainder of her outfits. Or trousseau, as Jean-Luc had referred to it. She was extremely relieved that he was taking no hand in proceedings, though it was ludicrous to compare his taste with Hopkins's, and even more ludicrous to compare the costumes, or their purpose.

And even more ludicrous again to compare the two men, Sophia chided herself. She must not allow the past to influence her present behaviour. Tonight, she had to prove to Jean-Luc that she could play as his loving bride. Sophia rolled her eyes at her reflection in the mirror, as she held out her wrists to allow Madeleine to button her long evening gloves. Playing the bride was one thing. It was the loving part that was more problematic.

They might be dining *à deux*, but when the footman threw open the double doors and announced her, Sophia felt as if she was walking on to a stage set. The room was quite magnificent, the pale green walls extravagantly adorned with plasterwork and cornicing gilded with gold. Two mirrors, hung opposite each other at either end of the long room, endlessly reflected the huge dining table and its array of silver and gold epergnes in the form of galleons sailing along the polished mahogany surface like an armada. A magnificent chandelier cast flickering shadows through two tall windows and out into the now dark courtyard.

Two place settings were laid at the far end of the table. A fire roared in the white marble hearth. Jean-

Luc, austere in his black evening coat and breeches, set down the glass he had been drinking from, and came towards her. His hair was still damp from his bath, combed back from his forehead, almost blue-black in the candlelight. He was freshly shaved, his pristine shirt and cravat gleaming white against his skin. His waistcoat was also plain black, though the buttons were gold. He wore no other adornment, save his diamond pin, a gold fob, and the gold signet ring, but the very plainness of his attire let the man speak for himself, Sophia thought fancifully. A man with no need of ostentation. A man without pretension. A man who exuded confidence in himself. Looking at him, refusing to acknowledge the flicker of attraction which she determinedly attributed to nerves, Sophia concentrated on the other, much more important thing about Jean-Luc. He was a powerful and influential man, but he was not a man who would abuse that power. Her instincts told her so. She decided that in his case, she could trust them.

'*Ma chère.*' He took her hand, bowing over it, his kiss as it had been earlier, bestowed on the air above her fingers. 'You look ravishing.'

He was waiting, Sophia realised, to take his cue from her. She smiled up at him, the practised smile of one dazzled. 'Jean-Luc, *chéri*,' she said breathlessly, 'as ever, you flatter me.' Catching his hand between hers, she allowed her lips to brush his fingertips in the most featherlight of kisses. It was entirely for the benefit of the three—no, she counted four footmen, and the butler, who were standing sentinel around the room, but the touch, voluntarily given, seemed to take Jean-Luc by surprise. He recovered quickly enough, enfolding her hands in his, pulling her towards him, smiling down at her besottedly in a manner she thought must be every bit as practised as her own.

'I could not flatter you, no matter how hard I tried. The reality exceeds any compliment,' he said. And then more softly, for her ears only: 'Bravo, Sophia!'

He ushered her towards the table, releasing her hand only when the footman pulled her chair out for her. She thanked the man, though she knew it was the custom in such large households to pretend that servants were invisible, but this was one habit of her own she would not break, and so she thanked the butler too, when he poured her a flute of champagne, receiving a small, startled nod of acknowledgement.

The food began to arrive in a procession of silver salvers, each set down by a footman, the domed lid removed with a flourish by the butler, and the contents solemnly announced. *Artichauts à la Grecque; rillettes; saumon fumé; escargot Dijonnaise; homard à la bordelaise; côtes de veau basilic; lapin Allemande; daube Avignonnaise; asperge gratin; salade Beaucaire...*

Sophia's mouth watered. 'How did you know to order all my favourite foods?' she teased.

Jean-Luc laughed, shaking his head. 'The credit must go to my housekeeper.'

'*My* housekeeper.' Sophia laid her hand over his. 'I look forward to meeting her tomorrow. From the little I have seen of my beautiful new home, I can tell she is most efficient, but there are certain aspects that I wish to attend to myself, to ensure your maximum comfort, *chéri*,' Sophia simpered. 'I intend to make you proud to have me as a wife.'

'My love.' Jean-Luc lifted her hand to his mouth, pressing a theatrical kiss to her palm, his eyes dancing with laughter. 'I have all the proof I need that you will be a perfect wife, now that you are here.' He raised his champagne glass, touching it to hers. 'To us.'

'To us.' The champagne was icy cold. The food looked absolutely delicious, her mouth was already watering. 'I would like to start by sampling some artichoke, if you please, they look delicious. Are they from Brittany?'

Handing her the dish, Jean-Luc casting an enquiring look at his butler, who bowed and informed him that Madame Bauduin was quite correct, that these were the first of the season.

'I had no idea you were a horticulturist, my little cabbage,' Jean-Luc said.

Sophia sighed theatrically. 'You have forgotten my passion for the culinary arts.'

'In my passion for you,' he replied fervently, 'I forget everything else.'

He was almost as accomplished an actor as she. If she did not know better, she would think the heavy-lidded, heated look he gave her was genuine. She could feel her own cheeks flushing, and reminded herself that she did know better. 'Have a care, my love,' she chastised, 'we are not alone.'

Jean-Luc responded by raising his glass. 'I am counting the moments until we are.'

'Then it would be prudent to have some sustenance first,' Sophia said, completely flustered. 'May I have some snails please. I find them a great delicacy.'

He laughed at that, a low rumble of genuine amusement as he handed her the platter. 'An English woman who likes snails. I truly have captured a prize.'

'These are not just any old snails, these are *escargot Dijonnaise*.' Sophia inhaled the delicate aroma with her eyes closed. 'A red-wine reduction, with shallots and bone marrow, garlic and truffles. You are very fortunate to have such an accomplished chef.'

Jean-Luc helped himself to the remainder of the snails, popping one into his mouth. '*We* are fortunate,' he corrected.

'We are. Please pass on our compliments to…?'

'Monsieur le Blanc,' the butler informed her graciously. 'I will indeed, *madame*.'

'So it seems I have married a gourmand,' Jean-Luc said. 'Would you like to sample some of this veal?'

'I'd prefer the rabbit, please. I would not describe myself as a gourmand, but I am very fond of cooking. Though of late I have not—not had the opportunity to indulge my passion.' The truth was, she had more or less lived on air since her return to England. She looked up to find Jean-Luc studying her once more. She wished he wouldn't do that. She returned her attention to her plate, absentmindedly sipping on the dry white wine which had seamlessly replaced her champagne.

'Paris has some excellent restaurants these days.

We will sample some of them, if you wish?' Jean-Luc smiled at her eager expression. 'In my view, the best places to eat are the cafes, but the type of women who frequent them are not the sort I would wish my wife to mingle with. There is a place near Les Halles, where the oysters…'

Sophia continued to smile, but she no longer heard what he was saying. What would he think if he knew his faux wife was, in her previous life, exactly the sort of woman he would not wish her to mingle with? A cruel paradox. She cursed under her breath. Hadn't she decided to leave that other life behind!

'…a great many new restaurants opened in the last ten years,' Jean-Luc was saying. 'Run by chefs who once ruled the kitchens of the grandest houses, and who lost their livelihoods when their former employers lost their heads. Chez Noudet in the Palais Royal, for example.'

'I had not thought—but I suppose many people depended for their livelihoods on the aristocrats who went to the guillotine.'

'*Absolument.* My own—*our* own chef, Monsieur le Blanc, is one such case I am afraid. And this town house too is a *victim* of the Revolution, in a way. I purchased it four years ago, from the heirs of the noble owners. It had, like most of the abandoned *hôtels particuliers* here in St Germain and more especially across the river in Le Marais, been looted. Tomorrow, when I show you round properly, you will see there are still bullet marks in the walls of the courtyard. It may have been almost thirty years since the Bastille fell, but the scars of the Revolution are still there, if you know where to look.'

'But now King Louis is back on the throne, surely things have changed?'

Jean-Luc shrugged. 'Superficially, perhaps, but it is *plus ça change, plus c'est la même chose*, I think. Some of us, like me, roll our sleeves up and get on with the business of trading, in an effort to restore our country's finances—and in the process, the fine buildings of our city such as this one. And others, many of our so-called nobility, sit complacently on their rears and expect others to spoon feed them.'

Sophia was somewhat taken aback by this. Would her own heritage place her in the opposite camp to him? Or would her determination to make her own way in life on her own merits be her saving grace? It didn't matter, she told herself, what Jean-Luc thought of her, provided she fulfilled her contract. But the assertion didn't ring true. Despite herself, she found him intriguing, his opinions interesting, his determination to be only himself admirable. 'Are they all so idle, these returning exiles?' she asked. 'Can none redeem themselves in your eyes?'

'Oh, they do. A large part of my business depends upon their custom and patronage. The heirs of the *ancien régime are* some of my best customers and a valuable source of contacts and new clients throughout Europe. Unlike them, I do not distinguish between old money and new. I can be very *charmant* when I wish to be. As you know, *mon amour*.'

This last was said with a smouldering look, and ac-

companied by another kiss pressed to her palm. Sophia
wanted to laugh, only she felt that she couldn't breathe.
Though she still wore her evening gloves, though his
lips did not touch her skin, his kiss sent a *frisson* up her
arm. The alarmingly visceral attraction made her feel
all tangled up inside. It made her forget that she was
playing a part. She looked down at her empty plate,
at her full wine glass, with dismay. Lost in their conversation, she didn't recall what she had eaten, after
the rabbit. She didn't recall the wine changing from
white to red. She didn't recall the footmen clearing
the table, bringing in a second course of fruit and ices
and mousse.

'Will you be so very *charmant*, as to serve me some
of that lemon sorbet?' Sophia asked, extricating her
hand. 'And perhaps you should have some too?'

'But yes, you are right, something cooling is what
is required. In your presence...' Jean-Luc placed his
hand over his heart. 'I burn like a moth drawn inexorably to the flame.'

Sophia bit back her laughter. 'Then perhaps you
should not come any nearer. I have no desire to cause
you pain.'

'Indeed, that I do believe. For when you agreed to
marry me, *ma chère*, did you not prevent my heart
from breaking?'

The soulful look he gave her was too much. Sophia
chuckled. 'Enough,' she exclaimed in English. 'I am
not sure whether you are aping Lord Byron or one of
his creations, but...'

'You think this is a performance! *Madame*, you stab me to the heart.'

'I will, with this cake slice, if you do not stop. It is the most lamentable—oh!' Sophia covered her mouth, casting a horrified glance over her shoulder, where the butler was making a show of arranging several decanters on a tray. 'I'm so sorry,' she mouthed, 'I quite forgot.'

He smiled at her warmly, his voice too low for any of the servants to hear. 'And so made your performance all the more believable. You have a most infectious laugh, though you do not have call to use it very often, *hein?* And now I have made you sad, by saying so. I'm sorry.'

Sophia tried to shrug. 'It doesn't matter.' With years of practice of shielding her emotions, both from those she loathed and the person she loved most, she found it unsettling that this man, almost a stranger, seemed able to read her thoughts. She ate a spoonful of lemon sorbet. 'This is delicious.'

'And so the performance resumes,' Jean-Luc said under his breath, before turning to dismiss the servants, telling the butler to leave the clearing up until the morning. 'Now,' he said, as the door closed behind the last footman, 'you may relax. If that is possible, in my company. I merely made a comment, based on a supposition. I was not attempting to pry into your affairs.'

Sophia pushed her sorbet aside. 'I am perfectly relaxed. It is better that you know nothing of me or my past. Then you will not confuse me with the creature you have brought me here to play.'

'Sophistry, Sophia?'

Which it was. 'Talking of which,' she said, ignoring him, 'we said we would agree our cover story. How we came to meet, I mean, and fall headlong in love.'

'Our whirlwind romance.' A cursory glance at her, Jean-Luc thought, getting up to pour himself a brandy, would be sufficient for any man to understand perfectly why he would wish to marry her. In her travelling dress, he had thought her slender, but her figure, revealed by the flimsy fabric of the evening gown, was certainly not lacking in curves. She was the kind of enigma that unwittingly brought out the most primal instincts in men: innocent yet sensual; fragile yet resilient; a woman who yearned to be protected, and one who desired nothing but to be left entirely alone. Was it unwitting? Impossible, surely, for any woman to be so accomplished an actress.

'Would you care to join me?' he asked, holding the decanter aloft, unsurprised when she shook her head. A woman who liked to keep a clear head. And who was, he told himself, simply doing the job she had been brought here to do. It was not her fault that he was distracted by her. Though one would have to be made of stone not to be.

Jean-Luc set his brandy impatiently aside and resumed his seat. He had his faults, but woolly thinking was not one of them. 'Let us plot the arc of our romance. Obviously, we met in England,' he said. 'Fortunately, I was there on business in February for a few weeks. It was not long after I returned, at the beginning of April, that Juliette de Cressy found her way to my doorstep.'

'So we met and married in the space of a few weeks,' Sophia said.

'We met and fell deeply in love and married,' Jean-Luc corrected her. 'It was a *coup de foudre*, for both of us. One look was enough.'

'You don't really believe that can happen? That one would decide to bind oneself for ever to a complete stranger, on the basis of a—a heated glance, without knowing anything of them, or of their intentions?'

It was, in fact, a notion he had always derided, but the scorn in her voice made Jean-Luc contrary. 'Doesn't love triumph over all?'

'Love does not put food on the table, any more than it puts a roof over one's head. In fact, in my opinion, love is the flimsiest possible reason for anyone to marry.'

'What would you consider more sound reasons?'

'It is a matter of quid pro quo, isn't it?' Sophia answered, as if this was perfectly obvious. 'Pedigree, wealth, position, influence, these are the bulwarks of marriage contracts. Where there is a fair exchange, then affection may flourish, but there are so very few fair exchanges, aren't there, and in most cases, it is the women who has least to offer, and so must sacrifice the most.'

She was staring off into the distance, having almost forgotten that he was there. 'And even then,' she continued coldly, 'it is often not enough. Lies are offered in exchange for promises. Could any such marriage flourish? No,' she concluded firmly. 'No. It is best that it does not even begin. No matter what the consequences.'

Could she be referring to herself? Fascinated, Jean-Luc had a hundred questions he was burning to ask and frustratingly, he could not ask any of them. 'Fortunately, we do not have to concern ourselves with that, since our marriage is entirely fictitious,' he pointed out instead.

Sophia blinked. 'You're right. It is just that, a figment of our imagination. They say everyone loves a romance, don't they? Why should they question ours?' She pursed her lips. 'So, we met in England. I expect you bumped into me when you were shopping for some shirts, and I was looking to match some ribbons for a new hat. I dropped my packages. You picked them up. Our eyes met, and we knew, yes?'

Her smile was as brittle as the spun sugar which decorated the honey cake. Jean-Luc returned it, like for like. 'I took you to tea,' he said, 'and then the next day for a carriage ride in Hyde Park, and we met every day after that. A week before I was due to return to Paris, I realised that I could not return without you, and so I proposed on the spot.'

'And I accepted with alacrity, and we were married by special licence—that is something one can easily accomplish, if you have sufficient funds,' Sophia added, her smile turning bitter. 'But I could not travel with you immediately, because I had…' She faltered. 'Why could I not come with you?'

'Perhaps you had family, loose ends to tie up?'

'No, none. Recently I have lived alone.' She blushed.

'Oh, you meant did the Sophia who married you live alone. No, she wouldn't have, would she, a genteel un-married woman like that? She would have had a com-panion of some sort.'

Which made him wonder what sort of woman that made Sophia, if not a woman like that? She had been completely confident with his servants, and quite at home taking this long, elaborate dinner. Her manners, her general air of refinement, were completely natu-ral, the product of good breeding and habit. His butler had taken to her at once, and like his chef, Fournier was another of the aristocracy's old retainers. Who was she? He itched to ask, but it would be futile. Sub-tlety was the key to extracting any information from the real Sophia. For now, he must concentrate on the fictional one. 'So, this companion of yours, she has to be settled elsewhere, then?'

'In the country,' Sophia said, nodding. 'In a cottage of her own, in the village where she grew up. I could do that for her. As the wife of a wealthy man, it would be the least I could do. And I'd want to make sure she was comfortable too, wouldn't I, since she had been my companion for so long? So I remained in England, counting the days until we were reunited.'

'And I waited here in Paris, counting the days until you came.'

Sophia frowned. 'Why didn't you tell anyone though?'

'I did, I told Maxime, my oldest friend. It would have been he who drew up the settlements. I wanted to keep you a secret, to unveil you in person, knowing that when they saw you, everyone would understand in a moment why I fell so madly in love with you.'

'And your servants?'

'Our servants,' he reminded her. 'Have known of your arrival from the day after I received confirmation of your appointment, from The Procurer, but they won't have talked.'

'You are very confident of that.'

'I have every reason to be. I pay very well, and I do not suffer insubordination.'

'So your intention then, is to present me to Mademoiselle de Cressy...'

'As soon as possible, now that we have our story straight.'

She smiled tentatively. 'Do you ever shop for your own shirts?'

He laughed, as much with relief that their story had lifted her mood, as at her acumen. 'Never, if I can avoid it. What if I had business with Berry Brothers, the wine merchants in St James's Street—a company I do have dealings with, as it happens. Walking back to my town house, I'd go along Bond Street, wouldn't I, and that was when I bumped into you. There, does that work?'

'I think so. Will you relate it?'

'We shall tell it together, just as we did there.' Jean-Luc grinned. 'Although we'll have to add in a few loving glances.'

She clasped her hands together at her breast and fluttered her lashes at him. 'Cornflower blue, the ribbons I was trying to match. You said they were the colour of my eyes.'

He smiled. 'Ah no, I would not have said that, for your eyes are no such colour. I was wondering to myself only this morning, what colour are they, those beautiful eyes of my beautiful wife, for I would not call it turquoise or cornflower or even azure.'

'What then would you call it, my love?'

She was not laughing, but there was laughter in her eyes, just as there had been before, when she had forgotten to act. Heat prickled down his back and his belly contracted as desire caught him in its grip. 'I have no name for the colour, but it is the blue of the Mediterranean in the south on one of those perfect days, when the sun is almost white in the sky, and the sea glitters, and the heat makes your skin tingle.'

Sophia nodded. 'I know,' she said softly.

He leaned closer. She smelled of flowers, like an English springtime after the rain, but at the same time he could swear there was an intoxicating heat emanating from her. 'You want to dive in,' he said, 'to feel the cool lap of the waves soothe your burning skin.'

'Yes.' She smiled. 'Like gossamer, that is how I always imagined it would be.'

Their knees were touching. He could sense the rise and fall of her breasts, only inches away from him, but he couldn't take his eyes off her mouth. 'Gossamer,' Jean-Luc repeated. 'No, it is like silk. Like your hair,' he said, his fingers brushing one long strand which had escaped her coiffure, then trailing down her cheek, her neck, to rest on her shoulder.

He heard her sharp intake of breath and waited, but she did not move. 'Jean-Luc, is this still—are we acting?'

He could lie, but that would be a big mistake. No matter how beguiled he was by her, her scent, her curves, the allure of her mouth, he could not pretend in order to take advantage. 'I am not,' he said, releasing her. 'Not any more. I forgot myself. Forgive me.'

'There is nothing to forgive,' Sophia said, shaking out her skirts as she rose. 'We immersed ourselves in our roles rather too enthusiastically, that is all.'

He chose not to contradict her. 'You play yours to perfection. No one will doubt you. But it is very late, and we have a very full day tomorrow. Come, I will escort you to your chamber.'

He knew he wouldn't be able to sleep, with her so tantalisingly close on the other side of the locked door. But at least tonight, it would be this astonishing creature who was to play his wife who would keep him awake, and not that other, deluded creature, the reason Sophia was here in the first place.

Chapter Four

The next morning Sophia joined Jean-Luc in the breakfast room, attended by Fournier the butler, who seemed to have taken a shine to her, and two footmen. Afterwards, Jean-Luc introduced his wife to the rest of the household, who were lined up in serried ranks in the entrance hall. She lost count of how many there were, but her determination to speak to everyone, down to the youngest scullery maid, met with Madame Lambert the housekeeper's approval, as well as Jean-Luc's.

The remainder of the day was spent acquiring her trousseau. Clothes had never held much interest for Sophia—a happy circumstance since, for most of her life, there had been little money to spend on them. She had refused to spend any of their meagre allowance on her previous trousseau, telling Felicity afterwards, in an attempt to make light of the situation, that she'd shown remarkably foresight. As to the silks lavished on her by Hopkins, she never considered those anything but garish costumes for the performance she was required to put on.

This latest, and hopefully last, part she would have to play required costumes too, but of a very different kind. Seated in the plush receiving room of one of Paris's most exclusive modistes, aided and abetted with enthusiasm by Madeleine, her dresser, Sophia momentarily abandoned herself to the seductive delights of high fashion. Morning dresses, carriage dresses, promenade dresses, evening dresses and ball gowns were paraded in front of her, in a flutter of silk and satin and lace, crape and gauze, figured muslin, plain muslin, zephyr and sarcenet. There were underdresses and over-dresses. There were nightgowns and peignoirs, chemises and petticoats of the finest cambric, silk stockings, corsets trimmed with satin and that latest fashion in undergarments, pantaloons. There were pelisses and coats and tippets and cloaks, boots and half-boots, sandals and shoes. There were pairs of gloves of every colour to suit every occasion, and so many bonnets that Sophia quite lost track of their various appellations and purposes.

'No, I've seen a plethora,' she said after several dizzying hours. 'I require only a few dresses, perhaps one evening gown, certainly no ball gowns. There is no point—' She broke off abruptly. Neither the modiste nor the dresser must suspect that her role as Jean-Luc's wife was temporary. 'What I mean is,' she amended, 'I would like time to consider my future needs, and will purchase today only what I require to see me through the next few weeks.'

'But of course, a most sensible approach,' the modiste said, smiling approvingly. 'Might I suggest Madame Bauduin leaves it to her dresser and I to make the initial selection? *Madame* is very fortunate that she has the figure to carry off any garment.'

'Yes. Thank you—though please, only the bare minimum for now,' Sophia said, already wincing inwardly at the expense which Jean-Luc would be put to, despite the fact that he had insisted, before she set out this morning, that she considered only her requirements to dress as befitted his wife, and not the expense.

Entrusting Madeleine with the task, Sophia returned in the carriage to the *hôtel*, a brief and uncomfortable journey through the narrow streets, the view from the mud-spattered window giving her frustratingly little sense of the city she longed to explore. This would be her only chance to see Paris. Under the terms of their contract, she had agreed to disappear from both Jean-Luc's life and his country when her task was completed. How would he explain his short-lived marriage? It was not her problem, she told herself as the carriage halted outside the gates of the town house and the footman folded down the steps. But she was curious none the less, and finding her husband waiting for her on the terrace, took the opportunity to ask him.

'I will say that you have returned to England to nurse your former companion. Is that not a plausible explanation?'

'Very plausible.'

'Good! Then, when time has passed, I will say that you had come to the conclusion that you could not settle in France and wished to remain in England. It would mean painting you in an unfavourable light, though.'

'Tell people whatever you wish. It cannot be any worse than—'

She broke off abruptly. *What they say already.* So obvious a conclusion to that sentence that there could be no possible alternative. But Jean-Luc did not finish it for her. Instead he pressed her hand, and there was something in those dark brown eyes, sympathy or pity or—whatever it was, it made her feel uncomfortable, so she looked away, fussing with the strings of her reticule.

'Did you have successful shopping trip, *ma mie*?'

A finger under her chin gently forced her to meet his gaze. 'It depends how you define successful. I suspect I have spent a great deal of your money.' Which, she thought sardonically, was the goal of every woman in her former situation, though it was one she had never shared. One of the things, she suspected, that had kept her under Hopkins's protection for so long, and had made him most reluctant to give her up. She had a much more precious use for his largesse.

'Welcome back.' Jean-Luc was eyeing her quizzically. 'Do you realise you do that? Something I say, or some remark you make, sends you to a place far away. Not a very pleasant place, either, judging from your expression.'

And he had done it again, Sophia thought, irked with herself. The man saw far too much. She really must be more on her guard with him. She pinned on her brightest smile. 'I can think of no place more pleasant to be now, however, than Paris.'

* * *

A tour of the town house had been the plan for the next morning, but Jean-Luc had a change of plan. 'I thought you would prefer a tour of my city instead,' he said to Sophia over breakfast.

'Oh! I was thinking only yesterday that I would like nothing better,' she exclaimed, clasping her hands together. 'But...' Her face fell. 'As your wife, surely my priority should be to explore my new home?'

'Paris is your new home. And though I am undoubtedly biased, for me, Paris is the most bewitching and beautiful city in the world. I wish to introduce you to it.'

His thoughtfulness touched her. She executed a deep curtsy. 'Then your wish is my command, Husband.'

'To be perfectly honest,' Jean-Luc said, as he tooled the small, open one-horse carriage out of the stables and on to the main road, 'the best way to see Paris is on foot. Our streets are very narrow, for the best part, but I wanted you to get a sense of the layout of our city. This is the Rue de Grenelle, in the Faubourg St Germain district. As you can see, there are a number of *hôtels particuliers* here. Some of them have been abandoned since the Revolution, but the Restoration has seen many reclaimed and restored to their former glory.'

'What happened to the family who previously owned your *hôtel*?'

'The are domiciled in England, with no plans to return—they left long before the Terror. *Naturellement*, I know them because they buy my wine.'

'*Naturellement,*' Sophia said, with one of her genuine smiles. 'I presume your wine has an excellent reputation then?'

'Premier Cru, of course,' Jean-Luc said. 'This is the Rue du Bac, which is the main route from the Left Bank to the Tuileries. Many carriages with insignia travel down this street every day, as the King's nobles make their way to the palace to pay court.'

'What makes your wine the best?'

'Just between us, I would not claim that it is absolutely the best. Many of the châteaux keep their finest vintages for their own consumption. People buy my wine and cognac and port and madeira because they know they are buying quality, and that they will get the same quality every time. The Bauduin name is one of the most prestigious in the wine trade, not only in France but in all of Europe. I do not adulterate wine, pass off poor quality spirit for cognac, or put new wine in old barrels. Those who do business with me do so because they trust me.'

'A man of principle. I can see why you are so successful. Do you have offices here? Or warehouses? Perhaps you could tell me a little of your business? A wife should not be entirely ignorant of her husband's activities.'

'I thought women were not interested in commerce. Maman actively disapproved of my taking up the wine trade.'

'But why? You had to earn your living.'

'She would have preferred me to continue my education for a few more years. I attended a monastery school, which meant living away from home during term time.'

'Goodness, those kind of establishments don't come cheap.'

'Which explains why my education was terminated at the age of twelve. Maman's ambitions for me were beyond her means.'

'And that's when you went into the wine business?'

'And broke Maman's heart, though I loved the business from the start, the almost magical alchemy of turning grapes into fine wines. I was industrious and had a good head for figures. My employer took me under his wing. I became his protégé and it grew from there. The fact that I was so successful relatively early allowed me to look after my parents. With hindsight, it was clear to me that they had lived beyond their means when I was younger, spending money they didn't have on my education, for a start. At least I managed to ensure that their later years were spent living in comfort.'

'No wonder your father was proud of you.'

'Unfortunately Maman, to her dying day, saw it differently. She lamented the fact that I was involved in business and not some loftier endeavour. If she had lived to see me settled in the *hôtel*, then perhaps she would have finally come to terms with my choice of career.'

'She clearly loved you very much,' Sophia said, surprising him by laying her hand on his arm. 'Is your place of business near here?'

'No, it is on the river, much further downstream. I will take you, one day, on a tour of the *halle aux vins*.

It is a new building, one of the more practical improvements which Napoleon managed to complete, along with the quays and the water supply.'

'So he was not wholly a monster, then?'

'That is how the English would like us to view him—or more particularly, your Duke of Wellington,' Jean-Luc said wryly. 'Here, they say he was a man whom no one liked but everyone preferred. He was certainly better for France than those he replaced and, I think, better than the King who has replaced him, over there in the Tuileries, which you'll see in a moment, when we cross the Pont Royal. But if you look to the right you will see...'

'Notre Dame?' Sophia exclaimed as he pulled over from the traffic to allow her a better view. 'I thought so. It is one of the few landmarks I recognised when I arrived.' She gazed around her wide-eyed as they crossed the grey choppy channels of the Seine. 'It is a beautiful city, I can see why you love it. There is something about a river running through a city, isn't there—and all those bridges. So much life. So many people bustling about, from a myriad of different walks of life.'

There was that rare sparkle in her eyes, her real smile curving her mouth. 'You are not someone who prefers the pastoral serenity of the countryside then?'

'I've had very little experience of it.'

'So you have spent most of your life in London?'

'Yes.'

The smile was still there, but there was an immediate wariness in her eyes. Jean-Luc turned the subject. 'During the Revolution, when the churches were deconsecrated, Notre Dame was used as a vast wine cellar.'

'Really? It must have held a positive lake of wine. It would have been quite a sight. Did you ever see it?'

'I wish I had, but the church was restored to its proper use long before I came to Paris.'

'When was that?'

'The first time, I think I would have been about sixteen, so 1804. By then, my employer was becoming very frail, and was not fit to travel on business.'

'That is very young, to have to shoulder so much responsibility.'

'I relished it, and when he died, he left it all to me.'

And you turned wine into gold.'

Jean-Luc laughed. 'You could say that. Many people claim that a fine Sauterne, from Graves, near Bordeaux is like drinking liquid gold.'

'Bordeaux is not far from Cognac, I think?'

'You know that region?'

'I have passed through the city.'

'You have friends there, acquaintances? Is that how you come to speak French so well?'

'No.'

And just like that, she was lost again, though it was not bitterness this time he saw in her beautiful eyes, but sadness, a yearning that squeezed his heart with compassion. 'Sophia?'

She blinked, and it was gone, as if she had raised a stage curtain, to reveal a new backdrop. 'I—I spent some months in the south last year. Do you like art,

Jean-Luc? Is it true that the walls of the Louvre hang empty, now that many of the works that Napoleon appropriated have been returned to their rightful owners?'

And that, he understood, was the end of the matter. Sophia was the mistress, he was coming to learn, of the carefully crafted answer, followed by the carefully crafted deflection. So he turned the carriage on to the bridge, and he let the vista divert her thoughts. Which, not surprisingly, it did. She leaned forward, throwing questions at him and pointing, her eyes once again alight with interest.

Laughing, Jean-Luc pulled over on the other side of the Seine, to give her a view of both palaces. 'That is the Tuileries on the left. What you see in front of us is the Pavillon de Flore, the part of the Louvre which joins the Tuileries. The main entrance, which is the Arc de Triomphe du Carrousel is behind there. We can drive round to take a look, or we can go for a stroll in the gardens. Which would you prefer?'

'Oh, the gardens, if you please.'

'So you do like to walk, even though you are not a country maid?' Jean-Luc asked, making a show of finding a safe spot to leave the carriage. He helped her down, handing the reins and a coin over to an eager urchin. 'I know London pretty well. I have a *pied-à-terre* in Jermyn Street.' She smiled blandly. 'Near St James's Park,' Jean-Luc continued doggedly, 'and Green Park, which I prefer since it is less manicured and more open. What about you?'

'I am more interested in this park—these gardens,' Sophia said, and he gave up, offering her his arm, which she duly took after hesitating for only a moment. 'Are we likely to encounter any of your friends or acquaintances?'

'The chances are slim, at this hour, but in the evening, these pathways are full of people taking a constitutional. You will have noticed the air is considerably fresher here.'

'I confess I have,' Sophia said. 'Paris is not the sweetest smelling of cities,' she added, wrinkling her nose.

'That is putting it very politely, though in the years since I first made it my home, considerable improvements have been made, believe me.'

'And how long is that?'

'Ten years, since my father died.'

'Though you acquired your town house only four years ago.'

'I lived in lodgings before that, in a much less salubrious location down by the docks. My house was very far from grand when I bought it. You'll see when I show you around, that there's still a deal of work to be done. One wing is still almost entirely derelict. I'd be interested to know what you think should be done with it.'

'You wish my advice? For all you know, I might have execrable taste.'

'On the contrary, I know you have impeccable taste. You married me, did you not?'

Sophia smiled up at him uncertainly. 'I hadn't realised we were playing our allotted parts, but you're right, when we are in public, it is best we make a habit of it.'

'I was not acting, I was simply making a joke. I'm sorry if it was ill judged.' Jean-Luc urged her over to a wooden bench set off the main path, covering both her hands in his. 'You are supposed to be my wife. My much-loved wife. Whose opinions matter to me.'

'I know. It is just that Paris is so very beautiful, and you have been so kind as to show it to me. I suppose in my excitement I forgot that it was actually your notional wife Sophia you were sharing with and not me.' She managed a very feeble smile. 'I won't forget again.'

'But I want you to forget,' he said. 'When you forget, when you relax and are yourself, that is when you are most convincing because your true nature shines through. I prefer you when you are yourself, Sophia.'

'Oh. Do you really?'

'Why wouldn't I?'

'I don't know. I'm here to play your wife, you didn't hire me to be myself. I'm not even sure that I know how—' She broke off, biting her lip.

'To be yourself?' She did not answer, but she did not contradict him. She looked so very lovely, and so very vulnerable, on the verge of tears yet determined not to give way to them. What had happened to her? What dark secret was she hiding?

'Who is Sophia?' he asked, gently teasing. 'I will start with the obvious. You are a breathtakingly beautiful woman. When you arrived on my doorstep the other day, I thought, this Procurer, she is a sorceress, for she has conjured up the woman of my dreams.'

She blushed. 'That's ridiculous.'

Jean-Luc shook his head, smiling. 'It is the truth,

but it is the formidable person behind that captivating face who truly interests me.'

'There is nothing remotely formidable about me.'

'I'm afraid I'm going to have to disagree with you. You are intelligent. You are perceptive. You are a most excellent listener. You are brave—no, don't interrupt me when I'm complimenting you. Consider this, Sophia—how many women would have the courage to do as you have done, to come to France alone, to take on this role—'

'A great many, if they were offered such a large fee,' she interrupted drily.

'Though very few I think, would be up to the part while you—not only have you embraced it, you have offered to do more, to help me. So that is another thing about you—you like to be useful. You have an enquiring mind. There—that is a good many things I know about you already, after only a brief acquaintance. But enough to state with certainty that I do indeed like you, Sophia.'

Her fingers tightened around his. 'I, on the other hand, don't know what on earth to make of you, but I find I like you too, Jean-Luc, and can say so with equal certainty. It seems such an odd thing to say to a man I barely know, but I do.'

They had drawn closer to each other on the bench. Her knee was brushing his. Her smile lit her eyes. Her skin was flushed with the late spring sunshine. Around them, people strolled, the trees rustled softly in the breeze, the birds sang, and yet for this one perfect moment they were entirely alone. 'If you really were my wife,' Jean-Luc said, 'if you were my heart's desire, just arrived from England, I would kiss you right now.'

Her eyes widened. Her lips parted. 'Here? In a public park?'

'This is Paris. Public parks are designed expressly for the purpose of kissing.'

'Then it is a pity that we are unable to put this unique design feature to the test.'

Dear heavens, was there anything so tempting. But she could not possibly be inviting him to—though she was leaning towards him, and when he dipped his head towards her, she did not pull away, and her lips were so tempting. With a supreme effort of will, Jean-Luc pulled himself back, cursing under his breath. She was only just beginning to trust him. He pressed a very poor substitute of a kiss to the back of her gloved hand. 'I think we'd better resume our walk.'

They strolled the length of the Tuileries Gardens and back, Jean-Luc describing the many changes he had witnessed in the last ten years. He was talking to set her at ease, she knew that, requiring only that she nod and smile occasionally, for which Sophia was extremely grateful. She couldn't fathom her contrary reaction. Jean-Luc was kind and thoughtful and understanding. He *liked* her, for goodness sake. She should be happy, not tearful. She was in Paris, living in the most luxurious of town houses, with a charming man who made no demands on her save that she cling to his arm and act the besotted wife. When set against what had been expected of her before, this was—well, there was simply no comparison. So why was she so emotional? Why couldn't she draw a clear line between herself and the performance he expected of her? Why, indeed, had she volunteered to cross that line, and to play significantly more of a role in his life than he expected?

Because he *liked* her! Because she *liked* him. Because he didn't expect or demand more than she was prepared to give. Because he seemed genuinely interested in her, her thoughts, her ideas, her opinions. Because, in essence, he was quite utterly different from any other man she had ever met. Would it be so wrong of her to do as he bid her, to be herself with him? If the result was that she was a more convincing, then that was to be welcomed. Of course she could never confide in him, her shameful history would revolt him, but if she could find a way to do as he asked, and be more herself—yes, it was a very attractive proposition.

'What have I said to make you smile?'

And Jean-Luc, Sophia thought, allowing her smile to broaden, was a *very* attractive man. 'I'm in Paris,' she said, 'reunited with my dashingly handsome husband, and the sun is shining. I have every reason to smile!'

He stopped abruptly and pulled her into his arms. 'Since, as you rightly point out, we are in Paris, the sun is shining, and I have been reunited with my beautiful wife, there is only one thing to be done.'

Her pulses leapt. She couldn't breathe. 'What is that?'

He dipped his head, blotting out the sun. And then in full view of the passers-by, he kissed her gently on the lips.'

It was the softest of kisses. Just the merest whisper of his lips on hers, but it made her head spin, forced her to cling to him, lest her knees give way, for she felt as if her bones had melted. And then the sound of an admiring whistle pierced the air, and it was over. Jean-Luc let her go, looking somewhat sheepish. 'Believe it or not, I have never done that in public before.'

'Believe it or not, neither have I. Shall we carry on walking, before we attract a full-blown round of applause?'

'We can go through the palace entrance here into the central courtyard, if you like. From there you can get a sense of the vast scale of the palace and the Louvre.'

'As you wish,' Sophia said compliantly. Unquestioning deferral was one of the earliest lessons Hopkins had inculcated in her. But she was no longer Hopkins's creature, and Jean-Luc did not deserve to be mentioned in the same breath, even if it was only in her thoughts. 'Actually,' she amended, 'I'd much prefer to see more of your beautiful city.'

'Your wish is my command.'

Jean-Luc smiled. By expressing her own wishes she had pleased him. Which was, Sophia thought as she allowed him to help her into the carriage, a truly novel experience.

The quay they drove along was very busy, forcing Jean-Luc to concentrate on his driving as they made slow progress, the Seine in contrast running at speed on their left, a muddy brown colour with grey choppy waves, and like the Thames, crowded with boats, barges and sculls. Despite this fascinating vista, Sophia was drawn to the view directly beside her of her erstwhile husband, his perfect profile, his disturbingly attractive person.

Very attractive, and very disturbing. She could easily have avoided kissing him, but she had not wished to. She, who had never in her life wished for such a thing had astonishingly, wanted Jean-Luc to kiss her. It was the way he looked at her. It was not lascivious. It was not covetous. It was not even that horrible, assessing kind of look of one weighing the odds as to her likely receptiveness, which she had always found revolting. It was a different kind of look altogether. As if he saw her—not the exterior which was her fortune and her misfortune, but the person inside. No man had ever looked at her in that way before. No man had ever made her feel this way before either. Tangled up inside, confused. Edgy, though not nervous but—anxious? No, not that either. Jumpy? She couldn't describe it. It was like looking forward to something while at the same time worrying it might not happen.

'The Place Louis Quinze,' Jean-Luc said, rousing her from her reverie and indicating a huge open space, dominated at the far end by two palaces. 'Or if you like, the Place de la Concorde, though you probably know it better as the Place de la Révolution.'

Sophia gazed at the innocuous civic space in horror. 'This is where the King was guillotined, and Queen Marie Antoinette?'

'And in the end Robespierre too, the man responsible for so much of the bloodshed—or at least the man who is most often blamed. Legend has it that for years afterwards, animals refused to cross the exact spot where the guillotine once stood.'

Sophia shuddered. 'I'm not surprised. Do you think this is where the Duc and Duchesse de Montendre met their end?'

His eyes were fixed on the *place*. She thought he had not heard her, but the tightening around his mouth betrayed him. 'It is probable.'

A tiny shake of the head followed, a dismissal of whatever grim thoughts had momentarily possessed him. 'We are heading into the Champs-élysées now. Some of the biggest of the noble palaces are near here, over on the Rue du Faubourg Saint-Honoré. They put my humble little *hôtel* to shame, but you can't see anything, they are all hidden behind imposing walls. One of them, I believe, belonged to the Montendre family. I have yet to ascertain which, since so many have changed hands in the last few years.'

'Oh, so you have already started your investigations? '

'A tentative start, not much more. Tell me,' Jean-Luc said, nodding at the road ahead, 'what do you think of that?'

'I have no idea,' Sophia said, eyeing the huge construction. 'What is it?'

'The new Arc de Triomphe. It was to be Napoleon's biggest tribute to himself. As you can see, he didn't get to finish it.'

'Are there any plans to complete it?'

Jean-Luc laughed sardonically. 'I doubt it's a priority for the King, and as for the people—Paris has far too many other urgent needs.' He drove in silence as they travelled the short distance towards the abandoned mass of stone covered in scaffolding, and once again pulled over. 'The Russian forces camped here during the occupation. Those were very dark days for Paris— to have foreigners claim our city—desperate times. It is a relief to finally put them behind us.'

'You really do love this city, don't you?'

'Yes. Though I have houses in London, Lisbon and Madrid, though I was raised in the south-west, it is Paris which is my home. I felt it here,' he said, touching his heart, 'from the first time I set foot here.' He consulted his watch, barking in annoyance. 'I'm sorry, but I must take you back now. I have urgent business to attend to.'

'Of course. We are supposed to be married, I would not expect my husband to sacrifice his business for me.'

'Then you will find that your expectations are aimed far too low. If I did not abandon my business—at least temporarily—for such a lovely wife, then I would be a fool. This meeting I have arranged, is to hand over some responsibilities to my secretary. Something which he believes long overdue, and will be delighted to accept.'

'But you must not—for my sake, you must not...'

'But I must. For my sake as much as yours, *ma belle*. Mademoiselle de Cressy must be utterly convinced of the veracity of our union. I promise you, Sophia, it will be no hardship at all to be seen to devote myself to you.'

The look he gave her made her skin heat. It made

her pulses jump. He was a very good actor, she reminded herself. Was he acting? 'And I, to you,' Sophia said, allowing herself the briefest of caress, her gloved hand on his cheek, her fingers fluttering along his jaw. He inhaled sharply. Was he going to kiss her again? She didn't care if he was acting or not. She wanted his mouth on hers. A kiss. Such a simple thing to desire, wasn't it?

He caught her hand. He pulled her closer. 'Sophia?'

Her hesitation was fatal. He sat up. Why had he asked her! If he had simply kissed her! She was well and truly hoist by her own petard and now it was too late to change her mind. When her body had stopped this strange clamouring, she would be glad she had not. 'There is a gap in the traffic,' she said, pointing sightlessly and stupidly, for Jean-Luc had proved himself an excellent driver.

But though he drew her a look—one of *those* looks—he said nothing, merely picked up the reins and carefully edged back out on to the thoroughfare.

Chapter Five

Jean-Luc's business meeting kept him away from the *hôtel* until long after dinner, and in the morning he left apologies for his absence once more. Deciding that she had better make a start on assuming her role as chatelaine, Sophia arranged to meet with the housekeeper for the long overdue tour of her new abode, then took a simple breakfast in her bedchamber of coffee and buttered baguette while she compiled her own list of domestic tasks. Jean-Luc was not the only one with a methodical mind.

Just as she was perusing her limited wardrobe, Madeleine burst into the room followed by a small army of maids bearing a very large number of boxes. 'Your trousseau has arrived, Madame Bauduin,' she announced.

Sophia looked on aghast as the boxes began to pile up in the bedchamber. Madeleine, with an uncanny knack for divining the contents of each box, directed gowns, hats, shoes, undergarments and overgarments into separate piles. 'Now, *madame*, we will select a

gown for you to wear this morning, and then I will
have all this put away—unless you wish to inspect…'

'No! There is no need.' She had no ambition at all to
see this mountain of unnecessary expenditure spread
out for her delectation and delight. She couldn't imagine what Jean-Luc would think when faced with the
bills. 'Not at the moment,' she said more temperately,
realising that she had spoken sharply. 'I have promised
to spend the morning with Madame Lambert. Madeleine…'

'*Oui, madame?*'

'How many gowns, exactly, did you order in the
end?'

Her dresser frowned as she did a quick mental tally.
'Morning gowns, seven, and the same of afternoon
dresses. Promenade dresses, four and four walking
dresses. Evening gowns, six, I think.'

'Twenty-eight dresses?' Sophia said faintly.

'*Oui, madame.* We can always order more if you are
concerned that is insufficient for your needs?'

Sophia poured herself the dregs from the coffee pot
and swallowed them. 'I suspect it will be sufficient for
the rest of my mortal days!'

Three hours later, Sophia entered the un-renovated
wing of the *hôtel* alone. Though Madame Lambert had
been very unforthcoming with her at first, by the end
of the extensive tour of the house she was fairly certain
that she had passed whatever examination the housekeeper had set her. The years managing house for her
father had stood her in good stead—the early ones, at

least, when there was still sufficient of Mama's money left to allow her to keep the house as it had been when Mama was still alive. Even then, their London town house had been nothing compared to this. Modest, is how Jean-Luc had referred to it yesterday, and she supposed it was compared to those on the Right Bank, or even compared to some of the grander houses she had visited with her father, when he was obliged to bring her along as his dining companion. Though none of those London houses had the spectacular light, the effortless sense of space of this house. None had those tall windows, the doors which opened on to the courtyard which, in summer, brought the outdoors inside.

Sunshine. Blue sky. Paris was not so very far away from London, yet even here, the air was different, and in the south...

A tear tracked down her cheek unchecked. Felicity had loved that fierce southern sunshine. 'I can feel it doing me good, heating my bones,' she used to say. She had a way of tilting her face up, as if she was drinking in the sun's rays, willing them to heal her. Her skin had become quite tanned. 'No respectable man will offer for me now,' she had said, laughing. 'I look like a peasant girl.'

She was always teasing. Always talking as if there was a future, as if there would be a time when marriage might feature, when tanned skin would then be an issue. She had the ability to live only in the present. Only occasionally could Sophia see that it was not a talent, but a hard-learned lesson. Only occasionally did she catch a glimpse of the other Felicity, the little sister who was terrified, and who tried so hard never to show it. So much life. And then, abruptly, none.

Tears cascaded down Sophia's cheeks. It was so unfair. So horribly unfair. She missed her dreadfully. It had been almost ten months now, but the pain felt so raw. She so rarely permitted herself to grieve. Since returning to England, all her efforts had been to survive without further compromising herself. Now here she was, on a beautiful day in a beautiful house in a beautiful city, and suddenly it overwhelmed her. With a sob, Sophia dropped her head on to her hands and gave way to a long overdue bout of tears.

It left her drained but oddly rejuvenated. She knew from experience that tears left no trace on her skin or eyes, a fortunate quirk of nature that had stood her in good stead many times in the past. She tucked her soggy handkerchief into the pocket of her gown. Enough tears! She had always prided herself on being firmly in control of her emotions. Those confrontations with her father had been very specific, always caused by the same contentious issue, and it had never been difficult to be anything other than patient with Felicity, who was adept at pretending all was well even when she was desperately unwell.

Jean-Luc would say that was a very English thing to do, but when it came to Felicity, Sophia's only motive had ever been a desire not to upset her sister by not being equally stoic. Pretence had become second nature to her, something else which had stood her in very good stead during the travails of her initial downfall and then the long endurance test which was her—did one call it a career?

She had never considered using this term before, and it amused her, in a dark way. Her father's career—his illustrious career, as he'd always referred to it—had brought his family to the brink of bankruptcy and left his daughters in abject poverty. Yet her choice of *career*—yes, she could, if she was so inclined, have labelled it illustrious with veracity. She had been successful. She had achieved what she needed to. It had been she who had instigated it on her own terms and ended it in the same way. Had she chosen to resume it on her return to London—ah, but she had not countenanced that. She would not live in shame ever again. Desperation had forced her down paths she would never have previously considered. The Procurer had provided a route to salvation.

She wandered over to the cracked mirror above the fireplace. The morning gown Madeleine had selected for her was an unusual colour of forest-green sprigged with white flowers, the hem weighted with white cotton lace. It was simply but beautifully cut, with a round neck and tightly fitting sleeves which tapered down to the wrist. It was not a colour which Sophia would have chosen, and as such, it quite transformed her. She was no longer any of her old selves, but someone quite new. Madame Bauduin was a confident woman, she decided, eyeing her reflection. Confident in her appearance. Confident in her ability to take up her new role. Confident in her husband's affections.

Her husband. Jean-Luc. It had become second nature for her to be on her guard with men, it should be a simple matter, especially since she had known him less than a week, but for some reason she was struggling. For a start, she felt as if she had known him for a great deal longer. The effect, she supposed, of how much he had been forced to tell her, but also the effect of how much he seemed to understand her, despite her resistance to telling him anything. And if she were being honest, she wasn't so resistant. In fact, quite the opposite. She had found herself on several occasions wanting to confide in him. And twice now, she had wanted to kiss him.

Sophia shivered. Not in fear, but in anticipation. Twenty-six years old, and she had never been kissed. Not properly. There had been kisses, but they had been perfunctory to say the least, a token prelude to another act, with no interest in her response. Just as well, since she had none, other than the urge to shield her mouth with her hand. Jean-Luc's almost kiss had not been token. It had been given—or not given!—in anticipation of nothing more than a kiss.

A kiss which made no demands. What would a kiss like that be like? She shivered again. No, not a shiver but a *frisson*. A word she'd never understood before. *Frisson*. Sophia closed her eyes and wrapped her arms around herself. She could almost feel the brush of his leg against hers. The scent of him, a clean scent, but with an undertone of—of Jean-Luc. His eyes would be dark with desire that she would pretend was not an act. His lids would be heavy, his lashes thick black, no man should have lashes so beautiful. His breath would be soft on her cheek. And his mouth…

'Ah, here you are!'

Sophia jumped. Her eyes flew open. Heat flooded her cheeks. He could not literally read her thoughts, she reminded herself. 'Jean-Luc. I did not expect…'

'My apologies. It took more time than I anticipated, but I am pleased to say that my business affairs are now temporarily in the capable hands of my secretary. I am now, as they say, all yours.'

He strode towards her, his hands outstretched. It was perfectly natural to allow him to clasp hers. As for his smile, it would be a very beguiling smile, were she the type to be beguiled, which she was not. Still, there was no harm in smiling back, was there, nor in proffering, as any newlywed wife in love with her husband would, a welcoming kiss.

'Sophia?'

This time she did not hesitate. 'Husband,' she said, disingenuously, closing the gap between them. 'It is lovely to see you.' And then she stood on her tiptoes, and she kissed him.

The touch of her lips on his made all thoughts of resistance flee. Husband, she had called him, Jean-Luc thought hazily, so this was part of their charade, though there was no one around and—and he didn't care. His senses were swimming at the nearness of her, at the light, fresh scent of her. And her mouth. Only then did he become aware that she was not actually kissing him, but simply pressing her lips to his. He could feel her breath, shallow and fast. Keeping one of her hands in his, he pulled her to him, wrapping his other arm around her waist, angling his head to kiss her properly. Her lips parted just a fraction. He kissed her, little darting kisses, all the way along her full top lip. She sighed, relaxing in his arms. He tried again, to kiss her properly. Her lips clung to his, but...

She was nervous, that was it. He slid his hand up her back, caressing the delicate skin on the nape of her neck, and fluttered more delicate kisses on her lips, until she followed his lead, giving fluttering, butter-fly kisses in return. He caught one of them, his mouth moulded to hers, and moved gently. She followed his lead this time, opening to him, and he deepened the kiss just a little, ignoring the sudden clamour of his senses, the stirring of his erection, coaxing her into a response, concentrating on coaxing her a little bit more, and a little bit more, until she was kissing him, her free hand clutching at his shoulder for balance.

Her kisses were so delightful that Jean-Luc stopping thinking, losing himself in her embrace for a long, breathless moment, until the tiny gap between them became an agony to maintain, and the desire to deepen the kiss from desire to passion became almost irresist-ible. Almost.

He sighed deeply, reluctantly, and let her go. Her lids were heavy over her eyes, her skin flushed, her lips—*mon Dieu*, he had better not look at her lips or he would fall into kissing her again. 'Sophia?' It took a moment for her to focus. 'I thought that you wanted—did I misunderstand?'

She shook her head. Her smile was faltering. 'No, I wanted—you didn't misunderstand.'

Husband, she had called him. Had she been acting the innocent? He could not believe it. And yet there had been a peculiar naivety to her kisses. But The Procurer would surely never have sent him a virgin to play his wife. Unless—was this the reason for the terms she had imposed? Impossible. But if it was true, he had no designs on taking her innocence.

'Was it an act, Sophia? I need to know, because I am confused. The kisses,' he elaborated, for now she looked just as confused as he. 'Were you playing the innocent, the wife who had not yet been kissed or...?'

'Why do you ask?'

She looked so vulnerable, he was tempted simply to tell her it didn't matter. But it did. He had to understand, no matter how painful the conversation. 'Because if it was not an act,' Jean-Luc said gently, 'then I won't do it again. It would not be right.'

'Why not?'

'Because I am not the kind of man to take advantage of a woman's innocence. I thought that this—this fear you have of my touch, I assumed it was because some other man—but if it is because there has been no other man at all, then I will not take advantage of this situation, to be the first.'

She was quite ghostly pale now, her beautiful mouth trembling. He longed to pull her into his arms and to comfort her, though for what, he had no idea. 'I'm not an innocent. It is just that I...'

He waited, holding his breath, expecting her to

change the subject, but to his surprise, she lifted her head to meet his gaze, reached out to touch his hand. 'You are a truly honourable man, Jean-Luc. I am not—I don't know if I have been unfortunate, but I have not met anyone like you before. I am not an innocent. You are not taking advantage of me.'

He took her hand in his. She did not resist, clutching at him as if she were drowning, and again, he had to fight his urge to pull her into his arms, to keep her safe, somehow, to protect her. He knew it was simply a reaction to her appearance. He'd noticed it the first day, hadn't he, that combination in her, of fragility and steeliness. It was simply that the vulnerable side of her was at the forefront at the moment. She didn't need him to protect her.

'Yet your kisses,' Jean-Luc persisted, 'were not the kisses of a woman experienced in the art of lovemaking.'

'I'm sorry to have disappointed you.'

He was surprised into a gruff laugh. 'I did not mean to imply they were not delightful. Merely unpractised.'

'Kissing is not—was not—I have limited experience.' Her colour had returned. 'Unlike you, I think?'

'How am I to answer that? I am not a gentleman but I am...'

'An honourable man.' Sophia astonished him by lifting his hand to her lips, pressing a brief but fervent kiss to his palm. 'Truly honourable.'

Their gazes were locked. The air around them seemed to sparkle with tension. He was breathing, he must be breathing, but it felt as if he was not.

Sophia raised his hand to her mouth again. This time her kiss lingered. 'I may be inexperienced, but that is not to say I would not be amenable to repeating the experience. Out of curiosity, you understand.'

He was hard. She had done nothing more than kiss his hand, and he was hard. 'Sophia, there is nothing I want more than to...'

'Then please,' she said, with a smile that sent fresh blood surging to his groin, 'do.'

He did, and this time Sophia gave herself over to the kiss, because this time it felt like another step in their conversation, and in that conversation she had felt herself sparkle. Like the blood fizzing in her veins as Jean-Luc kissed her, those fluttering, teasing kisses were like an invitation. She accepted, pressing little kisses back, and then following his lead to open her mouth, shaping her lips to his and tasting him. She wrapped her arms around his neck, tilting her head to allow him to kiss her more deeply. And then his tongue touched hers, and there it was again, a *frisson*, the most delightful sensation. His tongue touched hers again and she liked it. She liked it very much. And then the kiss deepened further, and there was heat, and tingling and his hand feathering up and down her spine, and his hair was silky soft where her fingers tangled in it, and their kisses made her weak, so that she leaned against him, and brushed against the unmistakable evidence of his desire, and when that happened, her body instinctively froze and went limp. Jean-Luc released her instantly. 'Sophia?'

She could not meet his gaze. What could she say? Her throat was dry. She cleared it. She shook her head. 'Please, don't be angry with me.'

'I am not angry, I am confused.'

She nodded. Tears were horribly close. She would *not* cry. 'Understandably.'

He sighed. 'At least you admit I have cause, even if you won't explain it.'

'I can't.'

He took a step forward, his hand raised as if he would touch her cheek, but clearly thought the better of it. 'I have had lovers. To make love, it is something that two people share, two people enjoy. If you wished me to stop kissing you, you only had to say. And if it was more than that, if you thought for a moment that because you asked me to kiss you, I would have demanded more...'

'I didn't.' Mortified, she forced herself to meet his gaze. 'I promise you, that's not what I thought.'

He was not angry. It was worse than that. There was pity in his gaze. 'You say that, but it's not how you acted.' He made a helpless gesture. 'You say you trust me. You say that you truly believe that I am an honourable man. But your actions reflect none of those assertions.'

'You are going to send me away,' Sophia said flatly. 'I've failed at the first hurdle, that's what you're trying to tell me.'

'For someone so very intelligent, you can be very foolish. Kissing is not part of your remit and we would probably both do well to remember that. I have no fault to find with you playing the role of my wife, and I am certain that when you meet Mademoiselle de Cressy tomorrow...'

'Tomorrow!'

'Tomorrow, we will easily persuade her that we are married.'

'We will, I will make certain of it.'

'Good.' He waited, but she had nothing she could think to add to this, and so to her utter relief, he shrugged, turning away. 'Well then, Madame Bauduin, perhaps you will share your wifely opinions on what should be done with this dilapidated wing of our home.'

They made their way through the connected rooms of the empty wing. Sophia, who had obviously inspected them already, had a host of ideas, which she recited from a notebook. They were excellent ideas, Jean-Luc thought approvingly. As he had suspected, she had impeccable taste, and what's more it chimed with his own, in her preference for maximising light, for muted colours, and for a lack of clutter. He listened. He encouraged her. He volunteered ideas of his own, which complemented hers. He occasionally disagreed with her. He gave the impression that his full attention was on the household renovation they were discussing, but mostly, he was studying her and trying to make sense of what had occurred between them.

The simplest solution would be to forget it. She was here to play his wife, he had no doubt that she would make an excellent job of it, but she was not actually his wife. He had the tangle of his own past to unravel without concerning himself with hers. But he was already far more intrigued than he should be. Was it precisely because she was so grudging with her history? What did he know of her? She was clearly well born. Her mother died young, her father died relatively recently. Most likely he had left her in straitened circumstances, else she would not be here. But why was she not married? She was twenty-six, well past what society would deem to be an eligible age. Had she devoted her life to her father? Was that likely, given that she admitted to having a difficult relationship with him? Surely marriage would have been preferable, a convenient escape route. And if not, when he died—even if she had no dowry, a woman like Sophia could not have lacked offers.

Perhaps she had been married. Why hadn't that occurred to him before! There had been a strange comment when they were concocting their own story over dinner on the second night—what was it she had said? Something about lies offered in exchange for promises. But hadn't she implied that such a marriage was better avoided? Or had he misunderstood her? Yet she had admitted she was not an innocent. So she had been married then, and she regretted it—yes, that made sense. Her marriage had been unhappy. That would explain a great deal. Except the kissing. Or perhaps it did. A loveless marriage, such as the English gentry were reputed to routinely make, based on bloodline and on land and on influence. The consummation of such a marriage would be—Jean-Luc baulked at trying to imagine such a union. Not lovemaking, but breeding. *Sacré bleu*, that would indeed explain a good deal.

Then why not admit to it? She had nothing to be ashamed of. It could be, he supposed, that she wanted to put it behind her, to forget all about it, or even pretend it had never happened. Small wonder that her aim was independence. Smiling, nodding in agreement with her suggestion that this salon would make an excellent library or snug, Jean-Luc felt quietly satisfied that he was beginning to understand her. Whether these insights explained her kisses—now that was a very different matter.

Why had she kissed him? Husband, she had called him. Was she practising? But there would no call to kiss in such a way in public. Why had she broken her own rules? Was it a simple matter of attraction? She could be under no illusions about his desire for her, but hers for him? Any other woman, he would be happy to accept such a simple explanation. But Sophia…

'What have I said to amuse you?' she asked.

Jean-Luc shook his head. 'It is nothing you have said. I was just thinking that you are like no other woman I have ever met.'

'That is why you married me, remember.'

Which, in Sophia's language meant, let us not discuss the matter. Jean-Luc smiled in token acknowledgement. If his little paradox was more relaxed playing Madame Bauduin, then so be it. 'You are perfectly correct, *ma belle*, that is exactly why I married you.' He took her arm, leading her into the last of the rooms.

'Jean-Luc, why aren't you married—I mean why aren't you really married?'

'I told you, I have been too absorbed in my business. And I have never met the right woman.'

'Yes, but you know it's quite unusual for a single man to purchase a house like this, unless he is thinking of settling down.'

'That is a very good point. We will tell people that it is evidence that I was already contemplating marriage, so that when I met you it was a case of the fates colliding.'

Her smile was perfunctory. 'That is not the real reason though.'

'I'm afraid the real reason is rather prosaic. My business is not about selling a few bottles of wine to men to drink with their dinner, Sophia. I sell to suppliers and to wealthy connoisseurs—men who wish to stock their entire wine cellars. And my trade is international. It is expected that I entertain these men from time to time, and I could not do that while in lodgings.'

'So it is a business asset, then?'

'You could say so. That is one of the reasons I've left this wing untouched. Under the previous owners, it was the nursery.'

'Of course, I should have realised. I'm assuming that you don't foresee the need for it in the near future?'

'You assume correctly. I currently have a wife who is not my wife, and a woman who claims that she should be my wife. That is more than enough for any man to wrestle with. Taking a real wife, and populating a nursery is not something I care to contemplate at all, for the near, middle or even distant future.'

'So, no nursery then.'

'No nursery. Your suggestions, with the changes we've discussed, are perfect.'

She beamed. 'I am glad to have been of help.'

'You have.'

Her smile faded. 'I should tell you that my trousseau arrived today.'

'Good. Is that one of your new dresses?'

Her face fell. 'It is one of twenty-eight.'

'Well, it is an easy enough matter to arrange another appointment, there is no need to be upset.'

'I'm not upset that I've ordered too few, I'm upset that I've ordered far too many,' Sophia exclaimed. 'Twenty-eight gowns and heaven knows how many pairs of shoes and boots and hats and coats and—and other items that need not concern you.'

Those *other items* interested him the most, but he doubted Sophia would wish him to tell her so. Nightgowns. Stockings. Chemises. Petticoats. Unfortunately, he'd never get to see her wearing any of those most alluring garments. 'I told you not to worry about the expense,' he said. 'It is important that you are adequately clothed.'

'What I consider adequate, and what Madeleine— but it is not her fault,' Sophia amended quickly. 'The fault is mine. I am so very sorry. I don't know if some of it can be returned, but…'

'You will do no such thing. How do you think that would look, for my bride to be sending back her trousseau?'

She grimaced. 'I hadn't thought. But you can have

no idea how much such clothing costs—oh, or perhaps you do.'

'No, I don't,' he snapped. 'I have never purchased any item of clothing for a woman in my life. I have had lovers, Sophia, not mistresses.' She flinched. 'I do not mean to offend you by being so blunt, but it is an important distinction to me.'

'And to me.' She bit her lip. 'Being Madame Bauduin is taking some getting used to.'

'Perhaps I was too modest when I informed you of my status. Let me assure you that I am a very, very, very rich man, and you, *ma femme*, must dress like the wife of one. Twenty-eight gowns does not seem to me such an outrageous number.'

'It does to me, but to Madame Bauduin—no, perhaps not.'

He smiled. 'Then that is an end to the matter. I trust there is something suitable in that vast collection to impress Mademoiselle de Cressy.'

'Oh, dear heavens, I had forgotten. Where is the meeting to be held? And at what time? Will it be just the three of us?'

'At Maxime's office, in the morning, so there will be four of us.'

'And what will you—what will we…?'

'We will tell our story. We will show to Mademoiselle de Cressy that we are madly in love. And we will tell her that though she is the first to have the honour of making your acquaintance, we have accepted any number of invitations. Soon all of Paris will be talking of the beautiful Madame Bauduin.'

'Will they? What invitations?'

Jean-Luc shrugged. 'They will arrive in numbers, once the marriage announcement, which Maxime has placed in today's newspapers, is circulated.'

'So you can't get rid of me now, even if you wanted to.'

'If that was a joke, it was a very poor one.'

'It was, a very poor one, I mean. I've lost my sense of humour of late.'

'And your self-esteem,' he riposted, 'has that been a recent loss too?'

He had not meant to speak so harshly, would have retracted the question instantly, but Sophia forestalled him. 'No,' she said, 'that is something I doubt I had to lose in the first place. My father,' she added, further astonishing him, 'was a man whose high opinion of himself could only be maintained by a correspondingly low opinion of everyone else.'

'He sounds like a man most *charmant*,' Jean-Luc said sardonically.

'He could be, actually, when it mattered. His public persona was very *charmant*.' Sophia's smile was mocking. 'At home, behind closed doors, we experienced the other side of his personality. Although you could say Mama had the last laugh. The greater part of her trust fund returned to her family when she died. My father blamed me for that. She had taken me for a walk in the park, you see. I slipped and fell into an ornamental pond. She fished me out but subsequently took a chill and never recovered. I don't know why I'm telling you all this, you can't possibly be interested.'

'And it is against the rules, do not forget that.'

'I did though.' She smiled tentatively. 'I have broken them twice today.'

'Once, to allow me to get to know you better and once, most delightfully, to allow me to kiss you. Do you regret your lapses?'

'No, because I know that you won't press me to confide in you unless I want you to, and I know that you won't kiss me again unless I ask you to. You really are an honourable man.'

'I fear your prior experience of men has led you to adopt very low standards. From what you have said of your father…'

She laughed at that, but shook her head. 'That is true, but I don't compare you to him or to…' She gave herself a little shake. 'It occurred to me that it might be a good idea for us to host a dinner or soirée. It is the custom, you know, for newly married people to do so, and since you said that it was vital that people believed in our marriage—what do you think? I'd be happy to take care of it. I have experience of both arranging and hosting such social gatherings. All you have to do is give me a list of the people you wish to attend. Obviously we can accommodate a good many more if it is a soirée.'

'Then it shall be a soirée. That way we can spend less time with more people.'

'Very well then. Canapes and a supper. I shall ask Monsieur le Blanc to compile a menu. How exciting!'

'My wife, the gourmand. I forgot. I think you were born in the wrong country. I'll tell you what, we will visit the market together, and you can instruct me on the best produce.'

Her eyes lit up. 'You don't need to, you know. I can go shopping with Madame Lambert.'

'I am perfectly happy that you do, but I would prefer you to enjoy your first taste of our renowned food markets in my company. You will find it both fascinating and enjoyable.'

'Won't you find it a chore?'

'How can making you happy ever be considered a chore?'

Chapter Six

For the momentous encounter with Mademoiselle de
Cressy, Sophia chose a full-length pelisse of navy-blue
satin, the bodice cut and fitted in the military style,
softened by full sleeves, which were gathered at the
wrist with a band of satin ribbon and trimmed with
white lace. White braiding and large white buttons
maintained the military effect, while the matching poke
bonnet had a jaunty white feather. Tan leather boots
and gloves completed the outfit.

She and Jean-Luc were driving to Maxime Sainte-
Juste's office in a town carriage pulled by two horses
and manned by two grooms, but Sophia was far too distracted to notice Paris passing outside the window. She
had hardly slept, had been unable to eat her breakfast,
and by now was quite sick with nerves. This was not
a game they were playing, not a play they were enact-
ing. In very different ways, this meeting could be the
key to both Jean-Luc's future and her own. And also,
she supposed, that of Mademoiselle de Cressy.

Beside her, his leg brushing her skirts, Jean-Luc was

also carefully dressed. A dark blue double-breasted tailcoat showed off his broad shoulders to perfection. The high, starched collar of his white shirt enhanced his tanned skin. Fawn-coloured knitted pantaloons and glossy, tasselled Hessian boots encased his long, muscular legs. Like hers, his gloves were tan. He held on his lap a simple, black beaver hat with a narrow curved brim.

'There is no need to be nervous,' he said. When we rehearsed our little romantic fable last night, you were word-perfect.'

'Yes, sitting at home, with no witnesses. Your friend, Maxime, what have you told him of me?'

'Nothing at all. Maxime is on our side, Sophia.'

On Jean-Luc's side, more specifically, she thought but did not say. The lawyer, she knew, had been party to Jean-Luc's signing The Procurer's contract. He would likely assume she was an actress, and he would probably assume that 'actress' meant courtesan, which was, Sophia thought slightly hysterically, a horribly reasonable assumption.

'*Ma belle*, you must stop worrying. You are my wife, remember.' Jean-Luc kissed her gloved hand. 'My beloved wife. Remember that too.' He kissed the tip of her nose. 'And most of all remember that you are my much-desired wife,' he said, his hand fluttering on her cheek, on her jaw. His mouth hovered over hers. 'Even though we have already made love this morning...'

'Jean-Luc!'

'Sophia.' His smile had a wicked edge to it that dissolved the butterflies in her tummy and made her blood tingle. 'I should warn you, Wife, that your husband is about to kiss you.'

He was not kissing her. He was kissing his wife. And as his wife it was her duty to surrender her lips to his. And to pretend to enjoy his touch. And if she did not have to pretend, it was simply because she was enjoying the novelty of it, and because it was just a kiss, nothing more, and…

His lips touched hers. Not just a kiss but kisses, gentle soft kisses, making her mouth soften, mould itself to his. Another kiss, a proper kiss now, his tongue barely touching hers. Her hands reached for him, pulling him towards her of their own accord, and their lips clung together and she felt the oddest sensation, of a connection, a yearning for something she didn't recognise, and when the carriage came to a halt, for a long moment their eyes met and he looked as surprised as she felt.

'Now you look exactly as a newlywed bride should,' Jean-Luc said, retrieving his hat from the carriage floor. 'Are you ready?'

A newlywed bride. She was his wife. He had not been kissing her, but his wife. He could not kiss her, because her own terms forbade it. Sophia straightened her bonnet. She was Madame Bauduin. Confident in her appearance. Confident in her position as the wife of one of France's richest men. Confident of her husband's deep affection. *'Absolument, mon cher.'*

'It was a *coup de foudre*, for both of us,' Jean-Luc said, casting Sophia a yearning look. 'One glance was enough.'

'It was in Bond Street, wasn't it, *mon cher*?' Sophia returned his look. 'I was looking to match some ribbons for a new hat.'

'I had business with Berry Brothers, the wine merchants in St James's Street, and I was walking back to my town house.'

'He ran right into me. I dropped my packages. You picked them up did you not, *mon amour*?'

Jean-Luc raised her hand to his mouth. 'Our eyes met, just like this. And we knew.'

Sophia smiled beatifically into her husband's eyes. 'We knew.'

'I took her to tea,' Jean-Luc said, returning his gaze to the other two interested parties. 'And then the next day for a drive in Hyde Park, and we met every day after that, until a week before I was due to return to Paris I realised that I could not live without her.'

'And so he proposed, on the spot.' Sophia clasped her hands together ecstatically at her breast. 'And of course I did not hesitate to accept. We were married just two days later by special licence. It was the happiest day of my life.'

'Until we were reunited four days ago, that is,' Jean-Luc chided her gently. 'Surely that became our happiest day?'

Sophia sighed. 'I think that every day we have together will be happier than the one before.'

There was a smile lurking in Jean-Luc's eyes. She dropped her gaze demurely, lest she betrayed herself by bursting into laughter.

'And there you have it,' Jean-Luc continued. 'The story of our whirlwind romance.'

'It is certainly a highly romantic story.' Maxime Sainte-Juste spoke with just sufficient irony to make Jean-Luc cast him a reproving glance.

The lawyer was not at all the stern, scholarly man Sophia had imagined, but rather boyishly good-looking, with dark brown wavy hair, blue eyes, and a mouth that seemed to smile, even when, as now, he was not doing so. As Sophia had suspected, the man had clearly made his mind up about her before she walked into the office. She treated the lawyer to one of her sweetest smiles. 'All the more remarkable for being a true story, *monsieur*.'

'But of course, Madame Bauduin, I did not...'

'You were married in March, you say, Madame Bauduin? Yet you did not arrive in Paris until four days ago,' Juliette de Cressy interjected.

As Jean-Luc smoothly launched into the story of Sophia's mythical companion and the need to settle her in the English countryside, Juliette de Cressy became increasingly agitated, and Sophia struggled not to feel sorry for her. Though only twenty-two years old, the French woman had about her a quiet air of sophistication, a poise and an elegance, combined with a cut-glass accent that lent a great deal of credence to her claim to be the daughter of nobility. She was also very beautiful, with hair which had the same blue-black lustre as Jean-Luc's, and skin like porcelain. She was tiny, of delicate build, with huge eyes, a retroussé nose, and a full mouth. The perfectly bred wife for a duke, rather ironically, Sophia thought.

'My husband was so kind,' she said, recognising her cue, 'as to purchase a little cottage for her, in the village where she grew up and though it was my heart's desire to be with him in Paris, it was a small sacrifice to make, to remain with her for a few weeks to ensure that she had every comfort.'

'And for me,' Jean-Luc chimed in, 'a small sacrifice to make, to ensure that my wife came to me knowing she had done her duty at home. Though I counted off every day on my calendar.'

'And I on mine.'

'And yet, despite your excitement and joy, you shared your happy news with no one,' Juliette de Cressy said, frowning.

'Maxime knew, for he drew up the settlements, didn't you, Maxime?'

'As you say.' The lawyer fidgeted with a brass paperweight, obviously deeply uncomfortable even with this half-lie.

'And the formal announcement was in the press yesterday. You will no doubt have seen it, *mademoiselle*? Yes, I thought so, though I brought a copy for you, just in case it had escaped your notice.'

'It did not.' Mademoiselle de Cressy was very pale. 'You are aware, Madame Bauduin, of my prior claim?'

'I know of the marriage contract to which you claim my husband is a party.'

'Ah. And like your husband, you think that I am a fraud, no? But of course you do. You are his wife, and it is very obvious that you are besotted with him.'

Which statement should please Sophia very much.

Clearly Juliette de Cressy believed their story. Unfortunately, it was equally clear that she believed her own too. 'No one is accusing you of fraud, *mademoiselle*,' she said gently.

'Your husband...'

'My husband,' Sophia said, putting her hand on Jean-Luc's to forestall him, 'most understandably, is extremely unsettled by your various claims. You will admit, will you not, that they are extraordinary?'

Juliette de Cressy shrugged. 'To me, no. It is a story Maman and Papa told to me, like many they told, of the days before the Revolution. Of course, I never thought that I would be forced to honour the marriage contract, but then I never thought that I would lose Maman and Papa while I am still so young.' She dabbed at her eyes with a delicate lace handkerchief. 'We were very happy in Switzerland. I was their only child, and they loved me very much, Madame Bauduin. Their loss, I feel it still, though it has been almost nine months now, since Papa—excuse me, I find it very difficult to talk about.'

'There is no need to apologise, *mademoiselle*. When one loses someone close, time has no meaning.'

'That is so true. However...' The Frenchwoman tilted her chin determinedly at Jean-Luc. 'We are not here to discuss my loss, but the consequences of it. Though I have no particular desire to be married to a complete stranger, none the less this particular stranger was selected as suitable for me by Papa, and so I must trust that he has, as in all else, my best interests at heart.'

'So close to his heart,' Jean-Luc said, 'that he died without making adequate provision for you.'

'Papa did make provision for me,' Mademoiselle de Cressy exclaimed. 'He provided me with you!'

'You cannot have me, *mademoiselle*, because I am already married.'

'But you cannot be, when you were already contracted to wed me!' Mademoiselle de Cressy wailed. 'I am very sorry, Madame Bauduin, but I do not see how your marriage can be legal. My marriage contract was made in good faith, and must take precedence. You must have your marriage annulled. Or you must obtain a divorce. Or you must—you must do something— because this man is obliged to marry me.'

'*Mademoiselle*, you must try to calm yourself. Hysteria will get us nowhere.'

'Calm myself! How can I calm myself? What do you think I will do if I cannot be married? I have nothing, *madame*, absolutely nothing, save the arrangement my father made for me with his best friend. And, yes,' she said, turning on Jean-Luc, 'it is true that he made no attempt to enforce the contract when he was alive, I admit that, but that is because he was loath to let me go. I was sixteen when Maman died. For the last six years, it has been just the two of us, myself and Papa. There was time, we both thought there was plenty of time, for me to find a husband of suitable standing of my own choosing, or for him to contact the one he had already agreed for me.'

'So I was your insurance policy? How romantic,' Jean-Luc said sardonically.

'I do not mean to sound calculating, but as it turns out I need to cash in my insurance policy after all. I am left alone and quite bereft, with no dowry and therefore no prospect of making a match with any respectable gentleman. All I ask for is what is rightfully mine, the marriage Papa arranged for me. Do you understand?'

'Mademoiselle de Cressy...'

'No, Jean-Luc, let me answer her.' Sophia got up to take the seat beside Mademoiselle de Cressy. 'I do understand, I assure you. I know that there are very few options open to gently bred women who find themselves on their own. I can see that you do feel quite desperate.'

'*Oui.* I do. It is not that I wish to deprive you of your husband, Madame Bauduin, I can see that you love him, and that he loves you, but he has no right to do so.'

'*Mademoiselle...* Juliette—may I call you Juliette?' Waiting for her nod, Sophia angled her body to give the illusion that they were alone. 'Your papa was very proud of your family name, your heritage, I think? Yes, I thought so. He would wish you to marry a man with a heritage he could be proud to be associated with, wouldn't he?'

'That is why he contracted me to marry the son of the Duc de Montendre.'

'But my husband is not that man.'

'He is.' Juliette crossed her arms and pursed her lips. 'I assure you, he is.'

And Sophia was forced to accept that Juliette truly did believe so. Aware that Jean-Luc and his lawyer were watching intently, she tried a different tack. 'Surely you would prefer to choose your own husband.'

'As I have already pointed out, despite being the daughter of a comte and of noble birth, I have no dowry whatsoever. That fact renders me unmarriageable in polite society, so choice doesn't enter into it.'

Maxime coughed. 'As to that, Monsieur Bauduin has already offered you a financial settlement which you rejected out of hand. My client has authorised me to table an improved offer comprising a lump sum dowry and an annual income. Which, if I may say so, is a remarkably generous gesture given he is under no obligation to offer you anything. I urge you to accept, so that all parties may move on from this most unfortunate situation.'

'No!' Juliette jumped to her feet, her eyes blazing with anger. 'What kind of woman would I be, to accept money to conveniently disappear? I am not some—some trollop to be paid off. If I accepted Monsieur Bauduin's offer, essentially a bribe to keep me silent, then I would be left quite without a character.'

'I'm sorry, I don't understand,' the lawyer said, 'why then are you so set on marrying my client?'

'I am not at all interested in marrying Monsieur Bauduin. I want to marry the Duc de Montendre.' Juliette twisted her lace handkerchief into a tight ball, breathing heavily, clearly trying desperately to regain control of herself. When she spoke again, she was still shaking, but her voice was calm. 'I cannot accept money, because it would confirm what you think, that I am a charlatan. I am not. My claim on the Duc de

Montendre is a valid one, and your client is the Duc de Montendre.'

'Mademoiselle de Cressy, if you would permit me, I would like to consult with Monsieur Bauduin,' Maxime said hesitantly.

'No, there is no need,' Jean-Luc said firmly. 'Here are my terms, Mademoiselle de Cressy. I assume that you are determined to press your claim?'

'I have no option.'

'Very well then, you will remain here in Paris for the time being. Maxime will ensure that you have sufficient funds to keep you in respectable lodgings along with your maidservant. The arrangements will be made in such a way that the proprieties will be observed. I leave that with Maxime to discuss with yourself. I will have no dealings with you other than through Maxime, and I will require your promise that you will speak to no one other than Maxime on this matter.'

'But why should I agree...?'

'I am coming to that, *mademoiselle*. I sympathise with your predicament. I understand that you are overwrought. I understand that your circumstances are straitened. But you must see that the solution is not for me to abandon the woman I love...' Jean-Luc paused to press a kiss to Sophia's hand '...for a complete stranger.'

'In our circle, such marriages are not uncommon. Maman said that she met Papa only twice before they were married, and they were very happy.'

'But your father was not in love with another woman,' Sophia pointed out.

'Of course not!' Juliette said indignantly. 'But...'

'I have not yet finished.' Jean-Luc spoke with quiet authority. Juliette, who was, Sophia was beginning to suspect, rather too used to getting her own way, stiffened, pouted, but was silenced.

'My wife and I have only just been reunited. We have better things to do than set about trying to disprove your claim, but none the less, that is what we will now do. I do not know how long that will take us, but I can promise you, Mademoiselle de Cressy, that we will succeed, and I will give you my word of honour that when we are done, we will lay all the evidence before you. You will now give me your word of honour that when we do, you will accept the proof and withdraw your claim.'

'The only evidence you will find will prove that I am telling the truth. And then—'

One look at Jean-Luc's face, and Juliette broke off.

'I think that Mademoiselle de Cressy understands,' Maxime Sainte-Juste said, breaking the short silence. 'Do you not, *mademoiselle*?'

Juliette nodded.

'And you are happy to give Monsieur Bauduin your word,' the lawyer said, encouraging her with a gentle smile, 'that whatever evidence he uncovers, you will accept the findings?'

Juliette heaved a sigh. 'I have no option.'

'That was ungracious, *mademoiselle*.'

Juliette turned to the lawyer in surprise, her big eyes wide. 'I'm sorry. I did not mean...' She heaved another sigh. 'You are quite right, it was most ungracious.' She turned to Jean-Luc. 'My apologies. You have my word of honour that I will accept your findings and my word that in the meantime, I will say nothing of this to anyone. Since I have no acquaintance in Paris anyway...'

'My sister,' Maxime Sainte-Juste said, 'will I am sure be most happy to make your acquaintance, and to show you the city. She is about your age, *mademoiselle*, and a most respectable young woman. As to your lodgings, I am sure that my mother will be able to recommend—' Sensing his employer's astonishment, he broke off. 'But we can discuss the matter later. I can see that Monsieur Bauduin is anxious to be away.'

'Monsieur Bauduin, it appears, can happily leave matters in your hands, Maxime,' Jean-Luc said, giving his friend a quizzical look. 'But you are quite right, I have a great many things to attend to, not least presenting my wife to Parisian society.' He bowed briefly over Juliette's outstretched hand. 'Your servant, *mademoiselle*.'

'Goodbye, *mademoiselle*.' Sophia dropped a curtsy.

'I am truly sorry,' Juliette said, returning the curtsy. 'If I had any other option, believe me, I would pursue it. I have no desire to ruin your life.'

'Which proves,' Sophia said to Jean-Luc as they settled into the waiting carriage, 'if nothing else, that she truly does believe her story, and more worryingly, is convinced that any evidence you produce will support it, rather than discredit it.'

'All it proves is that she is deluded.' Jean-Luc took

her hand. 'Though I do believe that she is now in no doubt of our marriage and our feelings for each other.'

'Yes, but it hasn't made any difference.'

'I didn't expect it to, not really.'

'Jean-Luc, you don't think her claim might have substance?'

'I don't think for a moment that I am a duke.'

'But?'

He shrugged, but it was unconvincing. 'Why do I know so little of my true heritage? Why did it never occur to me to ask questions of my parents when they were still alive?'

'Because you had no reason to.'

'Until Mademoiselle de Cressy came along,' he said wryly. 'And now, not only am I plagued with having to prove I am not a duke, she has inadvertently plagued me with doubts about who I really am. I always thought my parents were simply very private people, content in their own company, you know? But looking back, I wonder if there was more to it? Were they hiding something?' He sighed impatiently. 'It is driving me mad, the questions I should have asked them and now cannot.'

'But not so mad that you are imagining yourself the Duc de Montendre?'

He laughed. 'No. Mademoiselle de Cressy is—how do you say it, barking at the wrong tree?'

'Maybe so, but she is utterly convinced it is the right one.'

'She is also now convinced that we are married, and that we are madly in love.'

'That is very true.' Sophia leaned back on the squabs with a sigh. The parallels between Juliette and herself could not be ignored. Though Juliette's papa had loved his daughter, ultimately it had made no difference. She was left quite alone and without practical resources. For both of them, marriage was the obvious solution. Ironically, marriage was not a solution for either of them. Despite the shame and degradation Sophia had suffered, she had not once regretted her decision to forgo matrimony in favour of the less formal contract she had entered into. That, at least, she had been free to terminate when it had served its purpose. She shuddered to think of the alternative, which would have bound her for the rest of her life.

'I can see the wheels turning in your mind. What are you thinking?'

She opened her eyes to discover Jean-Luc resting his head beside hers. 'Poor Juliette,' Sophia said. 'You won't understand, but when she said she had no option but to press her claim, she spoke something close to the truth. Women in her position are reared only to be wives. Without a proper education, without any marketable skill, they have so few resources, only their body, their blood, their pedigree to barter with. You must not blame her for being so persistent, Jean-Luc.'

'I don't. When I said that I sympathise, I meant it. It does not square particularly well with my conscience to deceive her as we are doing, but she has given me no option. I will not solve her predicament by surrendering my own freedom.'

'No, that's not what I meant. Such a marriage, resented from the very beginning, would be doomed to failure. But the alternative for Juliette, to sell herself to a different kind of bidder...'

'It won't come to that! Whether or not she is the daughter of the Comte, as she claims, she is clearly gently bred. Women like that do not become courtesans, if that is what you meant. She is young, she is beautiful, she will find another man to marry her—with or without the dowry which I still intend to pay her. Though whether she will accept...'

'That is very generous of you.'

Jean-Luc shrugged. 'It's not. I can afford it.'

But he did not have to, Sophia thought. An honourable man. She smiled at him. 'She is very beautiful, quite exquisite in fact, and as you said, obviously gently bred. Were you the Duc de Montendre, she would be the perfect wife for you.'

'Well, I'm not. I'm Jean-Luc Bauduin, and the perfect wife for me is sitting right beside me. Thank you, *ma belle*, but I have had enough of Mademoiselle de Cressy for the moment. May I say that Madame Bauduin played her part to perfection.'

'Thank you. As did Monsieur Bauduin, which made my part considerably easier. There were times when I really believed you.'

He laughed. 'I almost convinced myself.

'We were good, weren't we?'

'Better than that. We were excellent.'

Their foreheads were almost touching as they rested on the squabs, his mouth only inches from hers. She felt that odd fluttering tension in her belly that she couldn't find a name for. She wanted him to kiss her. She knew, from that slumberous look in his dark brown eyes, that he wanted to kiss her, though he would not make the first move. Was there anything wrong with a kiss? There was a great deal right with it, she had learned yesterday. And no harm, not really. Compared to all the other physical intimacies she had been forced to endure, quite innocent. Innocently pleasurable, in fact, she reasoned.

'We were so good,' Sophia said, 'that were I really your wife, and were you really my husband, I think you might kiss me right now, don't you?'

'I think I might.'

She smiled. 'Then I think you should. In the name of authenticity.'

'In the name of veracity, I should tell you that I don't give a damn about authenticity. I simply want to kiss you, Sophia.'

'I'm not sure that I much care why you do, Jean-Luc. I just wish that you would.'

'Then it will be my pleasure,' he said. And did.

Kisses like before. Sweet kisses. Kisses that were safe, because they were only kisses, and because he had promised they would never be anything more. Safe kisses which felt dangerous in a dizzying way, as if she was on a precipice looking down. She knew she would not fall, but there was delight in imagining the thrill of tumbling into the abyss. That's what those kisses did. Kisses that took no liberties, and so she was free to return them. And when she did, and the kisses took on a more dangerous note, Jean-Luc stopped kissing her, releasing her before she even knew she needed to be released. Then she rested her head contentedly against his shoulder, feeling safe, for the first time in her life.

Chapter Seven

The next week was spent paying social calls in response to the flurry of invitations which, as Jean-Luc had predicted, poured in following the announcement of their marriage. His friends, business colleagues and acquaintances had all read the announcement of their nuptials in the newspaper. They were, to a man and woman, astounded to discover he was married. They could all, having now had the pleasure of meeting his English wife, understand perfectly his desire to renounce his bachelordom. After another exhausting round of visits earlier that day, Jean-Luc had declared that they had earned a treat, in the form of a night on the town.

Their destination was on the other side of the river in Le Marais, an area which had, before the Revolution, been popular with the nobility but which was now, he informed Sophia, notoriously unsafe and awash with unsavoury characters. 'Welcome to the Boulevard du Crime,' he announced as their carriage came to a halt. 'Named for the number of farces and melodramas performed here nightly, and not for the criminal activities which take place in the surrounding area.'

The wide boulevard was crammed with jostling carriages, lined with theatres from which lights and braziers blazed, the pavements awash with milling people from all walks of life. 'Goodness,' Sophia said, clutching his arm, 'it is busier than Drury Lane.'

There were hawkers selling nosegays, oysters, wine, cherries and a pale, potent spirit from the south which Jean-Luc informed her was called pastis. Outside each of the theatres, actors touted their shows, their cries and competitive banter adding to the general hubbub. Some people were strolling idly, enjoying the raucous atmosphere, while others were studiously examining the bills of fayre each theatre had to offer. There were groups of men in formal evening dress standing alongside groups of men still in their working clothes. There were courting couples in their Sunday best, oblivious to the hive of activity, with eyes only for each other. Women, in the tawdry plumage that formed the uniform of the street walkers called out their wares in competition with the other hawkers.

'Sophia, *ma belle*.' There was a warning note in Jean-Luc's voice. 'Two gentlemen of my acquaintance approaching. Jacques, Marc, may I have the pleasure of introducing you to my wife. Monsieur Jacques Burnell, and Monsieur Marc le Brun are rivals in the wine trade.'

'You flatter us, Jean-Luc,' the younger man said, bowing low over Sophia's hand. 'No one rivals your husband in the wine business, Madame Bauduin.'

'And now, it seems, none of us can rival him in the marital trade either,' the other vintner said, making his bow. 'Your husband has, as ever, picked the cream of the crop. It is a pleasure to make your acquaintance, Madame Bauduin.'

'We read the announcement of your marriage in the newspaper, didn't we, Jacques? None of us could believe it, but now the reason is very clear. No wonder he kept quiet about you.'

'You flatter me, *monsieur*.'

'Not possible, *madame*. Do I detect a trace of an English accent?'

'You do.'

'We met when I was in London on business,' Jean-Luc said. 'In February, as you may recall, for I missed your wife's birthday party, Marc.'

'Ah yes, how could I forget. My sister was most upset, Madame Bauduin. She has a little soft spot for Jean-Luc. She will be your sworn enemy now.'

'I should tell you, *ma belle*, that Marc's sister is only six years old.'

'And showing very early signs of excellent taste,' Sophia said, casting her husband a melting look to which he responded by kissing her hand.

'For pity's sake, Jean-Luc, you will melt her glove. I hope you have had the sense to purchase a box with a curtain at the theatre, else you will be providing the show.' Marc made Sophia another bow. '*Madame*, we must leave you or we will be late for our own show. I hope that you will allow my wife to do you the honour of calling on you? She will be delighted to be able to practise her English.'

'I look forward to it, Monsieur le Brun.'

'Alas, I do not have a wife to call upon you,' Monsieur Burnell said. 'But I dine tomorrow with the Corneilles, you will be there, I hope? Excellent. I look forward to it. Until then.' He made his farewell bow, and the two sallied off in the direction of the Théâtre de la Gaîté.

'You played the loving wife perfectly, as always,' Jean-Luc said, taking her arm once more. 'Now, hopefully we can relax and enjoy the show.' He directed her towards the foyer of the smallest of the theatres on the boulevard. 'I am hoping it will be a new experience for you.'

'Théâtre des Funambules,' Sophia read, frowning. 'What does that mean?'

'Theatre of Tightrope Walkers. You don't know what that is?' When she shook her head, he grinned. 'Then you are in for a real treat.'

The tiny theatre was packed to the rafters. In the stalls, men were crammed in, standing shoulder to shoulder. Fortunately, Jean-Luc had secured one of the few boxes. As he helped her out of her evening cloak, Sophia was relieved to discover that she was not, as she had feared, overdressed. Though many in the audience were plainly garbed, a significant number were in evening clothes. Her own gown was of cerise-pink satin with an overdress of net, the hem and puff sleeves embellished with an embroidered design of black poppies.

Her long gloves had been dyed to match the gown, an extravagance which Sophia would never have permitted herself but which, since Madeleine had taken it upon herself to order them for her, she guiltily treasured. They fitted so very perfectly, the soft leather encasing her arms like a second skin, that it was a pleasure to wear them. She couldn't resist running her fingers up and down the length of her arm. Looking up, she caught Jean-Luc staring at her. 'They are very nice gloves,' Sophia said, embarrassed.

'You certainly wear them beautifully, though I think you could make a hessian sack look fashionable.'

He took her hand, opening the two tiny pearl buttons which fastened the glove at her wrist, pressing a kiss to her pulse. For heaven's sake, she thought, it was absurd, to catch her breath over such a fleeting touch. Then he kissed her again, a mere caress of a kiss, but his lips lingered just enough for him to sense the delightful *frisson* which rippled through her.

'People are staring,' Sophia cautioned. 'Oh. That is why you are doing it.'

But he shook his head, smiling at her in a way that, oddly, made her stomach knot. 'It is a happy coincidence that what I wish to do is what I ought to be doing Namely making love to my wife.'

'Jean-Luc! One cannot make love in a public theatre.'

'Sophia.' The way he spoke her name was a caress. 'Don't you know there are any number of ways to make love?'

Any number, and she thought she had endured them

all, but this was a completely new experience. Not a performance, but a duet. The way their eyes met. The latent heat in his gaze which heated her blood. The tingling of her skin where his lips touched her wrist, surely the most innocuous of places, yet her pulse leapt in response, her body inched closer to his until their knees were touching. His smile, such a wicked smile, seemed to connect directly to her insides. It made her light-headed, that smile, made her want something she could not name, or did not care to.

'Sophia.'

He breathed her name again, his lips against her ear, the whisper of his breath on the nape of her neck another caress, so sweetly arousing. Arousing? He pressed another of those fluttering kisses to the skin behind her ear. And more, down her neck. And her hand lifted of its own accord to touch his cheek, and her mouth was already anticipating his kiss when there was a roar from the audience, and their private performance ended as the public performance got underway on the stage below.

'*Mesdames et messieurs,*' the Master of Ceremonies intoned from the stage, 'tonight, at the Théâtre des Funambules we have for your delectation a very special performance, a farewell to the European stage from one of its most talented duos. Tonight, for one night only, it is my great privilege to present the most extraordinary, the most graceful and indeed the most flexible acrobatic performers in the civilised world. Prepare to be both astounded and amazed. I give you brother and sister, Alexandr and Katerina, the fabulous Flying Vengarovs.'

The shouting and cheering subsided. Clothing rustled as the audience settled back in their chairs in anticipation. Painted fans wafted faces hot from the heavy, still air of the tiny candlelit auditorium. Tension, as taut as the rope stretched between two poles on the stage, was palpable. Sophia edged forward on her seat, leaning on the balcony of the box. Beside her, Jean-Luc also edged forward. She reached for his hand. His fingers twined with hers.

The Flying Vengarovs were a striking pair, he so tall, and she so tiny in comparison. Both wore long cloaks, hers dark blue and his jet black, studded with paste diamonds that sparkled and shimmered in the stage lights. There were paste diamonds in Katerina Vengarov's burnished auburn hair too. The couple seemed to float across the floor together like a constellation of stars tracking across the night sky. For a long, tense moment, they simply stood together in front of their tightrope, facing the expectant crowd. Then they made their bows and dropped their cloaks.

There was a collective intake of breath. The male half of the duo was half-naked, wearing only a pair of tightly fitted knitted pantaloons. His muscled torso gleamed, his sculpted physique drawing a chorus of whistles as he flexed his arms, the gesture rippling through his chest and stomach muscles. Beside him, tiny in comparison, the female acrobat looked quite naked. Closer inspection allowed Sophia to discern that she was wearing a flesh-coloured tunic studded with more paste diamonds clinging to her perfectly proportioned body. The pair were positively indecent, but Sophia found herself excited. They had an exotic allure that set them quite apart from their audience, as if they came from quite another world. She gazed rapt, as the girl put her bare foot on her brother's linked hands and he propelled her upwards on to the tightrope. He followed her, too quickly for Sophia to work out how he'd managed to leap so high, and the show began.

'I've never seen anything like it,' Sophia said for the third time, 'They seemed to fly through the air, as if they really did have wings. So graceful. So fluid. It was quite breathtaking.'

As was she, Jean-Luc thought, seating himself on the sofa beside her. They were back at the *hôtel*, sharing a nightcap in front of the fire in the small salon off the main dining room. Sophia had removed her precious gloves and had curled her feet up under her skirts. He had hardly been able to watch the Flying Vengarov duo for watching her, eyes wide with wonder, lips parted, her hand tightening in his, her breath held every time the brother released his sister to hurtle through the air. And every time he caught her safely, Sophia turned to him to share her relief and her joy, and he had been hard put not to kiss her on those pouted, parted, delightful lips, for his own sheer joy at being there with her.

'It was magical,' she was saying now, clasping her hands together at her breast. 'To see the perfection of the human body, such control, such shapes as they made together. I could have watched them for ever, they were so—so, beautiful, they made me feel so—' She broke off with an embarrassed laugh. 'What I'm trying to say is thank you.'

'There is no need to thank me, *ma belle*, your pleasure is my pleasure.' She smiled at him uncertainly. 'I mean you,' Jean-Luc hastened to reassure her. 'I wanted to please you, not my wife.' Though the boundaries between the two, the real Sophia and the part she was playing, were becoming increasingly blurred in his mind.

'It was a lovely thing to do and I'm very grateful but there was no need to.'

'Perhaps not, but I wanted to.'

'Oh.' She reached out to touch him, her hand resting fleetingly, disturbingly, on his knee. 'It was a—a pleasure, to watch them perform. It should have been shocking, they were all but naked, but it was...'

'Exciting?'

She blushed delightfully, nodding. 'Each time she flew through the air, there was a moment when I thought he wasn't going to catch her, a moment when she might fall, though she must know she would not. I was holding my breath every time.'

'I know.'

'You were watching me? But you must have missed...'

'I saw the entire performance reflected in your face. I assure you, I missed nothing. You were every bit as exciting to watch as the Flying Vengarovs.'

'It was like kissing,' she said softly, under her breath.

'That feeling. I've been trying to find words for it ever since we first—and that's what it was like.'

She smiled at him, and blood surged to his groin. A smile, that's all it was. He shifted on the sofa, preparing to get to his feet. 'It's late.'

Her face fell. 'Of course. We've probably had quite enough excitement for one day.'

'Sophia, it is more excitement that I am trying to avoid! I have no wish to break our agreement. If only you had not mentioned kissing...'

'But I did.' She shifted on the sofa, leaning towards him. 'Would it be wrong of us to kiss goodnight? As your wife...'

'No.' He eased himself away from her distracting presence. 'I want to kiss you, Sophia, and I won't pretend it is part of our act.'

He made to get to his feet, but she stayed him with a hand on his arm. 'Don't go just yet.'

'Sophia, what I'm trying to say is that you are a temptation I am finding increasingly difficult to resist.'

'You don't have to resist.' Sophia knew she was blushing, but she forced herself to hold Jean-Luc's gaze, her heart thumping at her boldness, the tension she would rather not name knotting in her belly. It was her own fault that he hesitated. He was playing by her rules. 'A kiss is not temptation,' she said, 'it is simply a kiss.'

Jean-Luc's smile had a sinful twist to it. 'Simply a kiss.' He pulled her into his arms. '*Ma belle*, I hate to contradict you, but I am fairly certain that there is no such thing.'

His mouth covered hers and her lids drifted closed as their lips met and the sweet, aching feeling that she could easily become addicted to flooded her veins. They kissed. Feathery kisses mirrored by the feathery touch of his hands on her bare arms, sending little *frissons* of delight shivering through her. Then deeper kisses, lips clinging, and her hands crept up around his neck, her fingers curling into the silky softness of his hair. Heat spread through her body as their kisses merged one into another, and she sank back on to the sofa, pulling him with her. Deeper kisses, and his tongue touched hers, sending a shock through her that made her nipples tingle and tighten. She followed his lead, sliding her tongue into his mouth, registering the answering sharp intake of his breath, the way his hands tightened on her arms, leaving her in no doubt of the pleasure she gave.

They were only kisses. Simply kisses. Nothing more. And so a complete delight. She let her hand drift down his body, smoothing over the line of his back, enjoying the presence of him, muscular, taut, reassured by the layers of clothing between them and at the same time revelling in it, the heat of his body, the roughness of his cheek, the day's growth of stubble rasping against her palm, the scent of his soap and his linen and the underlying, elusive Jean-Luc scent she could not even begin to describe.

He dragged his mouth from hers, but before she could protest, there were more kisses. On her lids. On her cheeks. The line of her jaw. The lobe of her ear. Kisses where no one had kissed her before, where she hadn't known kisses could be bestowed. Simply kisses, but they were making her restless now, sending her hands fluttering up and down his back, across the expanse of his shoulders, in search of something more. His hand skimmed down her body, brushing the side of her breast, and his mouth trailed kisses down her throat, to the swell of her breasts above the décolleté of her gown. She stiffened. He hesitated. She made no move, waiting. And then he kissed her again, his mouth gentle on her breasts, and his hand, cupping one of them through her gown, so gently, so carefully, that she knew she had only to move, to utter the tiniest word of protest, and he would stop.

She knew he would stop if she asked, and so she did not protest. She knew he would stop, and so she didn't want him to. Instead she surrendered to the sensation of his gentle caress, of his thumb, circling her nipple through her clothing, the delicious, delightful feeling of her nipple tightening, the tension connecting with the knot in her belly, sending new ripples of sensation through her. She bit her lip hard as an involuntary moan caught in her throat, and the echo of it, a noise which she had manufactured so often to order, threatened to rupture the mood. She opened her eyes, met Jean-Luc's gaze, his lids heavy, his desire reflected in slashes of colour on his cheeks. Jean-Luc, this was Jean-Luc not that despised other.

'Do you want me to stop, Sophia?'

He could not have said anything more reassuring. She shook her head. She caught his face between her hands, kissing him, her tongue sweeping over his lower lip, her kiss urgent, demanding. It was returned fervently, urgently, and her eyes drifted closed once more, and she was lost in a dark, vibrant, sensual world of endless kisses. His hand on her breast jolted new sensations from her, making her arch against him, as if her body was searching for something, seeking some place high up, where she must cling and kiss and where her hands must find skin beneath his coat and his shirt, where she must feel the ripple of his muscle with no barrier between them. She was lost in his kisses now, her mouth clamouring for more, her body clamouring too in a different way, coiled tight as a ship's rope. And then, before she knew what was happening, she unravelled, the tension inside her rent her apart, as if a knife had slashed through the ropes lashing her together, casting her adrift on a strange foreign sea.

Sophia cried out, a wild sound, which she caught instantly, covering her mouth, pushing herself free of Jean-Luc, and catching the wave of pleasure rippling through her before it had time to crash again. Mortified, she concentrated on suppressing everything that her body was intent upon doing to her, frantically gathering all the pieces together, wrapping her arms around herself, keeping her gaze fixed firmly on the ground, all the time aware of Jean-Luc beside her, keeping his distance, making no attempt to touch her, but watching silently.

She felt exposed. She felt both wildly elated, and at the same time on the verge of tears. She had always been able to hide her revulsion from Hopkins, why was it so difficult to hide these very different, utterly opposing feelings from Jean-Luc? She stumbled to her feet. 'It's late. I'm going to bed.'

'Sophia.' He got to his feet, though he made no attempt to touch her. 'There is nothing to be ashamed of.'

'I'm not,' she said, though even to her own ears, the lie was clear enough. She crossed her arms. 'You have made your point, Jean-Luc, if that is what you're trying to say.'

'My point?' He looked genuinely perplexed, and then he swore. 'Simply kisses. You think that I set out to prove you wrong? I had quite forgotten—Sophia, you cannot possibly be imagining that what you are feeling was one-sided? I assure you, I am every bit as aroused by our kisses as you are.'

Her cheeks burned 'I am not—you are not—you did not...' She stuttered to a halt. He had not made any attempt to demonstrate his arousal to her. He had, in fact, made every effort to keep sufficient distance between her and that part of him.

'You offered me kisses. I promised I would not take anything more than you offered.'

An honourable man who had not taken, but who had given. 'I'm sorry,' Sophia said helplessly. 'I didn't know. I have never....'

'That much is obvious,' he said gently. 'Your husband has a great deal to answer for.'

'My husband?'

'Arranged match or no, he should at least have tried to make it a pleasurable experience,' Jean-Luc said tightly. 'You may have been without experience, but that would almost certainly not have applied to him.'

He thought she was married. Or had been married. When she'd told him that she was not innocent, that was what he had surmised. She didn't know whether to be appalled or relieved. It didn't matter, Sophia told herself. What he thought shouldn't matter. But it did, and the sordid truth would appal him. It was kinder by far not to contradict him.

'It really is late,' Sophia said, pretending to yawn. 'And we have an early start tomorrow.' She forced a bright smile now. 'It has taken a considerable effort for you to obtain permission for us to cross the hallowed portals of the Montendre town house. I want to be fresh in order to help you make the most of it.'

'And you want me to discontinue this too painful conversation. As you wish, *ma belle*. I will bid you goodnight.'

He looked hurt, but there was nothing she could do about that. *'Bonne nuit,'* Sophia said, and turning on her heel, fighting the urge to flee, she left the room without a backward glance or another word.

Once alone, Jean-Luc retired to his study. Pouring himself a cognac, he leaned his head against the cool glass of the window. Light flickered through the curtains which had been drawn across Sophia's window. He knew her well enough by now. Any attempt to force a confidence would result only in her retreating further. That brittle smile of hers betrayed her every time. Was it his fault that their kisses had got out of hand? He sighed, taking a deep draught of his very excellent brandy. He hadn't intended them to, though he was forced to admit that he had, shamefully, wanted to prove a point. Which wasn't like him. He took another, smaller sip of his cognac and dropped wearily on to the window seat, turning his back on that flickering reminder that his wife was in the process of undressing.

His wife. Sophia had been here, playing that part for less than two weeks, but he felt as if she had been here much longer. He could not have said what it was she had done to change the already efficient running of the household, but there had been subtle changes. Dinners were less formal and more delicious. Breakfasts too, were more intimate affairs, taken not in the dining room but in a small parlour he didn't remember ever using before, but which caught the morning sun. At breakfast they planned their day, the time to be spent both together and apart—for his business, and the painfully slow process of trying to negotiate entrance to the town house belonging to the Montendre family, occupied him for a proportion of every day. Tomorrow, if matters went as planned, they would finally breach those hallowed portals together. He and his wife.

He had moved well beyond a passing interest in Sophia. He had desired her from the first, but he had very quickly come to enjoy her company. No, that was putting it too mildly. He relished her company. He looked forward to it. He wanted to please her. And those kisses—yes, he had been trying to prove a point. He wanted her to admit that they were not simply kisses. He wanted her to admit what he felt. That they meant something more.

Even though there could be nothing more. Sophia

was here to help him escape marriage yet ironically, Sophia was making him wonder whether marriage would be such a bad thing after all. Ridiculous! Jean-Luc drained his cognac. Absolutely ridiculous. He was frustrated, that was all. Though he did not like to think of himself as in any way a typical man, in this instance he was, wanting what he was told he could not have. Masculine pride was what motivated him, nothing more. He was certainly not falling in love with her. That was inconceivable, especially in such a short period of time. Now *that* was a preposterous notion!

Sighing, he allowed himself to look out of the window again. Sophia's bedchamber was in darkness. She was in bed. Asleep, or reflecting on what must surely be her first experience of pleasure? Could it be called pleasure, when she seemed to enjoy it so little? Maybe gratification was more appropriate. But that sounded too cold for what had been a shared sensual experience. Her response had clearly unsettled her. If only he'd known, he would have been more careful, but he had been so lost in the delight of arousing her, in watching her surrender to sensation, in wishing only to please her more and still more, that it hadn't occurred to him that the climax would be new territory for her.

Unwelcome territory? The clock on the mantel chimed the hour. One in the morning. The very morning in which he was to visit the Montendre town house, and perhaps finally obtain the evidence he needed to prove to Juliette de Cressy that he was not the man she wanted him to be. Though who he was—now that was a very different question. Not, however, one to ponder tonight. He should be asleep, so that he would be sharp, fully alert in the morning. He was wasting far too much time thinking about his wife, who was not his wife, and whom he would no longer require to be his wife, perhaps as soon as tomorrow. Which thought should make him happy. And not make him feel—no, he was not going to explore what it made him feel. He was going to bed. And to sleep. And he was not, most definitely not going to lie awake and think about the distracting, beautiful, intriguing woman lying alone in bed in the adjoining room.

Chapter Eight

To her surprise, Sophia had slept deeply, awaking as the morning light crept through a gap in the curtains, in a very different mood from the one in which she had fled from Jean-Luc the previous night. Pulling on a wrap, she padded over to the window and pulled the heavy curtains apart. The sky was changing from grey to pale blue, the few scattered clouds white and fluffy. She opened the window to lean out, relishing the welcoming kiss of the sun on her skin. It was going to be a lovely day.

She closed her eyes, surprised to discover that her memory of the previous evening's events was no longer tainted by embarrassment. Last night had been a revelation. Jean-Luc had been right, there was no such thing as simply a kiss. Until that shocking moment of release, she had been quite lost in those kisses and Jean-Luc's touch and his taste. Her hands roving over his body, she had relished the effect she was having, because it was an echo of the effect he was having on her.

Was that why it had happened? Startled, her eyes flew open. Last night, she had not set out to induce pleasure, but she had done, almost effortlessly. Last night, there had been none of the physical intimacies she had experienced before. They had been fully clothed, for heaven's sake, and yet she had surrendered to the wave of passion, the surging crescendo, in a way she never had before. She was not an expensively purchased toy for Jean-Luc to play with. She was not a well-trained automaton, dutifully responding to his cues. He had given her no directions, and he had expected nothing from her. He would have ceased at the merest indication from her. He had not gone galloping off intent on his own journey to completion. It was she who had galloped off uncontrollably! It was perfectly natural, Jean-Luc had said. And in the bright, revealing light of this June morning, Sophia saw that he had spoken the truth.

Hopkins, she supposed, had earned the right to affect indifference, having bought her body to do with as he wished, requiring only that she appeared to enjoy what gave him pleasure. It should have been different with Frederick. He had professed to care, but in the end had proved he cared only for himself. His subsequent behaviour demonstrated that beyond doubt. She'd thought it was the province of the male, to take pleasure from the female. She'd assumed that every woman did as she had learnt to do, to simulate her enjoyment. And she'd been wrong.

Though the circumstances, Sophia thought bitterly, until now had hardly been conducive. With both Frederick and Hopkins, she had been burdened by the bargains she had struck. She had knowingly sold herself twice, albeit the nature of the arrangements had been very different. Jean-Luc was also paying for her services, but on an entirely contrasting basis. He had no rights to her body. That was the enormous and very significant difference.

Last night. Tension curled in her belly, an echo of what had happened. Her first ever climax, and she had smothered it. She didn't want it to be her last. She was only twenty-six. When she left Paris, when she was no longer Jean-Luc's wife, then she would be free to take a lover if she wished. She tried to picture him, this mythical, considerate man, but she could only picture Jean-Luc. She didn't want another lover. She wanted him. Dare she dismantle the barriers she had been so determined to erect between them? What if she discovered it was a mistake? What if last night was unique? Could a yes become a no once more?

'Bonjour, Madame Bauduin.'

Madeleine's appearance with her morning coffee saved Sophia from answering this tricky question. But Madeleine's sidelong glances at the neat, undisturbed bedclothes as she poured the coffee and straightened the curtains made it clear that she was not the only one considering the subject. She knew that her dresser would not betray her to any of the other servants, just as she had assumed that Jean-Luc put similar trust in his valet, but it was clear that those two most personal of servants knew that their master and mistress were not sharing a marital bed. If she allowed Jean-Luc to make love to her it would enhance the charade of a happy marriage.

Sophia set her coffee cup down with a clatter. No! She would not sully her feelings for prosaic purposes. If she made love to Jean-Luc it would be for no reason other than genuine desire. And it was very much a question of *if*, for even if she wanted to, after last night there was no certainty that he would feel the same, she reminded herself, picking up her coffee again.

'I think the powder-blue half-pelisse, with the white promenade dress would be a good choice for today,' Madeleine said, holding up the garments for her inspection. 'Monsieur Bauduin has ordered the carriage for ten. He is taking you out to see more of our beautiful city?'

'No. I mean, yes.' Sophia set down her cup. 'And, yes, that combination will work perfectly.'

'You could wear the pale blue muslin with this pelisse, but I think...'

'No, the white is perfect. You have excellent taste, Madeleine. Thank you.'

'It is my job, *madame*, and you make it very easy for me. When Monsieur Bauduin engaged me, I had no idea that I would be working for such a very beautiful mistress. To be honest, I was very surprised to be engaged by the master of the house and not the mistress. It is very unusual, but yours is a most unusual love match, no?'

'Yes.' Sophia smiled thinly. She liked Madeleine, and did not like lying to her. 'I didn't realise you had heard the story of how we met.'

'*Monsieur*'s valet regaled us all with it. He had *monsieur*'s permission, rest assured. Some of the servants were a bit dubious—it seems *monsieur* had not even mentioned your name. But now all is clear. Such a *coup de foudre*, of course he wanted to keep you secret, in his heart, until you were reunited.' Madeleine sighed and clasped her hands to her bosom. 'I think it is *trés, trés* romantic.'

'Yes.' Sophia busied herself with a second, unwanted cup of coffee. Jean-Luc hadn't told her he'd disseminate their invented history to the servants. She understood why, but it made her uncomfortable.

'*Madame...*' Madeleine too was looking uncomfortable. 'I hope you will forgive me for being so bold, but I cannot help but notice *monsieur* does not...' She indicated the pristine bed. 'I am a married woman myself, *madame*. I know that even when one is in love as you are, the nature of—to some, it is a shock. If there is anything I can do to help, if you wish to talk...'

'No! There is nothing—I am perfectly—you must believe me, Madeleine, there is nothing to be concerned about.'

Her dresser looked unconvinced.

'Nothing at all,' Sophia said firmly. 'Now, if you would be so good as to fetch me some hot water, I do not wish to keep my husband waiting for his breakfast.'

The *hôtel particulier* which belonged to the Montendre dynasty had been closed up at the height of the Terror by the Duke, when he realised he had left it too late to escape Paris. Provision had been made for its maintenance if he were arrested, until such time as either he was released, or, if the worst should befall him, it was subsequently reclaimed by his son. This much Jean-Luc had managed to establish from the firm of lawyers engaged by the Duke to act as trustees, he informed Sophia over breakfast, 'Though the whereabouts of the son and heir are entirely a matter of indifference to them. They are paid on an annual retainer, as are the skeleton staff of the *hôtel*, and all seem content to continue with this arrangement indefinitely.'

'So if the long-lost son did turn up, it would be an inconvenience to them?' she asked.

'It would, but after all this time they don't believe it will happen.' Jean-Luc set aside his half-finished plate of eggs. 'They assume he must be deceased, and they are very likely correct in that assumption, though naturally, they don't wish to be proved so, for that would put an end to their stipends.'

'Which is why they have been obstructive, presumably?'

Jean-Luc grinned. 'Fortunately, I can be very persuasive.'

'And money talks,' Sophia added acerbically. 'As do servants. Madeleine told me this morning that you had shared our romantic history with your valet, who then told the entire household.'

'Best to put a stop to gossip before it begins. Not that I think our servants would gossip beyond the confines of the *hôtel*, but—as I said, it's best not to take the risk.'

'You think of everything.' No, not quite everything.

Sophia thought, biting her lip as she recalled the rest of her conversation with Madeleine.

'What is it, *ma mie*? You have that look of yours, the one where you are thinking dark thoughts and wondering whether or not to share them with me. If it is about last night...'

'No, it's not.'

'I went too far,' he continued, heedless, 'I know I did. I knew that with you there would be no such thing as simply a kiss—not for me, anyway. I should have stopped long before...'

'No.' She leaned across the table to touch his hand. 'No, I won't let you take the blame, that's not fair. I knew, you see, that you would stop any time, and I chose not to ask you to. I wanted you to continue, even though I did not know...' Her face was hot, but she was determined to carry on. 'Even though I was not aware of the—the strength of my reaction. In fact, I had no idea, and it—it took me aback.'

Jean-Luc laughed gruffly. 'Your English way of talking is some times—it took you aback? That is something of an understatement, no?'

'Just a little.' She was obliged to smile. 'I was angry this morning. Not with you,' she added hastily, 'but with—you see I really didn't know I could experience such release.' And she had thought she'd known it all. Why had no one told her? There had been opportunities, in the early days when she had been forced to ask so many mortifying questions, yet none of the so-called experts she had consulted had seen fit to enlighten her about that.

'And now you do,' Jean-Luc said. The silence between them stretched uncomfortably. 'I'm your husband, Sophia. You can tell me anything, ask me anything.'

'You are not really my husband. And even if you were, I can't, because even if you wanted to, which you probably won't...'

'But how will we know, if we don't discuss it, whatever it is?'

He was smiling, but he was not teasing her. There was tenderness in his expression. 'The fact of the matter is that I don't want last night to be the first and the last time,' she whispered. 'I know that the terms I insisted on forbid us to...' She paused to take a deep breath. 'What I'm trying to say is that I trust you enough to want to amend my terms. If you are amenable, that is.'

Jean-Luc exhaled sharply. 'Amenable? You can be in no doubt what I want. Ah, but of course you can, being you,' he added, studying her carefully. 'I think that your experience in affairs of the heart has been unsatisfactory, *ma belle*, am I right?'

'To put it mildly, which is why I want...'

'As I do.' He pressed her hand. 'Very much, but it would be a mistake to get too far ahead of ourselves. It is a leap, not just of faith, from what happened between us last night, to sharing a bed.'

'I know what size of step it is. I told you, I'm not an innocent.'

'But you are. You may not be a virgin, but you have no experience of making love. And now you are thinking, what an arrogant man my husband is, thinking that he can tutor me, but that's not what I'm saying.'

'What are you saying?'

'That to learn together, to make the journey slowly, to discover what pleases you, and what pleases me, would be so much more enjoyable.' His expression became serious. 'And for you, knowing that at any point you could call a halt, I think that is important, yes?'

'Yes.' She forced down the lump which had risen in her throat. 'And I know that you would. You see, I can trust you.'

Jean-Luc pulled out his watch with a groan. 'You do pick your moments. The carriage will be at the door in five minutes.'

'I need only three to get ready.' Sophia jumped to her feet, catching him unawares and pressing a kiss to his lips. 'I do not forget the reason you brought me here. A journey of a different kind for you. This could be a significant step, a momentous day.'

The Montendre town house, Sophia noted, was on a grand scale, a palace rather than a *hôtel particulier*, and one of the most opulent on the very opulent Rue du Faubourg Saint-Honoré. They were expected. As Jean-Luc drew the horses to a halt, the huge gates were opened by a liveried servant. Another awaited at the front door, ready to take charge of the carriage. And another stood at the top of the shallow flight of stairs.

'Welcome to the Hôtel Montendre, Monsieur Bauduin, Madame Bauduin. I have been instructed to show you around. You understand, there has been no one staying here since the Duke and Duchess were taken?'

Jean-Luc reassured the man that they understood perfectly well. In the drive across the city, he had been business-like, going over the little they had learned of the Montendre family and the questions which he hoped they would find answers to. He seemed not in the least nervous, while Sophia struggled to hide her own increasing tension. So much depended upon this visit, not least, the termination of their marriage. Which was the last thing which should be occupying her mind at this moment in time, she chastised herself, as Jean-Luc asked the servant whether there was anyone on the premises who had personally served the Duke and Duchess.

'No, not a single one,' the man replied. 'Some went with them to their fate, alas, and the others left Paris in order to avoid doing so. As far as I am aware, the château in Bordeaux is a ruin. Though the Duke made provision for a small staff here, he left limited funds for upkeep. The roof leaks like a sieve and the whole place is in dire need of repair. Now, would you like to begin your tour with the state rooms?'

'Actually, I wonder if it would be possible for us to inspect the place unaccompanied,' Jean-Luc said, slipping a coin into the servant's already outstretched hand.

'I see no reason why not, *monsieur*. If you have any questions, I'll do my best to answer them. The bells in the main rooms are still in working order. You only have to ring to summon me.' The servant bowed and withdrew.

'I had hoped there would be some survivors from the Duke's time,' Jean-Luc said, looking bitterly disappointed. 'Never mind, let us see what we can un-cover.' He produced a scroll of paper tied with a dusty red ribbon. 'A plan of the *hôtel* I managed to acquire at considerable expense,' he said, unrolling it on the huge circular table which was the only piece of furniture in the reception hallway. 'As you so rightly said this morning, money talks. Come and take a look.'

It was a melancholy and dispiriting experience, Jean-Luc thought, as he and Sophia climbed the stairs to the third floor. On first impression, the vast, ornate, interconnected state salons were awe-inspiring, seemingly palatial with their gilded cornicing, hand-painted wall coverings and brocade curtains. Some of the floors were marble. Others had oak floorboards. All were elaborately inlaid, the Montendre crest appearing repeatedly, not only on the floors but on the pediments above doors and windows, in the plasterwork, and in the very few pieces of dusty furniture that remained, presumably because they were too heavy and too large to sell. The portraits which had been taken down had left their ghostly outlines on the walls. On closer inspection, dark brown stains could be seen in the cornicing where water had made ingress. There were cracks and cobwebs everywhere. Many of the windows had been boarded over.

'The caretaker didn't exaggerate when he said this place was in dire need of repair,' Jean-Luc said, pulling up a rotten piece of floorboard in the window embrasure of one of the bedchambers.

'It must have been very beautiful in its day,' Sophia

said, brushing a cobweb from the bonnet of her hat, 'though I must confess, I wouldn't like to live here. I would need that map with me at all times, to stop me from getting lost.'

'I don't know. It has a certain something.' Jean-Luc pulled back the shutters, sending several startled spiders scuttling off. 'Look at those gardens.' They were at the rear of the house, looking out over what once must have been a magnificent garden. An ornate fountain, now filled with filled with leaves rather than water, stood at the centre of a network of geometric paths, the outline of the formal beds still barely visible. 'It's reminiscent of Versailles on a much smaller scale.'

'Decrepit magnificence,' Sophia said. 'Do you think ghosts haunt these halls and corridors?'

'I wish they did. Then we could talk to them, ask them a few pertinent questions. We haven't even come across a single portrait. I had hoped we'd at the very least get a likeness of the elusive Duke and his wife.' Jean-Luc pulled the shutters back across the room. 'Come on, we've still got the attics to investigate. Perhaps we'll find a helpful ghost lurking up there.'

'There are no such things as ghosts, you know,' Sophia said.

He had pulled out the map again, was casting an eye over the layout of the attics. It was the tone of her voice rather than the words which caught his attention, a terrible yearning that tugged at his heart.

'Death is final, no trace remains,' she said, turning away, making it clear she was speaking to herself. 'I wish that it were otherwise.'

And then she gave herself a little shake. And she flashed him her brittle smile. And he knew better than to ask her what she had been thinking, *who* she had been thinking of, though he longed to know. Her husband? Her father? She had not cared for either men, as far as he was aware. But absence, he supposed, gilded many memories.

Jean-Luc rolled up his map and took her arm, pulling Sophia tightly against his side as they left the room, which was all the comfort he dared offer. 'One conclusion we can draw,' he said as they made for the service stairs, 'is why there has been no pretender claiming the Montendre title. No one in their right mind would take this financial millstone on.'

The attics were, like the rest of the palace, built on a very grand scale, and similarly all but empty. Only one room, at the furthest end, contained a number of boxes and trunks. All of which, save one, contained woman's clothing.

'Shoes,' Sophia said, inspecting one trunk. 'Gloves. Petticoats. Goodness, look at this lace. Sleeves and jackets. These must be decades old. Stoles and scarves. Feathers. Oh, and look at this, Jean-Luc. How lovely.'

He turned from his inspection of the final trunk to find her standing beside him, holding a gown against herself. It was dark red velvet trimmed with gold thread. The sleeves were full, slashed to reveal a gold under-dress. There was nothing at all familiar about it, yet he had the oddest feeling. 'It's probably infested with moths.'

'No. I think there must be some sort of pomander in the boxes. Here, smell.'

Before he could turn away, she thrust the dress at him. His stomach lurched. And then he remembered. 'Bergamot,' he said, with relief. 'Maman had a little bottle of it, though she rarely wore it.'

'I'm not surprised. It's very expensive.'

Jean-Luc shrugged. 'We were comfortably off at one time, I thought I mentioned that.'

'You did. What happened to change your family circumstances?'

'I've no idea. Investments gone wrong, perhaps.'

Sophia bit her lip. She did that when she was pondering. 'Whatever the cause, I had to leave school go into the business—but you know all that,' Jean-Luc said impatiently, 'and it's hardly pertinent. I don't know why you've brought it up.'

He turned away, squatting down by the trunk to pick up a sheaf of papers that looked to be part of a set of household accounts. He made a show of examining them, confused by the nervous churning of his stomach. He heard the rustle of silk and damask as she folded up the gown, the soft sigh of the trunk being closed, and then felt her hand resting lightly on his shoulder. 'I think we have seen enough. We have found no evidence,' she said.

His relief was inexplicable. He smiled up at her. 'Nor any ghosts.'

The manservant was waiting for them in the reception hall with a decanter and glasses. 'One of the last bottles from the Duke's estate,' he said, pouring the wine. 'See what you think, Monsieur Bauduin, would it be worthy of your own prestigious cellars?'

Jean-Luc took a cautious sip, quickly setting the glass aside. 'I'm afraid it's corked, but thank you, I appreciate the gesture.'

'It was the gardener who recognised your name,' the servant said. 'I didn't make the connection with the celebrated Bauduin vintners. It is a pity the wine has deteriorated, but not surprising since there is no Duke in situ and our long-lost heir is highly unlikely to turn up now.'

'What will happen to the place?' Sophia asked, following Jean-Luc's lead and setting her own glass down untouched. 'If the heir never appears to claim it?'

'The annuity that pays our wages will run out eventually. Then I suppose the place will be closed up completely and left to fall into ruin. It's a real shame, but it's not exactly an uncommon story, though most of the other neighbouring town houses have been reclaimed. With these titled families, there's usually a third cousin twenty times removed happy to come forward, but the Montendre family pretty much all went to the guillotine. Save the boy.'

'And nothing is known of his fate at all?' Jean-Luc asked.

'Nothing. According to old Marie Grunot, he was sent away for his own safety, no one knows where, a couple of years before Madame Guillotine claimed his parents. But to be honest, Marie wasn't the most reliable of witnesses. Her husband, the Duke's valet, went to the guillotine along with the Duke and she was never the same again.'

'None the less I would be interested in speaking to her, out of curiosity you understand,' Jean-Luc said guardedly.

'Not possible, I'm afraid. She passed away last winter. Now, if there's nothing further, time is getting on, and my dinner...'

'What was the husband's name?' Jean-Luc asked sharply.

'Henri Grunot.'

Sophia shot Jean-Luc a startled glance but he shook his head imperceptibly.

'And the boy, do you know what age he was when he was sent away?'

The man puffed out his cheeks. 'Two? Three? Four, maybe? No, couldn't have been four, because the Duke and Duchess were taken in March of 1794, I know that because we were all appointed three months later, when the lawyer had the proof that they were both dead. He'd be—what, thirty years old now, the lad, if he'd survived.'

'How do you know that?'

'Because he was born in June 1788. It's recorded in the family bible. We keep it downstairs. Our gardener is very fond of a good pray at the end of the working day.'

'So my memory was not playing tricks on me?' Sophia asked. 'Henri Grunot, the valet, was indeed one of the signatories to the marriage certificate. Which proves it is authentic.'

Jean-Luc poured himself a glass of cognac, handing Sophia her preferred madeira, before sitting down beside her on the sofa. 'We always suspected it was. Now we also know that one of the witnesses is dead, but we still have no idea of the identity of the other.'

It was late afternoon. The sun cast shadows through the tall windows of the salon. Sophia took a small sip of her wine. It was honey-sweet, and as she had come to expect from Jean-Luc, a first-rate vintage. 'June 1788 is the date recorded for the birth of the Duke's son, and you were born in May of the same year.'

'Coincidence, nothing more. It's not even the same month.'

'That doesn't necessarily prove anything,' Sophia said carefully, for he had been in a strange mood since they left the Montendre residence, on edge, impatient, dismissive. 'The date recorded in the bible is that of the birth of the boy. Quite often what we call our birthday is actually the day we were christened or baptised. So it could be...'

'What?' He jumped to his feet, swallowing the cognac in one draught. 'You saw the list of names, not one of them refers to a Jean-Luc Bauduin.'

'No, but...'

'I know what you're going to say. Cognac is in the same part of the country as Bordeaux, but what of it? There are any number of towns near Bordeaux, no doubt full of numerous men my age, who could just as easily pass for the abandoned son of a long-dead duke.'

'Though it was you Juliette claimed,' Sophia said

tentatively. 'It is Jean-Luc Bauduin from Cognac who was named in the de Cressy family legend.'

'Legend, or a fable she has invented.'

'I don't believe she is a fraud, and I don't believe you think so either.'

'I don't know what to think any more.' Jean-Luc sighed, stretching his legs out in front of him. 'You were right, we are not just chasing one wild goose but a whole flock. I don't want to have to go to Bordeaux, but I can't think what else to do. You've been to Bordeaux before, I think you said?'

'I've passed through it.'

'It's a beautiful city. Not as beautiful as Paris, but lovely. You will like it.'

'I?'

'You don't think I'd go on my own, *ma belle*? We are only just reunited. I could not bear to tear myself away from you again so soon.'

'But we are due to host our soirée in three days' time.'

'And we shall. I'm not suggesting we leave immediately. You have put a great deal of effort into organising our soirée. I am, strangely, looking forward to it. I was thinking that tomorrow morning would be a good time to visit the market. You can see what there is, taste and try, as we say, and then send Madame Lambert off to do the shopping on the day with complete confidence.'

'If I wished our chef to tender his resignation. Sourcing ingredients is his province,' Sophia said, laughing, relieved to see his mood lifting. 'I can easily go to the market myself, Jean-Luc. You are not particularly interested in what food we serve.'

'But I am particularly interested in pleasing you, and I think that the way to your heart might well be through your stomach. I'm going to test that theory at the market, I warn you.'

'Oh, if you intend to feed me oysters and snails and *foie gras*, then my heart will melt like a perfectly ripe camembert,' she teased.

'Will it?' Jean-Luc touched her cheek. 'I have an insatiable appetite for camembert.'

There was something in his eyes that made her catch her breath, but she was spared the necessity of a response by a discreet tap on the door. A message had come from the *halle aux vins*, the footman informed Jean-Luc. A problem with a shipment required his urgent attention.

'I'm sorry, I'm going to have to leave you,' he said, after reading the note.

'May I come with you?' Sophia asked impulsively.

'It's likely to take some time to resolve.'

'I'm your wife,' she said, tucking her hand into his arm. 'My place is by your side.'

Chapter Nine

Sophia awoke as the dawn light filtered in through the windows. Bleary-eyed, she sat up, realising as she did so that she was wearing her petticoats and shift, not her nightgown, that she was lying on a leather sofa under her cloak and Jean-Luc's greatcoat, and she was not in her bedchamber but her husband's office in the *halle aux vins*.

Jean-Luc got up from the chair behind his desk to perch beside her. His chin was dark with stubble, his hair tousled, his shirt open at the neck to reveal a dusting of rough dark hairs on his chest. 'Good morning. Dare I ask if you slept well?'

'I am ashamed to say that I did, though I take it you did not?'

'Which is a polite way, I think, of telling me that I look a sight.'

'You look boyishly dishevelled,' she said, smiling shyly. 'It suits you.'

He smoothed his hand over her tumble of hair, pulling out a stray pin. 'Your crumpled, barely awake appearance is strangely appealing too.'

'With my hair on end, and my face creased? Thank you.'

He laughed softly, leaning towards her, sliding his arm around her waist. 'Sophia, you are adorable whatever the circumstances. Will you grant your husband a good morning kiss?'

She was not primped and prepared, yet there was no mistaking the heat in his eyes. And she could admit to herself, couldn't she, that she liked this unkempt version of her husband very much. She twined her arms around his neck. 'Good morning,' she said, and kissed him.

He tasted vaguely of the wine he had been sampling the night before, and of toothpowder too. He must keep a supply here, she thought hazily. He must be accustomed to spending the night on this sofa, where she had slept. He returned her kiss slowly, his fingers combing through her hair, freeing it from the remainder of her pins, and she slid her hand under the loose neck of his shirt, feeling the heat of his skin against her palm for the first time. Their kisses deepened, their tongues touched. She lay back on the couch, pulling him with her, for the first time wanting to close the space he maintained between them, sliding her hands down his back to pull him against her. Their kisses were languorous. Early morning kisses, slumberous, yet rousing every one of her senses.

She tugged his shirt free from his breeches, running her hand up his back, relishing the way his muscles tensed under her touch. More kisses, deeper kisses. He cupped her breast, circling her nipple through the thin cambric of her chemise. She shuddered with delight.

'More?' he asked, his lids heavy, his eyes dark with passion, and she nodded. 'More, please.'

He undid the ribbons to loosen the neckline of her chemise. He kissed her breasts, his mouth tasting every inch of her flesh, kissing as if there was no rush at all, which was both delicious and agonising. When his mouth covered her nipple, sucking, licking, she had to stifle a cry of delight. Her back arched, and she felt the ridge of his arousal, hard against her thigh, and it almost catapulted her out of her blissful bubble, but she screwed shut her eyes and refused to let the past spoil the present, shaking her head to forestall his question, pulling him back on to her, pressing her mouth fervently to his, and losing herself once more in their kisses.

Her nipples were tight, sweetly aching, with his ministrations. Her hands roamed more freely over his back, then, as he angled himself on to his side to lie beside her, on to the contours of his chest. She could feel his heart beating steadily, could feel the rough hair, then the flat, hardness of his nipples, and the sharp intake of his breath as she smoothed her hands over them. It was all so new, and all the more delightful for that.

The tension she now recognised was building steadily low inside her. She was hot. Restless. Wanting, but not wanting to think, afraid to act, anxious that Jean-Luc would misinterpret, that he would not know what she wanted, though how could he, when she herself did not?

'Hush,' he said, kissing her mouth again, gentler this time. 'Stop thinking.'

'I'm trying.'

He laughed softly. 'Stop trying.' He kissed her again, his tongue running along the inside of her lower lip, his hands on the swell of her hip, feathering, stroking, soothing and arousing, easing his body from hers, making enough room on the sofa to lay her on to her back. 'The slightest indication,' he whispered, 'and I promise I will stop.'

'Yes. No. Not yet.' Her body was a mass of contrary urges. Every one of her muscles felt taut. *Frisson* after *frisson* of sensation shivered through her as he stroked her breasts, her flank, and his fingers feathered under her petticoats, on to the soft flesh of her thighs. She mustn't think about it, but she couldn't help it, anticipating the rough intrusion.

But it was different. Whatever he was doing caused a coiling sensation to build inside her. And now his tongue, in her mouth, sliding and stroking in the same delightful, delicious rhythm, so that she finally forgot, lost herself in the spiralling pleasure he was giving her. Lost herself so completely that when her climax came it was like falling off a cliff and tumbling towards the ground, only it was not terrifying but freeing, a release. Finally, she understood as she bit down hard on her lip to stop herself from crying out. That was it, a primal visceral release.

Though it did not last long. As the last wave ebbed

away, Sophia opened her eyes, aware of her obligation to return what had been given. It was not the same as before, she told herself as she ran her hand over the length of his erection, and it was not, there was no need to disguise her distaste because she felt none. Though she still couldn't prevent herself thinking of it as a task which must be executed as quickly as possible. She briskly undid the fastenings of his breeches and was sliding her hand inside when he caught her wrist.

'What are you doing?'

'Don't you want me to?'

'I would, very much, if you wished to, but you clearly don't.'

'I do.' Her fingertips brushed the silky skin of his shaft. She discovered that she had not lied, though Jean-Luc didn't believe her. Or perhaps she'd misread his meaning. 'Would you prefer...?'

He caught his breath before gently but firmly removing her hand. 'What I'd prefer, Sophia, indeed what I insist on, is that you do nothing out of a misplaced sense of obligation.'

He sat up, pulling her cloak up over her exposed breasts. She had no idea what to think. Suddenly on the verge of tears, she sank down under the cloak, turning her face away. 'I'm sorry.'

'What on earth are you sorry for?'

She had expected him to be angry, but his voice was gentle, his tone genuinely perplexed. 'I don't know what to do. I don't know what you want.'

He sighed. He wrapped his arms around her, dropping his chin on to her head. 'All I wanted was to please you.'

'You did.'

She felt the shudder of his laughter against her back. 'I know, *ma belle*.' He kissed her hair. 'And when you are ready, then we will share our pleasure, but I don't think you are ready yet.'

'I want to be,' she whispered.

He tensed against her. 'What is stopping you, Sophia, what is holding you back?'

Though his back was to her, she could sense his focused attention. She had never tried to articulate her feelings. There had been pain some times, but experience had taught her how to avoid it. She had never believed her protector would harm her, not deliberately. 'Not fear of pain,' she said, her voice so low that she couldn't even be sure that he heard it, 'but of being violated.' The word shocked her, but it was the right word, she knew it as soon as she said it. 'Violated,' she said again. 'Though it was never against my will, it always felt as if it was.'

Jean-Luc swore viciously. His arms tightened painfully around her. He swore again. 'I had no idea.'

And he still had none. A tear trickled down her cheek. She had never allowed herself to pity her situation, knowing that it would be impossible to carry on if she did, and knowing that she had no choice but to continue.

'Do you want to tell me about it?'

'No!' She turned around, burrowing her face in his neck, clutching him tightly to her. 'It's over now, it's all in the past.' She knew it for a lie. The sordid details would stand between them for ever. Her only consolation was that he would never know. It was not too much to ask, surely. She pressed her mouth to his chest. 'I do want you, Jean-Luc.'

'I believe you, Sophia.' He kissed her forehead. 'But there is absolutely no rush.'

It was still very early when they left the *halle aux vins*, though the wharves on the Quai St Bernard were already busy with barges, stevedores working in an ordered chain to unload the casks and barrels. At Sophia's request, they abandoned the carriage and strolled along the quays, past the Île Saint-Louis, where the washerwomen were at work on the banks of the Seine, and on to the Île de la Cité, crossing in front of the majestic cathedral of Nôtre Dame. Once on the Right Bank, the streets became more crowded. Craftsmen and traders carried bundles, pushed carts. Horses pulled drays groaning with produce, heading for the huge food market at *Les Halles* where the crowds became a seething mass.

It was a place where the senses were assaulted, not always in a pleasant manner, though the laborious process of transferring skeletons from the nearby, notorious cemetery of Saints-Innocents to the catacombs, under cover of darkness had, thankfully, finally been completed. The Fontaine du Palmier had also delivered a much-needed fresh water supply to the nearby Place du Châtelet, thanks to Napoleon. But Sophia, Jean-Luc noted with amusement, seemed to relish rather than recoil at the sensory onslaught, her face alight with interest, her arm tucked safely into his, dragging him from one stall to the next with an eagerness that was both endearing and, disconcertingly, arousing. Though that was more likely the residual effect of their early-morning lovemaking.

They were standing at an oyster stall now, and Sophia was discussing the various grades of the shellfish knowledgably, the stall holder quite beguiled, as he offered her a selection of different oysters from Normandy and Brittany in the north, Marennes-Oléron in Aquitaine, and Arcachon near Bordeaux.

There was an unknowing voluptuousness in the way she tipped the shells back to swallow the briny molluscs, accentuating the clean line of her jaw, the length of her neck. The stall holder watched transfixed, colour tinging his swarthy cheeks. 'If she were my wife, *monsieur*, I would have no need for oysters,' he told Jean-Luc with a leering wink, as he handed over the careful selection Sophia wished to take back for the chef's delectation. And Jean-Luc, instead of being offended, permitted himself a smug smile.

They proceeded from stall to stall, with Sophia charming and sampling, the basket he had purchased for her slowly filling with cheeses, sweetmeats, savoury pies, delicate strawberries and juicy raspberries. She seemed utterly at home here among the jostling crowds, exchanging banter with the stall holders, male and female, examining the cages of rabbits and chickens with the experienced eye of a cook, rather than the sentimental one of a lady. He knew, from the dinners which she ordered for him, that she had not been teasing him about her love of food, but it was clear now, that it was a passion, and one she was indulging without restraint.

He remembered the way she had stroked the soft leather of her gloves at the theatre. The way she had luxuriated in the rich silks and damasks of the clothes they had discovered in the attic at the Montendre palace. She was a sensual creature at heart. Yet she struggled to lose herself in that most intimate of sensual experiences.

Violated. Jean-Luc swore vehemently. What kind of man had her husband been to make his wife feel so defiled! The man had not forced her, she claimed, but he struggled to understand why, if this was the case, she felt as if he had. Had his appetites been perverse? To imagine Sophia enduring—*mon Dieu*, no, he would not imagine, he could not bear it. No wonder that she wanted to forget, his beautiful wife.

His wife. Watching her dipping a crust of bread into a dish of Provençal olive oil, he decided that he liked being married. He had enjoyed introducing her to his place of business yesterday, her fascination with his trade, the unfeigned interest in every aspect of it, and her equally unfeigned admiration of his success had flattered his pride. There was a purpose to all his hard work, if it made her happy, if it kept her in comfort, a purpose that had been lacking since his parents died. He had not expected his faux-wife to have any real part in his life, but Sophia had fitted seamlessly into it, and it made him realise that there had been a gap he'd not even been aware of. He hadn't been lonely, but he would be, when she was gone.

A bottle of olive oil was jammed precariously into the overflowing basket, and Sophia rejoined him. 'I'm having the most wonderful time.'

Jean-Luc laughed, and couldn't resist planting a kiss on her lips, which were slick with olive oil. 'You astonish me.'

'There's only one thing more we need to do, to round off this perfect morning. If you will indulge me.'

'How could I refuse. What is that you desire?'

'A cup of coffee. I'm told the best stall is over there, in the corner with the red awning, and I'm told that the best way to drink coffee at this time in the morning is with a glass of pastis.'

'True, if you have a stomach lined with iron.'

'All one requires is the stomach of a Frenchwoman. I insist.'

'You will regret it.'

'I will if I don't sample it at least once.' She handed him her basket, smiling up at him. 'When one discovers a wonderful new experience, one is compelled to relive it. *Tu comprends?*'

There was a blush on her cheeks, and a glow in her eyes that squeezed his heart and stirred his blood. 'If you are referring to this morning, Sophia, then I both understand and heartily concur.' He tucked her hand into his arm, pulling her close. His wife. There was no need to think about the moment when she would leave. Their wild goose chase would take them weeks yet, more likely months, maybe even longer. Which should be a very worrying thought, but instead was oddly reassuring.

Sophia's evening gown for the soirée comprised white figured gauze layered over a white-satin under-dress accessorised with white slippers, long, tightly fitting white gloves and a white spangled scarf. She had been afraid, she told Madeleine, that people would take her for a ghost, but as ever, her dresser was proved correct when, her *toilette* complete, Sophia stood in front of the mirror. The simplicity of the gown accentuated her figure, the neutral colour made her hair seem more golden in contrast, her lips more coral pink, and her eyes a brilliant blue.

She had always been ambiguous about her beauty, for so few cared to look beyond it. Ultimately, it had served its purpose, but she had come to think of it as a mask behind which she could hide her true nature. Tonight should be no different. She was playing Madame Bauduin, it was simply another part, but it didn't feel like it. Sophia and Madame Bauduin had somehow inextricably become the same person, and Madame Bauduin wanted her husband to admire her.

It was clear, from his expression as she joined him in their parlour half an hour before the first guests were expected, that he did.

'*Ma belle.*' He made a sweeping bow, lifting her hand to his lips. 'You look captivating. I will be the envy of every man in Paris.'

Sophia dropped a little curtsy, delighted beyond

measure. 'And I shall be the envy of every woman,' she said. 'You look very dashing.' Which wasn't quite true, but she had no words to describe the way his dark, striking looks made her heart skip a beat and her pulses flutter. Like her, Jean-Luc had opted for simplicity, and it made the most of his lean, muscled figure. His tailcoat and breeches were black. His waistcoat was white satin embroidered with silver thread. 'One could be forgiven for thinking we had co-ordinated our attire,' she said, 'we are a perfect match.'

'That is because we are,' Jean-Luc agreed, 'though there is something missing from your own *toilette*, Madame Bauduin.'

He pulled a velvet box from his pocket. Sophia instinctively recoiled. 'No. Thank you, please do not be offended, but I cannot accept a gift. There is really no need.'

His smile faded to a frown. 'Actually, there is. It will be expected that I buy my wife jewellery as a wedding present, and it will be expected that you wear that present on the night of the first party we host together.'

'Of course.' Still Sophia could not bring herself to open the box. 'So it is part of my costume? I will of course return it when I leave.'

He sighed, setting the box down on the table. 'No, it's a present. Not from Monsieur Baudin to Madame Bauduin but from Jean-Luc to Sophia. And regardless of what assumptions you are making, it comes with absolutely no strings attached.'

'I wasn't making any—' But his straight look forced

her to cut short the instinctive denial. 'You're right. I'm sorry. I thought—I didn't think, that's the problem.'

'I believe you, Sophia. It is clear that your marriage has tainted your view of the world, but it is very wearing to be constantly judged by another man's standards.'

Guilt made her feel quite sick. '*Mon Dieu*, Jean-Luc I am so sorry.' It was the first time he had complained, the first time he had shown her that her behaviour hurt him. How patient he had been with her. How ungrateful she must have seemed, and selfish too, so concerned about her own feelings that she hadn't considered his. Was this Hopkins's true legacy? No! A thousand times no! 'I am truly sorry,' Sophia said, 'but I owe you more than an apology. I will endeavour to judge you on your own merits from now on, I promise you.'

'Perhaps I ask too much of you, to break such an ingrained habit in such a short period of time. We have known each other for less than three weeks. though I must admit that I feel as if it has been a great deal longer.'

'So do I.' She caught his hand between hers, pressing a kiss on his knuckles. 'I'm so sorry.'

'Stop apologising. All I ask is that you remember that I only ever have your interests at heart. I simply want to make you happy.'

It was the tenderness in his voice that touched her heart. 'At the risk of sounding pitiful, it has been some time since anyone has aspired to do that.'

'And at the risk of sounding like a domineering husband, I recommend that you choose your company more carefully in future.'

She smiled weakly. 'You are categorically not a domineering husband.'

'Then what kind am I?' His smile was teasing.

'A very caring one. But I hope by the end of tonight to have made you a proud one too,' Sophia said. 'I've never organised a party on quite this scale before.'

'It will be a triumph, Sophia. I have no doubts.'

'Thank you.' The velvet box still sat unopened on the table. If boxes could look reproachful, this one was making a good fist of it. She picked it up. 'May I?'

He shrugged, pretending to consult his watch, but she knew he was watching her. There was, however, no need to simulate her pleasure when she viewed the contents. A large oval turquoise, set with diamonds, hanging from a simple white-gold chain with earrings to match. 'It's perfect,' Sophia said, quite overcome. 'Absolutely perfect.'

'Not quite.' Jean-Luc fastened the necklace around her neck, kissing her nape. 'Nothing could match your eyes. This is the closest I could find.'

'I love it.' She slipped the earrings into place, standing on tiptoe to admire the effect in the mirror. 'You couldn't have picked anything more understatedly beautiful.' Or more of a stark contrast to the ostentatious baubles with which Hopkins had adorned her. Which came at a price, and which had been amongst the first things she had sold. And what was she doing, thinking of Hopkins at a time like this!

Sophia turned around. 'Thank you.' She reached up to kiss him, just as the doorbell rang, making her jump. 'Oh, goodness, our first guests are here already. How do I look?'

'In need of this.' He pulled her back into his arms and kissed her. 'Now,' he said with a wicked smile as he released her, 'you look absolutely perfect.'

'Monsieur and Madame le Foy, may I present to you my wife, Sophia?'

'Madame la Comtesse, may I have the honour of presenting to you my wife, Sophia?'

'Chevalier, may I have the honour...?'

'*Mademoiselle*, it would be an honour...'

For almost two hours Sophia stood by Jean-Luc's side to welcome their guests in person. Every invitation, it seemed, had been accepted, and several hundred had been issued. She knew that, because she had written them out herself. She was relieved to see not one familiar face among the throng. Jean-Luc, on the other hand, not only knew every single guests name, he had that rare knack of making them all feel as if their presence was crucial to the success of the soirée.

He was also extremely adept at whispering just enough background information into her ear as each guest approached. 'Fellow vintner, wife who has just had had their first child.' 'Widow, likes to buy wine, not so keen to pay for it.' 'Very rich, prefers quantity over quality, collects antique maps.' 'Loves cognac, her pug dog and her butler, in that order.' 'Breeds canaries, reputed to be worth her weight in gold. Given her extremely generous proportions that makes her very rich indeed. The man hovering at her side is her nephew, who hopes to inherit. The gold, not the canaries.'

Several times, Sophia had been hard put not to laugh, but Jean-Luc did not once betray himself. She was astounded by the breadth and variety of his acquaintances. As he steered her around the assembled company, she was even more impressed by his effortless charm, his ability to act as a social conduit, introducing merchants to countesses, chevaliers to wine growers.

The rooms were crowded, but a crush was avoided by using the courtyard as an overflow, which Sophia had organised to be lit with strings of lanterns. Slipping from his side to check on preparations in the kitchens, she returned to find Jean-Luc engaged in convivial conversation with a gaggle of their younger guests. If, by some twist of fate, he proved to be the Duc de Montendre, then he would, she thought, fit seamlessly into the role. For a man who had never hosted a soirée before, he was making a most excellent fist of it, effortlessly putting people at their ease.

He was a natural host. Unlike her father, who loved nothing more than the sound of his own voice, Jean-Luc was content to let others hold forth. He had no need to boast and to bluff in order to stamp his authority on a conversation.

'Your husband is a most singular man, Madame Bauduin, if you do not mind me saying so.'

Sophia turned to find herself addressed by the fabulously wealthy canary breeder who, was wearing a white confection that made her look like a galleon in full sail. 'That depends on what you consider to be the source of his singularity, Madame Rochelle,' she replied.

'Ah, a new wife who leaps to the defence of her husband. That bodes well for a long and successful marriage. I merely meant that your husband was a merchant with an aristocratic air. A man whose fortune is matched by his face. It is rare to find such a combination. I should know.' Madame Rochelle's face creased into a smile. 'Come, Madame Bauduin, there is no need for you to look so politely blank. It is my experience that suitors find my wealth to be very slimming.'

'It is my experience that wealth is in the eye of the beholder,' Sophia said.

'Ha! That is very good, you won't mind if I appropriate it?' Madame Rochelle raised her glass. 'I think you will do very well for our Jean-Luc. We are very fond of him, you know, and of his wine.'

'I am very fond of him myself.'

'An understatement I hope, *ma belle*?' Jean-Luc slipped his arm around her waist. 'I have missed you. Have you persuaded Madame Rochelle to give us a pair of her precious canaries as a wedding present?'

Madame Rochelle tapped him on the arm with her fan. 'Two love birds in this *hôtel* is quite enough. You have done well with your English wife, Jean-Luc. I heartily approve.'

He bowed with a flourish over her outstretched hand. 'I am very grateful for your approval, for you are the very arbiter of taste, *madame*.'

Which remark elicited a trill of laughter. 'You may

not think it to look at me, but it's true,' she said to Sophia. 'It is a little secret which your husband is one of the few privy to, that I have a regular little piece in a certain monthly magazine read by almost every lady present, telling them what to buy and where to buy it. I write under a nom de plume, of course.'

'And may I ask how my husband came to be privy to such information?' Sophia asked, amused.

'Oh, I told him. I hoped that he would manage to source for me a certain wine of rare vintage, and in exchange, I would use my magazine column to advise all of Paris to buy their wine from Bauduin's.'

'I will hazard a guess that he refused the deal.'

'You are quite correct. Though he did, some months later, send me a crate of the wine as a gift. A most generous gesture from a most generous man. I envy you, Madame Bauduin, as does every female here. Now, before I embarrass Jean-Luc any further, I see that your butler is about to announce supper, and if your wonderful canapes are anything to go by, then that is a treat I will not wish to miss.'

It was very late. The last of the guests had, most reluctantly left, and Jean-Luc had dismissed the servants, telling them to leave the clearing up until the morning. Picking up a bottle of champagne and two glasses, he joined Sophia in the courtyard, where she was sitting on her favourite bench beneath the covered terrace.

'That was a triumph, thanks to you,' he said, pouring Sophia a glass of the cold sparkling wine. 'You charmed the ladies and had the gentlemen eating out of your hands. No one doubted our story, I knew they would not, the moment they set eyes on you. We will be besieged with invitations tomorrow.' He raised his glass to her, unable to resist pressing a soft kiss to her mouth. 'To Madame Bauduin. The most perfect pretend wife a man could ask for.'

She smiled back at him, raising her glass in return. 'To Monsieur Bauduin, the most perfect pretend husband.'

He sat down beside her, sliding his arm around her, quietly pleased when, after only the tiniest hesitation, she let her head rest on his shoulder. Her hair tickled his chin. He could feel the soft rise and fall of her breathing. The night was still, warm for early June, scented with the lilac which was coming into bloom on the parterre. He sipped his wine, enjoying the peace and quiet after the noisy hubbub of the party. 'It is good to have the house to ourselves again, isn't it?'

'Have a care, Jean-Luc, lest you become one of those men who is forever advocating the delights of domesticity. Thus is Paris's most confirmed bachelor fallen from grace.'

'I was never a confirmed bachelor. I simply hadn't met the right woman. Now I have, I will be happy to advocate the delights of domesticity to any man who cares to listen.'

'Our guests have left, Jean-Luc. You may cease your performance.'

He tightened his arm around her. 'It requires surprisingly little effort, don't you find?' He kissed the top of her head. 'I enjoy being your husband.'

She sat up. 'Pretend husband, Jean-Luc. There is a world of difference.' She made a face. 'Perhaps that's why it is so enjoyable.'

'Was it so very terrible, your marriage, Sophia?'

She blanched. 'Jean-Luc.' She cleared her throat, took a sip of her champagne. 'Jean-Luc, I was not...'

It was obvious she was bracing herself to deliver a revelation, and suddenly he found he didn't want to hear it. Not tonight. He shook his head, placing a fingertip over her mouth. 'No. We agreed only hours ago that comparisons are odious. I should not have brought the subject up. Forgive me.'

He could sense her ambivalence and was mightily relieved when finally she shrugged, forced a smile, set her glass down on the paving and took his hand in hers, turning his signet ring over and over, emulating of his own habit. 'Where did you get this? It looks very old.'

'My father gave it to me. I've always assumed it belonged to his father though actually...' He frowned. 'I don't believe he ever said as much. There was an inscription on it once, on the inside, but it has faded too much to make out more than a few letters.'

Sophia ran her fingers over the worn contours of the gold. 'It feels as if there was once a setting, perhaps for a stone.'

'I've never noticed.' He did as she had done, noting the odd little nodules. 'You could be right.'

He poured himself another glass of champagne. Sophia, refusing a refill, snuggled back on to his shoulder. He kissed the top of her head. 'Aren't you tired?'

'Not in the slightest.' She slid an arm across his

stomach. 'Look at the stars up there. It's so peaceful, it's difficult to believe we are in the heart of Paris.'

'When I first moved here from Cognac, I couldn't sleep for the constant noise of the city. Which was just as well, since I had to work all hours to establish myself.'

'Do you still have a place of business in Cognac?'

'*Certainement.* It is where the business was founded. I would not dream of closing it. Besides, we buy most of our wine from the Bordeaux region. I visit there at least two or three times a year.'

'It was a portentous day for you then, when your parents became so poor they had to send you out to work.'

He laughed gruffly. 'I've been thinking about that. Why did Maman send me to a school they could not afford, do you think? There was a perfectly good school in Cognac.'

'Not good enough for her son, obviously.'

'She always did want the best for me. Was it as simple as that?' He drained his champagne. 'I can't help thinking there is more to it, Sophia. It is another thing I don't understand, another thing I've never questioned until now, the issue of money. Where did it come from, the money to pay for my schooling almost seven years? I don't know. My parents never worked, they didn't farm, they were not in trade. What did they live on, and why did it dry up? Again, I'm in the dark. In my younger days there was plenty. When I came home from school there was always a celebration. When I returned, there were new clothes and new books. And then there was less food. And less clothes, and no books, and then my clothes were patched and mended. And then there was no school.'

'So whatever their income was, wherever it came from, it dried up?'

'In about 1800. When I first started working, my parents were very poor.' He set down his empty glass. 'I don't know what I'm trying to say. I don't know that any of this adds up to anything, save my ignorance, their desire, perhaps to cover up some disreputable past, but...'

'You think it is something?'

'It is not nothing,' he said wryly. 'I'm not saying that I am this Duc de Montendre's son, I am still quite sure that I am not, but am I truly the son I think I am? And if not, what does that mean? Does it even matter? I only wish that I had thought to ask some of these questions while my parents were alive, that is all. This damned de Cressy woman, if she had not come along with her silly story, I wouldn't even have thought—but now it is too late, the damage is done. I feel as if I had a picture of my life, and now it has been torn up, and I can't make the fragments fit together into anything I recognise.' He swore softly. 'That sounds ridiculous. I think I have had too much wine.'

'Is there much to be gained by discovering the truth, Jean-Luc? If your parents came to Cognac to escape some sort of scandal, don't you think it would best to let sleeping dogs lie? You might discover something that might taint your memory of them.'

He cupped her face in his hands. 'I doubt very much

that there is anything sordid or scandalous in my parents' past. But if there is, I have to know, otherwise I will feel that I am living a lie.'

Living a lie. An hour later, lying wide awake in bed, Sophia realised that was exactly what she was doing, except the lines between their performance as husband and wife and the reality of their relationship as Sophia and Jean-Luc were now so blurred, she could hardly distinguish them. Tonight, when Jean-Luc had placed the turquoise necklace around her neck, she had felt certain she was turning a corner, finally putting her past completely behind her. Standing by his side, telling and retelling the story of their whirlwind romance to their guests, she had almost convinced herself that it was true. It had been so easy to cling lovingly to him, to gaze at him adoringly, to have him kiss her hand and her cheek. She wasn't aware that she was acting. She had always had to try so hard before, to pretend. With Jean-Luc, there was no pretence required.

Save that she maintained not a pretence, but a lie. A monstrous one, that with every passing day grew ever bigger. She curled her hand around the turquoise necklace which she'd been unable to bring herself to take off. A gift, for no other reason than that he wanted to please her. No man had ever bestowed such a gift on her. She had never known any man like Jean-Luc. Who had come to care for her. As she had come to care for him.

She would not be so foolish as to care too much— but how much was too much? He liked her. He trusted her. He thought he knew her. He did not want to live a lie, but she was forcing him to. He thought her married, for heaven's sake. She had to tell him. Before it was too late—though what the devil that meant, she wasn't sure. But she owed him the truth. Their marriage was well established now, she had served her purpose. If he chose to send her away, to tell everyone that her imaginary companion was desperately sick, then it would make no difference.

Sophia's hand curled more tightly around the turquoise stone. 'Please let him allow me to stay. Please let him…' *What? Forgive her? Tell her he understood?* The depths of her own folly struck her forcibly. She knew there could be no more excuses. Tomorrow, she would confess all. And most likely by tomorrow afternoon she would be on her way back to England.

Chapter Ten

'Maxime has just turned up, anxious to speak to me. It had better be important enough to warrant disturbing our breakfast.'

Sophia stood up. 'He will no doubt wish to speak to you in confidence. I will leave you to it.'

'Please sit down and finish your meal. I am happy for you to hear whatever he has to say,' Jean-Luc said firmly. He turned to the servant. 'Have Monsieur Sainte-Juste brought here, and set another place at the table.' He poured a cup of coffee and helped himself to some eggs. 'You are very quiet, Sophia, is something bothering you?'

Something was terrifying her. From dawn, she had been rehearsing her confession in various forms, none of them satisfactory. She couldn't decide whether to be relieved that Maxime's visit would force a postponement or frustrated, as the delay would only add to her anguish. 'I am just a little tired, it was a very late night,' Sophia muttered, realising that Jean-Luc was eyeing her with concern.

'And a very taxing occasion since so much was riding on the soirée being a success. So we will hear what Maxime has to say, and then you will go back to your bed, and I will have your dresser bring you a tisane, and—ah, Maxime, please join us.'

'Would you like coffee, Monsieur Sainte-Juste?' Sophia asked, 'Some breakfast, perhaps? We have eggs, and some very good cheese, and...'

'I thank you Madame Bauduin, coffee will suffice.' The lawyer made his bow, then took a seat beside Jean-Luc. Maxime took a sip of hot coffee. Jean-Luc waited patiently. The lawyer's expression was grave. Sophia's anxiety found a new focus as she watched him finish his coffee and pass his cup over for a refill. *'Merci.'* He took another sip. 'I hear that your soirée went swimmingly last night. I was sorry to miss it.'

Jean-Luc drew his friend a sceptical look. 'No, you weren't, Maxime. You hate parties. And besides, I seem to remember you had another engagement. Dinner, I think you said.'

'Yes. Dinner. With my sister, actually. And—and Mademoiselle de Cressy. The two have become very good friends.'

'Indeed?'

Jean-Luc smiled. It was his *I am waiting patiently* smile, Sophia knew, which preceded his *I'm not going to say anything until you do* ploy. The one that even she found difficult to resist.

Maxime's restraint lasted an unimpressive thirty seconds, by her count, before he spoke. 'I feel obliged to escort them, every now and then,' he said. 'My sister likes to think herself sophisticated, but she is—well, it does no harm, does it, to have a brother around to keep an eye on things?'

'Since I don't have a sister, how am I to answer that?'

Maxime drained his coffee cup for a second time. Sophia filled it for a third. The lawyer took a deep breath. 'Jean-Luc, I have to inform you that Mademoiselle de Cressy is—'

'Very pretty, and I am sure very distracting company, but I presume you did not come here to discuss Mademoiselle de Cressy.'

'You are, for once, quite mistaken. I came here to tell you that we now have incontrovertible proof that she is indeed the daughter of the Comte de Cressy. I am very sorry. I know it is not the news you were hoping to hear.'

'You are absolutely certain?'

'The agent I sent to Switzerland was very thorough, to the extent of bringing back with him one of the staff in service to the Comte and Comtesse de Cressy until Juliette was obliged to let him go, when her papa died.'

If Jean-Luc noticed Maxime's use of the familiar *Juliette*, he made no comment. Her husband's expression, Sophia thought, watching him nervously, was grim.

'So Mademoiselle de Cressy now knows that her story has been verified?' he asked.

Maxime looked affronted. 'Certainly not. I arranged for the servant to identify her without her knowing, but I must say, Jean-Luc, I think it only fair that Juliette—'

'You work for me, Maxime, not *Juliette*, as you so

fondly refer to her. I hope that the time you are spending in her company while chaperoning your sister is not clouding your judgement.'

The lawyer drew himself up. 'Jean-Luc, that was unworthy of you. I am very much aware of where my loyalties lie and my duty too. While you are in dispute with Mademoiselle de Cressy, I cannot possibly be more than a friend to her. As for Juliette, I am sure she has no thoughts save to marry you.'

'My sincere apologies.' Jean-Luc was immediately contrite. 'You did not deserve that. This news has come as a major shock.'

Which admission was a surprise to Sophia. 'But you always knew it was possible that she was telling the truth about herself.'

'I did,' he answered tersely, 'but it appears I hoped more than I realised, that she would turn out to be a fraud.'

He picked up his coffee cup only to find it empty. Sophia got up to pour him a fresh one, earning herself a grateful smile. 'It doesn't necessarily mean that the rest of it is true,' she said, placing her hand on his shoulder.

He caught her hand, pressing a kiss to her fingertips.

Maxime cleared his throat. Embarrassed, Sophia returned to her seat. The lawyer was eyeing her curiously. She had forgotten he was in the room. He was probably worrying that she was taking her role as Jean-Luc's wife too seriously. He might even be concerned that she would be difficult to dislodge when she was no longer required. He knew she was, unlike Juliette, a genuine fraud, so to speak.

'What will we do now?' she asked Jean-Luc, flustered.

'Before you reach any conclusions,' Maxime interrupted, 'I have more news to impart regarding the marriage contract.' He produced a parchment from a document bag and untied the ribbon which bound it. 'One of the signatories is, as you know, Henri Grunot. I have finally been able to gain access to the records at the Conciergerie—that is the prison on the Île de la Cité, Madame Bauduin, where the majority of those arrested were held before they were sent to the guillotine. Prior to their trial and execution they would have been in one of the many prisons scattered throughout Paris. To cut a long story short, the records confirm the story you were told at the Hôtel Montendre. Henri Grunot, occupation listed as valet to the Duc de Montendre, was convicted on the same day as his master, and both were executed that same day. The Duchesse de Montendre's summary trial was held two days later, and she went to the guillotine the following day.'

'*Mon Dieu,*' Sophia said, 'it is barbaric.' She had been in their home. She had walked through the rooms where they had lived. The clothes in the trunks must have belonged to the Duchess. This was no longer a story. It was horribly, tragically real.

'It is a piece of our history which we must be ashamed of for ever,' Maxime said, 'but we cannot deny it happened. The only thing we can do is ensure it never happens again. However...' he gave Sophia another of his thin smiles '... I did not come here to lecture you on the bloodthirsty history of France. The other witness, Jean-Luc, I have been able to trace him to Bordeaux. He is a lawyer, which is very good news for you. Even if he is not alive, his papers will be preserved. It is likely to be a family firm too. What I'm trying to say is, there's a good chance that we have a witness. Or at the very least, someone who is related to the witness.'

'At last. That is excellent work, Maxime. Thank you.'

The lawyer rolled up the marriage contract. 'You will need this, assuming that you intend to go to Bordeaux?'

'As soon as it can be arranged. Since Mademoiselle de Cressy has now been proven to be one party to that cursed marriage contract, it is absolutely imperative that I prove I am not the other.'

Maxime got to his feet. 'And do I have your permission to inform Juliette of the latest turn in events?'

'And how do you think *Juliette* will take the news?' Jean-Luc asked sardonically.

'If you're asking me if it's going to make her more determined to pursue her claim, then all I can say is that she's shown no sign whatsoever of relinquishing it.' Maxime frowned. 'I know you don't want to hear this, but from her point of view, the contract was made in good faith between her father and his closest friend. She feels she has a duty to honour it.'

'Though she might not feel so honour bound were she less poverty stricken.'

Maxime flinched. 'Perhaps not, but she is more or less destitute, Jean-Luc, her situation truly dire. As a gently bred young woman, marriage is her only option.'

'That is as may be, but I am not a viable candidate. I already have a wife.'

'Not in the eyes of the law.'

'But in the eyes of Paris and Mademoiselle de Cressy I do, and that's what matters,' Jean-Luc said firmly.

'Have you considered the possibility—Jean-Luc, what if your trip to Bordeaux proves inconclusive either way?'

'If I cannot prove that I am not the Montendre heir, nor can she prove that I am. As far as I am concerned that will be the end of the matter.'

'What if she does not accept this?'

Jean-Luc shrugged. 'Whether she accepts a settlement as a gesture of goodwill is up to her, but I repeat, her claim would not be enforceable without cast-iron proof. And as my lawyer, I would expect you to persuade her that was the case. In the meantime, I trust you will ensure that Mademoiselle de Cressy continues to honour our agreement by keeping her own counsel? Good. I have no idea how long we will be away, but I will keep you informed of any significant developments.'

He shook Maxime's hand, bidding him good morning. His polite smile faded as soon as the door closed behind him. 'Now we know why Mademoiselle de Cressy was so convincing.'

'So now you must leave Paris on a long trip which, if Maxime is correct, may not even prove to be conclusive.'

'*We* must leave Paris, I'm not going without you. As to Maxime—he is a lawyer, they are trained to be pessimists. But it is as I told him: if, after Bordeaux, we have exhausted all avenues of enquiry, Mademoiselle de Cressy will be forced to accept that no proof is proof enough. I am anxious to be rid of that woman from my life.'

'And this woman too,' Sophia said, forcing a smile.

'Ah, this woman is a very different matter.' He pulled her into his arms. 'I am not remotely anxious to be rid of you, *ma belle*. You must know that.'

Were any words ever so bittersweet? They warmed her heart, but they terrified her too. She could not afford to let him care too much. One certain way to prevent that would be to confess to her scandalous past as she had planned, but how could she possibly do that now? He needed her by his side while his future was uncertain, and she couldn't bear the thought of being forced to continue to play his wife, when she had destroyed the trust that had blossomed between them.

Sophistry, Sophia? No, she told herself firmly. The contract she had signed with The Procurer obliged her to remain with Jean-Luc until he dismissed her. Until he could rid himself of Juliette de Cressy, he could not dismiss her. Why estrange him, make an endurance test of the time they had together by telling him the sordid truth, when she could instead be a support to him? A wife to him. Why pretend that she didn't care, when she did? Why not make the most of it, for heaven's sake, when it would be over soon enough?

'I don't intend to leave your side any time soon.' Smiling up at her husband, Sophia buried her guilt in the corner of her heart she reserved for such things. It was becoming a crowded spot.

City of Bordeaux

As Jean-Luc had predicted, their triumphant introduction into society had resulted in a rash of invitations to the newlyweds from friends and business colleagues, delaying their departure for almost two weeks. But eventually, they quit the city, leaving the business in the charge of Jean-Luc's secretary and Mademoiselle de Cressy seemingly happy under Maxime's care.

A scheduled meeting with one of Jean-Luc's established customers was reorganised to take place in Bordeaux rather than Paris. 'I can't put him off,' he had informed Sophia just before they boarded the coach, looking harassed. 'He's getting married, and he wants me to stock the cellars of his new country estate from champagne to cognac, as well as to supply some more exclusive vintages for the celebration of the nuptials. It's a distraction I could well do without, but business is business.'

Though the wine business was the furthest thing on either of their minds as they finally arrived in the bustling port of Bordeaux in the late afternoon five days later. The trip south, made at speed in a private carriage, had been so very different from Sophia's prior experience of the journey, that until she stepped out of the carriage on to the Place Royale, she had not thought of that earlier, tragic procession south. Now, the beauty and symmetry of the square, the buildings extending on either side like welcoming arms as they ran down to the bank of the Garonne River, jolted her memory. Though it had only been an overnight stop, the city had made an favourable impression on her. She had never been back, for her other journeys, including that last return to England, cloaked in such grief she barely registered her surroundings, had been made via Lyon.

Standing on the cobblestones of the huge square, facing out to the wide, sedately flowing river, Sophia closed her eyes, breathing in the warm air, which did not quite have the distinctive sweetness of the true south, but was so very different from Paris. Despite the heat, she shivered. Fifteen—no, sixteen months since she had been here. Almost ten now, since...

'Sophia? Our hotel is just a short walk away. The streets are too narrow for the carriage.'

'Would you mind sending the bags on ahead? I'd like to get some fresh air.'

'But of course. I would like to stretch my legs too. We'll walk along the quayside, if you like.' Jean-Luc instructed the coachman, then slipped her hand into his arm.

The quays were relatively quiet, the work of the day done, the warehouses closed up, the ships at anchor creaking in the light breeze. 'A great deal of my time was spent here when I first started in the wine trade,' Jean-Luc informed her. 'Though our offices were in Cognac, all of the wine from the region was shipped from here.'

'Why didn't your employer establish his business here, then, rather than in Cognac?'

'In those days, the main trade was still brandy rather

than wine. I have thought often of moving my business premises to this city, but it doesn't feel right. Though it is I who have expanded it into an international concern and given it the Bauduin name, I feel that I owe it to the old man, to keep something of his heritage, you know?'

'And Cognac is also close to your heart too, isn't it?'

'Of course, even if it turns out not to be, as I have always assumed, the place of my birth.' Jean-Luc drew them over to a wooden bench, positioned at the deserted far end of the quays with a view over the river. 'Will you tell me, Sophia, what has made you so maudlin?'

'I'm not...' Catching his eye, she bit back her instinctive denial, shaking her head.

'You know so much about me. This whole journey south, we have talked and talked of my family and the Montendre family, but never of you. I know I have no right to ask, but...'

'It's not that I don't want to tell you, Jean-Luc, it's just that I don't think I can.' Sophia stared out across the river. The tide was changing, making the boats rock rhythmically, the rigging seeming to sigh. There was the faintest tang of salt in the air. She licked her lips and realised she was crying silently. Days had gone by of late when she had not thought of her sister. Now, with the change in air, it all came back to her, and she longed, desperately, to spend one more day, one more hour with her. Ten months. How could it have been ten months?

Jean-Luc handed her a kerchief. She dabbed at her eyes. He did not press her, but there was such tenderness in his expression that something inside her shifted. This man, despite all the turmoil and uncertainty in his own life, cared about her. He understood her as no one else ever had. Not even…

'Felicity,' Sophia said. 'It was because of Felicity that I was here, on my way south. She was my sister. She was resident in the spa at Menton. She was dying of consumption.'

It was as if a dam had burst. Sophia's story tumbled out, an outpouring of tender love, raw grief and aching loss for her beloved sister that touched his heart. Jean-Luc had thought he knew her, thought he understood her, but here was a huge, significant part of her that she had kept completely secret, a wound too painful for her to reveal to anyone. Save that now, she was talking of it to him. He was honoured, but helpless. He wanted to pull her into his arms and tell her, ridiculously, that he would make it better. But he dared not touch her, lest he interrupt the flow.

'She was five years younger than me, and such a lovely, loving child,' Sophia was saying now, her big blue eyes aglow, focused on the distant past. 'When Mama died, Felicity was just turned six. My father dismissed our governess, and so it fell to me to school her while trying to school myself. Despite the fact that he purported to be an advocate for formal schooling for boys…' She blinked, turning her gaze back to Jean-Luc, curling her lip. 'One thing you could say about my father, he was consistent in his hypocrisy.'

'What kind of man was he!' he exclaimed with

barely suppressed anger. 'Did he blame your younger sister too, for being the wrong sex in his eyes?'

'It was worse than that. Felicity was never strong and my father—I don't think he ever cared for her. That is a terrible thing to say, I know it is, but it is the truth, though even now, it pains me to admit it. She was often ill, you see, and she was painfully shy, consequently of little value in furthering his career.'

'His career?'

Jean-Luc watched her weigh up whether or not to elaborate. She was the daughter of someone of standing, clearly. He was beginning to wonder if he knew anything about her at all.

'He was a politician, a fairly eminent one, though never as successful as he believed he ought to be. He was too outspoken and opinionated, he alienated many potential allies. And after Mama died, when he lost the funds which had helped cover the cracks in his popularity, when he could no longer sponsor dinners and grease palms—you can imagine.'

'A bitter man with a small mind who blamed everyone but himself for his failures?'

Sophia laughed drily. 'That is him in a nutshell.' Her brittle smile faded. 'And who, when his youngest daughter's health began to fail, claimed that it was nature's way of sorting the chaff from the wheat. I disliked him heartily before that. I hated him then, though no more, I suspect, than he hated himself in the end, when even he was forced to confront his demons. He drank himself to death. After we had paid his debts, there was pretty much nothing left. That was almost four years ago, and by that time Felicity...' Her voice trembled, but when he made to take her hand, she shook her head. 'No, let me finish, if you please. If I stop now, I don't think I'll be able to carry on again.'

She twisted his handkerchief into a knot, her brows drawn fiercely together. 'She needed sunshine and heat. She knew that her lifespan would be limited, the signs of the consumption advancing and ravaging her body could not be ignored. We had heard such good things of the air on the Mediterranean, people with her condition who lived much longer than those who remained in England, so I determined to find the funds to send her to convalesce there.

'My sister—Felicity—she was so stoic, Jean-Luc, not even at the end would she admit to suffering. I don't know how she endured it, knowing that her life would be cut short. She never would admit to it, I suppose that was her secret. Always with her it was tomorrow this, and next month that, and sometimes, she was so very good at it you see, I believed her.'

'She was very brave.'

'Yes. She was very brave.'

'But it must have made it very difficult for you.'

'I didn't think of it, because she did not.' Sophia gazed down at her lap. 'It was a shock when I did lose her, more than a shock. I should have been prepared, but I wasn't. It has been ten months now, and there are still days when I wake up and I've forgotten that she is gone. Though it has helped, coming here to be with you. I have had a purpose again.'

Now she did allow him to take her hand, and to pull

her head on to his shoulder. He held her, feeling her gradually relax, and together they watched the river, until finally she sat up. 'I was only here, in this city, for one day. I thought I'd forgotten, but when I stepped out of carriage this afternoon, I remembered it very clearly.'

'You found the means to send her to live in the south then?' Jean-Luc asked.

'Yes.'

Her withdrawal was almost palpable. 'And you found a way to be with her too,' he said gently, 'before the end?'

'Yes.' It seemed he did know her, after all, enough to sense her silent thanks for the change in tack. 'For six months, I stayed with her,' she added.

'And while you were with her, you improved your grasp of my language?'

'Felicity teased me at first, for she was fluent by that time, of course, having been in Menton for about two years, but it turned out that we both had an ear for it. There was a Frenchman, another resident at the spa for the same reason as Felicity, who had taught at onc of our English boys' schools, and he helped. Felicity used to say that...'

Jean-Luc listened without interrupting as Sophia spoke, her eyes once again aglow with memories, her soft smile unbearably tender as she confided in him, laughing at this tale, grimacing at that, never once even hinting at whatever sacrifices she must have made, at the silent suffering she must have endured, crediting her sister with the brave heart, not for an instant imagining how much braver hers must have been, for it had to endure the aftermath.

'That is more than enough,' she said, cutting herself short in the midst of an anecdote. 'Forgive me, I have prattled on.'

'At my request.' He kissed her gloved hand. 'Thank you, Sophia. I am honoured.'

'It is I who should thank you. I have not, as you'll have gathered, spoken of her at all. It has helped enormously.'

'Now I know why you are an excellent listener. And were, I think, a most dutiful sister.'

'I couldn't save her, Jean-Luc. I couldn't do that for her.'

'I suspect you did a great deal more than she ever knew. Two years, I think you said, she was in Menton, before you joined her for the last six months?'

'Yes.' Sophia had got to her feet, shaking out the skirts of her pelisse. 'We must have been sitting here for an age. The hotel will be thinking us lost.'

'So you didn't see her in the interim?'

'Twice I was permitted to visit for a month each year. I made it a—' She broke off, horrified. 'We really should get back before the light fails, Jean-Luc.'

'Condition,' he finished for her. 'Of your marriage, I presume?' For it all made sense now. Horrible sense. Admirable sense. Brave, sacrificial sense. 'Sophia.' Jean-Luc caught her hand between his, struggling with the wealth of emotions coursing through him. '*Ma belle*, what you did, what you sacrificed—' But seeing her face, he broke off, cursing under his breath.

'You cannot possibly be ashamed. It was a noble thing to do.'

'You think I married for Felicity's sake, don't you? But I didn't.'

'Sophia, you know there is nothing you can tell me that would make me think ill of you?'

She gazed at him for a long, painful moment. 'I believe that is what you think,' she said, finally, 'but you deserve better than me.' She turned away. 'We must get back. I have the headache. You will have to excuse me from dinner.'

Chapter Eleven

Jean-Luc had secured the most luxurious suite in the hotel for their stay, the two bedchambers separated by a drawing room and a small dining room. Conscious of his far-too-perceptive gaze, Sophia drew on her vast experience of affecting indifference, keeping her face blank, her smile bland, as the housekeeper showed them round their accommodation. She turned down the offer of a lady's maid, closing the door of her bedchamber firmly on Jean-Luc as soon as they were alone. And then she stood rooted to the spot in a maelstrom of regret and uncertainty and guilt. She had done the one thing she had promised herself she would not do, and spoilt things with her impulsive confession.

In despair, Sophia tugged off her hat and cast off her pelisse, only then noticing that a bath had been prepared, the steam rising from behind the screen. Jean-Luc must have ordered it. He knew how much she enjoyed the luxury of bathing after a day's travel. She did not deserve such an attentive, kind, thoughtful husband. He did not deserve such a lying, deceitful, ungrateful, tarnished wife. So it was just as well she was not actually his wife. Even if she wished she could be.

No! Sophia stopped in the act of unlacing her gown. 'No, no, no, no, no,' she whispered viciously, 'you must not be so stupid, so reckless.' Her fingers shaking, she continued to undress. She wasn't stupid, she was simply over-emotional. An understandable response to talking about Felicity, Jean-Luc being so understanding, the relief of finally confiding details of her personal life in him. Yes, that was it.

She wriggled out of her corset, casting her remaining undergarments on to the bed. Stepping into the deliciously hot, scented water, sinking down into the bath, she closed her eyes as the water began to soothe her tense limbs, and clear her fogged brain.

You think I married for Felicity's sake, don't you? But I didn't.

Meaning that she had not gone through with marriage to Frederick. She'd thought it obvious, but it was actually quite ambiguous.

You think I married for Felicity's sake, don't you? But I didn't.

Meaning that she *had* married, but for quite another reason. Sophia sat up, reaching for the soap. Was it wrong of her to hope that this was the interpretation Jean-Luc had put upon her words? Another lie. Though she hadn't actually lied. And she would have gone through with it for Felicity's sake if Frederick had kept his promise.

Sophia shuddered. Thank the stars he had not kept

his promise! To be married to Frederick, to *still* be married to Frederick without even the comfort of knowing she was supporting Felicity, did not bear thinking about. How very different it would have been, compared to marriage to Jean-Luc. Not that she was married to Jean-Luc, she reminded herself once again as she stepped out of the bath, wrapping a large towel around herself. Though it felt like marriage. Or what marriage ought to be. Perhaps because it was not marriage!

Her husband was on the other side of that door, most likely having his customary glass of madeira before dinner. Tomorrow, she would accompany him to a lawyer's office in the next stage of their quest to find the lost Duc de Montendre. He had been adamant, on the journey down, of the impossibility of he and the Duke being one and the same, but less and less certain of who he was. It was difficult to watch him struggling to reconcile the love he knew his mother had for him, with the possibility that she had been lying to him all his life.

These last few nights Sophia had been so exhausted after each leg of the journey that she had been fit for little more than to bolt down her dinner and fall into bed. Now, on the eve of what could be a momentous day, she could not in all conscience simply abandon Jean-Luc and leave him to fret in solitude. He, who had listened to her outpouring of grief and love, regardless of his own concerns. He had comforted her. And though he had leapt to the wrong conclusion, he had understood what drove her to do it.

You cannot possibly be ashamed, he had said.

Sophia gazed at herself in the mirror. She was not ashamed of her motives. She had not lied, when she told Jean-Luc she would have done more if required. She had succeeded in what she had set out to do, and she had freed herself at the end of it. Was she ashamed? Yes, of what she had endured in the interlude, forced herself to do, but of what had compelled her to do it? 'No,' she said firmly to her reflection. 'No, not any more.'

It would make no difference to the world. She would be judged by her actions, not her motives. Let them judge! She was not returning to that world. And Jean-Luc? Sophia sat on the edge of the bed, wrapping her arms around herself. Jean-Luc was a very different matter. He was a respectable, honourable man, with an impeccable reputation and a business which prospered in no small part due to the integrity which she so admired in him. She didn't just admire him, she liked him. A great deal too much to burden him with the truth. There could be no future for her with Jean-Luc, but it was her duty to support him in whatever way necessary while he uncovered his past.

Smiling, Sophia set about dressing in fresh underclothes, selecting a muslin gown of rose-pink with three-quarter sleeves which was loose enough not to require a corset. Some times, doing one's duty was astonishingly pleasant.

Jean-Luc was in their drawing room, gazing out at the busy street in front of the hotel. Like her he had bathed and changed, exchanging his buckskin breeches and travelling coat for a pair of knitted fawn pantaloons that clung to his muscled legs, and a black tailcoat that emphasised the breadth of his shoulders. He turned as Sophia closed her bedchamber door behind her, a surprised smile lighting up his face. 'Your headache has receded?'

'I didn't have a headache.' Sophia took the madeira he poured for her, touching the rim of the delicate crystal glass to his. 'Thank you for ordering my bath.'

'Your nightly pleasure, and my nightly torture, imagining you soaping yourself in it.'

'You do not!'

He kissed her softly on the lips. 'Oh, but I do. And now you have a complexion to match your gown. You blush so very charmingly it is a delight to tease you.'

She set her glass down beside his, on a side table. 'Are you teasing me?'

'Would you prefer me to lie to spare your blushes? Or would you prefer me to tell you the truth?' He pulled her into his arms. 'Which is that I picture you lying naked, the water lapping around you,' he whispered in her ear, 'your skin flushed with the heat, your hair streaming down your back like a river of gold, and your eyes closed in bliss.'

He kissed the pulse behind her ear. His hands were resting lightly on her arms, barely touching. There was still a gap between their bodies, yet Sophia was sure she could feel heat emanating from him. Though perhaps it was from her. She reached up to touch him, smoothing her hand on his freshly shaved cheek. 'I do close my eyes,' she said, pressing a brief kiss to the corner of his mouth. 'I do find it blissful.'

Jean-Luc groaned. 'Now I think it is you who are teasing me.'

She stepped closer, twining her arms around his neck. 'Do you like it?'

He slid his hands around her waist. 'Very much.'

She closed the last few inches between them, pressing herself against him, feeling the unmistakable ridge of his arousal, for the first time in her life, pleased to discover this proof of his desire. He wanted her. She caught her breath. She wanted him. She smiled up at him, a smile she hadn't known she possessed, that let him see just how much she wanted him. She kissed him, not a fluttering kiss but a real kiss, shaping her mouth to his, touching her tongue to his, arching her body against his. A kiss which could leave him in no doubt of what she wanted. How far she had come, she thought hazily, in learning the unspoken language of kissing. How naive she had been, thinking kisses the most innocent of endearments, when they were actually the most intimate act of all.

But when she angled her mouth to deepen it still further, Jean-Luc dragged his mouth away from hers, his breathing ragged. 'Sophia, if you are still teasing me...'

'No.' She kissed him again. 'I promise you, I am entirely serious.'

'Then I should tell you, *ma belle*, that so too am I. More serious than I have ever been in my life.'

He gave her no time to ponder his meaning, but when he kissed her, it was different, though she could not have said how. She very quickly ceased to care as his kisses woke the fire in her belly and heated her blood, welcoming the building tension inside her that she now knew for her own arousal. As before, there were kisses trailing paths from her mouth, down her neck to her breasts, but now she followed his lead, pushing aside his coat, tugging his shirt free from his pantaloons, wanting to touch flesh, skin, no barrier between them.

They sank down on to the thick rug in front of the fireplace, where a huge bouquet of roses filled the hearth, kneeling face to face, kissing and touching and stroking. His coat was quickly discarded along with his waistcoat. She pulled his cravat free, burying her face in the warm skin at his throat, pressing feverish kisses that made him groan, made his breathing quicken like her own, left her in no doubt of the effect she was having on him, of how much he wanted her.

There had been no doubts with Hopkins either. He had never attempted to rein in his passion. Experience had taught her the little tricks which would bring him quickly to a conclusion. It was her only satisfaction, knowing she could play him like an instrument, make him dance to her tune.

'Sophia?' Jean-Luc's eyes were heavy-lidded, his cheeks flushed, his breathing ragged, but his expression was one of concern. 'You were miles away. Do you want me to stop?'

'No.' His asking the question encapsulated the difference, which was vast. She was his lover, not his mistress. He wanted to make love with her, not to her. 'I'm fine, I promise. Don't stop. I don't want you to stop.'

'Sophia.' Her name was a caress. He kissed her. 'Sophia,' he said again, softly, '*mon amour*, I want you so much.'

He untied the sash of her gown, then the laces at the back, easing the muslin over her shoulders, down her arms, until it pooled on the rug where they knelt. Her chemise was next, his sharp intake of breath as he gazed at her naked breasts stilling any embarrassment. Then his mouth on her nipple, his hands cupping and stroking, making her forget everything save his touch and the mounting excitement building inside her.

Fighting it, wanting to prolong the ecstasy, she tugged at his shirt, watching with another newfound pleasure as he pulled it over his head, drinking in the sleek, muscled strength of him, her hands following her eyes, relishing the contrast of the rough hair on his chest with the smoother skin of his belly. And then her lips followed her hands, adding taste to touch and to sight, as she pressed a kiss to the dip in his chest, then dared further, to lick where she had kissed, making him moan, a feral sound that set her heart racing. He wrapped his arms around her, easing her on to her back.

'You test my resolve to its limits,' he said, kissing her.

She twined her arms around him, lost in the sensation of his chest against her breasts, of his mouth clinging to hers, and now the urgent clamour inside her for release. He sensed it, helping her to wriggle free of her gown, her chemise, her pantalettes. his hand cupping the heat between her legs.

She bit back a moan. He said her name. A question. 'Yes,' she answered, wanting, desperately wanting, afraid it would stop if she thought about it. He touched her, sliding inside her so easily, so delightfully that this time she barely managed to stifle her moan. And then his mouth covered hers, his tongue sliding into her mouth and his fingers sliding between her legs, and she struggled to cling on because she didn't want it to stop, suddenly afraid that the memories of all those other encounters would pollute this one. But then he said her name again, and she opened her eyes and met his gaze, saw passion mixed with tenderness.

'Jean-Luc.'

'Sophia, *ma belle.*'

'I want you so much.'

'No more than I want you.'

And then she was lost as he kissed her again, and she kissed him back, and he stroked her to a shuddering climax, and this time she surrendered to her instincts, pressing herself against him urgently, caught up in a primal need to be part of him, to meld with him in a way that she had never before even imagined possible.

It was nothing like before. He slid inside her so easily, so carefully, each push making her muscles clench around him, and each clench making her shiver with delight. Higher, and more, his breathing harsh, his arms braced at her side, his eyes locked on hers. Time froze, and then he moved inside her, and this time Sophia couldn't bite back her guttural moan of pleasure. And then he moved again, and she moved with him, and his mouth covered hers, and he thrust higher inside her, and she wrapped her legs around his waist, and he thrust higher, and she cried out as her climax reached a second wave, lost and yet not alone, clinging to him, mouths locked, bodies conjoined, as he thrust again and again and again, each thrust a shivering delight which she never wanted to end, tightening around him, until he cried out, tearing himself away from her as he came, spilling on to her belly with a hoarse, guttural cry that echoed her own.

'I am sorry,' Jean-Luc said, dabbing at her stomach with his kerchief, 'I was not expecting to make love to my wife for the first time on the floor of a hotel-suite drawing room. Your bedchamber is ten steps away, but it was ten steps too many. It is your own fault for being so irresistible.'

She threw her arms around him, burrowing her face into his chest. 'You are so lovely.'

He laughed, smoothing his hand over her hair. 'I think that is my line.'

She pressed a kiss over his heartbeat. 'I mean what you did, at the end, to take such care...'

'No man worthy of the name would do less.'

She could think of one man not worthy of the name, but he had no place here. She shook her head to banish the unwelcome intrusion on what they had just shared. 'I feel—different somehow,' she said kissing him. 'In the most delightful way.'

He pulled her tightly against him, rolling on to his back to take her with him. 'Different, in the most delightful way. Strangely, that is exactly how I am feeling.'

Astonishingly she could feel his shaft stirring between her legs. Even more astonishingly, Sophia felt herself stirring in response. She wriggled and he stiffened. 'Jean-Luc, how you are feeling is not at all like a man who has just been delighted.'

'Sophia, I am feeling like a man who hopes to be delighted again.'

She laughed. 'What a good thing it is then, that I am a woman who feels exactly the same way.'

'What did you order for dinner?' Sophia, dressed only in a navy-blue silk wrap embroidered with improbably large sky-blue roses, was curled up on the sofa in their drawing room.

'You said earlier you didn't want dinner.' Jean-Luc, wearing his shirt and pantaloons, sat down beside her, planting a kiss on her mouth.

'That was before I ravished you. Now I am ravenous.'

'Then it is as well that I ignored you and ordered *entrecote* bordelaise with *boulangère* potatoes, haricots verts, asparagus and peas. Does that meet with *madame*'s approval?'

'Very much. I should get dressed before it arrives.'

'Wait in here until they have served it in the dining room, then there is no need.'

'I can't eat my dinner in my dressing gown.'

'I can think of nothing more delightful. Save you

eating dinner wearing nothing at all, of course, though I would starve, not being able to concentrate on the food.'

'Then perhaps it would be better if I got properly dressed. I would not want to spoil your appetite.'

'Talking of appetites, I should warn you that I plan to undress you again, straight after dinner.'

Her eyes widened. 'You do?'

'With your permission.'

She looked charmingly flustered. 'In that case, perhaps it would be best if I spared us both the effort and kept on my wrap after all.'

'I think that is a very good idea. Then I can have the pleasure of unwrapping you.'

He kissed her again, and only a sharp rap on the main door of their suite prevented him kissing her yet again. 'Dinner is served,' Jean-Luc said.

Later, much later, with both culinary and carnal appetites totally sated, they lay with their limbs tangled together in Sophia's bed. 'Are you worried about tomorrow?' she asked him, turning on to her side to face him.

He pushed himself upright against the pillows. 'My greatest concern is that the outcome is not definitive. Until Mademoiselle de Cressy came along, I had no reason to question my history, but since her arrival, I really do feel that I know nothing at all about myself, and I feel so—so stupid, for never having asked the many questions now rattling around in my head when my parents were still alive.'

'Are you starting to think the unthinkable,' Sophia asked tentatively, 'that they are not your real parents?'

'In all honesty, I don't know.' He pulled her against his chest, resting his head on the silky softness of her hair. 'Perhaps tomorrow, this lawyer will produce some incontrovertible proof that the lost Duc de Montendre and myself cannot possibly be one and the same person, and then I can get on with my life.'

'And I with mine.'

Which thought was even less palatable than speculating about what revelations lay in store for him at the lawyer's office tomorrow, Jean-Luc discovered. 'When you first arrived in Paris, you told me that you didn't know what your plans were.'

It was a tiny movement, but he felt it all the same, a slight tensing of her body against his. 'That's true. I still have no fixed ideas as yet.'

'But you are still set on living an independent life? I thought you enjoyed being married to me as much as I enjoy being married to you. Does that not give you pause for thought about being committed to a solitary existence.'

'No, because this is not real, it's fantasy.' She freed herself from his embrace. 'We have your future to settle before I can even think about mine. That should be our focus, not indulging ourselves in fanciful conjecture.'

He laughed wryly. 'We have just indulged ourselves rather delightfully in another way. I hope you don't view that as an unwelcome distraction.'

She plucked at the sheet. 'Very far from unwelcome

but a distraction we can't afford, Jean-Luc. Not at the moment.'

'As always, you are quite right. We both need a good night's sleep.' One step at a time, he thought, getting out of her bed. Time enough to worry about the future when the doubts he had about his past were resolved. Grabbing his shirt and pantaloons, he leaned over to kiss her softly on the lips. '*Bonne nuit*, Sophia. Sleep well.'

Sophia had taught herself how to fall sleep at an early age. How to lie perfectly still, empty her mind of thoughts, and to force her body to relax, from her toes to her calves, fingertips to shoulders, focusing only on this until she fell into oblivion. It almost always worked. An argument with her father, a long day spent nursing Felicity, a night spent enduring Hopkins's attentions, all could be obliterated by forced unconsciousness. There were a few exceptions. The first night with Hopkins. Her only night with Frederick. The last nights of Felicity's life and Sophia's first nights without her.

Tonight was another exception. Hardly surprising, she thought as she watched the sun rise over the Bordeaux rooftops. Jean-Luc was exceptional in almost every way. The first man she had kissed. Not the first man she had shared a bed with, but tonight, it had felt like the first time. The first time she had relied upon her instincts, and not the instructions she had been given or the lessons she had been taught. Not one person exacting his pleasure from another, but two people pleasuring each other. Uniting, to become one. Astonishingly, it really had felt as if that was what had happened. As if they were made for each other, shaped to perfectly fit each other.

It would be easy for her to tell herself it was so very different from her other experiences because those other men had cared only for themselves, but she wouldn't lie to herself. Yes, Jean-Luc was a generous, attentive and thoughtful lover. But it was because he was Jean-Luc that made their lovemaking just that. Making love.

Her heart sank like a stone, and she saw herself for a fool. A stupid, stupid fool. She loved him. She had fallen in love with her husband. Who could never, ever be her real husband, though just for a moment, she allowed herself to imagine it, the blissful idyll of their time in Paris, only with no end.

But if they were really married, then things would be different, wouldn't they? Real marriage would require her to bend her will to his, it would mean she was no longer Sophia, but someone else's property. That's what she'd always thought. Independence, that's why she was here, wasn't it? To imagine herself as a wife, that was to go against everything she was working towards.

But she was Jean-Luc's wife, and she liked being Jean-Luc's wife, not because it wasn't a real marriage, but because it was marriage to Jean-Luc. It wouldn't change, he wouldn't change, just because they made their vows in front of the Mayor.

As if that could ever happen! He might excuse her

Frederick, but Hopkins—no. Even in the most sympathetic light, her dealings with him had been wholly mercenary. The plain truth was that she had prostituted herself. The body which she had shared so freely and so pleasurably with Jean-Luc, had been for two years the instrument which sated another man's appetites, bought and paid for to do with as he saw fit. It mattered not that she had loathed every second, that every encounter was a violation. She had served him willingly. Jean-Luc would be revolted. For such a truly honourable man to marry such a dishonoured woman as she, was unthinkable.

So she had better stop wasting time contemplating it, and turn her mind to more important matters. A tap on the door preceded the maid with her hot water and morning coffee. From her sister, Sophia had learned how to live in the moment, and to make the best of what she had. What she had, she reminded herself, was a great deal more now than she could have imagined, the day The Procurer came calling. She could never be more than a temporary wife to Jean-Luc, but when this faux marriage was over, she would have the means to her independence. She would be free to live, if not free to love. She was much more fortunate than most women.

Chapter Twelve

'Monsieur and Madame Bauduin, it is indeed a pleasure. Welcome to our humble premises. Please, step into my office, make yourselves comfortable. I must say, *monsieur*, your letter was something of a bolt from the blue.'

It was immediately apparent to Sophia as she sat down in front of the desk beside Jean-Luc that the rotund, luxuriantly moustached Monsieur Fallon facing them was far too young to have been the co-signatory on the marriage contract.

And equally apparent to Jean-Luc. 'Your father is not able to join us?' he hazarded.

'That would require a miracle of Lazarus-like proportions, *monsieur*. I'm afraid my father stands before a very different jury these days. But I indulge myself in lawyerly verbosity. In a nutshell, to summarise, he is dead, sir. His case was dismissed in March of last year, so to speak, with no prospect of an appeal.'

Sophia sought Jean-Luc's hand, an instinctive gesture of comfort, knowing how disappointed he must be. He cast a fleeting smile in her direction, as if it was she and not he who needed reassuring.

'So it falls to me to discharge my late father's obligations, which I will endeavour to do both humbly and with due diligence,' Monsieur Fallon said earnestly, stroking his moustache. 'I take it you have your copy of the marriage contract with you?'

'There is more than one?' Jean-Luc produced the document, placing it on the desk.

'Three copies were made. I have one in my possession, as you see.' A second, red-ribboned scroll was produced. 'You have one which I think your letter indicated was held by the Comte de Cressy? And the third, naturally, would have been held by the Duc de Montendre.'

The lawyer busied himself with comparing the two scrolls. It did not take him long. 'As you see, both are signed by my father. The contract was drawn up in this office a year after the birth of the Duke's son, as was the Montendre tradition. Our family law firm served the Montendre family for generations, so this was not the first such contract executed here. My father often lamented the fact that it was likely to be the last, however. He was much affected by the tragic death of the Duke and Duchess.'

'Were any provisions made for the maintenance of the estates?'

Monsieur Fallon pursed his lips. 'Were the circumstances not so extraordinary, Monsieur Bauduin, I would tell you that I cannot discuss such matters. As it is—well, you will see for yourself if you visit them.

The château itself still stands, but it is a shell. There was a fire, the result of looting, I am afraid to say. When it became common knowledge that the Duke and Duchess were dead—alas, so it was with many other such estates. All the family papers, every remaining portrait, all destroyed. Of course the lands are still there, and the vineyards, and many of the farms are still cultivated, but there has been no one to collect the rents since the Duke's man of business fled. I was too young myself to remember those times very clearly, but from what my father told me—not pleasant, Monsieur Bauduin, not pleasant at all. You know, I can't quite believe this is happening. When I received your letter—if only my father had been here.'

'Unfortunately he is not,' Jean-Luc said crisply. 'In fact, I would much rather circumstances had not brought me here at all—with all due respect to yourself—but as it is, you will understand my eagerness to hear if you have any information which can be of assistance.'

'As to that.' With an air of repressed excitement that gave Sophia a horrible sinking feeling, Monsieur Fallon produced a leather book and pushed it towards Jean-Luc. 'As you can see, it is a statement of account. A lump-sum deposit was entrusted to my father by the Duc de Montendre. Here you see the record of withdrawals over a number of years. And then the closing statement in…'

'1800,' Jean-Luc said. 'The year I was taken out of school.' He looked, Sophia thought, as if he had been punched in the stomach. 'But who was the recipient of these payments?'

'Ah, now that is a mystery my father never fully resolved.' Monsieur Fallon settled himself more comfortably in his chair. 'Once a year, a fixed sum of money was to be withdrawn from the safe and transported to the church of Saint-Pierre in the little hamlet of Archiac—do you know it, Monsieur Bauduin? It is about two or three days on horseback from Bordeaux.'

'And about half a day from Cognac, where I was raised,' Jean-Luc said.

Monsieur Fallon's brows shot up. 'We always assumed that Angoulême was the money's final destination. It is the largest town, and also less than a day's ride from Archiac.'

'Forgive me, *monsieur*,' Jean-Luc said, 'but I am afraid I'm not privy to your assumptions yet.'

His clipped tone made the lawyer sit up. 'I can see this has come as a shock to you. I understand your wine business, Monsieur Bauduin, is based in Cognac? Yes, I see, it is beginning to make sense.'

'Not to me.'

'No.' Monsieur Fallon shook his head several times. 'Well, the story is quickly told, albeit the cloak-and-dagger nature of it offends my lawyerly sensibilities. The money was deposited in a leather purse, on the same day every year, in the same place, hidden behind the altar of the church. We had no idea who collected it and, as I said, my father assumed that whoever it was resided in Angoulême.'

'But I note that the amounts diminish significantly in the later years.'

'I applaud your observational skills, sir. The lump sum was sufficient for the payments to be made for five years from the initiation of the fund in 1790, with a little contingency built in. A prudent suggestion of my father's, I believe. He taught me to consider all eventualities. Advice that has stood me in good stead. In 1790 you were, Monsieur Bauduin, two years old, I think?'

Waiting only for a nod from Jean-Luc the lawyer continued. 'The Duke and Duchess died in 1794, as you know, but they were, like almost everyone else, trapped in Paris from the previous year, when The Terror began. If they tried to communicate with my father, word never reached him. As you can see, after 1794 he reduced the sum each year in an effort to eke it out, but by 1800 there was nothing left.'

'The Duke's financial arrangements are obviously fascinating, but what do you think this account has to do with my visit here and the marriage contract?'

Monsieur Fallon spread his hands. 'My father's view was that the only explanation which made sense was that the money was payment for the care of the Duke's son. The boy was being raised in the château, as all the Montendre children always were. In the autumn of 1790 the Duke and Duchess returned to Paris, to protect their palace in the turmoil of the Revolution. They let it be known that they were taking their son with him. This account was opened by the Duke before he left, as you can see. Only my father guessed the reason, and only then when he had word from a connection in Paris that the boy was not, as everyone believed, with his parents.'

'So your father surmised that the Duke had placed his son into hiding as a precaution, given that members of the aristocracy were starting to be executed? Yet when your father heard the Duke himself had fallen victim to the guillotine, he made no attempt to recover the child?'

'My father was sworn to secrecy by the Duke, Monsieur Bauduin. He made a solemn vow never to speak of this fund, never to make any attempt to trace the recipient, under any circumstances whatsoever. It was imperative that the boy's identity remained a secret, for his own safety. That vow gave my father many sleepless nights after the Duke's death, he told me, but there was nothing to be done. This little account book seemed set to be a mystery never to be resolved.' Monsieur Fallon's eyes brightened. 'Until I received your letter. I cannot help but think from your expression, that this document means something to you.'

'It proves that the money paid for the upbringing of the Duke's son dried up at exactly the same time as my parents' finances dried up. But that is all it proves. It certainly is not evidence enough to conclude that I am the lost heir of the Duc de Montendre.'

'Not on its own, of course not. But a most persuasive case can be made when all the other circumstantial evidence is taken into account. The marriage contract. Mademoiselle de Cressy's family tale which makes a direct link between your name and the Montendre one. This little account book here, which ties in with the changes in your own youthful circumstances. And the fact that you have been able to find no trace of your birth—or more correctly I should say the birth of Jean-Luc Bauduin.' Monsieur Fallon pursed his lips. 'That is a great accumulation of evidence. You are, Monsieur Bauduin, in my legal opinion, in a very strong position to press a claim to be the rightful heir to the Montendre title. If I may say so you look much less excited than I would be, in your shoes.'

Jean-Luc got to his feet. 'That is because I am not yet certain in whose shoes I am standing. I would be very much obliged if you would keep the content of this meeting confidential, for the time being.'

'But there is so much to do if you wish to reclaim your title. The château, the Paris house...'

'A shell and a ruin,' Jean-Luc said, sardonically. 'You get ahead of yourself, *monsieur*, nothing is yet proved irrefutably.' He got to his feet, holding his hand out for Sophia. 'I need time to assimilate all you have told me. I will be in touch when I have decided what, if anything I wish to do. In the meantime, I rely on your discretion, and bid you good day.'

Jean-Luc hired a carriage to take them to the Château Montendre, which was an hour's drive south-west of Bordeaux on the Garonne River. The majestic ruin looked to have its origins in mediaeval times, judging by the huge keep, which had formed the original structure. The main building, four storeys high and now roofless, was built between two other, smaller towers whose steeply pitched roofs, perched like witches' hats, had survived the fire. Ivy covered all the south-facing façade. The carriageway and formal gardens were almost entirely overgrown, though the crumbling walls of the kitchen garden still stood on three of the four sides, small, hard fruit from the peach and apricot trees which had once been espaliered, rotting in the tall grass.

It was a melancholy place, Sophia thought as they followed the remains of a path into a cluster of outbuildings built around a courtyard. A row of broken barrels sat outside one of them. This must have been where the estate wine was produced, though on the slopes which surrounded them, the endless rows of vines looked dead. The hot, arid air of the summer afternoon was permeated by the sweet scent of decay.

Jean-Luc had said almost nothing since leaving the lawyer's office, shaking his head in answer to her anxious enquiries, lost deep in thought on the drive, a heavy frown drawing his brows together.

Standing now, shading the sun from his eyes with his hand, for he had abandoned his hat and coat in the carriage, he sighed heavily. 'Absolutely none of this is familiar. Nothing strikes a chord, not a single thing. Perhaps if the interior had not been destroyed...' He grimaced. 'But like everything else in my history, it no longer exists. I have no idea who I am, never mind who I am not.'

'You are the person you have always been.'

'I most sincerely doubt it.' Sweat trickled down his temples. He mopped it with his kerchief. 'I forget how hot it gets here. Come, let us see if we can find some shade.'

There was a stone bench on the north-facing wall of the kitchen garden. Sophia removed her pelisse, fanning her face with her bonnet. 'You think it is true, then?'

'Fallon was right. Taking all the circumstances together, it's simply too much of a coincidence. My parents are not my parents. My name is not even my name. I can't take it in. Why didn't Maman say anything? Why couldn't she have explained...?'

A pulse beat in his cheek as he fought for control, but he sat so rigidly, Sophia was afraid if she tried to touch him he would break. 'Monsieur Fallon's father was sworn to secrecy. Your parents probably were too. The Duke...' The Duke! Jean-Luc's father. She was finding it almost as impossible to believe as he.

'I know,' Jean-Luc said, with a poor attempt at a smile, as if he had read her thoughts, 'it's preposterous.

And dreadful. If she'd thought any future with Jean-Luc Bauduin, wine merchant was impossible, how much more preposterous would it be to imagine herself the wife of a duke? Sophia's stomach lurched. Not that she had imagined herself as Jean-Luc's wife, she reminded herself. In fact she'd cautioned herself against imagining just that this morning. Was it only this morning? It seemed like a lifetime ago. And if she felt that, what must Jean-Luc be feeling?

She risked taking his hand. To her relief, his fingers curled tightly around hers. 'You were only two years old. They must have loved you a great deal, Jean-Luc, to send you away for safekeeping, as they did. It must have been an agony for them to part with you.'

'You think so? They abandoned me.'

'To a woman who loved you as her own. Perhaps she was your nurse.'

'I'll never know now. One of the many things I'll never know. I don't even have any idea what my real parents looked like. Do I resemble them?' He thumped his free hand on his thigh. 'What the hell do you think they were playing at, Sophia? What did they imagine would happen to me?'

It was an agony to see him, normally so certain and confident, now so vulnerable, and to be able to do so little to help. 'You heard what Monsieur Fallon said. The Duke left enough funds to support you for five years, with a little more besides. It was 1790, long before the Terror. He would not have imagined that he and the duchess would be trapped so long in Paris, and it would have been beyond his wildest imaginings at that point, thinking that they would be executed, else they would have escaped, don't you think?'

'I don't know.'

'Perhaps they tried to get a message to Cognac, but it didn't make it.'

'Or perhaps it did,' Jean-Luc said heavily, 'and the instructions were to keep me in the dark for ever.'

'I don't believe that.' Sophia gave his arm a shake. 'To have gone to such lengths to protect you as the Duke and Duchess did proves how much they cared. And as for your *maman*—'

'Who was not my mother,' he interjected bitterly.

'No, but she was the next best thing. She loved you. She tried to do the best she could for you, under very difficult circumstances, making sacrifices, never complaining.'

'As you did, for your sister?'

'It's not the same.'

'No. At least my—my father made some provision for me. What you did for your sister, Sophia, it was beyond admirable. I hope she appreciated it.'

'She never knew.'

Jean-Luc's brows shot up. 'She did not know you were married?'

Sophia's mind went blank for a horrible few seconds. 'Don't change the subject. What I'm trying to tell you, Jean-Luc, is that you were loved. Not by one set of parents, but by two.'

If he noticed it was she and not he who changed the subject, he made no comment. 'Now I understand why my father—my adopted father—resented me a little.'

'No doubt he too thought that situation was temporary. It must have been a terrible strain for him, when the money began to dry up. And he'd have known, don't you think, that the Duke and Duchess were executed?'

'I suppose so.'

'You said he was proud of you in the end, Jean-Luc. Don't forget that.'

'I should be grateful to him. It was he who found me work at the vintner's. As the son of a duke, I would have been permitted to drink any amount of the wine

I sell, but trade in it—no!' He nodded at the château. 'They would have been appalled.'

'Or perhaps they too would have been proud,' Sophia countered. 'Not of the way that you earned your living, but the reasons for it. You worked hard so that your parents—adoptive parents—could live comfortably, didn't you? And as I believe I have informed you on several occasions,' she added softly, 'you are the most honourable man I have ever met. I think they would be proud of you.'

He kissed her hand. 'Thank you, you are a very loyal wife, but… What is it, Sophia?'

'Juliette,' she exclaimed, horrified. 'The contract. Her claim is valid. You are legally obliged to marry her.' She clutched at her heart, which seemed to be intent on lurching out of her chest.

'No!' Jean-Luc leapt to his feet. 'Under no circumstances!'

'You gave her your word of honour that you would inform her of the outcome of our investigations.'

'There is no definitive outcome yet! There is not yet irrefutable evidence…'

'And yet your own instincts tell you otherwise.'

'No!' He swore, kicking a stone, sending it flying high into the ruined succession house where it shattered one of the few remaining panes of glass. 'There goes one of the last pieces of my heritage,' he said sardonically, but the action seemed to calm him. 'It is too soon to be making decisions about anything. I need time to become accustomed, to consider my options.'

'Of course you do.' Sophia tucked her arm into his.

'To say that today has been momentous is one of the great understatements.'

They made their way back round to the front of the château, where Jean-Luc had left the carriage in the shade of what had once been an alley of lime trees, but which was now a veritable forest. Tying the ribbons of her bonnet, Sophia wandered up the shallow flight of steps to the main door, a massive affair of oak and iron, which lay off its hinges at a crazy angle. 'There is a crest above the door,' she said over her shoulder to Jean-Luc, who was pulling on his coat. 'It's Latin, I think. *Ab Ordine Libertas.* Something about freedom?'

'From order comes freedom.' Jean-Luc said. 'I may have left school prematurely, but while I was there, I was a most attentive pupil.' He rolled his eyes. 'A monastery boarding school to learn Latin and Greek! Why the devil didn't I question that!' He held out his hand. 'Enough. If we don't leave now, we'll miss our dinner. I've ordered a seafood extravaganza for you.'

'Then let us make haste,' Sophia said, taking his hand. Her fingers encountered his heavy gold signet ring. 'Jean-Luc.'

'What is it?'

'This. You said it was given to you by your father—Monsieur Bauduin, I mean—but do you remember, we thought there had once been a stone set in it. And on the back...'

'The inscription.' He twisted the ring off, frowning down at it. 'I always assumed it was two words, a name.'

'A... R... D... N... L... B... S...' Sophia said, tracing the faint outline of the few remaining letters. 'Do you think…?'

Jean-Luc's gaze was fixed on the Montendre family motto above the door. *'Ab Ordine Libertas.* From order comes freedom.' He turned back to her, his eyes stormy. 'The irrefutable proof I was referring to. My family motto lauds freedom. That is appropriate, because I do not intend to surrender mine.'

Although Jean-Luc took dinner with her, he was present in body only throughout the lavish meal, eating little, saying less, and staring often, distractedly, at the engraving on the back of his signet ring. He excused himself immediately after, telling her rather unnecessarily that he was not fit company for her, and that he needed time to think. Though Sophia desperately wanted to help him, she understood his need to be alone. Waking in the night, she heard him pacing in the drawing room of their suite, but forced herself not to go to him, trusting that he would come to her when he was ready.

He arrived while she was finishing her breakfast the next morning, freshly shaved, only the dark shadows under his eyes testament to his sleepless night, but she was relieved to see he seemed in good spirits, that his smile was not forced when he leaned over to kiss her. 'I'm perfectly well, I promise.'

'I heard you pacing in the night. I confess, I was very tempted to join you, but I didn't think you would welcome my presence.'

'Just this once, you were right. I needed to be alone, to try to accustom myself to the situation.'

'Your world has just been turned upside down, I imagine it will take more than a day for you to accustom yourself to this particular situation, which is almost unprecedented.'

He took a cup of coffee from her, draining it in one gulp, pulling out a chair to sit down beside her. 'Yesterday was a shock, a huge shock, but it was being faced with the evidence, rather than the outcome itself. You know, because I've told you, that I've been questioning, doubting my own history—the history that I thought was mine,' he added wryly. 'None of it made sense, and now it does. I couldn't prove who I thought I was because I wasn't who I thought I was.'

'So you believe you are the Duc de Montendre?'

He laughed, shaking his head. 'That will take a great deal of getting used to. I believe that I am the lost heir. At least now I can start to uncover my history. There are people here who knew my family, some who may even remember me as a child, servants, estate workers. I called on Monsieur Fallon first thing this morning to ask him to find some of them for me to talk to, and to set my claim in motion. I've also asked him to liaise with Maxime in order to obtain a sworn statement from Mademoiselle de Cressy. Her testimony, ironically, is vital, since it establishes the link between the Bauduin and the Montendre names.'

'She will be very happy to help, I am sure.'

'Don't give me that forced smile, *ma belle*, I can see right through it.'

'She's the perfect wife for you. It was your father's dearest wish…'

'No.' He took her hand, pressing a kiss to her palm. 'Throughout all this, from the very beginning, I have been certain of one thing. I am not going to marry Juliette de Cressy. And as time has passed, I have become even more certain. Now, it is as you say, my world has been turned upside down, but even were I to be sent to live on the moon, and even if she was the only woman there, I wouldn't marry her.'

'But…'

'No.' He got to his feet. 'I have far more important matters to talk to you about. I have plans I want to share with you.'

'Ah.' Sophia stood up. 'You have a plan. That explains why you look more like yourself, Jean-Luc.' She stood on her tiptoes to kiss his cheek. 'Or should I call you…?'

'My name is Jean-Luc. I have a very long list of other names too, but I have no intentions of assuming any of them. Now, I have something to show you.'

'What?'

'Patience, Sophia. Go and get your hat.'

'I remembered last night.' They were in the courtyard which had once been the centre of the Château Montendre's wine-making business. Jean-Luc closed his eyes, trying to recall the image which had popped into his head. 'I think it is this one.'

He led the way to the largest of the buildings. The fire had not reached here, but the looters had. Empty bottles and shattered glass covered the floor. On one long wooden bench, the heavy iron lever which was used for corking the bottles was still fixed in place, a box of crumbling corks by its side. Crates, on which the Montendre name could still be read, stood stacked but empty. 'Yes, it is here,' Jean-Luc said, examining the floor, kicking the dust away to reveal the outline of a trapdoor. 'See?'

'The cellars?' Sophia asked.

'Yes. That is what I remembered. I must have escaped from my nurse. I remember running, chasing something, I think it was a cat. Anyway, it came in here, and I ran in after it and this hatch must have been open and I fell, head first down the stairs.'

Sophia gasped in horror. 'You could have been killed.'

Jean-Luc shrugged. 'I don't even have a scar.'

'Then you must have borrowed one of the cat's lives. The cellars here are probably built into rock.' Sophia looked around the bottling store, shaking her head. 'They must have produced thousands of gallons of wine here.'

'It was quite an enterprise, according to Monsieur Fallon. They didn't just grow it to stock their own cellars.'

'How odd, don't you think, that you happen to be a wine merchant? Perhaps it wasn't a coincidence after all. I think wine must be in your blood.'

'I hadn't thought of that,' Jean-Luc said, much struck by the notion.

'So you see, you did not escape your heritage after

all. In fact, by selling wine, you could say you were continuing the family business that was based here.'

He laughed. 'I don't think my father—my father the Duke, that is—would see my trade in quite such a light, but we are, as ever, thinking along the same lines.'

'Are we?'

'It will take years. The vines will have to be completely replaced, and you can see for yourself that all of this will need to be rebuilt, but I'm thinking of extending my business empire to include wine produced from my own vineyards. What do you think?'

Sophia clasped her hands together, her eyes shining. 'I think it's a wonderful idea. It's perfect. It is so—so perfectly you.'

Which was exactly what he'd felt when he'd had the idea in the middle of the night, but somehow her saying so made it even more perfect. He picked her up, whirling her around, making her laugh, clutching at his shoulders.

'Put me down. You're making me dizzy.'

He did as she asked, though he kept his arms around her waist. She was making him dizzy. Looking into her eyes, he felt as if his heart was being squeezed, as if the ground was once again shifting under him, as it had done yesterday. Only this time, he was not overwhelmed by uncertainty. Quite the opposite, for he saw clearly, for the first time ever, that he belonged here. And that she belonged here with him. He had fallen deeply and irrevocably in love.

'Jean-Luc?' She reached up, pushing a lock of damp hair from his brow. 'Are you feeling quite well?

There is a flask of water in the carriage, shall I fetch it for you?'

Dazed, he nodded, watching her as she walked with that floating, graceful sway despite the rooted-up cobblestones and the wine-making detritus covering the courtyard. He loved her. It seemed so obvious now, explained so much. The way she had fitted so seamlessly into his life, his desire to talk to her, to consult her, to please her, to be with her. And that feeling he'd been ignoring, when they made love, of it being somehow right, a feeling of harmony that he'd never felt with any other woman. It was because he loved her.

He drank from the flask she passed him, watching as she took delicate sips after him, her lips touching the rim where his had been. Such an intimate gesture. And arousing. He dragged his eyes from her. He loved her. The need to tell her was almost irresistible. But as she recapped the flask, Jean-Luc forced himself to bite his tongue. It was too sudden. There were too many matters unresolved, not least of which was Sophia's oft-stated desire for freedom. She had not said she wouldn't ever marry again, but she had made it clear it was not one of her ambitions. And then there was the small matter of Juliette de Cressy, the bride his father, the Duc de Montendre had selected for him, though she hadn't even been born until after he died.

No! He would fulfil his duty to the Montendre name by restoring his heritage. *From Order Comes Freedom.* The *ancien régime* was over now. He was the new order. Yes, there were a good many things for him to sort out before he asked Sophia to be his duchess, but—*sacré bleu*, look at her, was there ever a more perfect duchess?

'What are you smiling at?' Sophia asked him.

He took her hand, leading her out into the courtyard. 'All this. Not just the winery, but the château, it's beautiful, isn't it?'

'Very. Are you thinking of restoring the château too?'

'I could not make wine here, and live in Paris.'

'But you love Paris.'

'I do, but I've just discovered something. You know what they say, a home is where the heart is?'

'Your heart is here?'

He pulled her into his arms and kissed her lingeringly. 'It is right now,' he said. Once again, the urge to tell her was almost too much to ignore, but there was too much at stake for him to be precipitate. So instead, he took the map which Monsieur Fallon had miraculously obtained for him. 'Château Montendre and the estate,' he informed Sophia. 'Let's set about making some plans and then we'll have some lunch.'

'Lunch? We're in a ruined château miles from the nearest hotel.'

'I think you'll find that I have prepared for every eventuality.'

Chapter Thirteen

~~~~~~~~~~~~~

They ate the sumptuous picnic the hotel had assembled on his instruction in the shade of what had been, in the château's heyday, the impressive lime-tree walk. Poached eggs in aspic gleamed with little emerald jewels of parsley and chives. A fish terrine comprised of layers of trout and turbot smooth as silk, separated by spears of white asparagus. The *rémoulade* of celeriac was tart, the *rillettes* of duck rich and creamy. *Cabecous*, the little discs of goat's cheese from nearby Périgord, spread on Sophia's favourite country bread made her close her eyes in bliss, and the wine, a young red from a château just a few miles down the river, was served, to her surprise, chilled.

'That was one of the best meals I've ever had,' she said, accepting a quartered apricot from Jean-Luc.

He laughed. 'You say that after every meal.'

'At the risk of sounding extremely unpatriotic, French food is undoubtedly the best in the world.'

'It would be extremely unpatriotic of me to disagree, but Portuguese cuisine is responsible for the world's greatest pastry—Pastéis de Nata. I always make a point of sampling some when I am in Lisbon.'

Sophia finished her apricot, and gave in to the temptation to relax, lying on her side, her head resting on her hand. 'What kind of pastry is it?'

'A custard tart.' He lay down beside her. 'But not just any custard tart. Pastéis de Nata are made with sugared pastry, rolled very thin and cut so that you can see all the little spirals on the base, like a snail's shell.'

He had removed his coat, waistcoat and cravat. His shirt was damp, clinging to his chest, the dark shadow of hair clearly visible through the white cambric. He smelt of sweat and dust and soap. A trickle of perspiration ran down Sophia's back. 'And the custard?'

'Flavoured with vanilla, cinnamon and lemon.' He trailed his fingers down her bare arm. 'Sweet.' He licked into the corner of her mouth. 'And yet tart.' His hand travelled back up her arm, brushing the side of her breast.

She shuddered. 'Jean-Luc, are you trying to seduce me with recipe ingredients?'

'Yes. Is it working?' His fingers drifted over her breast, unerringly finding her nipple, which immediately peaked in response.

'Yes.' Sophia said. 'Dear heavens, yes.'

Taking him by surprise, she pushed him on to his back, leaning over him to claim his mouth with a slow, sensual kiss. He tasted of wine and sunshine. She loved him so much. He could never be hers, she would never see this beautiful château brought back to life, but she could claim this perfect day for her own. She kissed him again, aroused by the way her kiss made his eyes darken, made his breath quicken. He might not love her as she loved him, but she could be in no doubt about the depth of his desire.

He pulled her on top of him and their kisses changed from languorous to passionate. His hands roamed down her back to cup her bottom. She could feel him, hard between her legs, and the driving need to have him inside her made her forget all about their surroundings. She whispered his name, arching against him.

Desire took over, hot and fierce as the summer sun which dappled through the leaves as they touched and kissed, tearing impatiently at their clothes, his boots and his breeches, her shoes and her undergarments, cast heedlessly aside as their bodies strove for that most intimate connection. And then, as he lay on his back beneath her, she caught her breath, wanting, suddenly, just to touch him, curling her fingers around the sleek, thick length of him. The tension of her own arousal tightened inside her as he pulsed in response, as he watched her, as she watched him responding to her touch, taking her cue from his response, for the first time in her life relishing what she did, not thinking about what she did, wanting only to please, confident that she did.

His chest heaved. The muscles of his belly rippled. She could see, in his eyes, and in his mouth, that she was testing him, taking him to the brink of his self-control, and it was exciting, very, very exciting, but she wanted more from him. She wanted all of him. So she leaned over to kiss him on the mouth, and as she did, she slid up his body and took him inside her.

He bucked under her. The movement sent her right to the edge of her own climax. Not yet, she thought, forcing herself to slow down, to lift herself then thrust slowly, and then again, eliciting a deep groan from him as he slid his hand beneath her gown and touched her. She lost control then, in a wild, frenzied drive to completion that made her cry out in astonished delight, her own climax triggering his, his self-control better than hers as he lifted her away from him only seconds before he came.

But afterwards he pulled her tightly against him, as if he wanted to meld them together, and she burrowed her face into his chest, listening to the pounding of his heart and wishing she could stay like this for ever. *I love you*, she thought, sealing the thought with a kiss. *I love you so much.*

The silence was broken by the distinct, rhythmic, sawing sound of a cicada. She stirred, but Jean-Luc's arms tightened around her. 'I don't want to move. Not yet.'

'Nor I.' She kissed him softly. 'Not yet.'

Scowling, Jean-Luc picked up the visiting card which the maid proffered on the tray as she arrived to clear breakfast away the next day. 'I can't believe I forgot I had arranged this meeting. You remember,' he said to Sophia, 'the customer who is getting married. He is waiting in the foyer.'

'The one who wants to buy a whole warehouse-worth of wine? You had better not keep him waiting. Business is business.' She got to her feet. 'I will leave you to it. 'I can go for a stroll, call on Monsieur Fallon if you like, and postpone our appointment with him till later?'

'There's no need. I'll have the hotel porter deliver a message to him. Why don't you stay here, meet my client? I had Maxime make arrangements for a tasting at a premises down near the docks, you'll enjoy that. I have the details in my bedchamber. You go through to the drawing room. I will have him sent up and will join you both momentarily. I just need to take a quick look through my notes. I hate to be unprepared. I'm so sorry.'

'It's absolutely fine. As you said, business is business, especially if it allows you to keep me in the manner to which I have become accustomed,' Sophia teased.

Though she had better not become too accustomed, she reminded herself firmly, wandering through to the drawing room, where she checked her appearance in the mirror. Fortunately, she had dressed for the visit to Monsieur Fallon, in a walking dress of white muslin designed to be worn with a mint-green half-pelisse. The sleeves were long, the neckline high, perfectly suitable attire for her to receive morning callers.

A polite tap and the door was opened to reveal the maid and a tall, well-dressed gentleman. A tall, well-dressed and horribly familiar gentleman.

For a terrible moment, time stood still. Sophia had the distinct impression that the ground was opening

up beneath her. There was a rushing sound in her ears.
The room appeared to spin before her eyes.

'Sir Richard Hopkins, Madame Bauduin,' the maid
announced.

The man who had been her protector for two years
stood on the threshold. 'Sophia! In the name of all
that's sacred, what are you doing here?'

She stood rooted to the spot, utterly appalled, sick
to the pit of her stomach. It was unmistakably him.
Handsome in a swarthy way. Immaculately garbed.
Suave, sophisticated and utterly vile. 'Get out,' she
hissed. 'Get out right now.'

'Since when do I do as you tell me, Sophia? Don't
you recollect that it was always the other way around,
when you were my—'

'I was never yours.' A gust of anger coursed through
her. 'You merely rented my body for a period.'

'Describe our arrangement how you will. I came
to meet my vintner, not call on damaged goods.' Col-
lecting himself, Hopkins closed the door and strode
towards her. He caught her hands. 'So, you are now
plying your trade in France. You look very well, at any
rate. A deal better than when I last saw you.'

She snatched her hands away. 'Four weeks after my
sister died! You called not to offer your condolences,
but to make me an offer you thought I could not refuse.'

'Yet you did refuse it.'

'Yes, I damn well did.' Resentment rose like bile in
her throat. 'The bargain we made was complete, I no
longer needed to subject myself to your ministrations.'

'I do not recall that you found me repulsive.'

He spoke in that cold, clipped tone that she remembered so well, and which she had always appeased with compliance, if necessary with feigned affection. But she no longer needed to appease him. 'Our contract required me to please you. What I actually felt about you was another matter entirely.'

He took a step towards her, then halted. 'Women of your sort, Sophia, cannot afford the luxury of feelings.'

'We can certainly not afford to show them.'

'You entered into our liaison of your own free will. You knew exactly what my terms were, I made them perfectly clear.'

'And then duly breached them out of spite.'

'What do you mean?'

'When I refused to resume our arrangement after my sister had died, no longer having a pressing need for your bribes, you blackened my name. Do no deny it, sir, it is the only explanation for the plethora of other offers of protection I then subsequently received from your friends. You promised you would not talk, and you did.'

'Not while you were mine.'

'I was never yours.'

'Sophia, come back to me. Perhaps I was hasty. I will make you a proper settlement.' Hopkins grabbed her around the waist. 'An annuity as well as a quarterly sum.'

'Let me go.'

'Sir Richard! What the devil are you doing?' Jean-Luc threw down the bundle of papers he was holding. 'Take your hands off my wife.'

'Your wife?' Hopkins drew Sophia a baffled glance then stepped hastily away, holding his hands in the air. 'Monsieur Bauduin. There has been a grave misunderstanding.'

'Get out,' Jean-Luc said, his hands curling of their own accord into fists.

But though Hopkins put some distance between himself and Sophia, he made no move to leave. 'Let us not be too hasty, Monsieur Bauduin. I swear that I had no idea this lady was your wife, otherwise—in any event I have travelled all the way from England in the expectation of placing laying before you an extremely large order...'

Jean-Luc took a step towards him. 'Get out before you need wine for your funeral rather than your nuptials.'

Sir Richard turned tail. The door slammed behind him, and Sophia's knees buckled. She sank on to a sofa.

Jean-Luc was at her side in an instant. 'Forgive me. I would never have left you alone with him for an instant if I had thought—but he always appeared to me to be a perfect gentleman. I am so very sorry.'

'It's not your fault.' She couldn't resist clinging to him for a moment, burrowing her face into his shoulder.

'But it is my fault, I should not have left you alone, though I did not imagine—*mon Dieu*, that he could think for a second that placing an order for wine entitled him to molest my wife!'

Sophia lifted her head. She freed herself from his

embrace for the last time, for he would not want to touch her after what she was about to tell him. 'Jean-Luc, it's not what you think. Sir Richard and I, we are already acquainted.'

'You know him? But that makes it even worse, why would he...?'

'I *know* him.' Something in her voice alerted him. He went very still. Her throat was dry, but she no longer felt sick, only a dull, aching sense of loss. It was over. She met his gaze without flinching. 'I was his mistress.'

He must have surely have misheard, Jean-Luc thought, but the expression on Sophia's face gave him pause. She was ashen, but there were no traces of tears, and she continued to hold his gaze. 'His mistress? I don't understand.'

'You will, in a moment. I know it is early, but I think we are both going to need a stiff drink,' she said, getting up to pour them both a cognac.

He took his, setting it down on the table by the sofa. When Sophia downed hers in one swallow, his heart sank. When she sat down opposite him, he knew that whatever she was about to tell him, he didn't want to hear.

'I convinced myself it was for the best, not to tell you the truth,' she said. 'I knew you would be appalled and disgusted, and who could blame you? I knew you would hate me, and I couldn't bear that.'

'Sophia! I could never, ever hate you. If you only knew...'

He reached for her, but she shrank away from him.

'Don't. You won't want to touch me, not after you hear what I have to say.'

She wrapped her arms around herself, obviously girding her loins. Jean-Luc reached for his cognac, bracing himself.

'When my father died,' Sophia began, 'he left us penniless. I think I told you that? And Felicity, I told you that too, didn't I, that the only way to extend her life was to send her here, to a reputable spa. I tried to persuade my father to provide the funds. He made a series of empty promises, but he never made good on any of them. His money was earmarked for more important things, such as advancing his political career. He never did believe that Felicity's life was worth preserving.'

'While it was his own which was not,' Jean-Luc said viciously.

'Well, he made a good job of destroying it in the end, and as a result he left us with almost nothing.'

'Had you no relatives who could help? Your mother's family?'

'My father estranged all of them. To be fair, Mama's sister did offer to take us in, but she lives in Yorkshire, and my sister needed a better climate, not a wetter and colder one.'

'And so you married? Or have I got that wrong? I thought you said you were Hopkin's mistress?'

'I told you I was not an innocent, and you assumed that meant I must have been married. I didn't contradict you. In fact I did try to marry. Like Juliette, I had no dowry, I had nothing to offer save my looks and my bloodline.'

'I've just realised that I still don't even know your surname,' Jean-Luc said.

'No. I have always been Simply Sophia to you.' For the first time, her voice wavered. It took a Herculean effort not to wrap his arms around her. 'My name is Lady Sophia Acton. My father was Lord Jasper Acton. He served in various positions in both the Duke of Portland's government and that of Spencer Perceval.'

'*Sacré bleu!* I knew you must be gently born, but I had no idea…'

She shrugged contemptuously. 'Being gently born, Jean-Luc, is the equivalent of being born to be useless, if one is a female. I was not exactly a prize catch. I had no dowry, and I had my sister to care for. If it were not for her I would never have considered such a marriage—but then my story would not end with my sitting here, telling you all this. I would not have met you.' She stared down at her lap, lacing and unlacing her fingers. 'I'm sorry, this is turning into a very convoluted tale.'

'Take all the time you want.' Jean-Luc poured them both another glass of cognac. He was no longer apprehensive but angry. Whatever she had done, it was clear her motives were utterly altruistic. He hated, loathed that she should have suffered, but what was the point in telling her so. All he could do was listen, and once he understood, try to make it better.

Sophia took a small sip of her brandy, but set the glass to one side, taking a deep breath. 'To cut a long story short, Frederick, my second cousin, offered for my hand. I was honest with him, I thought he'd value that. I did not pretend to return the love he claimed to have for me, but I promised to make him the best wife I could, provided he agreed to send Felicity to Menton and pay for her treatment.'

'And how did this Frederick take your candidness?'

'I thought he appreciated it,' Sophia said, with a mocking smile. 'You are thinking that was naïve of me, I can tell.'

'I suspect he would have preferred to go to the altar under the illusion that you had chosen him for the same reasons he had chosen you,' Jean-Luc said drily. 'I presume that this love he avowed for you preceded the death of your father? That the proposal he made to you was not his first?'

'That is very astute of you.'

'No, Sophia, it is very obvious. He knew he was not worthy of you. He took advantage of your circumstances. You were honest with him, but he chose to delude himself.'

She sighed. 'He deceived me too. The date of our marriage drew nearer, and still he had not set up the trust fund for Felicity's convalescence. When I pressed him, he told me that he was concerned that when the fund was put in place I would renege on my promise to marry him. I was shocked that he'd even consider me capable of such dishonesty, but none of my protestations swayed him. He demanded tangible proof of my intentions.'

Jean-Luc set his cognac glass down, afraid it would shatter in his hand, he was gripping it so tightly. 'He wanted you to pre-empt your wedding vows as some sort of obscene test of good faith,' he said, striving to keep his tone even.

Sophia nodded.

Let her have broken the engagement, he thought. But her face told him the truth. 'You agreed.'

She nodded again. 'For Felicity's sake. I felt I had no option. And then, afterwards, he told me...'

'That there were no funds for your sister. But because he had seduced you, you would still have to go through with the marriage.'

'He didn't seduce me,' Sophia said scrupulously. 'I acceded to his request.'

'He lied to you.' The suppressed rage in his voice made her shrink. 'I am sorry, I did not mean to frighten you. I am so—it is so—I want to eradicate the whole ghastly episode, make it so that it never happened.'

'But it did, and one thing you have learned of late, Jean-Luc is that there is no escaping the past.'

'But it is done now, Sophia. Your husband is dead, no?'

'No. I never married him, you see.' She lifted her eyes from her hands, her expression defiant. 'Are you shocked?'

He laughed gruffly. 'I am surprised, though I should not be. You told me, didn't you, over dinner that first night in Paris.' He searched his memory for her words. 'Lies offered in exchange for promises, I think you said. No marriage could flourish under such conditions. I thought you spoke from experience. I thought that your marriage had been a bitter one.'

'When in fact it was simply non-existent, despite

Frederick's best efforts. He begged and he cajoled and he threatened. I called his bluff. He called mine, and broadcast my deflowering to anyone who would listen.'

'*Salaud!*'

'My thoughts precisely. I had lost my one asset, and my sister's days were numbered. And then Sir Richard Hopkins came calling.'

And now Jean-Luc felt sick again, but across from him Sophia's expression almost broke his heart. Such shame mingled with defiance. He wanted to hug her. He wished he had thrown Sir Richard head first down the stairs, breaking his aristocratic neck. He didn't need to know the tawdry details, he understood her meaning completely, but he could see that she needed to confess, and he hoped that doing so would be cathartic. 'Go on.'

'He offered to act as my protector and establish me as his mistress. He knew that I had no experience, but he was willing to teach me.'

He could not disguise his revulsion. Such a dilettante, with Sophia in his clutches. His beautiful, innocent, selfless Sophia. Now, he was finally beginning to understand the enigma that she was.

'Whatever else he was,' she said, 'he was very generous, Felicity was able to live in comfort, and I was permitted to visit her once a year.'

'At a cost, I suspect,' Jean-Luc said grimly, for another piece of the puzzle had fallen into tragic place. 'There is no such thing as a free gift, no?'

'I thought so, until I met you.'

Which remark should have warmed his heart, but

instead made him even more furious. Sophia was heroic, but so far her life had been a tragedy. 'So for two years you were his...' Victim, was the word which sprang to mind.

'Mistress,' Sophia said. 'His own little bird of paradise, he called me, which was apt enough, I suppose, for he kept me in a gilded cage, in the form of an apartment on Half Moon Street. He would visit me there. It suited me,' she added hastily, noting his exclamation of disgust. 'I told Felicity that I had married Frederick. The fewer people who knew that I had sold myself, the better.'

'Do not talk of yourself in that way.'

'What other way is there to describe it?' she demanded harshly. 'I could not claim that Hopkins seduced me. He paid me. I gave myself to him.'

'And every time, it felt like a violation, that is what you said. He callously took advantage not just of you, but your desperate situation.'

'I know, and I despise him for it,' Sophia said bitterly, 'but I hate him even more for breaking his promise.'

'What promise?'

'To keep his mouth shut.' Sophia jumped to her feet. 'I terminated our arrangement when I went to Menton to share Felicity's last months with her. When I returned to London, he offered to take me back into his bed. I had completely misjudged the costs of everything associated with my sister's demise. I was in dire straits, but not that dire. I refused. He took it very badly. His punishment was to broadcast my activities and laud my accomplished technique. This generated many offers of varying degrees of disgustingness which I rejected out of hand. And then, out of the blue, The Procurer arrived with your offer. So there you have it. The sad and sorry tale of my fall from grace.'

She picked up her cognac, draining the glass. Jean-Luc ran his fingers through his hair. The extent of her bravery, her endurance, her determination to do her best by her beloved sister could not be quantified. The treatment meted out to her, the sheer injustice of it, and her stoicism in the face of it, there was nothing and no one to compare with her. All of this he would explain to her, he would force her to see how wonderful she was, but at this moment he could think of only one thing to say.

He removed the cognac glass from her hand. He put his arms around her. 'I love you so much.'

'What did you say?'

'I love you, Sophia.'

'You can't.' She struggled free of his embrace, using the sofa to create a barrier between them.

'I know you want your freedom, I understand that. *Mon Dieu*, who could not understand that, after all you have been through. I did not mean to speak yet...'

'Please, I beg you, don't speak at all. You can't possibly love me, Jean-Luc, I'm not fit to be loved by you. Weren't you listening to me? I know what I've done. I know that it's shameful and disgusting. It *was* shameful and disgusting, but I would do it again if I had to.'

'You will never have to. Sophia, I love you. I want to marry you, to marry you for real, I mean. I did not intend to declare myself, not until I have dismissed this claim of Mademoiselle de Cressy's but…'

'Ironically, Juliette is the perfect wife for you.'

'No. The real irony is that my pretend wife is the perfect wife for me.'

'I couldn't be less perfect, and when you reflect on it, you will see that I am right. I would bring such dishonour to your noble family name, a name you have only just reclaimed for yourself.'

'Sophia…'

'No, listen to me,' she interrupted desperately. 'You have to listen to me. You would be ruined by association with me, which is bad enough, but it is not the worst aspect of it. No matter what you think you feel for me now, it won't last. Every time we make love, you will be thinking, did she do this with him, did she do that, and I couldn't bear that, not after it has been so perfect.'

'Sophia, when you make love with me, do you think of my other lovers?'

'Of course not, but it's not the same. They were your lovers. I was Hopkins's courtesan.'

'Not any more. You are my lover.'

She flinched. 'It is over. My past will fester in your mind, eroding all that is precious between us. It will taint everything it touches. You would come to find me revolting, and then you would resent me, and eventually you would hate me. When you have had a chance to think through all I have told you, you will thank me for refusing to let me ruin your life, I know you will. Please, don't say any more, I beg you.'

'I am saying what is in my heart, Sophia.'

'Tomorrow, you will know in your heart that it was a mistake.' He made to protest, but she shook her head violently. 'Please, no more. It's bad enough that I have spoiled things between us. Regardless, I will continue to assist in whatever way I can. We will maintain the charade of our marriage until such times as you judge it appropriate for me to take my leave.'

He wanted to sweep her into his arms, to tell her over and over and over until she believed him how much he loved her, but she looked so fragile, and she was in the right of it too, in a sense. His mind was reeling. Though he was certain of his love for her, he was not at all certain he could persuade her, and he was beginning to doubt the strength of her feelings for him.

'You are right,' he said. 'We both need time to reflect.'

'Thank you. I will leave you alone with your thoughts. You will come to see that I am right.'

She turned away, shoulders slumped. The door closed behind her, and Jean-Luc picked up his notes from the floor, tearing every single page of his very lucrative wine order for Sir Richard Hopkins into tiny pieces. It did not make him feel better, but as he dropped the pieces into the grate and watched them burn, the one thing Sophia had not said struck him.

I don't love you. Those words would have put an end to his declaration once and for all, but she had not said them. The world, which had seemed so bleak, was once again a blaze of southern sunshine. If Sophia loved him, he would find a way for them to be together. All he needed was a plan.

But first he had unfinished business with a certain English aristocrat.

Chapter Fourteen

'This is where Louis VII married Eleanor of Aquitaine,' Jean-Luc informed Sophia the following morning, as they entered the huge Gothic Cathédrale Saint-André. 'More importantly, as far as I am concerned at least, it is where my parents were married.'

The cathedral had that familiar smell of ancient stone, candle wax and incense, but unlike churches in England, there was a mellow warmth to this one, a welcome sense of sanctuary and peace, an intimacy at odds with the austere, massively vaulted interior. Sophia felt some of the tension generated by yesterday's traumatic revelations and her long sleepless night, begin to ease as she walked up the huge central aisle at Jean-Luc's side. She loved him, of that she was utterly certain, and though it was her heart's desire to be by his side for ever, she loved him far too much to ruin his life by being selfish.

Did he love her? The question had tormented her throughout the long, lonely hours of darkness. It mattered not, she'd told herself time and time again, but she could not bring herself to believe the lie. If he loved her even a fraction as much as she loved him, how happy she could be. If he loved her, if he truly loved her, then surely nothing else mattered? If he loved her…

And on it went, until she returned full circle. His love would wither and die when the full price he must pay for it became apparent. He would not want to touch her. She was tainted, damaged goods, a social pariah. And from that, nothing but misery could spring. No, she could not inflict herself on him. Better to cling to the notion that he did not love her, than torment herself in the future over what might have been.

Jean-Luc would be glad that she had rejected his declaration yesterday. Though what he was actually feeling right now, she had not the remotest idea, Despite studying him covertly over breakfast and on the short stroll to the cathedral, she could not discern his mood at all. Her confession did not seem to have disgusted him. So far. As for her rejection—far from being angry or even depressed, he bore an air of suppressed excitement.

Which, when he led her to one of the side chapels, where a huge tome had been set on a table, she thought she finally understood.

'Monsieur Fallon organised this,' Jean-Luc said, pulling what Sophia surmised must be the Parish Register towards him. 'Monsieur Fallon, I am rapidly discovering, despite being both verbose and pedantic, is a man capable of pulling strings in this city. I look forward to doing a good deal more business with him.'

He rapidly flicked through the ledger until he reached the appropriate year, and then began to turn the pages more slowly, running his finger down the columns, coming to a halt at one particular entry. 'See here, Sophia.'

'"Baptism, 2 July 1788",' Sophia read. '"Nicolas Frances Henri Maximillian, Marquis de Montendre, son of Nicolas Charles Frances Claude, Duc de Montendre, Born 2 June 1788." My goodness, that is you.'

'Finally, a tangible fragment of my true history.' Smiling, Jean-Luc ran his hand over the copperplate writing. 'It doesn't change who I am, I see that now. You were right about that, I am, exactly as you said, the man I have always been. But knowing where I have come from makes a huge difference to my future.'

'I know.' She covered his hand with hers. 'I understand.'

'No.' He closed the register and turned to her. There was a light in his eyes that seemed to contradict what she was sure he was about to tell her. 'You don't understand at all, Sophia. You are thinking that you were right yesterday, when you told me that you could not be part of that future, are you not?'

'You are the Duc de Montendre.'

'I am also Jean-Luc. The man who loves you more than all the stars in the heavens.'

'You can't. It's impossible.'

'I can. And with you by my side, anything is possible.' He shook his head when she made to speak. 'I know what you think, *ma belle*, and I understand why you think it, but you're wrong. You put forward your case yesterday, let me put mine now, but not here in this sacred place. Let us go somewhere more appropriate, where we can talk freely.'

Bordeaux's public garden was a ten-minute walk away. Bordered by town houses, it was a pleasant, open space, consisting of parterres bounded by paths, and a small boating pond where two little boys were sailing their toy yachts.

They sat down together on a wooden bench in a shady, secluded spot. 'First of all,' Jean-Luc said, 'I want to assure you that I speak from the heart, but also from the head. I have thought long and hard about all the terrible things you told me yesterday, and I do not dismiss any of them lightly. But I want to try to show you that your thinking is muddled.'

'You won't ever persuade me that I'm worthy of you. I wish that I could wipe the slate clean, but I can't.'

He took her hand, his fingers twining tightly around hers. 'If we are to talk of worthiness, it is I who am not worthy of you. As for the past, we both know, in our own ways, that it cannot be undone. I hate what you have been forced to endure. If I could have spared you a second of suffering at the hands of that vile cabal of men, your father, your fiancé, and that other abomination of a man, then I would, but I cannot. We can't alter the past, Sophia but we can make a much better, brighter future together.'

Her heart was an agony of longing, but her resolve was made of sterner stuff. 'I would not make you happy, Jean-Luc. My past would haunt you.'

'No, it haunts you, not me. It is time to lay the ghosts to rest.' He let go of her hand to pull off his hat, mopping the sweat from his brow. 'You think that you will be judged for your actions. Perhaps so, by those who do not know you or those who are eager to judge others rather than themselves, but why should you care what such people think? I do not give a damn about them.'

'You do business with at least one of them.'

His lip curled. 'Not any more. I had a subsequent meeting with that man not worthy to be called a gentleman, and made it very clear that my wine will not be sullied by residing in his cellars. I have also made it clear,' he added, his hand curling into a fist, 'that he will be well advised not to mention your name or his recent encounter with you to anyone. Ever.'

'But how can you prevent him?'

'You need not concern yourself with the particulars. Content yourself with the knowledge that I have considerably more influence in high places than he. Something else which he now understands.' He unfurled his fist, flexing his fingers. '*En effet*, he is gone from your life for ever.'

Ruthless, Sophia thought, was the perfect word to describe Jean-Luc at this moment. His cool eyes, his satisfied smile, his utter assuredness. It was a side of him she had not seen before. What had he said to Hopkins? She could not imagine, but she could easily imagine Hopkins's reaction. He liked to think of himself as all-powerful. She would have liked to have witnessed that encounter. It was wrong of her, but she found this iron-fisted side of Jean-Luc more than a little alluring.

'He is not a man who reacts well to being bested,' she said, making no attempt to hide her pleasure.

Jean-Luc shrugged. 'We have wasted enough time on him. Let us concern ourselves with the future.' He gathered her hands between his again. 'Our future.'

Oh, but it was so tempting to be swayed by his certainty. When he looked at her like that, it was easy to believe that love shone in his eyes. 'We have no future,' Sophia said, the words sounding strangled as she forced herself to utter them. 'Even if you are indifferent to the gossip, the fact that I will be shunned by society, and you too by association...'

He laughed at that, shaking his head. 'You think yourself so worldly, but you are such an innocent in many ways. For a start, this is France, not England. We have been through a Revolution, Sophia. The *ancien régime* is dead.'

'You forget that you are now a member of the ruling class.'

'Yes, one who intends to create a new order. Not only do you overestimate the impact of what you view as your fall from grace, you underestimate my influence. The guests who attended our soirée adored you, Sophia. Did you not feel welcomed into the heart of Paris society?'

'Of course, but they didn't know the truth.'

He shook his head. 'And they will remain in blissful ignorance, unless you feel obliged to wear your shame like a—a badge of dishonour. Can't you see, Sophia, this is all in your head? It is time you realised you have nothing to be ashamed of.'

'Nothing!'

'Absolutely nothing. At every step in your life, you have put others first, even that domineering fool of a father of yours. Your love for your sister was pure and deep and utterly unselfish. You sacrificed yourself for her, and you did all you could to ensure that she never knew the cost.' His hands tightened around hers. 'It makes me want to weep, thinking of your suffering, but when I think of your reasons, my heart swells with pride. How can you talk of dishonouring me by becoming my wife, when it is I who would be privileged and honoured to call myself your husband?'

A lump rose in her throat. 'That is the nicest thing anyone has ever said to me.'

'It is what anyone would say, who really knew you. You are the most beautiful woman I have ever met, but your inner beauty shines even more brightly than this ravishing exterior. I love you.'

She could no longer doubt it. For a moment she allowed herself to bask in his love, but only for a moment. 'Unfortunately, it doesn't alter the facts. You are the Duc de Montendre, for goodness sake.'

'Yes, I've thought of that too. If I decided not to claim the title, I wondered, would Sophia be more likely to marry me?'

'No!'

'That is what I concluded. You see, I know you almost better than you know yourself, and you understand me too, in a way that no-one else does. You understand that I owe it to my heritage to restore the lands and to restore the livelihoods of those who lost them during the Terror.'

'You wish to make the Montendre name great again?'

He laughed. 'I'll settle for making Château Montendre wine the finest in France. I can't do any of those things until I claim the lands, and to do that, I must claim the title. I've set Monsieur Fallon on the case, and asked him to do all he can to expedite the hearing. He seems to think that by presenting me as a philanthropic duke, the courts will be sympathetic.'

'And will you like being a duke?'

'Only if you will be my duchess.'

'Juliette expects to be your duchess, Jean-Luc. In fact, she has a legal right to be.'

'I wondered how long it would take you to bring her into it.' Once again, he released her, frowning down at his hands. 'From the very first, I have been determined not to marry her. It has been the one constant, through these last tumultuous months. At first, it was because I thought she was a charlatan, but from the moment you walked into my life, I could not help comparing my faux wife with the woman who, it now turns out, was the wife my family arranged for me.'

He angled himself towards her again. 'I do not take any account of that. I am prepared to sacrifice a great deal to restore my family heritage, but I won't sacrifice my happiness. I don't love Juliette de Cressy, I love you, Sophia, and I know in my heart that I will never,

ever love another woman in the same way. No matter what happens, I'm not marrying Juliette de Cressy.'

'But what about the contract? You gave her your word of honour that you would tell her the truth, and the truth is that you are the Duc de Montendre.'

'I will do as I promised. It has always sat ill with you to lie to her, I know. To be honest, it has of late sat very ill with me too. She is desperate, as you said. You see in her parallels with your own situation.'

'She has no other resources. She has been bred to make a good marriage and is equipped to do nothing else.'

'If you had not had to support your sister, would you have agreed to marry this Frederick person?'

'No, but I am more resilient than Juliette.'

'Because experience has forced you to be. It has made you the woman you are. The woman I love with all my heart, and the only woman I want to marry, which is what I intend to tell Mademoiselle de Cressy when I see her. I will tell her the unvarnished truth, that we deceived her, that we are not married, but I will make it clear I don't give a fig for her claim. It changes nothing.'

'What if she threatens legal action?'

'I will inform her that I am prepared to fight it all the way to the highest court in the land. She can then either accept a generous settlement from me made in good faith, or decline it, but I will make no offer for her hand and that is the end of the matter, *tu comprends*?'

Sophia was beginning to understand, and she was

beginning to hope. In fact, she was finding it very difficult now, to rein in her hopes. Had she been nurturing her shame? She had most certainly been allowing others to judge her, or to imagine that they would. Did she care? Yes, she did, though for Jean-Luc's sake much more than herself. 'I may sympathise with Juliette's predicament, but I confess I find the prospect of you marrying her distressing,' she conceded.

His smile was tender. Her defences were crumbling rapidly. 'Which brings me to the most important point. After all you have suffered and all the sacrifices you have made, you deserve to be happy, my love. If I can make you happy then I will spend the rest of my life doing so. But if I can't, if what you want is your freedom, then I will let you go, for the same reason that I dare to hope you have been so determined to let me go, because I love you, Sophia.'

She could not restrain herself any longer. 'And I love you Jean-Luc, more than I can ever put into words.'

He caught her to him, wrapping his arms tightly around her. 'My beautiful Sophia, you will try to put it into words, yes?'

She beamed. 'I will, and there's no time like the present. I love you, Jean-Luc.'

'I know how much your freedom means to you,' he said fervently. 'I want you to share every aspect of my life, but I don't want to smother you. I want you to feel free to live as you choose.'

'What I choose is to want to live by your side. I know you would never smother me. I *know* you. I trust you.'

'I want you to accept the fee you have earned from our contract…'

'I can't take that.'

'It is yours, Sophia, you have earned it. Stash it away somewhere, use it as you see fit, but have the security of knowing it is there.'

'Thank you, that means a great deal to me.'

'It is nothing compared to what you deserve.' He let her go, only to drop to his knee in front of her, her hand in his. 'I do not deserve you, Sophia, but I dare to ask you all the same if you will make me the happiest man on earth. Be my duchess and my wife.'

Her heart was making a very determined attempt to leap out of her breast. She thought she might burst with happiness. Was the sun shining brighter above them? It felt as if it was. 'You could not be happier than I, *mon amour*. Yes,' Sophia said, kissing his hand fervently. 'Yes, please.'

He gave a shout of joy, leaping to his feet and pulling her into his arms, and kissing her. And kissing her. And kissing her. Until they were both breathing raggedly.

'You told me once that public parks were designed expressly for the purpose of kissing, but I don't think you meant this kind of kissing,' Sophia said.

'You are quite right.' His smile was wicked. 'This kind of kissing requires some privacy.'

'Should we return to our hotel? Then, I can not only tell you how much I love you, but show you.'

He shook his head. 'An excellent plan but I think we can improve on the location.'

* * *

The light was fading when they reached Château Montendre, having postponed the drive until the worst heat of the day had subsided. Jean-Luc led her to a terrace built between the two protective arms of the towers, with a prospect overlooking the slopes of the vineyards. The tent was pitched on the old cobblestones, secured to the façade of the building. 'How on earth did you manage to organise this?' Sophia said, eyeing the billowing canvas in astonishment.

'As I said, Monsieur Fallon is a man who can pull many strings. And I am a man in love,' Jean-Luc said, pulling her to him for a long, tender kiss. 'We have to return to Paris tomorrow, but I wanted us to have this special night here first. It marks the beginning of our new life together.'

'Home is where the heart is, you said.'

'Which means that my home is wherever you are, my love. Though I hope that we can be happy here.'

Sophia looked around her in wonder. The sky was turning from azure to indigo, the stars tiny pinpoints of light high above. The air was humid after the heat of the day, heady with the scent of the verdant green all around them. The dusky light masked the worst effects of the destructive fire, turning the overgrown gardens into a magical wilderness, giving her a breathtaking glimpse of how beautiful Château Montendre would be, restored to its former glory. 'I could be happy anywhere with you,' she said, 'but here—it feels like home, don't you think?'

'I do,' Jean-Luc said, 'but the time for thinking is over.'

He swept her up into his arms, shouldering aside the layers of gauze which formed the doorway of the tent to set her down inside. A table was set for two, silverware glinting, crystal glasses gleaming, candelabra ready to be lit. Red wine had already been decanted. Champagne was cooling on ice. An array of covered salvers were set out on a long, low table. 'You have gone to an enormous amount of effort to arrange all this. Did it ever occur to you that I might turn you down?' Sophia asked.

'I could not allow myself to imagine such a disaster. You could have told me that you didn't love me, you see, and you never did. I clung to that and hoped. And prayed. And now my prayers have been answered. Would you like to eat now? I have ordered...'

'Jean-Luc, for once, I'm not remotely interested in food. What I'd like...' She could feel herself blushing, but she was determined to do as he bid her, and put her past behind her. 'What I'd like more than anything,' Sophia said, twining her arms around his neck, 'is for us to make love. I have promised to be your duchess, and I can't wait to be your wife, but what I want above all is to be your lover.'

She kissed him then, letting her lips and her tongue show him what was in her heart, and when he returned her kiss, the last tiny shreds of doubt disappeared. He loved her. Gazing into his eyes, she saw her love reflected there, and knew that he thought only of her. Both their pasts had been settled, laid to rest. There was now only a glittering future to look forward to. Though first, there was the small matter of the here and now to be savoured.

She kissed him again, murmuring over and over, in the space between kisses, that she loved him, she loved him, she loved him, and her kisses were returned, tenderly, lovingly, and then ardently. There was a bed, discreetly set behind a veil of curtains at the rear of the tent. This time there was no need to rush as they shed their clothing item by item, kissing every inch of skin revealed, sinking on to the piles of soft blankets, lost in a haze of passion and love.

Jean-Luc's mouth was on her breasts, her nipples. The sweet, dragging ache of desire began building inside her as he kissed his way down her belly, then the top of her thighs, untying her garters, kissing the back of her knee, her calf, her ankle, as he removed her stockings. He set her on fire with his kisses, making her writhe and moan under him, until his mouth claimed that most intimate kiss of all, and she cried out in astonishment and delight.

Honey, she thought, as his tongue licked over her sex, her veins felt as if they were sweet with honey, fizzing like an icy cold champagne. She had never experienced such sensations, longing for surrender but desperate not to give in, for she wanted this to go on for ever. These kisses took her to a place she had never been before, where passion soared to new heights, where she floated, like a billowing cloud, until somehow, the sensation changed, deepened, and she was rushing mindlessly, desperately, towards completion.

She cried out her pleasure when her climax came, unrestrained, wanting to unleash the same passion in Jean-Luc. She tugged at his shoulders, arching herself shamelessly against him. His eyes met hers, drugged and dazed with desire. And then he thrust into her, and she was lost again, clinging, thrusting with him, in a wild, feral rhythm that was not hers or his but theirs. Harder, faster, deeper, he drove until he cried out too, and she held him fast as he spilled inside her, and finally Sophia knew what it felt like for two people to truly be as one.

Epilogue

Paris—three months later

An invitation to the soirée to be held later that evening to celebrate the nuptials of the Duc and Duchesse de Montendre was the most sought-after card in the social calendar. When Jean-Luc Bauduin had been officially declared as the long-lost heir to the Montendre duchy, the news had caused a sensation.

No one more befitting the title could have emerged, Paris raved, for not only did the former Monsieur Bauduin epitomise the looks, demeanour and stature of such a distinguished noble, he had the financial where-withal required to restore the Montendre estates and châteaux to their former grandeur.

When it became clear that the new Duke was very much his own man, choosing to expand his business empire rather than retire from the trade for a life of lei-sure, tongues wagged, but the weight of opinion was very much in the new Duke's favour. This was France, after all—unlike England, a country which had freed itself from the stifling conventions of the past. Could England boast such a fine example of a thoroughly modern duke? *Certainement pas!*

Unfortunately for the matchmakers, this perfect example of a duke was already married, but Paris agreed that no more perfect duchess could be found than the beautiful Madame Bauduin, and no couple could be more obviously in love than the Duke and his Duchess.

To be invited to attend the wedding ceremony taking place this morning would have been a coup, but it was understandable, since the Duke and Duchess had already been married in England, that they wished this second ceremony to be conducted in private.

As the much-anticipated day arrived, those fortunate enough to be in possession of the coveted invitations busied themselves with their preparations for the soirée. The Duc and Duchesse of Montendre were already renowned for their fabulous dinner parties. Madame la Duchesse's menus were so incomparable one would think she had been born a Frenchwoman. As for Monsieur le Duc's selection of wine to accompany tonight's feast—rumour had it that he had somehow managed to source a select few cases of the very last burgundy produced at his father's estate, secreted away from looters deep in the cellars of Château Montendre.

Much discussion and speculation was taking place over breakfast coffee and croissants in the various Paris *hôtels particuliers* as to whether or not the rumour was true that the happy couple would be quitting Paris for Bordeaux within the month. If so, the continued restoration of the Hôtel Montendre surely guaranteed their residence in the city for a portion of the year at least.

But all that was for the future, the ladies of Paris informed their husbands dismissively. For them, the subject of most interest right now was what the new Duchesse de Montendre's wedding gown would look like.

Sophia and Jean-Luc were due at the Mairie for the civil ceremony in half an hour, with the church service scheduled to take place an hour later. Sophia stood in front of the mirror as Madeleine put the final touches to her *toilette*. She was not nervous as such, but she was in something of a daze. So much had happened these last three months, her life had been quite utterly transformed, and she still could not quite believe it. She had laid the ghosts of her past to rest. Jean-Luc had been right about that, they had resided in her head and not his. She was no longer ashamed, but accepted what she had done, and put it behind her, embracing every day of this bright new life, and the man who loved her.

'*Magnifique,*' her dresser declared, stepping back with justified pride, for she had played a key role in the design of the gown. 'Never has there been a more beautiful duchess, *madame*.'

For once, Sophia was inclined to agree. A simple underdress of silver-grey silk which clung to her slim figure was transformed by the over-dress of silver gauze and lace. The sleeves were elaborately gathered at the shoulders, then tightly fitted to the wrist where a fall of lace covered her hands. The skirt of the overdress was made of the same gauze, the hem trimmed with the same lace, the material shimmering with a myriad of tiny diamonds, like stars in the twilight sky. The décolleté was an elaborate leaf design formed of silver lace, seed pearls and larger diamonds. The largest diamond of all, a wedding present from Jean-Luc, was suspended on a delicate chain around Sophia's neck. He had urged her, when the date of the wedding was set, to dress like a duchess. His Duchess. Turning around to hug a tearful Madeleine, Sophia hoped she had done him justice, that he would be proud of her.

Jean-Luc was waiting for her in their private parlour. Dressed in his customary black, his cravat more elaborately tied, his silver waistcoat, embroidered with the Montendre coat of arms, adding a touch of ducal splendour. But he needed no badge to proclaim who he was, Sophia thought, making her curtsy. He was as he had always been, his own man, and in her view, the perfect man.

'Well? Am I fit to be your Duchess?'

'You are fit to be my Queen,' Jean-Luc said. 'How long is it since I told you that I love you?'

'At least three hours.'

'I have been remiss. That is two hours and fifty-nine minutes too long. I love you, Sophia.'

'And I love you, Jean-Luc. Even more than I did when I told you this morning after we made love.' She stood on her tiptoes to kiss his mouth. 'What's more, I think I can safely promise you that I will love you even more when we make love again tonight as man and wife.'

He groaned, pulling her carefully towards him for another, deeper kiss. 'Our wedding night.'

'Patience, or you will crush my gown. Besides, our witnesses, Juliette and Maxime will be here any minute.'

'The only couple in Paris almost as much in love as we are,' Jean-Luc said, smiling. 'Maxime told me that they are waiting only until our nuptials are formalised before they announce their own.'

'I am so happy for them. How poor Maxime must have suffered, forced to stifle his feelings for Juliette in those weeks when your true identity was unclear. What an agony he must have been in that day when you told them both that you really were the Duke.'

'Unbeknown to me, it was not only Maxime's hopes I was shattering, but Juliette's too,' Jean-Luc said ruefully. 'I'm not sure which revelation was the biggest shock to her. The fact that I was the Duke, or the fact that we were not married. My best friend thought that I was honour bound to marry the woman he was secretly in love with, and she thought she was going to have to honour the loveless contract she had come all the way to Paris to enforce, and forgo the man she had, most inconveniently, fallen in love with. When I confounded them both by announcing that, notwithstanding the two facts, I had no intention of marrying her under any circumstances, Juliette was quite unable to disguise her relief. And as for Maxime, he almost punched the air in delight. He did not fall on his knees before her, but he made his feelings clear enough. Which came as a very welcome surprise to Juliette, sparing me the need to persuade her my mind could not be changed.'

Sophia chuckled. 'And now they are to be married, and I gather from Juliette, sooner rather than later.'

'Maxime doesn't like her being in any way beholden to me. He won't accept the dowry I offered.'

'No, but we will find a way to give them a wedding present he cannot refuse. Talking of which,' Sophia said, producing a small leather box from the reticule she carried, 'I have a wedding gift for you.'

'You are the only gift I want or need.'

'My love, you have showered me with gifts, including this latest,' Sophia replied, touching the diamond at her throat. 'I wanted to give you something to remember the day by. Open it.'

She watched as he did, his eyes widening as he took out the signet ring, in which a large, finely cut emerald had been set. 'Of course it's not the original stone,' she said. 'As you surmised, that was most likely sold by Monsieur Bauduin to keep the family solvent when the trust fund began to dry up, but we know from the various tenants you've spoken to since, that it was an emerald, for several of them commented on the fact that your father was never without it, so I thought— do you like it?'

Jean-Luc turned the ring over, to find the engraving newly etched. '*Ab Ordine Libertas.* You told me you were having this cleaned, not restored. This must have cost a small fortune. I can guess where the money came from.'

'From Order Comes Freedom. Our new world order, Jean-Luc, is what's provided me with my freedom. I don't need all that money you insisted on giving me.

I don't need an insurance policy or financial security. All I need is you.'

His throat worked with emotion. His eyes were alight with love as he crushed her to him and she wrapped her arms tightly around him, the pair of them quite heedless of her wedding gown. 'I love you so much, Sophia. You too are everything I need.' He kissed her softly, then let her go, holding out his arm for her. 'My most perfect, beautiful, admirable Duchess. Our wedding party, and the rest of our life, awaits.'

* * * * *

Historical Note

As you may have gathered from reading this book—if the dedication didn't give it away—I have a long-standing love affair with Paris. I spent much of the time writing this story sighing nostalgically over maps and photographs and longing to jump on a plane and travel there. *Again!*

Of course the city in which Jean-Luc and Sophia fall in love bears little resemblance to Baron Haussmann's radically transformed version of today, with its wide boulevards, parks and, perhaps most critically, modern sewage and water supplies. In 1818, Paris was, frankly, a very smelly place. But this is a romance, and when it comes to that city I'm a hopeless romantic, so I glossed over a few of the gritty realities.

If you would like to know more about Paris at the time, though, then I can recommend either Alistair Horne's *Seven Ages of Paris*, or Andrew Hussey's *Paris, the Secret History*—both of which are highly readable and guaranteed to make you want to go there to explore all the history for yourself.

Napoleon was the first to encourage those who fled France during the Revolution to return home, and they came flooding back after the Bourbon Restoration in 1814, when Louis XVIII, brother of guillotined Louis XVI, came to the throne. In case you're wondering what happened to Louis XVII, he was the Dauphin, Louis XVI's son, and uncrowned King during the two years between his father's death and his own.

Claims by purported relatives to titles were not exactly common, but they did happen. My thanks to Dr Jonathon Spangler for drawing my attention to the case of the Prince of Lambesc, who tried to establish his post-Revolution claim to property using feudal documents. He failed. In an effort to make Jean-Luc's claim less complex, I turned to two English *causes célèbres* instead. The Tichborne Claimant and the Douglas Cause. Thank you yet again to Alison Lyndsay for these. Both relied heavily on circumstantial evidence, identification of the claimant by servants, et cetera.

Would Jean-Luc have been forced to renounce Sophia in favour of Juliette had they really been married? The jury is out on that one, but it is likely either that Jean-Luc would have bought his way out of the problem, or that Juliette's counter-case would have been conveniently 'lost' in the system if Jean-Luc was prepared to cough up the bribe money! Thanks to Dr Spengler again for this information.

As ever, there's a ton of other reading and history in this book—and, as ever, I'm running out of space to cover it all. If you want to know more about the Revolution and The Terror, Christopher Hibbert's *The French*

Revolution is an excellent place to start. If you want to see more of the fabulous Flying Vengarovs in action, then you can read my story *The Officer's Temptation* in the fun duet I wrote with Bronwyn Scott: *Scandal at the Midsummer Ball*.

And if you want to talk books or history or, for that matter, food or sewing, or any number of other things, then please do join me on Twitter or Facebook.